LETHAL GAME

A JONATHAN GRAVE THRILLER

JOHN GILSTRAP

PINNACLE BOOKS
KENSINGTON PUBLISHING CORP.
www.kensingtonbooks.com

PINNACLE BOOKS are published by

Kensington Publishing Corp.
119 West 40th Street
New York, NY 10018

Copyright © 2022 John Gilstrap

All rights reserved. No part of this book may be reproduced in any form
or by any means without the prior written consent of the publisher, except-
ing brief quotes used in reviews.

If you purchased this book without a cover, you should be aware that this
book is stolen property. It was reported as "unsold and destroyed" to the
publisher, and neither the author nor the publisher has received any pay-
ment for this "stripped book."

All Kensington titles, imprints, and distributed lines are available at special
quantity discounts for bulk purchases for sales promotions, premiums,
fund-raising, educational, or institutional use.

Special book excerpts or customized printings can also be created to fit
specific needs. For details, write or phone the office of the Kensington special sales manager: Kensington Publishing Corp., 119 West 40th Street,
New York, NY 10018, attn: Special Sales Department; phone 1-800-221-2647.

This book is a work of fiction. Names, characters, businesses, organiza-
tions, places, events, and incidents either are the product of the author's
imagination or are used fictitiously. Any resemblance to actual persons,
living or dead, events, or locales is entirely coincidental.

PINNACLE BOOKS and the Pinnacle logo are Reg. U.S. Pat. & TM Off.

ISBN: 978-0-7860-4556-3
ISBN: 978-0-7860-4557-0 (e-book)

First printing: July 2022

10 9 8 7 6 5 4 3 2 1

Printed in the United States of America

Praise for John Gilstrap and His Thrillers

CRIMSON PHOENIX

"A nonstop roller coaster of suspense! *Crimson Phoenix*
ticks every box for big-book thrillerdom."
—Jeffery Deaver

"Don't miss this powerful new series
from a master thriller writer."
—Jamie Freveletti

"A single mother's smart, fierce determination to protect
her sons turns this vivid day-after-tomorrow scenario
into a gripping page-turner."

—Taylor Stevens

"*Crimson Phoenix* snaps with action
from the very first page. It's certain to hit the 10-ring
with old and new readers alike."

—Marc Cameron

STEALTH ATTACK

A BOOKBUB TOP THRILLER OF SUMMER
"Nobody does pacing and suspense better than Gilstrap.
And in Grave he continues to grow with each entry.
Stealth Attack is riveting and relentless reading
entertainment."
—*The Providence Journal*

TOTAL MAYHEM

"Propulsive . . . Not everyone survives the
final confrontation, but series fans can rest assured
that Grave will fight again. Straightforward plotting,
amped-up action, and amusing banter keep
the pages turning."
—*Publishers Weekly*

SCORPION STRIKE

"Relentlessly paced as well as brilliantly told and constructed, this is as good as thrillers get."

—*The Providence Journal*

"A sizzling beach read for military action fans . . . the perfect summer read for thriller fans."
—*Publishers Weekly* (starred review)

"The series deserves attention from anyone who enjoys plot-driven thrillers. . . . Grave is, as always, a solid series lead."
—*Booklist*

FINAL TARGET

"Fast paced and well plotted."
—*Booklist*

"Exciting. . . . Fans of epic adventure stories will find plenty to like."
—*Publishers Weekly*

FRIENDLY FIRE

"If you only read one book this summer, make sure it's *Friendly Fire*, and be ready to be strapped in for the ride of your life."

—*Suspense Magazine*

"A blistering thriller that grabs your attention and doesn't let go for a second!"
—**The Real Book Spy**

NICK OF TIME

"A page-turning thriller with strong characters, exciting action, and a big heart."
—**Heather Graham**

AGAINST ALL ENEMIES

WINNER OF THE INTERNATIONAL THRILLER
WRITERS AWARD FOR
BEST PAPERBACK ORIGINAL

"Any John Gilstrap novel packs the punch of a rocket-propelled grenade—on steroids! Gilstrap grabs the reader's attention in a literary vise grip. A damn good read."

—BookReporter.com

"Tense, clever. . . . Series enthusiasts are bound
to enjoy this new thriller."
—*Library Journal*

END GAME
AN AMAZON EDITORS'
FAVORITE BOOK OF THE YEAR
"Gilstrap's new Jonathan Grave thriller is his best novel to date—even considering his enviable bibliography. *End Game* starts off explosively and keeps on rolling."

—Joe Hartlaub, BookReporter.com

DAMAGE CONTROL

"Powerful and explosive, an unforgettable journey into the dark side of the human soul. Gilstrap is a master of action and drama. If you like Vince Flynn and Brad Thor, you'll love John Gilstrap."
—Gayle Lynds

"Rousing. . . . Readers will anxiously await
the next installment."
—*Publishers Weekly*

"It's easy to see why John Gilstrap is the go-to guy among thriller writers, when it comes to weapons, ammunition, and explosives.
His expertise is uncontested."
—John Ramsey Miller

"A page-turning, near-perfect thriller, with engaging and believable characters . . . unputdownable!"
—*Top Mystery Novels*

"Takes you full force right away and doesn't let go. The action is nonstop. Gilstrap knows his technology and weaponry. *Damage Control* will blow you away."
—*Suspense Magazine*

THREAT WARNING

"*Threat Warning* is a character-driven work where the vehicle has four on the floor and horsepower to burn. From beginning to end, it is dripping with excitement."
—**Joe Hartlaub,** *Bookreporter*

"*Threat Warning* reconfirms Gilstrap as a master of jaw-dropping action and heart-squeezing suspense."
—**Austin Camacho,** *The Big Thrill*

HOSTAGE ZERO

"Jonathan Grave, my favorite freelance peacemaker, problem-solver, and tough guy hero, is back—and in particularly fine form. *Hostage Zero* is classic Gilstrap: the people are utterly real, the action's foot to the floor, and the writing's fluid as a well-oiled machine gun. A tour de force!"
—**Jeffery Deaver**

"This addictively readable thriller marries a breakneck pace to a complex, multilayered plot. . . . A roller coaster ride of adrenaline-inducing plot twists leads to a riveting and highly satisfying conclusion. Exceptional characterization and an intricate, flawlessly crafted story line make this an absolute must read for thriller fans."
—*Publishers Weekly* (starred review)

NO MERCY

"*No Mercy* grabs hold of you on page one
and doesn't let go. Gilstrap's new series is terrific.
It will leave you breathless. I can't wait to see what
Jonathan Grave is up to next."
—**Harlan Coben**

"John Gilstrap is one of the finest thriller writers on the
planet. *No Mercy* showcases his work at its finest—taut,
action-packed, and impossible to put down!"
—**Tess Gerritsen**

"A great hero, a pulse-pounding story—and the launch of
a really exciting series."
—**Joseph Finder**

"An entertaining, fast-paced tale of violence and revenge."
—***Publishers Weekly***

"No other writer is better able to combine in a single novel
both rocket-paced suspense and heartfelt looks at family
and the human spirit. And what a pleasure to meet
Jonathan Grave, a hero for our time . . . and for all time."
—**Jeffery Deaver**

AT ALL COSTS

"Riveting . . . combines a great plot and realistic, likable
characters with look-over-your-shoulder tension.
A page-turner."
—***Kansas City Star***

"Gilstrap builds tension . . . until the last page,
a hallmark of great thriller writers. I almost called
the paramedics before I finished *At All Costs*."
—***Tulsa World***

"Gilstrap has ingeniously twisted his simple premise
six ways from Sunday."
—*Kirkus Reviews*

"Not-to-be-missed."
—*Rocky Mountain News*

NATHAN'S RUN

"Gilstrap pushes every thriller button . . . a nail-biting
denouement and strong characters."
—*San Francisco Chronicle*

"Gilstrap has a shot at being the next John Grisham . . .
one of the best books of the year."
—*Rocky Mountain News*

"Emotionally charged . . . one of the year's best."
—*Chicago Tribune*

"Brilliantly calculated. . . . With the skill of
a veteran pulp master, Gilstrap weaves a yarn that demands
to be read in one sitting."
—*Publishers Weekly* (starred review)

"Like a roller coaster, the story races along on well-oiled
wheels to an undeniably pulse-pounding conclusion."
—*Kirkus Reviews* (starred review)

ALSO BY JOHN GILSTRAP

Blue Fire

Crimson Phoenix

Stealth Attack

Hellfire

Total Mayhem

Scorpion Strike

Final Target

Nick of Time

Friendly Fire

Against All Enemies

End Game

Soft Targets

High Treason

Damage Control

Threat Warning

Hostage Zero

No Mercy

Six Minutes to Freedom (with Kurt Muse)

Scott Free

Even Steven

At All Costs

Nathan's Run

For Joy

CHAPTER 1

Jonathan Grave hadn't moved in nearly three hours. He sat at the base of a towering cedar tree, his knees pulled up to his chest, his rifle draped across his lap as he scanned the sloped bank on the other side of the river for sign of his prey. The November Montana air felt clear and sweet. Not yet cold by local standards, weather reports predicted that the mercury would dance around fifteen degrees after dark—about where it was when he'd started out this morning.

Somewhere in the woods on Jonathan's left, his giant friend, coworker, and Army buddy Brian Van de Muelebroecke—a.k.a. Boxers—presumably was scanning his own horizon.

Jonathan was certain he'd seen a bull elk along the far side of the river, but by the time he'd settled into position for a shot, the beast had disappeared into the trees. The elk hadn't run, though. Jonathan took that as evidence that he wasn't spooked. There was a good chance, then, that the bull—or one of the cows he was no doubt trying to impress with his big rack of antlers—might follow the same trail back this way. Jonathan had allotted five days for this hunt, and today was only the first. He had plenty of time to show patience.

This was his favorite part of any hunt. He didn't get enough silence in his life these days. Sometimes solitude worked against him, dredging up images and events that he'd rather forget, but so far, the demons had all stayed away. He considered those demons to be an occupational hazard, having spent so much time in nasty places doing nasty chores to protect innocents from nasty people.

In many ways, on a hunt like this, pulling the trigger and dropping the animal was a letdown. Not that he felt guilty about filling his freezer with two hundred pounds of deliciousness, but because the gunshot marked the end of the silence.

The radio in the pocket of his chest rig popped as it broke squelch. "Scorpion, Big Guy."

He and Boxers had had those radio handles since their Army days with the Unit, and old times died hard.

Jonathan reached under the blaze orange vest he wore over his camo'd chest rig and keyed the mic. "Go ahead," he whispered. God had blessed elk with amazing ears. He didn't want to waste these past hours by making noise.

"Gotta take a break, Boss," Boxers said. "We got a visitor. We're coming your way."

Boxers knew better than to break a moment like this, so whoever the visitor was, it had to be important. Smart money said it was a game warden. Jonathan muttered a curse under his breath as he flexed his knees, straightened his back, and stood. He let his Vortex Viper binoculars fall against his chest by their lanyard and slung his rifle. "Are you coming to me or are we meeting in the middle?"

"We'll come to you."

As he waited, Jonathan brought his binoculars back up to his eyes and scanned the opposite bank again. Believing with all his soul that Murphy and his law ruled the universe, he knew that if Mr. Elk were going to make a surprise appearance, it would be now, when Jonathan was out of position, or in a few minutes, when he'd be locked in conversation.

Rustling leaves and heavy footsteps preceded Boxers' arrival with exactly the person Jonathan had been expecting. The game warden looked to be little more than a kid—maybe twenty-five—and he carried himself with the stern authority of a street cop. Topped with a wide-brimmed cowboy hat, the warden wore the standard uniform of the Montana Fish Wildlife and Parks Department—a khaki shirt and blue jeans, along with a Sam Browne belt packed with a big Glock, handcuffs, and enough spare mags to engage a militia.

Jonathan adjusted his rifle on his shoulder, put a smile on his face, and walked toward the others. "We can't be in trouble yet," he said, offering his hand. "We haven't been here long enough."

The warden looked at Jonathan's hand, then tucked his thumbs into the armholes of his ballistic armor. The name SIMONSEN was stitched into a patch that was Velcro'd onto the vest.

Jonathan didn't appreciate being dissed by a child, but he also didn't want to get sideways with the one agency in Montana that could turn this adventure into something unpleasant. He decided to roll with it and see what the guy wanted.

"Are you from DC, too?" Simonsen asked.

"Nope. Virginia."

"He said you two are hunting together." Simonsen flicked a thumb at Boxers.

"We traveled together," Jonathan said. "Not sure we're exactly hunting together, with him being a couple hundred yards away. Have we done something wrong?"

"I don't know," Simonsen said. "Have you?"

Boxers made a sound and rolled his eyes.

Simonsen turned on him. "Did you just growl at me? Get around with your friend, where I can see both of you. Let me see some identification."

Jonathan reached around to his back pocket for his wallet. "I've got my nonresident hunting permit, too," he said as fished out his driver's license and handed it over. "But it's on my phone." Every bit of information on the license was fiction.

Simonsen held the license with two fingers on his left hand while he jotted the information into a skinny, lined reporter's notebook. "Won the permit lottery, did you?" he asked as he wrote.

"Been trying for years and finally struck. Both of us did." Elk licenses were distributed by lottery every April 1, and they cost nearly one thousand dollars to get.

"How'd you get here?"

"We flew."

"What airline?"

Jonathan hesitated. There was no inoffensive way to say the next part. "I have my own plane."

"How many stops between home and here?"

"None."

"Not even a fuel stop?"

This was all beginning to sound strangely intrusive. "Not even," Jonathan said. "My plane has the range."

"And a lot more," Boxers said. As the designated pilot for their team and the man who had speck'd out the two planes that comprised Jonathan's fleet, he showed a parent's pride.

Simonsen handed back the driver's license. "I'll see your permit now."

Jonathan returned his license and wallet to his back pocket and pushed his hand into his left front pocket for his phone. The fictional identity on the permit matched that on the driver's license.

Simonsen pointed at the binoculars hanging from the strap around Jonathan's neck. "I guess that a man who can afford his own plane has plenty of scratch for those eight-hundred-dollar field glasses."

They were only six hundred, but Jonathan let it go. He pulled up the electronic image of his permit, but Simonsen barely looked at it. "Put it away," Simonsen said. "I figure if you were that ready to show me, I got no reason to look." He nodded to Jonathan's slung rifle. "What're you shooting?"

"MR seven-six-two," Jonathan said. "It's the civilian version of—"

"The Heckler and Koch four-seventeen. Yeah, I know. Same as your tall buddy." Simonsen's mood lightened as he spoke of weaponry. "I carried the four-sixteen over in the shit pile." He glanced at Jonathan, then gave Boxers a long look. "You guys serve?"

"A long time," Jonathan said. "Been out for a few years, though."

"Why are you wearing body armor?"

"I'm not," Jonathan said. "Just the plate carrier. Easiest way to keep the essentials at hand."

Simonsen pointed to the camo-patterned rucksack that rested against the base of a tree. "You and your buddy dress together every morning?"

"That was the best Uncle Sam could buy. Why try to improve on it?" This whole interview felt two clicks too adversarial.

"What would I find if I opened it?"

"Socks, shirts, some underwear. Can I ask why you're so curious about Boxers and me?"

"You guys are drivin' a Suburban, right? A rental?"

"Yep."

"The way you parked it up there," Simonsen said. "Most people when they hunt, they just pull off to the side of the road and go at it. You folks tried to hide your vehicle. Pulling it into the trees, well off the road." His eyes narrowed. "Mind tellin' me why?"

Jonathan had no idea why. It was just the way they'd parked. He looked to Big Guy for help.

"Old habits die hard, I guess," Boxers said. "I never like leaving a vehicle too close to the road."

"It's the way poachers behave," Simonsen said. "I didn't have a lot else to do, so I thought I'd seek you out and find you." He pointed briefly to Boxers' boots. "Them size fifties make tracking pretty easy. I saw where you guys split from each other, so I followed the easy one first."

Now it made sense. Sort of. "You walked all this way just to ask questions?" Jonathan said. "That must be two miles."

"Every bit of three," Simonsen corrected. "It's my job and my pleasure to arrest poachers. Not everyone has the patience to wait the years it can take to win the permit lottery."

Jonathan had grown tired of the jaw flapping. "Are we free to go?"

"As far as I'm concerned. Unless you need to confess to something."

Jonathan chuckled. If only the warden knew what Jonathan could confess about the last many years. "I've got a question for you about elk. This is my first time with game this big. Is this spot—"

Simonsen's vest dimpled, and he made a burping sound as he sat down hard. He was still moving when the sound of a gunshot reached them.

"Shit!" Jonathan and Boxers said it together. They reacted instantly—reflexively—by likewise dropping to the ground and crawling for cover. Jonathan had just dived behind another cedar when a bullet tore through it at what would have been the level of his head if he hadn't ducked. The report reached them about a second later.

"You okay, Boss?" Boxers asked.

"Fine. You?"

"Peachy. Who'd you piss off this time?"

Simonsen had been hit hard, drilled through his center of mass. He'd collapsed onto his back, staring up at the flawless sky. Jonathan had no idea whether he was dead or alive, but he knew he was unacceptably exposed.

"Cover me," Jonathan said. "I'm going to pull him to cover."

"He's dead."

"We don't know that."

Jonathan watched as Boxers shifted his butt around so he could better stabilize his rifle. "You do what you want," Big Guy said, "but I don't think Ranger Rick is the shooter's target."

"Why?"

"Watch. Keep an eye on the slope on the other side of the river." Without any warning, Boxers darted back into the clear for half a second and then ducked back behind cover. A bullet tore into the trees behind where he would have been, accentuated after the fact by the sound of the rifle's report.

"Big Guy!" Jonathan yelled. "What the hell?"

Boxers had made himself small—as if that were possible—behind his tree. "Did you see muzzle flashes?"

"Seriously?"

"I told you to watch the other side."

Jonathan settled in deeper behind his cover and tried to think. The fact that the shooter had not anchored his kill of the game warden with another shot made it clear— well, mostly clear—that Simonsen was not his intended target. That left only the two of them.

"What do you figure the time delay between the impact and the report?" he asked Boxers.

"I give it about a second."

"That's what I got. Speed of sound is three hundred forty meters per second, right?"

"Three forty-three," Boxers corrected

"What's that, three hundred seventy-five yards?"

"Give or take."

Jonathan pulled his laser range finder from its pocket on his vest and scanned the other slope. The trees were thick and the hill was steep. At the three-fifty- to three-seventy-five-yard mark, the woods were especially thick.

"I don't see a spot at that range where he could get a

shot off without hitting another tree," he observed aloud. This was not a long shot for a talented sniper, but it was a challenging range for a hunter. Even twigs and leaves can make a difference in the flight path of the bullet.

Maybe that's what happened.

"Hey, Boss," Boxers said. "Take a look at the rock ledge about ten meters to the left of the massive red tree."

Jonathan pulled the range finder away to locate the landmark with his bare eyes and then brought it up again. An outcropping of rocks rose from the trees. From it, a shooter could have a clear field of fire. Mother Nature had built a perfect sniper's nest—an elevated platform for taking the shot and lots of cover in the event of return fire. And it was at the right distance.

"Okay," Jonathan said. "Now that I know where to look, jump out again and I'll watch for the muzzle flash."

"I already rode that horse," Boxers said. "I believe it is your turn."

It was hard to argue the logic. Besides, since Big Guy's stunt had clearly been a ruse to get the guy to show himself, the shooter would be foolish to fall for the same trick a second time. "He's probably moved on to get a different angle," Jonathan said.

"Definitely," Boxers agreed. Neither of them moved.

"You're still going to make me do this, aren't you? After all the good times we've had together."

"Nah," Big Guy said. "I'm not making you do anything. I don't mind sittin' here till dark. It'll get damned cold, though."

Jonathan peered through the range finder again. He supposed there were other options. They could just pound the outcropping with a shit-ton of ammo, but if they did that and the bad guy wasn't there, that would just reduce the bullets available to them to fight off the real attacker.

"Well, shit," Jonathan said. "I'm gonna do this thing, okay?"

"If you insist."

"But I'm not going to just duck in and out. I'm going to make a dash for that thick oak on the other side of the warden." He was betting on the fact that the shooter wasn't good enough to lead his target effectively.

"Want me to keep his head down?" Big Guy asked.

"That'd defeat the purpose, wouldn't it? I mean, the whole point is to get him to show himself."

"You're right," Boxers said. "I was just testing your commitment. What about that orange vest?"

"I'll keep it on for the mad dash. It'll add to his temptation to shoot."

"Good thinking," Boxers said. "I'd hustle, though, if I were you. Sometimes you run like a girl when you're scared."

"I hate you."

Boxers answered with a loud smooching sound.

"I'm counting it down," Jonathan said. "Three . . . two . . . one . . ." He launched himself into the opening at what would have been *zero* if he'd continued the cadence. He sprinted out into the clearing, bent low at the waist to create as small a target as possible, and beelined to cover behind the stout hardwood. As Jonathan passed Simonsen, a quick glance showed that his eyes were fixed and lifeless.

As Jonathan slid into place, Boxers opened up with a barrage of ten shots.

"Did he shoot at me?" Jonathan shouted after Big Guy was done.

"Negative, but I saw a flash. I figured it for the lens of a rifle scope."

"Game warden's dead," Jonathan said.

"I told you he would be."

Now that they could eyeball each other across the clearing, Jonathan tugged at the lapel of his blaze orange vest and unzipped it. This was not a time for high visibility. As he shrugged out of it, Boxers did the same.

"Well, this is exciting," Big Guy said. "What do you want to do next?"

CHAPTER 2

The stamp in the cornerstone declared to the world that Godfrey's Hardware established its Fisherman's Cove roots in 1959, but to Gail Bonneville's eye, it might as well have been a hundred years earlier. Ike Godfrey, the third-generation proprietor, sported a beard that would have made ZZ Top jealous. The color of dirty snow, his whiskers extended to the top of his prominent belly, which itself strained the seams and suspenders of his ever-present denim coveralls. With the approach of cold weather, he'd only recently replaced the ever-present faded T-shirt he wore underneath with an ever-present three-button Henley.

If the faded portraits on the wall inside the front door were accurate, Ike was the image of both his father and grandfather. Gail was too new to Fisherman's Cove to remember either one, but she'd heard that every generation of Godfreys had served valiantly in their generations' wars and lived well into their nineties.

A bell slapped against the glass as Gail pulled the door open. She stepped aside to let Venice Alexander enter ahead of her. Spelling be damned, the correct pronunciation for her colleague's name was "Ven-EE-chay." It had something to do with a teenage temper tantrum, and the moniker had stuck.

Ike greeted them with a big smile and a little wave. "I know I'm blessed when two beauties enter my store at the same time," he said. As he approached, he wiped his hands on a rag that he conjured from his back pocket. His Popeye forearms bore wartime tattoos that Gail didn't understand yet respected, nonetheless. "How are my favorite private eyes doing today?"

"Only one of us is a PI.," Venice corrected. "I'm just an IT nerd."

Gail suppressed a laugh at Venice's understatement. In reality, that IT nerd was one of the most feared hackers on the planet. Of course, no one was allowed to know that. In a town this size, where everyone knew everything about everybody else—or at least thought they did—it suited Gail's and Venice's purposes for the world to believe that their employer, Security Solutions, was a plain vanilla private investigations firm, when, in fact, it was much more than that.

"And I'm more of a manager than an investigator," Gail said. Hey, if the meme of the day was understatement, why shouldn't she do her part?

"What can I do for you?" Ike asked.

"It's that time of year," Venice said. "RezHouse needs new batteries for the smoke detectors."

"Standard nine-volts?"

"I need thirty of them," Venice said.

Ike gave a low whistle. "I remember when there were

only a few students," he said. Then he laughed. "Okay, I remember when there were no students at all."

Resurrection House stood on the grounds of the mansion where Jonathan and Venice had both grown up, albeit with him in the nice part and she in the servants' quarters. Those were the days when Digger went by Jonny and his last name was Gravenow. The days before his father, Simon, had finally been caught doing the things that had made him rich on his way to earning a life stretch in a SuperMax. Today, the mansion served as home for Venice, her son, Roman, and for Mama Alexander. Modern academic buildings and dormitories on the mansion's land served as Resurrection House, a boarding school for the children of incarcerated parents.

In a kind of temper tantrum of his own, Jonathan had years before deeded the land to St. Katherine's Catholic Church for one dollar on the single condition that it be used for the purpose he dictated. Since then, the school had lived off of charitable funds raised through the RezHouse Foundation, which was subsidized with hundreds of thousands of dollars in contributions from Jonathan's own pockets.

"If it's for the school, the batteries are on the house," Ike said. "And don't waste your breath arguing."

He spun on his heel and led them farther back into the store, into the canyons of shelves that were stuffed with everything from hammers and saws to garden furniture. Bullets to arrows to firearms. Gail felt confident that if they looked hard enough, they'd find elements of Grandpa's original inventory buried in the stacks somewhere.

Gail loved the place. Keep your big-box hardware

emporiums. It was worth a few extra bucks to deal with people who knew not just where everything was inside the store but also how to work every piece of equipment they sold.

Venice's order stripped the spinning display rack's supply of two-pack nine-volt batteries.

"We have to stay on schedule with these things," Venice explained. "You can't let the batteries go low and start chirping. It always happens at two in the morning, and it takes forever to find out which one is the problem."

Ike agreed. "I tell people all the time, when you replace one, replace them all. Saves a lot of heartache."

They carried their armfuls of battery booty to the front counter, where Ike produced what looked like a paper lunch bag from underneath and shook it open. "This should hold them all," he said. "By the way, when does the gala happen this year?" The RezHouse Foundation hosted a fundraiser every year at the Kennedy Center in Washington, DC, and Ike was a regular.

Gail groaned. She'd come along on the trip to the hardware store to take a break from office drudgery, but now that Venice was dialed into a RezHouse confab, she knew that the visit would extend an extra ten minutes. She excused herself to dig a little deeper into the museum that was the stock on the shelves.

As she approached the front window, a display of coiled-spring leg-holder traps caught her attention. Gail wasn't a hunter. She didn't mind that Digger and Boxers were off on their critter-kill in Montana, but she didn't understand the allure of meeting your food before you ate it. These traps, though, sized for everything from foxes to bears, were cruel. If you're going to kill a thing, kill it. She saw no need to torture it first. That's why she favored snap traps for mice over the "humanitarian" glue traps that drove little Mickey to rip off his own hide as he struggled to get away.

A glance out the front window made her stop perusing and pulled her closer to the glass.

A green Toyota pickup truck sat parked across the road and down a ways to the right. The driver sat behind the wheel, and the waft of exhaust from the tailpipe told her that the engine was running. Something about this wasn't right.

Before joining on with Digger's team, Gail had been a sheriff in Indiana, and before that, she'd been an operator on the FBI's HRT—Hostage Rescue Team. Some elements of training never dim. This was the second time she'd seen this vehicle today. The first was when it was parked near a stop sign at the base of Church Street, outside the converted firehouse that served as the offices for Security Solutions. She'd noticed it then because the vehicle was occupied and running, but she'd dismissed her concern because there were a thousand reasons for an idling truck to be curbed in the middle of town.

Out here, though, Godfrey's was the only business within a hundred-yard stretch of road, and she and Venice were the only people in the store.

"Hey, Ven?" Gail called.

"I know, we're almost ready to go," Venice replied.

"I need you to come over, please. Ike, you, too, if you don't mind."

Ten seconds later, they were with her at the window. "Does that vehicle look familiar to either of you?"

"It's a pretty generic truck," Ike said.

"I don't recognize it," Venice said. "Why?"

Gail explained about seeing it across from the office.

"Are you sure it's the same one?" Ike asked. "How many green pickups must there be?"

"There's no reason for him to be sitting there," Gail said. "Unusual means potentially dangerous."

Ike scoffed. "You have any idea how many vehicles drive up and down this road every day?"

"How many park and watch your door?" Venice asked. She turned to Gail. "Do you want to call Doug Kramer?" He was the chief of police for Fisherman's Cove.

That was probably the smart move, but Gail didn't want to pull that trigger just yet. Though Doug and Digger had grown up together, a cop was a cop, and so much of what Security Solutions did fell outside the rule of law that she didn't want to invite eyes and ears that didn't need to be there.

"If it turns out to be nothing, that will be embarrassing," Gail explained.

"I'll call him if you'd rather," Ike said.

"Not yet."

"You look like you have a plan," Venice said.

It wasn't the first time that Gail had been outed for her lack of a poker face. "Sort of," she said. "Are you carrying your pistol?" she asked Venice.

"It's in the car."

Of course it was. Venice had a carry permit and she had a weapon, but she never liked having it around. Gail pressed her elbow against the grip of the holstered Glock 19 on her right hip, under her coat.

Ike produced a .38 snubby from the front pocket of his overalls. "Use mine if you want. What are you thinking?"

Gail explained.

After they'd finished listening, Venice said, "So, you want to use Ike and me as bait."

"A distraction," Gail corrected.

"Why don't I just go out and confront the son of a bitch?" Ike offered.

"I don't want to put you in the middle of our troubles," Gail said.

"If he's up to no good, how do you know I'm not the target?"

"Because he started at our office," Gail said. "It's the nature of our business that we sometimes piss people off. I'm thinking this might be one of those people."

"Angry that he got his windows peeped into?" Ike quipped.

Gail let that go. She was thinking more along the lines of the Chechen terrorists they'd crossed, the Russian plots they'd spoiled, or even the politicians whose careers they'd destroyed over the years.

"Something like that," Gail said. "Just be as nonchalant as you can manage. Keep an eye on him without looking like you're doing it."

"I don't like you out there by yourself," Venice said.

"If I need help, you'll be close."

"You're a tough gal," Ike said. "I like tough gals. The back door is past the pet food." He pointed to the canyon of stuff farthest to the left.

Gail wasted no time. Winding her way back through the stacks, she tried not to think about what a fire trap this store was, comforting herself with the thought that it had been this way for a long, long time.

Predictably, the exit light over the back door was burned out, as were the overhead fluorescents—or maybe Ike hadn't turned them on. The light on her phone helped her navigate the final few feet to the steel panel door. She lifted the steel crosspiece from the keepers that had been mounted to the masonry wall, pulled the dead bolt out of the slot, and pushed the door open.

Gail hadn't realized how warm it was in the store until the cold afternoon air rushed over her. Moving quickly but without running, she hooked to the left and crossed to what she thought of as the green side of the building. She kept her Glock holstered, but she opened her canvas farm coat to allow for quicker access if it came to that.

A patch of woods in the store's side yard gave her some measure of cover to get down the road a bit, then she crossed to a point where she would be behind the Toyota. A glance over her shoulder revealed that Ike and Venice were exactly where they were supposed to be, engaged in conversation at the hood of Venice's new Chevy Blazer.

At this angle, Gail could see only a sliver of the driver's face, but he appeared to be watching the diversion.

She told herself that this didn't have to be the threat she sensed it to be. There could be a thousand reasons why this guy was following them. Just because she couldn't think of one that wasn't an inherent threat didn't mean that it didn't exist.

She approached the Toyota from its seven o'clock position, doing her best to stay out of the sideview mirror's range. She didn't want the driver to see her until he was at full disadvantage, but she also didn't want to startle him too badly.

Again, it was possible that an innocent explanation existed.

She was still ten feet away when the driver saw her reflection. He reacted with startling speed, pivoting in his seat and whipping his hand up to the window.

Gail never saw the gun—at least not yet—but she recognized the body mechanics for what they were, and she sure as hell recognized the boom of the shots as the driver fired through his closed window. She dove to the street and rolled to the left rear wheel.

The Glock was in her hand before she realized she'd drawn it. From a seated position, she saw the driver's door fly open as the shooter started to roll out of the door. She saw his leg from his thigh down, and she drilled his knee with her first shot. She saw the denim of his jeans pucker with the impact, and she thought she heard him yell, but he kept coming.

Half a second later, the driver pivoted out of the door, somehow landing on his good leg. His right hand gripped what looked to be a short-barreled MP5 pistol.

Gail threw herself backward on the pavement to pose as small a target as she could. Aiming past and between her raised knees, she pumped as many rounds into the man's exposed torso as it took to make him collapse and stop moving.

For what felt like minutes but couldn't possibly have

been more than a few seconds, she held her position and her aim, ready to drill him again if he moved. Between the assault to her eardrums and the percussive hammering of her heart, the world seemed without sound.

Still holding her aim, Gail sat up. By the time her legs were under her again, Ike and Venice had arrived at the scene.

". . . okay?"

They were speaking to her, but she hadn't yet rejoined the real world.

"Gail!"

She pivoted her head to see Venice leaning into her face. "Are you okay? Are you hurt?"

Good question. "I think I'm fine," Gail said.

Ike moved in closer. "Do me a favor and put that piece back in its holster," he said. "Sumbitch is dead. Let's check you for holes."

Working from muscle memory, Gail pushed her jacket out of the way, lifted the tail of her shirt, and slid her pistol back into its Kydex home till it seated with a click.

"Hold your arms out," Ike said.

Gail knew the drill. All too often at the end of a gunfight, people discovered after the fact that they'd been hit. Another set of eyes could see things that the potential victim couldn't.

"I don't see anything," Ike said.

"I think I'm fine," Gail said again.

"What was that all about?" Venice asked. She'd been calm a few seconds ago, but now the nerves were kicking in. Her voice trembled when she spoke.

"I don't know," Gail said. "I think it was a hit. Clearly, the driver intended to kill me. Maybe us."

Venice and Gail locked gazes as the same thought occurred to them. "RezHouse." They said it together.

"We've got to lock it down," Venice said. "Now."

CHAPTER 3

Boxers kept an eye out for ongoing threats while Jonathan pulled Simonsen's body behind some rocks, where he wouldn't be visible to someone on the other side of the valley. Jonathan knew it was silly to worry about a corpse, but he wanted to allow the man as much dignity as conditions would allow.

Once behind cover, Jonathan released the Velcro closures for the ranger's ballistic vest and flopped it over his head so he could slide it off the body. The lack of blood from the bullet wound spoke of instant death. Once he'd removed the ranger's vest, Jonathan started going through his pockets.

"Do you think you could leave a little more DNA on the body?" Boxers said. "The dumbest prosecutor on Earth will be able to build a case of robbery and murder."

"We're going to report it all, anyway," Jonathan said. "We've got nothing to hide."

"The hell we don't. We could sink a cruise ship with the shit we have to hide." Along with Venice and Gail, Jonathan and Boxers ran a covert side of Security Solutions that operated far outside the lines of the law. It started as an effort to rescue kidnap victims more . . . *efficiently* than law enforcement officers could. While feebs and local SWAT teams were consumed by cumbersome procedures designed to cover their asses and protect the rights of bad guys, Jonathan and his team did what had to be done and left with their precious cargoes—the hostages that they'd rescued—healthy and ready to be reunited with their loved ones. As for the kidnappers, well, missions often ended badly for them.

"We haven't done anything wrong here," Jonathan said. "I want to find this guy's radio."

"You know, if you get arrested, I'm not bailing you out."

"I always figured you'd just blow the wall out of the jail and walk me out."

"Now you're flirting with me," Boxers said. At once gentle and lethal, Big Guy loved blowing shit up. It might have been his favorite thing. But only for the forces of good. "What's the plan from here? We gonna look for the body across the valley?"

Jonathan sat back on his haunches, frustrated. "This guy has a couple hundred rounds of ammunition, but no radio. How does that make any sense?"

"Am I talking to myself here?" Boxers asked. "What the hell is our next move?"

"And the ammo is all nine-mil while we're both shooting seven-six-two and forty-five." Jonathan stood, but kept low, behind the cover of the rocks as he draped Simonsen's vest over the dead man's face. "No, we're not going to go look for the body." He led the way deeper into the surrounding forest and deeper into cover.

"Inquiring minds want to know why."

"What's the point?" Jonathan asked. "If he's dead, he'll be dead for quite some time. If he's wounded, he'll have all the advantage as we go to him. I don't see an upside to walking that far out in the open."

"You're not even curious about who was trying to kill us?" Boxers asked. "Because I have to tell you I'm curious as shit."

"We'll let the police handle it," Jonathan said.

"What police? We're in the middle of nowhere."

"That's what nine-one-one was invented for."

"Have you tried your phone out here?" Boxers said. "I've got *negative* bars."

"Same here. And the sat phone is in the truck," Jonathan said.

"I told you, you should have brought it along."

"Really?" Jonathan said. "That's where you want to go?"

"I'm just sayin' I told you it was a bad idea to leave the phone in the truck. I told you that if one of us got hurt, you might want to have it."

"We have the radios," Jonathan countered. "If one of us got hurt, the other could go back to the truck and make the call."

"How's that workin' for you now?"

"Are you really going to make me shoot you?" Jonathan said.

"I'm just sayin' that next time . . ." Boxers let it go with a laugh.

They stood in an awkward silence for a few seconds.

Big Guy said, "So, are we hiking back now or what?"

"What are the chances that that guy was working alone?" Jonathan asked. He sat back down on a rock.

Boxers leaned against a tree. The tree groaned.

Jonathan said, "Can we agree that the shooting was intentional? That we were the targets?"

"As opposed to who else?"

"As opposed to *anyone* else," Jonathan said. "And I mean specifically you and me. Digger Grave and Brian Van de Muelebroecke."

Boxers took his time answering. "I won't dispute it," he said. "I mean, I can't say that's *not* the case, but I don't see that it has to be. There are easier ways to kill us than to follow us out to the land of elk and moose."

Jonathan saw the point, but he felt confident that his instincts were right. For the moment, it didn't matter *why* someone tried to kill them. It mattered *that* they tried.

"You know what?" Jonathan said. "We *don't* know that they were trying to kill *us*. We only know that they were trying to kill *me*."

Boxers puffed up, feigning insult. "You're saying I'm not good enough to want to kill?"

Jonathan laughed. "I'm sure I could fill a ballroom with people who'd be delighted to kill you."

"Damn straight you could."

"But in this case, the shooter lined up to take *me* out. You were set up hundreds of yards from here."

Boxers' eyes got big as something dawned on him. "Well, there's your answer," he said. "Yes, there's another shooter out there."

Jonathan saw it, too. "Setting up to take *you* out."

"Exactly."

"But Ranger Simonsen arrived and screwed it up." Jonathan tried to fold his arms, got annoyed when his rifle got in the way. "That means we're still being hunted."

"Unless he got scared off by what happened to his buddy."

"*Their* buddy," Jonathan corrected. "That's what we have to assume, anyway. That there's more than one left."

"I wonder if they thought to bring a satellite phone with them," Boxers said.

Jonathan let him have his gloat.

"So, I guess we need to work our way back to the Suburban," Boxers said.

Jonathan wasn't so sure. "They'll know that's the one place we have to go," he said. "Whoever these shooters are, they're ambitious enough to come all the way out here to take us out, and they're talented enough to nearly make a pretty long shot. If any are still alive, they're smart enough to use our Suburban as bait to set a trap."

In his mind, Jonathan inventoried what they'd left in the Suburban. Pretty much everything.

"Here's what we know," Jonathan thought aloud. "It's gonna get damn cold tonight, and all of my cold weather gear is in the Suburban."

"We can always cuddle," Boxers said.

"You'll crush me when you turn over," Jonathan said.

"Wait till dark and go to the Suburban then?"

"If we assume competence, then we have to assume they've got NVGs." Night vision goggles.

"Staying put is not a good idea," Boxers said. "If we're going to stay in the woods overnight, we'll need to build a shelter and put it someplace with better advantage."

Jonathan didn't relish the idea of camping out in sub-freezing weather. Big Guy was right that they needed to find shelter, but Jonathan wasn't so sure that they'd have to build it.

"I think I have a solution," he said. Laying his rifle on the ground at his feet, Jonathan straightened his right leg to gain access to the pouch pocket on his thigh, where he kept a map of the forest where they'd set out to hunt. It was one thing to choose to remain incommunicado by leaving the satellite phone in the truck, but it would have been suicidal to enter any forest without a map and a compass and the know-how to use them.

"When we scoped out where to set up, I remember seeing a cabin around here somewhere," he explained. He kneeled and spread the map out on the ground so they both could see. In this part of Montana, there wasn't much to see if you didn't know what you were looking for. Squiggly rust-colored contour lines showed the various elevations, blue lines showed the locations of streams, and tiny squares showed man-made structures, so far as those structures were known.

"Our truck is here," Jonathan said, pointing to a piece of tape he'd placed on the paper map. It took a few seconds for him to get his bearings and trace his finger along the route they'd taken to get to the spot where they were kneeling. "And here we are now."

"Longer way than I thought," Boxers said.

"Simonsen said three miles." Jonathan leaned in closer for a better look, then shifted his body to get out of his own shadow. When he'd gone through this exercise last night at the hotel, he'd had better light. "If I'm remembering properly, there's a house about a mile west of here."

"Which side of Death Valley?" Boxers asked, gesturing to the shooter's location.

Jonathan stabbed the map with his finger. "Here," he

said. "And better still, it's on this side. We don't have to walk through the kill zone."

"The *known* kill zone," Boxers corrected.

"Ever the cheerful one," Jonathan said. He folded the map in on itself until the rectangular paper showed their current location and the one where they wanted to go. Next, he produced a compass from the same pouch pocket and shot a quick azimuth toward the cabin. He pointed up the hill with a bladed hand. "That way."

Renaldo Vega cursed himself quietly as he patched his wounds. The first missed shot was a forgivable sin, but an unfortunate one. At this range, there was always a possibility that a target would move while a bullet was in flight, and that was exactly what had happened as he tried to execute Jonathan Grave. That the bullet hit a cop, instead, would muddy the waters for Renaldo's boss, but as far as Renaldo was concerned, prey was prey. If collateral damage occurred, such was the price of doing business, as the Americans liked to say.

What angered him was the fact that he fell for the trap of drawing out his fire. That's what happened when emotions were allowed in invade what is supposed to be a calculated application of force. The miss had angered him. When the second target, Brian Van de–something unpronounceable, had stepped out from behind cover, Renaldo had assumed he was making a stupid mistake and he'd fired. He didn't realize until after the bullet had left the muzzle that he was being goaded into revealing his position.

His error had earned him a thigh and neck full of bullet

and rock fragments from the fusillade of what must have been ten rounds unleashed at him. He figured they had to come from Brian the Giant because Jonathan Grave was still in motion when they arrived. They were not well-aimed—thank God for that, or Renaldo would have already passed through the gates of Hell—but they were effective at keeping his head down as he tried to present as small a target as possible.

Renaldo never saw where the bullets themselves impacted, but they were close enough to launch white-hot fragments into his flesh. He felt more than a little foolish as he cowered now behind the rocks that provided his cover, using his knife blade to pry the bits of metal and stone out of his flesh.

So far as he could tell, none of the fragments had penetrated deep enough to cause life-threatening issues, but they hurt like hell and a few of them bled with surprising enthusiasm. Nothing his medical kit could not handle, but it would take some time to patch himself up. He kept his rifle close in case Grave and his friend wanted to verify their kill, but he didn't think they would. That would be a stupid move on their part. They'd been ambushed, and they'd survived. They had ample cover to be swallowed into where they could be safe. Renaldo had been told to respect these men as worthy adversaries, and he had every intention of doing so.

He'd let them have a head start while he did as good a job as he could on patching himself up.

When he'd dressed this morning in his heavy camo gear and quilted long underwear, he'd done it for the warmth the clothing would provide. He'd had no idea that they would serve as body armor. Nowhere near enough to even slow a direct hit, they provided at least a little protection against the much slower and oddly shaped fragments when they hit.

He was able to pull most of them out with the tip of his blade. In the case of the two in his neck, he'd been able to leverage them out with his fingernail. Of the wounds he could see—a couple of the ones on his backside were out of sight—only the one on his right thigh could probably have benefited from a couple of stitches. On that one, the fragment had avulsed a wad of subcutaneous fat that Renaldo just pushed back into place, and he covered it up with a two-inch-square adhesive bandage.

The whole process of repairing his wounds took the better part of twenty minutes. When he was done, it was time to rejoin the hunt.

Renaldo had planned this encounter carefully. Once he had read the email string between Grave and the officials at the Montana Fish, Wildlife and Parks Department, the task of tracking them had become fairly easy—and was made even easier through the purchase of a drone that could track them as they drove.

If Renaldo hadn't whiffed his shots, he'd be a quarter of the way back to his vehicle by now. As it was, the day was going to get a lot longer.

A *ranger* for God's sake. How could he possibly have planned for the intrusion of a ranger? Who would have seen that coming?

In retrospect, Renaldo probably should have aborted the job as soon as Fabian Ramirez reported that Grave's giant friend had walked away from his hunting position, thus ruining Ramirez's shot.

Instead, Renaldo had instructed Ramirez to return to

the vehicle. Renaldo figured that two people in the same shooting location would be too visible, especially since Ramirez would not have had time to establish a strong sniper position before it would have been time to shoot.

It never occurred to Renaldo—not for even an instant—that he would whiff the shot.

He felt the emotion returning to his gut, and he willed it away. As inexcusable as the events of this morning were in his mind, he could not tolerate even the thought of letting his heart get in front of his head again.

What was past, was past. He still had a job to do, and he had every intention of doing it.

Grave's choices at this point were limited. Renaldo knew what they were—knew what they were *likely* to be, he corrected himself. Hubris was often deadlier than emotion.

There were only a few places he could go. The most likely one was their vehicle, and that was already covered by others in Renaldo's team.

That left the single least likely place to go, which he decided would be his next stop.

Renaldo walked to the fine specimen of horse that his sponsor had provided, and he mounted up.

If he could get there first, the day might still end on a good note.

CHAPTER 4

Roman Alexander knew that he was supposed to be paying attention. He knew that Mr. Moranian, the squatty little man in the frayed sweater who was droning on about the Marshall Plan and the aftermath of World War Two, would lose his shit if he caught Roman daydreaming again, but there was too much crap spinning around inside Roman's head for him to focus.

Roman wasn't sure what he'd done to piss off Mateo Lopez, but clearly, something had happened. There was a time—not long ago—when Roman wouldn't have given a crap about what another student thought of him, but much had changed in the few months since he'd transferred into RezHouse from the Northern Neck Academy. At the Neck, he was one of many just like himself— smart, wealthy, and aware. Here at RezHouse, though, academic barriers to entry didn't exist. You just had to be a kid.

And kind of an orphan.

Resurrection House was a residential learning center for kids whose parents were in jail. The students here came from all over the country, while the students at the Neck came from all over the world.

Here, the finer points of math, science, and literature were not high priorities, and Roman had run himself crosswise with a bunch of the kids by being quick to raise his hand and presenting the correct answers in class. The defining conflict happened in history class on Roman's third day at RezHouse. He'd known that the Civilian Conservation Corps had been a part of FDR's New Deal, and the speed of his response had pissed off Richard Goldsbury, the most persistent rider of Roman's ass.

Goldsbury had assembled his posse to beat Roman down as he crossed the basketball courts on his way to the dormitory.

"Hey, Smart Boy," Goldsbury had yelled to him. "You've got things to learn about how things work here at Rez-House." Four of Goldsbury's buddies followed him like geese—V formation and everything—as they moved in to take Roman down.

Roman rolled his shoulders to let his backpack slide to the ground and braced for what was coming. Goldsbury's lips were pressed into a thin line, his fists were clenched, and his eyebrows had knitted into a single line. Violence was coming.

Goldsbury was the kind of bully that Mr. Jonathan and Mr. Boxers had told Roman about for years—one who won by frightening his opponents. Goldsbury could probably hit hard and probably enjoyed doing it, but he clearly had not been trained. He'd squared off instead of angling his body, and he held his hands way too low.

Goldsbury had closed the distance to four feet when Roman launched a right cross that connected the heel of his hand with the spot where the left side of Goldsbury's lower jowl joined his upper. The attacker spun halfway on his own axis and dropped. He wasn't knocked out, but he wasn't getting up for a while, either.

The trailing geese slid to a stop. Schoolyard fights at RezHouse usually lasted longer than this, no doubt with different results.

"I don't want to hurt anyone else," Roman said.

"You think you can take us all out?" That question came from a nasty piece of work named Settlemeyer. His teeth were a shade of yellow that Roman had never seen before.

"I'd rather not have to," Roman replied. He never talked about the black belt he'd earned, but he'd gained confidence recently when he'd had to use it against a no-shit real-life killer.

Settlemeyer feinted drawing back to throw a punch, but he remained out of range and Roman didn't react.

Neither did the other geese.

"You're an asshole, Alexander," Settlemeyer proclaimed. "You just started a war."

It had been three months, yet the second battle never materialized. Maybe it would never come.

Still, Goldsbury had made it clear to the rest of the school that a choice needed to be made. To be Roman Alexander's friend was to be Richard Goldsbury's enemy. Remember that fear thing? Yeah, it was real.

One exception was Mateo Lopez. Tall, athletic, and a magnet for girls' attention, Mateo seemed to fear no one and somehow commanded everyone's respect. Even Richard Goldsbury stayed out of his way, yet they seemed to be friendly with each other.

For the high schoolers, every dormitory room was a single, unlike the doubles and even quads for the younger kids. Smaller than the closet in Roman's bedroom back at the mansion, his room still had a private sink and room enough for a bed and a desk. Mateo's similar room sat directly across the hall. On most nights, the two of them spent the final hour or so before lights out sitting in one room or the other and shooting the shit.

They talked about nothing important and about everything that was not. One of the critical RezHouse rules—one that Father Dom D'Angelo had specifically mentioned on Roman's first day—was that no one asked questions about anyone's family. The school itself was born of trauma, and no one wanted to dredge up bad times while trying to create new good ones.

If any of the students had pieced together the fact that Mama Alexander was his grandmother, they hadn't challenged him with it yet. Fact was, Roman didn't belong here. The only reason he had left Northern Neck Academy was for the security surrounding RezHouse and its residents. Guarded 24/7 by armed and uniformed officers, the school and dormitories appeared to Roman to be impenetrable.

His mom, Mr. Jonathan, and Father Dom had all agreed that it was the only option for him after a kidnapping thing that had happened to him several months ago—a thing that he wasn't allowed to ask questions about. He wasn't supposed to be curious about how Mr. Jonathan and Mr. Boxers ended up following him down to Mexico and sinking a submarine.

No, really. A goddamn submarine.

Roman tried never to think about what would have

happened if the timing of that night had been even a little bit off.

Father Dom was pastor of St. Kate's, and he was also a shrink. A psychologist. Apparently, he and Mr. Jonathan had grown up together or maybe gone to college together, and they were best buds. When Roman got back to the USA after being beaten and shot at and sinking a god-damn submarine, the adults all agreed that he needed to spend some time with a head specialist.

Roman liked Father Dom. He'd known him—or at least who he was—for as long as he could remember, but before the kidnapping shit, it was hard to see past that white patch on his collar. Now that he thought about it, Father Dom never wore his collar when they had their talks. They happened in the living room of Father Dom's house—in the rectory—and Roman liked the way that the priest spoke to him as if he were a regular guy instead of a patient or even a kid.

Roman's wandering brain shifted gears to his most recent chat with Father Dom. It got very real after the priest asked him whether he was still sleeping well.

"I have nightmares," Roman said. He described some of the violence in them.

Father Dom scowled. "That's a new development."

"No, it's not. I've been lying to you."

The priest's eyes narrowed. "Why would you do that?"

Roman made a point of saying nothing as he held his gaze.

Father Dom leaned back into his cushioned plaid chair and crossed his legs. They did a staring contest for the better part of a minute before the priest said, "It's not like you to play games."

"Who says it's a game?" Roman sat in an identical chair, but with both feet drawn up under his thighs. "I've been having nightmares. They keep me from sleeping."

"I know you have," Father Dom said. "I hear from your mom that the house mothers hear you yelling out in the night."

Roman felt his gut tighten. "You said everything we talk about is secret."

"It is. That doesn't stop her from telling me things."

"So, you're just keeping secrets from *me*."

Father Dom chuckled. It wasn't a mocking thing. He looked genuinely amused. "Says the pot to the kettle. Look, Roman, these meetings are all about you. You've been through a lot, seen a lot, and these talks are all about helping you sort things out in your head."

"Because I'm crazy, right?"

Another laugh. "Young man, you are many things, pain in the ass among them. But as far as I can tell, *crazy* is nowhere on the list."

"But if you knew I was lying, why didn't you say anything?"

Father Dom hiked his shoulders. "I assumed you had your reasons. These meetings are about *you*, Roman. You can use them however you want."

Roman was still thinking that through when the priest raised his right hand as if taking an oath. "We've known each other a long time, and you know what I do for a living. When I raise a hand to God, it's a pretty serious thing. So here I am swearing to you that I will never repeat a word of what happens in here to anyone else."

Roman didn't know why he had such a hard time believing him. Everybody loved Father Dom, and perhaps more importantly, he'd never heard anyone say a bad word against him. If there was anyone in his life worth taking a risk with, maybe this was the one.

"Okay," Roman said. "What does my mom *really* do for a living at Security Solutions?"

Something flashed behind the priest's eyes, there and gone in a second. "As far as I know, she pretty much runs the place."

"That's not what I mean."

"Then ask what you mean."

"When Mr. Jonathan goes away on his trips, Mom will stay up all night—either at the firehouse office or the one in the house. When it's the house office, she'll lock the door, and no one is allowed to go near it."

"Have you asked her?" Father Dom asked.

"Sure. But she won't give me a straight answer. I mean, Jesus—" He heard the word pop out of his mouth, and he retreated. "Sorry."

"The Lord understands stress," Father Dom assured him. "After all, he invented it for us."

"Remember Derek Halstrom? Mom's boyfriend? I mean, people *attacked* our house. Why would they do that?"

Father Dom said nothing to that. He seemed to be waiting for more.

"Then, when Mr. Jonathan gets back from his trips, he's always bruised and cut and stuff. What are they doing?"

"What do you think they're doing?"

"Oh, come on, Father," Roman said, slapping his thighs. "What's the point of talking if all you're going to do is answer my questions with more questions?"

"That's the way this works, Roman. During the time

we're together, what *you* think on any topic will be more important than anything *I* think. You're what, fourteen years old now? You've seen a lot, and you've been through a lot. You're smart. You've asked questions of your mom and, I presume, Mama Alexander. Maybe Digger and Boxers. What have you pieced together?"

"You know they're the ones who rescued me down in Mexico, right?"

"I've heard rumors to that effect." Father Dom winked.

"I mean, they had guns and they had grenades and all kinds of shit. Oh, sorry."

"The Lord understands cussing, too. He doesn't like it, but He understands it."

"Why is all of this happening?"

Father Dom's patient smile never wavered.

"Why won't anyone answer my questions, Father? I mean, they're not stupid, are they? The questions, I mean?"

"No questions are stupid," Father Dom said. "But there are a few that can't be answered easily."

Roman decided to change his approach. "Okay, after we got back from Mexico—no, when we were getting off the plane—Mr. Boxers gave me this real serious talk about how I should never tell anyone about what happened down there. He wouldn't tell me why, but he was, like, scary-serious. He said that if I told anyone, people's lives would be threatened. I mean, come *on*."

"You're angry."

"Of *course* I'm angry. Wouldn't you be? I mean, I have to go to a different school, I have to leave all my friends behind, and now I can't tell anyone why. How can I not be angry?"

Father Dom took a deep breath and recrossed his legs.

"Let me ask you this: Are you angry because you don't know what happened or because you can't tell people about it?"

That one rocked Roman back a little. "What do you mean?"

"Just what I said. If you understood what happened, would you tell your friends about what you knew?"

"Not if it would threaten people's lives."

"Might knowing those things threaten *your* life?" Father Dom asked. "Could it be that that's why they don't tell you what you want to know? Could it be safer with you not knowing?"

"I have the right to make that decision."

Father Dom gave a little shrug that said, *maybe*.

Roman leaned forward in his chair and drew his legs even deeper under him. "Do *you* know what they really do at Security Solutions?"

"Remember that stuff about what we say being secret between us? That pretty much cuts across the board. We priests aren't allowed to talk about a lot of stuff. Throw in the part about me being a psychologist, and you understand why I don't talk much."

Roman had been dancing around his real question, hoping for a way to slip it in without sounding totally paranoid, but now he felt he had no choice. "Am *I* the one people are trying to kill? Is that why I had to quit the Neck and come here?"

He'd been hoping to get a dismissive laugh and an *of course not*. Instead, he got a furrowed brow and a softer tone. "I don't know how to answer that," Father Dom said. "I think it's safe to say that your mom thought the security here is safer than at Northern Neck Academy, but I don't think that translates directly to you being anyone's target."

"Was Derek Halstrom a target?"

"Come on, Roman. You're asking questions I can't possibly know the answers to. What happened to Derek was terrible. What happened to RezHouse that night was terrible, too. Surely you don't think you were the target that night."

The thought had occurred to him.

"Again, I suppose it's possible," Father Dom said, "but hardly likely. Think about who your classmates are. Think about who their parents are. Given the nature of many of the crimes they've committed, you know they must have enemies."

And that's why no one was allowed to talk about family histories.

"Mister Alexander." The sound of Mr. Moranian's voice broke through Roman's wandering thoughts and brought him back to the present. He had no idea what they were talking about anymore.

Roman stood. "Yes, sir?"

"Are we keeping you from something more interesting?" Roman imagined that Mr. Moranian, with his red face and thick neck, might have been the previous generation's Richard Goldsbury.

"I'm sorry, sir." He didn't say that it was impossible to think of anything that *wouldn't* be more interesting than anything Mr. Moranian had to say.

"At least you could open your notebook and pretend to take notes," Moranian said.

Roman responded with a nod and returned to his seat,

making a show of opening the black and white speckled notebook that was filled more with doodles and drawings than with notes.

Moranian wasn't thirty words into the next phase of his monologue when Roman slipped back into his head. He had to figure out what he'd done to piss Mateo off. The smile that never left his friend's face was gone, replaced by a scowl.

When Roman said good morning to him, Mateo had walked away without speaking. That had been hours ago. Even though they sat next to each other in most of their classes, Mateo barely made eye contact.

Roman had resolved to ask directly after Moranian's class, but as it turned out, he didn't have to. As the bell rang and the students all stood in unison, Mateo grabbed the sleeve of Roman's shirt and pulled him closer. "We need to talk," he said.

"What about?"

"Not here."

Before Roman could ask for the details, Mateo was headed for the door, no doubt confident that Roman would follow because people always followed when Mateo led.

Roman's Spidey sense was chiming like a church bell as he followed his friend past the lockers in the hallway and past the ramp that led to the gymnasium—the spot where most conspiratorial conversations went down. Mateo turned left, down the short hall that led to the boys' room, and then beelined toward the exit door that would dump out into the cold air of the south courtyard.

Roman whisper-shouted, "The alarm!"

Mateo slammed his hip into the door's crash bar, and the door blew open. No alarm sounded.

"That alarm hasn't worked in six months," Mateo said. "That's when I broke it." Again, where there would normally have been a smile, there was only a look of stress.

"Where are we going?" Roman asked. The elements weren't adding up. Being alone, out in the courtyard where no one was supposed to be, normally cheerful guy anything but.

"Just over here," Mateo said. "Don't be such a bitch-boy. We need to be in private."

Probably by design, Roman figured, privacy was hard to come by at RezHouse. He knew from his mother that security cameras were hung everywhere and that there were many more than the ones people could see. Everyone could see the unblinking eye that had been installed in the left front corner of every classroom and lab. Students and teachers alike knew that their classroom activities were continuously scrutinized.

What most didn't know, Roman imagined, was that the security teams had hidden lenses in air ducts and on bookshelves. Roman didn't know where they were, exactly, but he knew that the cameras were recording all the time and that they could be monitored in real time via banks of monitors in the guard station, in his mom's office, and from the Zulu Room—the bunker built into the third floor of the mansion that served as an evacuation place if such a thing were ever necessary.

"There's no camera coverage over here," Mateo said as he drew to a halt, and pressed into an inside corner of the courtyard.

How could he know that? Roman wondered. "Tell me what's going on, Mateo."

His friend was nearly vibrating with nervousness. "You need to be careful," Mateo said. "These next few days in particular. You need to be careful."

"Careful about what? Richard Goldsbury?"

"Shit no," Mateo said while coughing out a laugh. "Goldsbury is a pussy. After you beat him down, he's done with you."

"Not Settlemeyer."

Another laugh. "No, not him, either. Shut up and I'll tell you."

Roman waited.

Mateo turned away from the corner—away from Roman—and pivoted his head, scanning.

"What is it?" Roman pressed. "Jesus, you're about to blow apart."

"You can't tell anyone we had this conversation."

"Why?"

"Promise me."

Roman held out his hands, a gesture of frustration. "This is a conversation?"

"This is important, Roman. You have to promise me."

His Spidey sense went nuclear. Mr. Jonathan had lectured him a thousand times about never making a promise ahead of knowing what you're promising. "Okay, I promise."

Mateo scanned the entire horizon again, then turned back to Roman. "Stay on campus for the next few days," he said.

That was it? "Where would I go?"

"Anywhere. Don't go to the church. Don't go to your

mother's office. And don't go back to your house down the hill."

"You know about that? You know about the mansion and my mom?"

"Don't change the subject," Mateo scolded. "Promise me."

"I already did."

"No, you promised not to talk about this conversation. You never promised not to go anywhere."

Roman took a step back and scanned the horizon on his own. "Mateo, you're not making any sense."

"I've made all the sense that I need to. Promise."

"I'll do my best," Roman said.

Mateo grabbed Roman by both shoulders. "You are in a lot of danger," he said. "Please don't ask me how I know or what the danger is. I'm in danger, too, by telling you this."

"God *damn* it, Mateo. You haven't told me anything."

"If you leave the campus you might get killed," Mateo said. "There, is that enough for you? And now that I've told you that much, if people find out that I have, now I can be killed, too."

Roman's heart leaped and kept hammering harder. Talk of killing cut way too close to home after the events in Mexico. He knocked Mateo's hands off his shoulders and gave his friend a shove. "You can't just say shit like that and not explain," Roman said. "Who is going to try to kill me? And if they are, why wouldn't I just call the police?"

Everything changed in Mateo's face. He took a step forward. A very menacing step. "Keep the police out of this."

"But I—"

"The police will just make everything worse for everyone," Mateo said. His eyes grew red as he shoved his hand into his hair. "Shit, I shouldn't have said anything."

Roman moved to stay in Mateo's eyeline. "I promise, okay?" he said. "I don't have any idea what's happening, but I promise that I'll stay here on campus."

Mateo seemed a bit stunned. Confused, maybe.

"Talk to me," Roman said. "What the hell is going on?"

Mateo wanted to say something. Roman could see it in his eyes. But then it passed. "It's nothing. Just remember. You promised."

Roman wanted to press harder, but sudden movement from behind startled him. A parade of three security guards streamed out of the exit he and Mateo had just used. Only these weren't just school guards. One was the chief guard from the mansion, Moses Brinkman, and he looked pissed.

"Jesus Christ, Roman, what are you doing out here?" A black rifle dangled across his front from a sling, and he was wearing a bulletproof vest that had been stuffed with extra ammunition.

"We were just—"

"You need to come with me," Moses said. He grabbed Roman's biceps in his fist and pulled.

Roman tried to pull back, but that was a nonstarter. "I can't, Moses," he said.

"We're not taking votes," Moses said. Six-four and built like a fighter, his expression and grip both told Roman that his choices rested between walking or being dragged.

"What's happening?" Roman asked.

"The school is on lockdown," Moses said. "You need to come with me to the mansion."

"No!" Roman shouted. He brought his elbow down on

Moses's wrist and pivoted to break his grasp, which didn't work.

The chief guard's eyes grew hot. Homicidal.

"If we're locking down, my place is in my dorm," Roman said. He shot a look to Mateo, who'd cast his gaze down to his feet. "I'll be with my friends."

Moses moved faster than you'd think, this time grabbing Roman by his biceps *and* the back of his belt. "You'll go where I tell you," he said, and he lifted, hiking the seam of Roman's jeans into his soft parts.

"Ow! Shit, Moses, you're hurting me."

"Good," the guard said. "Raise a hand to me again if you want to see what real pain feels like."

Moses let Roman's feet touch the ground again after only a couple of steps, and Roman didn't resist anymore.

Inside the school, the hallways looked like a prison. All the classroom doors stood closed, and guards armed with rifles had positioned themselves every forty or fifty feet. All of them wore vests just like the one Moses was wearing.

The image was startling only because Roman knew it was real this time.

Lockdown drills at RezHouse were different from the ones Roman had endured at Northern Neck Academy. At the Neck, an alarm would sound and students would be directed to cower in a corner. Here at RezHouse, the kids didn't have to do much of anything. The guards would swarm the halls and prepare to fight off whatever the threat might be.

The procedure then called for the classrooms to be released one at a time and for the kids to be escorted back to the dormitories, where more guards would keep an eye on everyone.

At this moment, though, Roman was the only student in motion, and judging from the set of every guard's eyes, really serious shit was going down.

Roman's promise to Mateo wasn't yet five minutes old, and already, it was clear that he was destined to break it.

CHAPTER 5

"We should go back into the store to wait for the cops," Ike said. "This guy might have friends, and if he does—did—they're gonna be pissed."

While Venice had been on the phone with the security team at RezHouse, Gail had taken care of the 9-1-1 call to the police. The call taker had seemed unnerved by the report of a shoot-out. Those things rarely happened in Fisherman's Cove. And it would escape no one's notice that when they did, the cast of good guys was nearly always the same.

"Not yet," Gail said. "Ven, you go in with Ike. I'll be there in a second."

"We're not leaving you by yourself," Venice said.

Gail didn't respond. If they were going to stay, that was fine with her. In reality, if there were more shooters, she figured that they'd be shooting by now. She kept that to herself, though, if only to not tempt fate with cocky comments.

The dead man had crumpled faceup at the base of the open driver's door. His eyes and mouth both drooped open, but in a subtle way that left him recognizable. That's what Gail hoped, anyway, as she leaned in close with her phone to take a picture.

"Hey, Ven, do you have any blank paper in your car? I want to get some fingerprints."

Venice spun around and hurried back to the Blazer. Half a minute later, she was back with several plain white note cards, which she handed over.

Gail settled onto her haunches—an effort that still hurt, but not all that long ago was impossible for her to do—and manipulated the shooter's right hand to pat it in the blood pooling under him. That done, she rolled the bloody fingertips across the card to get prints.

"Isn't that tampering with evidence?" Ike asked.

"I'm not taking the prints away," Gail said. "I'm just getting a record of them."

"And that's not tampering?"

"It most definitely is tampering," Venice said.

"And I most definitely don't care," Gila said. "We all saw what happened. Forensic reconstruction won't be necessary."

She let his right hand fall back to the ground and shifted her attention to the left hand. This was more of a challenge, though, because the pooled blood was all on the corpse's right side, making her have to dip the finger-tips one at a time into the bullet wounds themselves.

"No one gets to shoot at me and not expect me to try to find out why," Gail continued.

"You have access to a fingerprint database at your office?" Ike asked. The surprise in his voice was obvious.

Gail realized in a flash that her actions were exposing secrets that should be kept, but the genie was already out of the bottle. "You'd be surprised what you can find if you know where to look," she said. She was going for just the right balance between dismissive and knowledgeable.

When the prints were documented, Gail handed the cards to Venice and said, "Why don't you head off to Rez-House and check in on Roman. He's going to be scared."

"What do you think this is all about?" Ike asked.

Gail ignored the question. "You'll both need to give statements, I'm sure. It's probably best if we're not seen here together chatting."

"Why not?" Ike asked.

Venice placed her hand gently on Ike's arm and eased him away from the scene. "If you watch police work a crime scene, you'll see that one of the first things they do is isolate witnesses from each other. That way, their testimony doesn't get contaminated by other witnesses' memories."

Venice's explanation was correct, learned, perhaps through the many crime scenes that Security Solutions had created over the years.

When the others' backs were turned, Gail went to work on the shooter's pockets, looking for anything that might reveal the man's identity. The dead man wore khaki tactical pants and a nondescript black wool sweater with a plain gray T-shirt underneath. His pockets were empty. Not even a tuft of lint.

As the sound of an approaching siren grew in the distance, Gail picked up her pace and turned her attention to the Toyota's cab. The seats and the floor were a lot like his pockets—clear of anything she might want to see. The glove box revealed a receipt from Old Dominion Car Rentals, and the date stamp showed Richmond.

The siren was getting louder, probably no more than a

half mile away. She quickly took photos of the front and back of the rental agreement before depositing it back in the glove box.

Across the road, Venice was pulling away in her Blazer, taking a route that would prevent her from crossing paths with the police. They had nothing to hide in this case, but theirs was a world wherein the less the police knew about anything, they better off everyone was.

Chief Doug Kramer was the first to arrive at the scene. He drove a police-modified Ford Explorer that was painted in the blue-and-white colors of the Fisherman's Cove Police Department.

Kramer killed the siren as soon as he was in sight of the scene. When he parked, he angled his buggy in a way that effectively shut the road down to other traffic. More sirens wailed in the distance.

Gail stepped away from the shooter's vehicle and stood still while the chief said something on his radio before opening his door and climbing out into the chilly air.

"Are you okay?" he called as he closed his door. Built like the love child of a bullet and a fire hydrant, Kramer could have been a linebacker if he were six inches taller.

Gail clicked SEND on the email to Venice that contained the photos she'd taken. On the off chance that Kramer might insist that she surrender her phone, she wanted to make sure they still had access to the data they would need.

"I'm fine," she said.

Clearly not truly interested in Gail's wellness, Kramer walked to the far side of the truck to look at the corpse.

"He's anything but fine," the chief said. He stooped for a look, but he didn't touch anything. "Tell me a story."

Gail filled him in on the details of the attack and her response. The whole story didn't take a minute.

"How many times do you reckon you shot him?" Kramer asked when she was done.

"I lost count," Gail said. "I can check my mag to see how many are left." As she spoke, she pulled her jacket away to let her Glock be seen.

"I'm gonna have to call in the state PD crime scene guys for this," Doug said.

"There's not a lot to investigate at this point," Gail objected. "He tried to shoot me, and I beat him to the punch."

"I don't question any of that, Gail," Kramer assured. "But shoot-outs on public roads are going to draw attention— the kind that our stalwart governor won't like to have."

"Are they going to try to give me a hard time for this?"

"I hope not," Kramer said. "I'm in your corner if you need it, but you know Governor Asshat's views on guns. The fact that you've got a concealed carry permit and actually used it to save your life is going to weaken his political stance. If the incident gets a lot of attention, he's going to want to change facts to fit his agenda."

"The press won't be on my side, either," Gail said.

"Ah, the press," Kramer mused with a chuckle. "P-R-E-S-S. Professionals Reversing Everything Sacrosanct in America."

Gail laughed.

"You come up with that yourself?"

"I'm not as stupid as I look, I guess." The chief scowled as he noticed something he clearly didn't like. He stooped back down. "Have you been playing with the body?"

Gail waited for him to clarify what he meant.

"Don't just gape at me," he said. "This body's clearly been moved. Did you do that?"

"I wanted to see if he had any identification on him."

Kramer stood, and his ears turned red. "That's not for you to do," he said.

"Now I know."

"Don't bullshit me, Gail. You used to be an FBI agent. And a sheriff. And if I'm not mistaken, you're still a lawyer. You know better than that."

"I have a right to know who is trying to kill me." She opted not to share the fact that thanks to Irene Rivers, the director of the FBI, she still carried a Bureau badge and credentials assigned to Gerarda Culp.

Kramer placed his hands on his Sam Browne belt, the webbing between his thumbs and forefingers straddling the butt of his SIG Sauer nine millimeter on his right side and his yellow Taser on his left. "You don't have a right to screw up my crime scene."

"Sorry, Chief, but it was my crime scene before it was yours. That asshole tried to gun me down. He might have been trying to gun down both Venice and me. I opted not to stop him."

"Venice was here?"

"Yes," Gail said. "And Ike, too."

As if on cue, Ike emerged from his store across the street.

Kramer held out his hand. "Ike, do me a favor and stay inside, okay? I'll be there in a bit to take your statement." To Gail: "Where is Venice now?"

"Out of an abundance of caution, she ordered RezHouse to be locked down. She went back to be with Roman."

"What evidence did she take with her?"

Gail took a step back. "Questions like that make me wonder if I should lawyer up."

Kramer gave a noncommittal shrug.

"Oh, for God's sake," Gail said. "I went through his pockets and found nothing. I took his picture, and I dipped his fingers in blood to get good fingerprints."

"What are you going to do with the prints?" Kramer asked.

"Exactly what you'd think we'd do with them. I want to know who this guy is."

"And armed with that information, what do you intend to do?"

Gail considered that before answering. "I guess that will depend on what the information shows. This is a voyage of exploration, Chief. Why are you being so weird about it?"

Kramer held his hands out to his sides, a gesture of frustration. "Why would you think, Gail? Not that long ago, RezHouse was attacked by parties unknown and a lot of people got hurt. Now, there's this attack on you and perhaps on Venice. I don't pretend to know all that you and your team do, but I'm also not an idiot. I see how bruised and battered y'all are after you've been gone for a while. I can only imagine that you're busy out there making enemies."

He pointed at the body on the ground. "If this is what happens to enemies and you are independently seeking the identity of this guy, the dots I connect are pretty ugly."

Gail knew that Digger and Kramer had been friends since childhood and that they had a certain understanding between them about what Security Solutions could and could not get away with. She wasn't sure what that understanding was, exactly, but she knew that Kramer had only recently looked the other way when he had Gail dead to rights on a burglary rap.

She settled herself and tried to let her armor down a little. "Doug, I don't know what to tell you. This altercation went down exactly as I told you it did. When you talk to Ike, I'm sure he'll give you a version that is substantively the same as mine. So will Venice when you speak with her, but you're not going to be able to give much credence to what she says because you know that we will have talked."

She let those words hang. The conversation was back on him.

"You said you saw this guy and this vehicle outside your office," Kramer said. "Then you saw it here, and you got suspicious. Why was that?"

Gail's defenses shot back up. "There's no rational explanation for him to be here. Clearly, he was following us."

"That's not a crime."

"No, it's not. But it's suspicious. And given our line of work as private investigators, it's threatening."

"So, why didn't you call it in?" Kramer asked.

"Call what in? That a guy in a car might be following us?"

"That's what most people would do if they thought they were in danger. They would call the police—the people who are responsible for protecting the community."

Gail didn't understand this change in questioning. "I'm perfectly capable of fighting my own battles, Chief." As she heard her words, she knew they were mistake.

"So, you came out here itching for a fight?"

Gail's shoulders sagged. "Don't do that, Chief. That's

not like you. Don't play *gotcha* games with me. You know what I mean."

"I do," Kramer confirmed. "But it's the Commonwealth's attorney's favorite game. Might want to keep that in mind. When the state guys get here, they're the prosecutor's butt boys, and you know as well as I that self-defense runs counter to the narrative."

Gail felt herself scowling, trying to read between Kramer's lines to figure out what he was trying to tell her."

"Political times, Gail. That's all I'm telling you. While you might not need an attorney when you talk to me, you might want to consider one when you're talking to them."

Kramer's cell phone rang. He held up a finger as he reached for it, and while he pulled the phone from his pocket, Gail felt a flash of anger. There was a lot going on right here. In a community like Fisherman's Cove, what could possibly be more important?

After a few seconds of listening, the chief tossed a nervous glance toward Gail and then turned his back as he took a few steps away from her.

This couldn't be good, she thought. In the distance, she heard more sirens on the way, and she was growing impatient. If she was still on the scene when the state police investigators arrived, God only knew how long it would be before she could break away. Still, she took a couple of steps away to give the chief the privacy that he obviously craved.

She was still moving when Kramer clicked off and turned back to her. His face was a mask of dread.

"Something wrong, Chief?"

Kramer scowled and pulled at his ear as he searched

for words. "Look, Gail, I don't know what's happening here, but it's got to be something."

"What are you taking about?" Her own sense of dread boiled hot.

"It's Mama Alexander," he said.

Gail's breath caught in her throat. "Oh, my God, what?" Mama Alexander was Venice's mother, but she was also the adopted mother of every child in Resurrection House and more than a few residents of Fisherman's Cove.

"She's in the hospital, Gail," Kramer said. His eyes were wet and red as he spoke. "She was in a car wreck. Witness said that it looked like somebody ran her off the road."

"How badly is she hurt?"

"I don't know. The responding officer didn't know, either. All I know is that she was conscious at the scene and they medevac'd her to the shock trauma center."

"But she's alive?"

"As far as I know. I'm so sorry, Gail."

"I need to get word to Venice," Gail said.

The sirens were growing nearer.

"Git," Kramer said. "Go tell Ike that I said he could drive you into town."

Gail spun and headed toward the store. She'd taken three steps when Kramer called her name, drawing her to a stop.

"I hope she's okay."

Gail acknowledged the sentiment with a subtle dip of her chin, and she continued on to get Ike.

When she was out of sight, the first thing she was going to do was change out her spent magazine for a fresh one and maybe buy a box of nine mil from the store. Coincidences did not exist in the real world. These two incidents, timed so close together, meant that someone was coming after the Security Solutions team.

Somehow, after she broke this news to Venice, she was going to have to find a way to reach out to Digger.

CHAPTER 6

It had been a long time since Jonathan had been this far north. He was surprised at how quickly the sun slipped behind the trees at this time of year. It was barely one o'clock when they approached the cabin they'd been searching for, and already it felt like dusk. The structure itself was a Montana cliché: hand-hewn tree trunks stacked atop each other with batting of some sort to keep out the cold. If he wasn't mistaken, the roof was built of giant logs, as well.

"I think we need to be careful, Boss," Boxers whispered. "Somebody chooses to live this far off the grid, they probably don't welcome visitors."

"I'm hoping this is a summer getaway," Jonathan said. "That it's empty for the winter."

They both jumped when an amplified voice boomed, "Show yourselves or get shot!" The voice sounded nominally female, but in the three-packs-a-day way that makes it a hard call to make.

They both ducked behind trees for cover and dropped to a knee. "Don't you ever get tired of being right all the time?" Boxers asked.

"We mean no harm!" Jonathan yelled.

"You got a lot of guns for not meanin' no harm!" The voice had the tinny sound of a cheap megaphone.

"We're hunting!" Jonathan said.

"Not on my property you ain't."

Boxers said, "Do you want to tell her that this is public land?"

"That'd help," Jonathan said. But Big Guy was right. They were on park land. Homesteaders were tolerated, but they had no land rights.

"We're not hunting on your property," Jonathan shouted. "We ran into some trouble, and we need help!"

"Ain't got none to offer. Now you two feds go back to your fed friends and leave me the hell alone. I ain't done nothin' to neither one o' you. Yet."

"I'm thinking Mrs. Unabomber," Boxers mumbled.

"We're not feds!" Jonathan yelled.

"That's exactly what feds would say."

"She's got a point," Boxers muttered.

"I swear to God I'm going to shoot you," Jonathan whispered, triggering a rumbling chuckle from Big Guy. "Can we come out and chat?" he called to the hidden threat. "If you're not satisfied that we're not feds, you can shoot my friend."

"Good one," Boxers said.

"I done told you that I don't got nothin' for you."

This wasn't going anywhere. The argument had gone circular and at high volume. Nothing good could come from more of that.

"All right, this is what we're going to do," Jonathan

hollered. "My friend and I are going to step out and show ourselves."

"Like hell we are."

"We'll have our guns with us, but our hands will be up."

"What's with the *we* shit, Kemosabe?"

Jonathan ignored him. "We are not feds," he continued. "You can believe that or not, but I'll tell you that killing us in cold blood will not make your life any easier. Know what I'm saying?"

No response.

"Come on, Big Guy."

"You're seriously going to do this? You're going to turn yourself into a target for a crazy hermit with a megaphone?"

"Yep. And so are you."

Boxers growled as he stood. "What the hell?" he mumbled. "Now that I hear the words out loud, it's not the craziest thing we've done."

"Not by a long shot."

"Just so you know, if we get whacked, I'm going to make Hell a miserable damned place for you."

"We're coming out now!" Jonathan shouted. As he rose to his full height and stepped out from behind his cover, every hair on his arms and his neck jumped to attention.

"We're going to walk toward the cabin now!" Jonathan announced.

Twenty-five yards separated their tree line from the squatty structure. They'd only taken a few steps before the tinny amplified voice said, "You can stop there."

They stopped.

"You told me who you ain't," the voice said. "Now you can tell me who you *are*."

"My name is Jim Shaffran," Jonathan said, randomly pulling up the name of an opera star he'd gone to school with back in the day. "This is Brian Halleck." That name came from a long-ago Army buddy.

"Tell me your story," the voice said.

Jonathan had had enough of this. "Ma'am, you are wearing out my patience. If you're going to shoot, shoot. I'm putting my hands down." He lowered them to his sides, keeping clear of his weapons. "We need help, and I'm tired of being treated like an invader."

"You *are* an invader."

"Well, there you go," Jonathan said. "Can we talk or not?"

"Not."

Boxers laughed.

So did Jonathan. "Actually, that's the wrong answer. Please, just step to the doorway so we can see each other. This stalemate crap makes everybody nervous."

Fifteen seconds passed in silence. Jonathan and Boxers exchanged looks.

"Not what I was expecting," Boxers mumbled. "What's my last name again?"

"Halleck."

Finally, a figure appeared in the door of the cabin, a bolt-action hunting rifle at low-ready, but out of position to take a quick shot. Five-foot-four with dark hair pulled back into a tight ponytail, she looked a decade younger than her rasp had led Jonathan to believe.

"I'm here," she said. "Say what you've got to say."

"The simple version is that we need shelter for the night,"

Jonathan said. "It's hard to explain, but we're separated from our vehicle."

"Why don't you *un*-separate from it?"

Jonathan looked to Boxers. *Should I tell her?*

Big Guy shrugged. *What choice do we have?*

"Here's the thing," Jonathan said. "Some people are trying to kill us. Our truck is a logical place to set up an ambush. It's getting dark, and we think they probably have night vision."

"How far away is your truck?"

"A few miles. Three or four."

"Why don't you call the police?"

"Our cell phones don't work out this far."

"You didn't bring a satellite phone?"

"Yeah," Boxers said, his first words at full volume. "You didn't bring a satellite phone?"

"It's in the truck, ma'am. Along with our cold weather camping gear."

The woman watched them for a solid fifteen seconds, saying nothing, clearly evaluating their story.

"Can I ask you for your name?" Jonathan asked.

"What makes you think people are trying to kill you?"

"Because they already shot at us." Jonathan answered without hesitation, hoping that the honesty would make her feel more comfortable.

"Maybe they thought they were trying to bag the Yeti," she said, pointing to Boxers with her forehead.

Big Guy growled. He didn't like it when people made fun of his size.

"What'd you do when they shot at you?"

"We shot back."

"Did you hit anybody?"

"We don't know."

"You didn't go check?"

"It wasn't safe. We'd have to step into the open."

"But you're certain they were firing at you," the woman said. "You saw someone."

"Saw the glint of his scope," Jonathan said. "Well, Brian did, actually."

The woman looked confused, as if she'd lost track of what they were talking about. "So, this guy. He shot at you, you shot back at him, and then you just wandered here? Why this place?"

"Because it's the only one on the map," Jonathan said. "I think I mentioned that we need shelter. The temperature's going to be a problem tonight."

"Snow, too."

Jonathan looked to Boxers again. "You said it was going to be cold and clear."

"I didn't say anything," Big Guy pushed back. "I just read the National Weather Service report."

"Those jackasses don't know nothin' about the weather up here," the woman said. "Yeah, you can come in." She spun on her own axis and disappeared back into the darkness of the cabin. "Have the Yeti watch his head. The ceilings are a little low."

Jonathan couldn't suppress his laugh this time.

"All you had to do is bring the goddamn sat phone," Boxers grumbled. Watching him navigate the six-foot-tall doorway was a little like watching a child climbing back into the womb. "One more snicker from you . . ." He didn't finish the sentence. He didn't have to.

The interior of the cabin was spartan at best. An ancient potbellied woodstove sat in the middle of the room.

To the right of the door sat a saggy bed made of hewn logs and a worn mattress that was likely as old as·the stove. A white gas camping stove sat on a shelf in the back right-hand corner, and a handmade table with four chairs dominated the far corner on the left. To the left of the door sat an overstuffed chair with a hurricane lamp on the table next to it. On the wall behind the chair, a rickety bookshelf sagged under the weight of hundreds of books.

The woman didn't watch as they entered, but rather busied herself with placing her rifle onto hooks designed for the purpose on the front wall immediately to the left of the door. "It ain't much, but it's better'n freezin' to death I imagine."

Jonathan closed the door behind him, cutting off all light except for what little beamed through the one front window and one back window.

"My name is Looney," the woman said. "And just as the Yeti don't want to hear no sniggerin', neither do I. First name Holly. Holly Looney. Sit wherever you like so long as it ain't my chair or my bed."

"I prefer Brian," Boxers said. The patience and polite-ness in his tone startled Jonathan.

"Now, untie yourselves from those rifles so you don't start knockin' stuff off the tables and shelves."

Disarming oneself was always a risky step, and after having already been threatened, responding to a command to disarm was even stupider. But Jonathan and Boxers both complied. The unslung their rifles and stacked them muzzle-up next to the front door.

Holly moved to her chair in the corner and sat down. "Pull up some floor," she said. "Oh, but before you do that, Brian, do me a favor, please, and put some sticks on the fire in the stove."

Without a sarcastic remark or even an annoyed grunt, Boxers did just that while Jonathan lowered himself to the floor and drew his feet under his thighs. Thirty seconds later, the stove was fed and Big Guy was seated next to him on the floor. It occurred to Jonathan that if anyone took a picture of the scene, it would look like they were two kids being lectured to by a schoolteacher.

"Okay, fellas," Holly said. "What have you two done that has the laws is tryin' to kill you?"

The abruptness of the question startled Jonathan and triggered a snort. "I never said—"

"No, what you *said* was that some stranger out in the woods decided to take a shot at you for no reason at all. I ain't buyin' that, and you need to know."

"So, what are you buying?"

"I'm buyin' that you got sideways with the laws, and they're comin' after you. I'm buyin' it because that's what I want to believe. That's the reason I let you in here at all. I don't like the laws myself all that much."

Jonathan noted the construction of her sentences, her use of *the laws*, which to his ears spoke of living in the country for a long time. Now he found himself in a dilemma. He made a career and stayed alive by not telling the truth to strangers—certainly not to strangers who hadn't earned the right to hear said truth—but he saw little upside in pretending to be a criminal.

He decided to tell her the whole story, including the death of the ranger.

"You've got to be shitting me," she said when he was

done. Her tone hovered somewhere between anger and disbelief. "This is what you've decided to bring down on me?"

"I'm sorry, ma'am," Jonathan said, "but we had no choice."

"The hell you didn't!" Holly yelled. "Do you think that the laws are just going to look the other way when there's a dead ranger a couple miles from my cabin? They're not just going to shrug that off and say, *Oh, a couple of hunters were getting shot at, and the shooter hit the wrong guy.* I'm not sure I believed the story while you were telling it, and now that I hear the words coming from my own mouth, I know I don't. You need to get out of here. Like, now."

"I've already explained to you—"

"That people are trying to kill you. I don't care."

Boxers stood, rising to his full height by staying under the ridge pole, seemingly filling the room. "Well, I do, care," he said. "I don't mean to threaten you, and I don't mean you any harm, but Mr. Shaffran and I are not going to just walk out of here into an ambush. Not with night falling."

Holly stood, as well. She barely came up to Big Guy's shoulders. She stepped closer to force him to either step back or crane his neck to stare down at her. "You don't impress me as no murderer," she said. "A killer, yes. I see that in you, but you ain't a murderer. I killed a bear once with a huntin' knife, so your size don't matter much to me, either."

Jonathan likewise got to his feet. This was the time to find some middle ground. "Tell you what," he said. "If I'm right and shooters are out there looking for us, laying a trap for us, they'll be expecting us to come through the woods. You have a vehicle out there. I saw it."

"I ain't lettin' you steal my pickup."

"I don't want to steal it," Jonathan said. "I want you to drive us back to our Suburban."

Holly's face twisted into a mask of disbelief. "You want me to drive you to where you think a bunch of killers are. Is that what you're suggesting?"

"That's exactly what I'm suggesting," Jonathan said.

"Why in a million years would I do such a thing?"

Jonathan was making this up on the fly now, so he hoped his manufactured logic held up to scrutiny. "The way I see it, you don't have a lot of choice," he said. "It wasn't my intent to back you into a corner, but I think that's where you are. When we don't show up at their ambush site, they're going to come looking. They have the same maps we have, I'm sure, and this is the only logical place for us to be.

"You don't impress me as a murderer, either, so I don't expect you to kill us. And I urgently discourage you from trying. The inconvenience alone of disposing of my friend's body will keep you from killing us."

That got the chuckle from her that he'd wanted and the growl from Boxers that he'd been expecting.

"So, let me be completely honest with you. We're not leaving here to go wander through the forest at night. That's just not happening. That leaves you with three choices, as I see it. You can either drive us back to our vehicle, you can let us drive ourselves back to our vehicle, which will leave you with quite a hike ahead of you to get your truck back, or we can spend the night here and hope for the best. What's your pleasure?"

"My pleasure is that you didn't come here."

"Noted for the record," Jonathan said. "And that's a shame."

Holly spun around and walked back to her chair, where she plopped down. "This isn't fair," she said.

"You're right," Jonathan agreed. "And for what it's worth, I'm sorry we had to involve you."

She looked away and stared at a spot on the floor for a long time. "Why do you think I'm out here all by myself?" she asked, finally.

Jonathan stayed quiet, figuring she'd get to it on her own.

Didn't take long. "I got me somethin' of a past," she said. "A couple of decades ago, I might have thrown something I shouldn't have at someone who shouldn't have had somethin' thrown at them. I had me some anger issues back then. The laws looked for me for a while, or so I'm told, but I also heard they gave up after a while. Maybe it was a statue of liberations kind of thing. Anyways, I started out here to hide, and then I stayed out here 'cause I liked not bein' around people. When I thought maybe you was on the run from the laws, I thought it was kind of exciting to help you out."

Jonathan saw the sadness in the way her shoulders drooped.

"That weren't the right way to feel, I know, but it is what it was. Now, you bring all this shit down on me. On this place. You know, I don't even own this cabin. I don't own the land. I don't own nothin' about none of this. Just my truck and my stuff. I own that. I been squattin' here for fifteen years, and people pretty much left me alone. Rangers came by every now and again to put a mirror under my nose to see if I was still alive, but nobody never asked no questions.

"Now, with this shit you've brought down on me, God only knows what's going to happen. God only knows what new questions people gonna ask."

Her eyes hardened as they came back around to Jonathan, and she thrust a forefinger at him. "You had no right to do this."

Jonathan stayed silent. He didn't explain that none of this was his plan and that given the opportunity to plan this trip out more carefully, he still wouldn't have built in an assassin's bullet. He didn't mention that he and Boxers literally had no other choice but to be here.

He didn't mention these things because they were all irrelevant. Because Holly Looney was one hundred percent correct. They had no business being here, and all of it was damned inconsiderate and unfair.

Yet he still had no intention to wander out into the woods and tempt more bullets being thrown at him.

"If I drive you up to your truck, ain't they still gonna see you comin' and take shots at you?" Holly asked.

Jonathan took it as a good sign that she was considering the options.

"They might be expecting us, but they're not going to expect us to arrive in a vehicle," he explained. "And if shooting starts, we'll have better odds given the light of the day. When it gets dark, if they have night vision, all of the advantage falls to them."

Holly's shoulders relaxed some as she leaned back and crossed her legs. "If I heard you right—and there ain't nothin' wrong with my hearing—wish I could say the same about my knees—you want me to drive you into a gunfight with a team of assassins."

Jonathan hadn't thought about his request in quite those terms, but he couldn't quibble with her words. "You don't have to go into harm's way with us," he said.

"The alternative is to let you steal my pickup truck."

"*Borrow* is a better word," Jonathan said.

"I'll stick with steal. And no, you ain't gonna do that."

"I have an alternative," Boxers said. He still hadn't moved from when he'd stood and planted his fists on his hips. "You can drive us close and drop us off." He looked at Jonathan. "It's still from a direction they won't be expecting, and if we get moving soon, we'll be there before they'd reasonably expect us to arrive."

Jonathan liked it. He'd known Big Guy for many years and knew him to be whip smart, but it was often easy to let his hulking size diminish that.

"What do you think, Holly?" Jonathan asked.

Her gaze returned to that spot on the floor as she thought it through. Ten seconds later, she shot to her feet, startling him.

"Okay," she said. "If we're going to do this thing, let's do it for real." She walked across the room and over to her bed, where she stooped to all fours and reached under the bed frame. As she pulled out a loaded AR15, Jonathan's hand instinctively went for the pistol on his hip.

Holly saw his reaction and rolled her eyes. "You two are strung tighter'n banjo strings. I just want to be ready if the shit hits the fan." She placed the rifle on the mattress and reached under again. This time, she came up with a ballistic vest that was stuffed with extra magazines.

"I think I might be falling in love with you," Boxers said.

"You can't handle me, big boy," she said. As she slipped the body armor over her head and fastened it, she explained, "One o' the things I worry about when I'm up here without enough to think about is what crazy people might come wanderin' this way." She fastened the Velcro flaps by pressing them tight against her ribs. "You hear about militias and such nonsense, and I realize that my little squatter's camp is just about perfect for them. If they want it, they'll have to fight for it."

"And what about the FBI if they decide to put you back on their radar?" Jonathan asked with a smirk. He was pretty sure he knew the answer.

"Let's put it this way," she said. "Holly Looney ain't gonna die in no prison cell."

"That settles it," Boxers said. "I'm definitely going to marry her."

CHAPTER 7

Roman felt like a prisoner as Moses and three other security guards surrounded him and quick-marched him from the academic building across the giant yard to the mansion. From there, they forced him all the way upstairs to the Zulu Room, where he was ordered to stay until further notice.

He asked Moses what this was all about, but after three tries, he decided to stop giving the guards the satisfaction of telling him they didn't know. He didn't believe that for a second. What he did believe was that they'd been ordered not to tell him anything.

"I'll make you a deal," Moses said with his signature smile when they arrived at the Zulu Room. "If you stay put, I'll leave the door open. But if you force me, I'll have to close it and lock you in."

Roman took the deal. For the past hour, he'd been trying to lose himself in Fortnite and the sheer pleasure of blasting strangers, but it wouldn't take.

The Zulu Room was an armored and reinforced apartment on the third floor of the mansion, designed to be the place to go when "the shit hit the fan," whatever that meant. The place reminded him of the bomb shelters he'd read that people built in their backyards during the Cold War—except the Zulu Room was brightly decorated and had all the plumbing, cooking, and electronic needs that anyone could ever want. The only thing about the room that screamed *I am a bunker!* was the fact that when the door was closed, from the outside it looked like an ordinary bookcase. Also, the room had no windows.

What it did have, though, was a bank of monitors that allowed you to toggle from one security camera to another to see pretty much every corner of RezHouse and the mansion. Mom had assured him that there were no cameras in the private spaces of the house or the school—the bedrooms and bathrooms. He chose to believe her because what choice did he have? But given all the technology to make cameras as tiny as a flea, how could he be sure?

The monitors were off limits to Roman, but what his mom didn't know couldn't hurt him. There was something fascinating about watching people who didn't know they were being watched. It wasn't just the underwear adjustments and nose picking, either—though those were pretty funny. People stood and walked differently when they thought they were alone. Their whole body language changed. People who slouched stood a little taller when they knew people could see them.

Roman wondered if the RezHouse residents had noticed how many cameras had been mounted inside the school. Even the dormitory hallways had cameras—though, true to his mom's assurances, the camera images stopped at the doorways to the rooms. Locker rooms and bathrooms were out, too.

But the stairwells were all covered, and that's where most of the nasty stuff went down. Just two days ago, Roman had had to bust a kid in the face for trying to steal his phone out of his pocket. That was the problem with looking two years younger than you really were. People thought they could push you around. That came with an upside, too, though. The bullies were that much more surprised when they learned that you'd been studying martial arts since, like, forever. Mr. Jonathan had insisted on it.

And unlike the Northern Neck Academy, where bullies and victims were punished equally when a fight broke out, here at RezHouse, kids' fights were recognized as inevitable. They weren't supported, exactly, but when they were done, if there was a clear aggressor and a clear defender, the aggressor was punished by the administration and the defender was, well, defended by the system.

Roman was surprised to learn that even Father Dom was supportive of students resolving their own problems, even to the point of violence. He considered that to be a *life skill*—that was his term for it. People who didn't fight well learned to work their way out of difficulties in different ways, whether as a class clown or as a good runner.

Roman considered his skill set to be somewhere in the middle. Back when he was at the Neck, he'd been editor of the middle school newspaper, so he was pretty good with words. That allowed him to talk his way out of most problems, but when that didn't work, he had the wherewithal to resolve things otherwise.

If only he were bigger. The extra height and weight carried by his peers always gave them an advantage until a quick kick to the nuts or the solar plexus evened the odds.

Now, all the classrooms were empty and all the students had been evacuated to their dormitories, where the doors remained open and the kids partied under the watchful eyes of the armed security guys.

Except for Roman, of course, who had to serve his evacuation in isolation in his little prison room.

Movement from a parking lot caught his eye, and he saw his mom pulling her new Blazer into the garage. Halfway in, though, she stopped. She was clearly on the phone with someone. She looked stressed. And then she looked horrified. Her eyes grew wide, and she brought her hand to her mouth. She became much more animated and spun in her seat to look out the back window while she handled the transmission shifter and the Blazer shot backward out of the garage bay.

Roman watched as she backed the Blazer onto to the lawn, crushing some of Mama's prized flowers to execute a T-turn to head back down the driveway to the newly in-stalled guard shack.

She stopped long enough to speak with the guard at the end of the driveway, and then she shot off again.

Immediately after the gate guard reached for the mi-crophone on his shoulder, he heard Moses's radio rasp, and then he heard an urgent tone in words he couldn't understand. As the two guards spoke, the gate guard closed the gate at the end of the mansion's driveway. Roman had never seen that done before the dead of night.

A few seconds later, Moses appeared at the door to the Zulu Room. "Roman?" he said.

Roman jumped, caught off guard watching the monitors that were none of his business. "I'm sorry, son, we need to lock you in."

"What's happening?"

"That's not for me to tell you," Moses said. "I'm sorry. I know that's not what you want to hear, but that's the way it is."

"How long?"

"I don't know. You won't be forgotten about, I can assure you of that. You have all the snacks and stuff that you can need, I think, and we'll get a meal to you soon."

"Where did my mom hurry off to?"

Moses looked genuinely embarrassed. "Again, I can't tell you." Maybe because he was in a hurry to change the subject, Moses closed the door, and Roman heard the lock set in the jamb.

"This is stupid," Roman said aloud. He slid his phone out of his pocket and dialed his mom's number. When it went to voice mail, he clicked off and dialed again. And then he did it again.

Finally, she answered. "Hi, sweetie," she said. He recognized her tone. It was the one she used when she'd been crying and she was trying to sound cheerful—trying to hide the truth from him.

"Mom, what's going on? Moses locked me into the Zulu Room, the school is on lockdown, and I saw you tear out of the driveway—where the gate is now closed. What's happening?"

"I don't know for sure—"

"I have a right to know, Mom. Are we under attack?"

When she didn't answer for ten seconds or more, Roman wondered if maybe she'd hung up.

"Mama's been in an auto accident," she said, finally.

"Oh, shit."

"Don't cuss. I'm on my way to the hospital to check on her. I'll let you know what I find."

Roman nodded and was about to let her off the hook when he realized that she hadn't answered his question. "That explains why you tore out of here," he said. "Why is the school locked down? Why am I locked in?"

More silence.

"Mom, I was here for Derek. I was kidnapped. I have a right to know."

His mom remained silent on the other end, but he wasn't going to interrupt it. Sooner or later, she'd get around to saying something. "There's another thing," she said. "Someone attacked Miss Gail and me a little while ago."

"Attacked?"

"Miss Gail had to kill him."

"Oh, shit."

"Don't cuss. A man we'd never seen was going to shoot us."

"Why?"

"I have no idea."

"Are you okay?"

"Yes, Miss Gail and I are both okay."

"And what about Mama's accident?" Roman asked. He

heard his voice catch in his throat. "Was it really an accident?"

Silence again. "I hope so," his mom said.

"But you think it wasn't?"

"I *fear* that it wasn't."

Her emphasis on the word *fear* told him that she saw some great distinction between thinking and fearing, but he didn't get it.

"Mom, is this about Derek?"

"I don't know what it's about, Sweetie. All I know is that things are very scary right now."

"What about you, then?" he asked. "Why don't you have a security guy with you?"

"I'll be fine," she said.

"You don't know that."

"I'll be fine," she repeated. "Look, Roman, I have to go. I need to get in touch with Mr. Jonathan as soon as I can."

"Is he being attacked, too?"

"He's with Mr. Boxers on his hunting trip," Mom said. "If they are, some attackers are in for a very bad day."

Mom laughed, but Roman didn't find it very funny.

Renaldo Vega smelled the cabin in the woods long before he saw it. Since it was the only structure within miles, he figured it to be the only option for Jonathan Grave and Brian the Giant to go to for help. He knew that they had left their satellite phone in their vehicle, which meant that there would have been no communication with the outside world yet. There was a better chance of cell reception from the inside of a lead-lined coffin than there was from these mountains.

He thought about relaunching the drone that he carried in his backpack, but the leaf canopy was too thick to get it aloft without wrecking.

The horse made too much noise in the dry leaves, so he dismounted, wrapped the reins around an aspen tree, and unslung his Remington seven-millimeter magnum rifle. Designed to shoot big animals at great distances, the two-hundred-grain bullets he'd loaded were plenty for human prey, as the poor ranger had learned only a couple of hours earlier.

The air smelled of wood smoke.

Even the most vigilant warriors lost a step when they were settled in to get warm.

He was ready to return to civilization. He was also ready for the ten thousand dollars he would receive when he delivered the scalps of the two men he was here to kill. His boss had originally wanted their entire heads, but Renaldo had convinced him of the impracticality.

Scalps smelled awful enough on their own after a few hours. He wanted nothing to do with drippings and secretions of severed heads. What was it about his boss's countrymen that made them so thirsty for blood, and in such dramatic ways?

Killing had been Renaldo's business for more years than he'd like to count, and for him, dead and invisible was every bit as deceased as dead and on display. This was just one of the reasons why he preferred working for governments rather than private entities. Governments were happier when bodies were never found.

And Renaldo prided himself in his abilities to make dead things disappear.

He winced as he took his first few steps, adjusting to the stiffness of his wounds and the annoying tug of the adhesive bandages against the hair on his legs.

He placed his feet carefully as he advanced on the structure he still couldn't see. He stopped every few steps to listen for sounds that might interest him, and he scanned the surrounding foliage in search of anomalies that would verify that his prey had come this way.

If they had not—if they had chosen the only other option that Renaldo had imagined and returned to their vehicle—they would be cut to pieces by the two members of the assault team who had been left behind to man the fort.

The urge to rush was nearly overwhelming. While noise and fast approaches often worked to his benefit when he was charged with killing unskilled, unsuspecting victims—it startled them and made them uneasy—it was precisely the wrong thing to do with this prey. He knew that they would be tuned to any sign of other humans approaching, even if they were thoroughly engaged in enjoying a meal.

If he could catch them by surprise, the first shot would be a guaranteed kill. He would take his second shot as the remaining living target was reacting to the death of his friend.

This job was not a difficult one if you took your time.

He stopped again and listened. Mostly, he heard the sound of the breeze through the branches of the surrounding trees, but there something else now.

It was the sound of people talking.

Moving very slowly, Renaldo pulled the Remington's bolt back halfway to verify that he had a cartridge in the chamber, and then he slid it home again. He set the safety with his thumb and started his final approach.

In just a minute or two—five, at the most—this would be over.

CHAPTER 8

Jonathan pointed to the spot on his map where Boxers had parked the Suburban.

"You're right," Holly said. "That *is* a long walk. How close do you want me to get you?"

"As close as you're willing," Jonathan said. "Drop us off, we'll make our way to the rental and get the hell out."

"Suppose they've disabled it?" Boxers asked. "We'll be stuck in the middle of nowhere without wheels."

"I don't want Holly to be exposed," Jonathan said. To Holly, he asked, "Are you willing to stop about a half mile down the road and wait for us?"

"I agree with the Yeti," she said. "We're talking what, a fifteen, twenty-second difference? If the vehicle is dead, you grab your shit and we come back here."

Jonathan recoiled at the words. "I thought—"

"I changed my mind," she said. "I'm like that. Too much time without anybody to talk to, I guess. I want you out of here, but I don't want you dead. Especially him. I've buried a horse before. That's a lot of work."

This time, Big Guy laughed. Maybe they really were destined to be a thing.

"Sooner is better than later," Jonathan said, and they piled into the bed of Holly Looney's Dodge pickup truck.

Renaldo heard an engine turn over and roar to life.

Was that his prey? Of course it was. Who else could it be?

Renaldo took off at a run. Stealth no longer mattered. Not at this point. If they got away, there was no telling where they would run off to.

As he crashed through the underbrush, the branches tore at his already damaged flesh, but he ignored the pain. At this range, all he needed was a clear shot. Just one, and at least half of his mission would be solved.

He carried his rifle vertically in front of his body to keep his silhouette as small as possible as he skirted the trees and bushes and creepers that seemed intent on making him fall.

The engine noise got louder as the driver found the right gear and started to move. He could tell that the vehicle was an old one, not well kept and having gone far too long without a tune-up.

Seconds mattered now.

The outline of the cabin emerged from the tableau of foliage. A small thing, not the least bit *charming* (a word Americans loved to use), with white smoke curling out of the chimney.

The engine noise crescendoed, then it started to Doppler away from him.

"Dammit!" He shouted it in English as he looped around the near side of the cabin in time to see the vehicle approaching a curve that would take it behind a tree and away from his sight picture.

Renaldo thumbed the safety off as he snapped the Remington to his shoulder. In the half-second remaining to see his target, his eyes recorded that both Grave and his friend were in the bed of the old pickup truck. That meant that there was at least one other person with them.

As he turned and hurried back to his horse, he pulled his radio from his belt and keyed the mic. Here in the clearing, he hoped that the signal would be strong enough to be heard. "Unit Four to Team," he said in Spanish.

"This is Unit One," came the reply, also in Spanish.

"Our friends are coming in your direction. They number at least three."

More primer than paint, more rust than metal, the once-yellow Dodge looked to be at least twenty years old, but it started easily, and it had power to spare after they loaded up. Jonathan and Boxers rode in the bed, rifles up and at the ready, while Holly navigated a rutted road that only she could see, slaloming around trees and boulders, all the while shifting and downshifting like a pro to compensate for the steepness of the slope. Jonathan had to hang onto the sides of the truck bed to keep from being ejected.

After eight or ten minutes of riding the paint shaker, they finally found a solid surface. Holly stopped and spun in her seat to look through the cab window into the bed. "Good," she said. "You're still there.

And they were off again. This time, the acceleration damn near sent Jonathan over the tailgate.

"Tomorrow's bruises should be interesting," Boxers quipped.

Ten minutes later, the pickup slowed to a crawl and then to a stop.

Holly looked out the window again. "I put us about a half mile out," she said. "If there's folks out there to shoot you, this would be the time."

"I think we should sit here a while longer so they can zero their scopes," Boxers grumped.

"We need to go in fast and hard," Jonathan said.

"Okay," Holly said. "Remember, you asked for this." She launched like a rocket.

"She's doing this on purpose!" Boxers laughed.

"Damn straight I am!" she shouted over the roar of the engine.

Jonathan cringed. This was the wrong time for making a lot of noise. Boxers knew better. Holly should have.

Less than a minute later, they skidded to a stop alongside Ranger Simonsen's truck. Its windows had been smashed, and at a glance, Jonathan could see that the interior had been ransacked. Given the timing of events, that had to have been done while Simonsen had been hunting them down.

"We were right," Jonathan said. "There's more than one of them."

He was just rolling over the side of the truck bed when the vehicle trembled with the characteristic impact of bullets, two in rapid succession—*tonk, tonk*—followed almost immediately by the sound of the rifle reports.

"God *damn* it!" Boxers yelled. "I'm hit!" He tumbled out of the bed and onto the ground, where he scurried across the road to find shelter behind a boulder. Blood streamed down the left side of his face.

"How bad?" Jonathan asked. He'd taken cover behind the front wheel well and the engine block and didn't want to take a look to assess the wound if he didn't have to. His time and eyesight were better spent searching the tree line for the shooters. He had to dodge the passenger side door as it swung open and Holly Looney crawled out and dropped to the ground.

"My ear, goddammit," Boxers said.

Holly log rolled herself along the ground and propped herself behind the rear wheel well. She clearly was in pain.

"Just the ear or the brain behind it?" Jonathan called to Boxers.

"Just the ear, I think."

"You okay, Holly?" Jonathan asked.

She was breathing funny, and when she coughed, blood bubbled from her nose. "Not enough vest," she said.

Jonathan started toward her, but she waved him away. "Kill the bastards first," she said. "Then you can take your time saving me."

"Holly's hit!" Jonathan called to Big Guy. "Did you see where the shots came from?"

"The woods on the other side of the truck," Boxers said. Not a lot of help.

"Are you functional?" Jonathan asked.

"If I can breathe, I can fight," Boxers said.

"These guys are good," Jonathan said. "They've got good trigger control." Less experienced attackers employed a spray-and-slay mentality that wasted a lot of ammo.

"Not the greatest marksmanship, though," Boxers added. "Thank God."

Jonathan wasn't sure about that. By hitting the driver, they'd taken the vehicle out of commission. Assuming the other vehicles were likewise disabled, their opfor—opposing force—had created an effective trap.

"We need to flank these guys," Jonathan said. "Joking aside, I need to know if you can run and function."

"I got a floppy ear," Boxers said. "I can do whatever we need to do."

"Holly?" Jonathan asked. "You still with us?"

"I'm not dead yet."

Jonathan closed his eyes and brought back his memories of the map that led them here. This section of the mountain road was pretty level. Plenty of swales and defilades to hide in, but no significant elevation advantage. In Jonathan's mind, that made ducking and dashing behind trees and rocks a workable defense as they tried to get the enemy to reveal their locations.

"We've got to seal this deal before nightfall," Jonathan said.

"No argument from me."

"Okay, we're going to go old-school," Jonathan said.

"Full frontal assault?"

"Samurai style," Jonathan said. "But with zigging and zagging. I go right, you go left, shoot at anything that shoots at you first." He shifted his attention. "Holly, do you know what covering fire is?"

"Shoot to keep their heads down."

"Have you got it in you to do that?"

"Better to bleed to death shooting than it is to bleed to death sitting here."

"Don't talk that way," Boxers said.

"It'll be what it is," she said. She coughed a wad of blood. "But if you need my help, I think the clock is ticking."

"You don't even have to aim," Jonathan said. "Just point your gun straight out across the bed and keep pulling the trigger till slide lock. Can you do that?"

"Count it down," Big Guy said.

"Holly?"

She took a deep breath and with considerable effort, rose to her hands and knees, then pulled herself up against the side of the truck. "This shit really hurts," she said. "Do it now or leave me alone."

"On zero," Jonathan said. "Three . . . two . . . one . . ." The zero was implied in the cadence.

He bolted away from the black side of the vehicle— the side away from the opposing force—and dashed through the open across the road and into the woods where he imagined the shooters to be. Behind him, to his left, Holly's rifle slammed away into the woods. If they had more ammunition, it would have made sense for Jonathan and Boxers to be unleashing their own covering fire to keep the enemy's heads down. If they had body armor . . . If they had their fully automatic weapons . . . If they had explosives . . .

Ifs didn't matter much once *now* became reality.

After what felt to be about twenty shots fired, Holly's gun fell silent. A part of Jonathan hoped that the bad guys would take advantage of the silence to return fire and reveal their positions, but apparently, they were too good for that.

Jonathan didn't like facing opponents who knew what

they were doing. Tactical knowledge on the part of the bad guys made the good guys' lives way more dangerous. Often, it made them shorter, too.

It seemed to Jonathan that this was going to be a stalker's battle.

He hated stalker's battles. They were far too close to being a fair fight, and no one survived the battle business for as long as Jonathan had by fighting fair. Overwhelming force and speed of action brought down on unsuspecting bad guys was the path to a long life.

Jonathan put himself in the position of the hunters he was hoping to kill. Presumably, they understood that he and Boxers were no ordinary prey, that they'd danced this number more than a few times in the past, so they'd be on their toes. That was more bad news.

With that knowledge came the certainty that the bad guys had blown their second opportunity to make a clean kill and that Jonathan and Boxers would thus be hunting for them. If the shooters had thought it through all the way to the end, they would know that this final battle had to come before sunset.

Jonathan hunkered in behind a stout tree and tried to put himself in the enemy's shoes. What would he do if the roles were reversed? Since the shooters had already shown themselves, the smart move would be to displace and relocate. On the other hand, relocating would mean abandoning what Jonathan could only assume was a prepared defensive position—the kind of position that could make the difference between winning a fight and losing one.

One thing Jonathan felt sure about was that the enemy was seated deeper into the woods than he was now, which was only twenty or thirty feet from the edge of the road. It would make no sense for them to set up an ambush with long guns so close to the road. But there was another hand to be considered here, too. Without the elevation advantage they'd had when shooting long range across the valley, additional distance meant reduced sight picture, which made a good shot more difficult.

Stalking at this level was a game of patience and observation. It would be foolish to stay put and allow the enemy to get an angle on you, but it was equally foolish to move too much and announce where you were. Sooner or later, someone would make a mistake, and when he did, the hunter needed to recognize it for what it was and capitalize on it.

From behind his tree, Jonathan surveyed the woods surrounding him. Boxers was out there somewhere, no doubt doing the same thing, as were the people who were hunting them in return.

Keeping low, Jonathan moved quickly but smoothly to better cover, this time a massive boulder that had erupted no doubt a million years ago. It was easily fifty yards deeper into the forest, which was as deep as he felt safe to be.

He pulled his army-green wool cap down to his eyebrows and tucked in the tips of his ears. The fewer odd angles he presented, the less visible he would be to his prey. He positioned himself as comfortably as he could with his chest pressed into the eroded surface of the rock and settled himself in to be perfectly still.

His movement to this position may have alerted his prey to his location. If so, they knew where to watch for him. It was time to be invisible.

Spotting human prey was as much about seeing what was unusual or disturbed as it was seeing the prey itself. People were good at hiding behind and under things, but they were less good about covering the indicators of how they had found their hiding spot. If people covered themselves with branches and twigs, those branches and twigs had to come from somewhere. When they were dragged through the woods to the hidey-hole, they would disturb the ground, perhaps bending plants and shrubs that otherwise grew straight.

Tracking and stalking was less about finding actual tracks than it was about seeing anomalies and trusting your gut.

Jonathan willed his breathing to slow. He cupped his gloved hand over his nose and mouth to break up the cloud of condensation when he exhaled. He cleared his mind as best he could, and he stared into the trees. He tried to unfocus his eyes to keep from being distracted by individual images and to take in everything at once. Thanks to years of training and forced survival, he knew that natural patterns would emerge for him sooner than later. Once those were visible, exceptions to the ordinary would reveal themselves.

Twenty or thirty yards ahead, maybe ten degrees off his centerline, something moved. He shifted his eyes and brought them into focus. Whatever it was could have been an animal, but it couldn't have been the breeze. Breezes moved everything at once, perhaps in a passing wave or perhaps in an extended gust, but they never moved a single point in space, and that's what Jonathan had seen.

Whatever was there had gone dormant. Jonathan allowed himself a satisfied smile.

One of the hazards of stalking human prey was the very human tendency to second-guess that which you knew to be true. Inexperienced gunmen would convince themselves that the movement they saw was nothing, merely a figment of their imagination.

It was a propensity that snipers counted on.

Most people are incapable of remaining perfectly still for long periods of time. At one level, Jonathan supposed, everyone was incapable of that, but in a battle of experienced shooters, to be the first to move was often to be the first to die.

Truthfully, that first move was rarely the one to prove fatal because awareness that a target exists is worlds apart from actually acquiring said target. That's how Jonathan figured he got away with his dash from his shelter behind the stout tree to his current shelter behind the rock. If the shooters had seen anything at all, they clearly had not had enough time to squeeze off a shot. Or, they were staying stealthy.

With the target area identified, it now was time for Jonathan to watch intensely. Every detail became important.

Movement of a different sort.

The first time, he'd seen physical movement, whether it was foliage or maybe even an errant arm twitch. Now, the movement was in the air itself. It was a puff of condensed water vapor—an exhalation cloud.

Whatever was there was breathing. Only animals breathed. Only humans remained so still in this part of the world.

Moving with impossible slowness, he keyed the mic on his radio to break squelch and then let go. He did it again. Twice breaking squelch had long been Jonathan and Boxers' code for spotting danger.

Never shifting his eyes from the condensation, Jonathan moved with impossible slowness, a fraction of an inch at a time, to bring his rifle to his shoulder. It took him well over a minute to bring the weapon into play. One check of the angle of the sun in the sky assured him that the lens of his scope would not betray him, and he flipped up the lens caps.

With both eyes open, he settled in behind the scope, welded his cheek to the stock, pressed the butt plate into the soft spot of his shoulder, and observed his prey at four-power magnification.

The other shooter was dug in pretty well, pressed behind rock cover of his own. His rifle looked like it might be a Remington 700, the civilian version of the U.S. military's vaunted M24 sniper rifle. It was bolt action and was typically chambered in 7.62-millimeter NATO, but it could be .30-06 or any number of other rounds, any of which would render anything or anybody quite dead.

The shooter was looking the wrong way to see Jonathan, presenting his left shoulder and ear as a sight picture. He wore digital camouflage clothing, and he'd painted his face to blend in with the woods. This guy meant business.

As Jonathan settled in to take a shot, he stopped himself.

He thought back to the cadence of the rounds as they'd hit Holly Looney's pickup truck. They'd come much faster than a single shooter could spit out with a bolt-action rifle.

His target was not one of one. He was working with a partner, and Jonathan needed to locate him before he gave away his position.

Thirty seconds later, Jonathan's target pivoted his head and eyeline to his left and made a subtle shrug with one shoulder. He was communicating with someone.

Jonathan kept his shoulder lock on his prey, and with his naked eye, followed the shooter's sightline. Sure enough, a second shooter, equally well camouflaged, was nestled in a swale, concealed by a deadfall and a rock. The way he was dug in, Jonathan wasn't sure that he'd have seen him at all if it had not been for the glance by his first shooter.

Jonathan rehearsed the next step in his head, visualizing what he needed to do before he committed to the shots he needed to take. If he could make his two kill shots in three seconds or less, the second target would have no time to react effectively. After three seconds, the second target could either pull away to become invisible or he could start returning fire. Jonathan ran the sequence through his head.

Right target first. Pivot twenty degrees and take out the second on the left.

Right, then left.

Right, then left.

He even imagined the recoil and the time it would take to reacquire the sight picture.

Jonathan settled the reticle as close to Target One's center of mass as the angles would allow—more or less the middle of his shoulder blade—and placed his finger on the trigger.

He focused on the rudiments. Breathe in. Breathe out

halfway and hold. Add pressure to the trigger. Just as the trigger broke, the target looked back over to his partner.

Jonathan's muzzle flashed as the rifle boomed. He allowed the recoil to break his forestock weld to the rock, and he pivoted left. That target was in the process of spinning to react when Jonathan shot him twice in the chest and once in the forehead.

Certain that Target Two was dead, Jonathan pivoted back around to Target One, who'd disappeared behind his cover. He saw blood spray on the rocks, but that wasn't enough. Dead wasn't dead until the body was checked.

On the chance that there were still more shooters, Jonathan stayed behind his cover. He keyed his mic. "I got two, Big Guy."

"I don't see anything," Boxers replied. "Hang tight for a bit, and I'll come your way."

For the next forty-five seconds, Jonathan stayed perfectly still, watching for some kind of movement from the men he'd shot. He saw nothing. He was in the process of shifting from the target on his right to the one on his left when a shot from close by split the ever-colder air.

Jonathan dropped back to his butt and brought his rifle close to keep from presenting an obvious target. In the seconds following his instinctive response, he realized that if he'd been targeted, the shooter was not very good because nothing hit near him.

His radio broke squelch. "Scorpion, Big Guy," Boxers said. "That was me. Seems they sent a team of four. I nailed a new one as he was trying to close in on you. On horseback, if you can believe that. My gut tells me that's all of them."

"I concur," Jonathan said. Shooters like to work in

teams of two unless they preferred to work alone. Clearly this group was a team, not a collection of loners. These three, plus the guy across the valley accounted for everyone. "Can you confirm that yours is dead?"

"Dead with an exclamation point," Big Guy said.

"Do you have eyes on me?"

"Affirm."

"Okay, I'm going to step out and confirm my kills. "

"Gotcha covered."

"Go see to Holly," Jonathan said. "I've got this."

CHAPTER 9

Venice parked her Blazer in one of the short-term slots just past the ambulance entrance to the emergency room and hurried toward the electric doors. As she crossed the threshold, a teenager in a scrub suit told her that she couldn't use that door.

"Good to know," she said without slowing. A second set of doors brought her into a scene of controlled pandemonium as medical staff and God only knew who else moved around and past each other with a kind of grace that might have been choreographed. A young man in the uniform of a maintenance staffer swirled a mop through a blood trail, to Venice's eye making a bigger mess than he started with.

She told herself that the blood had spilled from someone other than Mama.

"Ma'am, you can't be here," said someone else wearing scrubs, this one a young lady.

"I'm looking for my mother."

"I understand, but you can't come this way. You need to go around to—"

Venice walked away. The emergency department was

arranged like a wheel without spokes, with the hub being a massive nurses' station and a dozen or more operatories circled around it.

"Ma'am, I'll call security if I have to."

"Do what you need to do," Venice said. She heard herself channeling Digger and felt a surge of pride.

It had been a while since Venice had visited the ER. The walls were cheerier than they used to be. White subway tiles were broken by a ribbon of navy blue tiles that swooped up and down in a continuous line around the circle of operatories. Sliding glass doors had replaced the shower curtains of days gone by.

But the lack of privacy remained a constant, with the clear glass providing a clear view of patients and their assembled families. Venice walked with purpose—neither fast nor slow—around the interior perimeter, scanning each room for Mama.

One guy she figured to be well into his eighties lay back in his bed with his eyes open, his hands crossed on his lap. She didn't know if he had died, but it was only a matter of time. In the next operatory, a scrum of medical people were working with intense effort on a patient she couldn't see, but judging from the floor in there, she knew where the blood slick at the front door had originated.

At the next station, Venice spotted Mama's massive purse before she saw Mama herself. The purse and other personal items had been shoved into a clear plastic bag and placed on a shelf under the hospital bed.

"There she is!" Venice heard from behind. A glance showed an approaching security guard with the bitchy lady in tow.

"Ma'am, you can't go in there," the guard said.

Venice crossed the threshold into Mama's room. She had a lump on her forehead but otherwise appeared to be sleeping.

The guard rushed in after her. "You need to leave," he said. "Now."

"She's my daughter," Mama said without opening her eyes. "I'd like her to stay with me."

"You need to check in at the visitor's desk," the guard said.

"But she's already here," Mama said. "Don't be difficult, Billy."

The guard looked startled.

Mama opened her eyes. "Billy Anson," she said. "You remember me. Your mother played mah-jongg at my house every month for years. Don't make me tell her you're being difficult."

Billy clearly had no words. "Um."

"Venny's my only baby, and she's worried about me. She knows I don't approve of breakin' the rules, but now that she's here . . ."

The bitchy nurse seemed entirely unsatisfied when Billy turned and left without saying anything.

"Rules exist for a reason," the nurse said as she turned to leave.

"I'd like to speak to the doctor at the first opportunity," Venice said.

As the nurse left, Venice closed the door and then pulled the privacy curtain shut. She moved to the side of Mama's bed and took her hand. "Are you okay?"

"I think I am," Mama said. "But the doctor said something about a bruised liver and waiting for test results. Other than that, some bumps and bruises."

"No broken bones?"

"Maybe my ankle. They took a picture of it, but only a doctor can tell me what it says,"

Venice shifted her gaze to Mama's feet. Her right ankle had puffed up a lot, and there was bruising down around her toes. Broken or not, she wasn't going to be walking on it for a while.

"Do you remember what happened?" Venice asked.

"Every second of it," Mama said. "I'd been to Miller's to order up a roast for Christmas. You know how over-booked they get for the holidays, so I thought I'd get our order in early. I was thinking about inviting—"

"The wreck, Mama. What can you tell me about the wreck itself."

"Venny, that's what I was doing. You interrupted. You do that a lot, in fact. Remember—"

"Mama!" Florence Alexander was the queen of tangential conversation. If you didn't rein her in, she'd go on forever.

"Okay, straight to the ugly part, then," Mama said.

She was driving down Loggins Road, a twisty two-lane passage through the corn fields of the Northern Neck whose posted speed limit was fifty-five, but the safe limit was more reasonably capped at forty-five as the landscape changed from flatland to woods. Mama had noticed a big black pickup truck behind her on the road. She thought it was either a Chevy or a Ford but allowed for the possibility that it was one of those big Toyotas.

The truck would fall back a ways and then race up to follow way too close to her bumper, only to fall back again.

"I figured they were trying to mess with me," Mama

said. "You know, maybe teenagers or something. Boys without enough to do."

"So, you saw them? Venice asked. "You know they were men?"

"Well, no," Mama admitted. "I guess I assumed that part. Are you doing an investigation or something? Is that why you're asking all these questions?"

"I think we need to know all that happened," Venice said. "You know, after the attack on RezHouse a while back, we need to be vigilant."

"Do you think someone was trying to kill me?"

"I don't know, Mama. You haven't finished telling me the story."

As she approached the sharp turn near the Nelsons' farm, the one that leads into Myers' Woods, Mama slowed down, both to take the turn more safely and to give the boys in the truck a chance to get around her. After all, if it was so important to them, maybe they had a family emergency or something that they needed to get to.

"So, I slowed to about thirty-five, and that's when they hit me. Oh, Venny, it was a terrible thing. They started to pass me on the left. Not a very smart thing, really, when you think about it, being on a curve and everything."

But rather than passing cleanly, the driver hooked the left rear bumper of Mama's Ford Focus. Instead of slowing down, though, they sped up, pushing Mama's car into a spin that ended when she hit a tree and flipped over, the front of her car facing the wrong way.

"I'm tellin' you, Venny, I don't think I've ever been that scared. Never in my life." Mama's brow furrowed. "No, *scared* ain't it. It happened too fast for me to be scared. What I was, was startled."

"Then what happened?" Venice pressed.

"Then I came here."

"Between there and here. What happened in that time? Did the boys in the truck stop and help you?"

"You know I was upside down, right? So it was hard to tell the details, but yes, I think they did stop. I mean, I heard doors open and close and I heard footsteps coming. But then, I saw another car approaching from the same direction I'd been coming from, and then the boys started running the other way. Well, not running, I guess. More like jogging."

"And?"

"And then a nice lady named Anita—or maybe Antigua—she stopped and asked me if I was all right, and then she called nine-one-one and here I am."

"The police came?"

"Oh, Lordy, yes. The police and fire trucks and an ambulance. It must have been a boring day for the first responders." Mama chuckled at her joke.

"So, you told all of this to the police?"

"Pretty much," Mama said. "Though they didn't seem near as interested as you."

"And what have the doctors told you so far?"

"No very much. I imagine I'll be free to go after I hear about the x-ray and they do whatever they need to do to my ankle before I can leave. And that liver thing."

"Does that hurt? Your liver, I mean?"

"Venny, my whole *body* hurts. I guess maybe that's a blessing, right? Better than not being able to feel the hurt?"

Leave it to Mama to find the bright side of pain.

Mama reached out and squeezed Venice's hand. "Now, tell me what you're not tellin' me."

Venice recoiled. "Excuse me?"

Mama squeezed the hand harder. "Venny, Darlin' I've known you since you were bloody and naked comin' outta me, and you've never once for one day in your life been good at hiding concerns when they're weighing on you. Now, what is it?"

Venice's mind raced. What did Mama need to know, and what should she definitely *not* know?

"Just tell me the truth, sweetie. I'm gonna find it out one way or the other. I always do."

That statement was truer than it was false. Mama was a world-class busybody, and when she wanted to know a secret, she'd pursue it like an arrow flying to its target. Only, arrows lost momentum. Mama only gained momentum as frustrations got in her way. The only secrets she didn't know, as far as Venice was aware, were the ones associated with the covert work of Security Solutions. And even there, she had her suspicions. That she didn't know the details was mostly due to the fact that she probably didn't *want* to know.

Venice steeled herself with a deep breath and relayed the details of the shoot-out in front of Ike's store.

"Good Lord, and you want to know if *I'm* all right? What about you, Venny? And Gail?"

"We're fine," Venice said. "But you can imagine when I heard about your attack—"

"Who said it was an attack? It was more of an auto accident."

"You know better than that, Mama."

Mama's features darkened as her eyebrows knitted together. "Are you saying that our family is under attack again?"

"I'm saying that it might be."

"Why would someone want to do that?"

Venice didn't try formulating an answer. She had no firm evidence of anything, and any guess she posited would only trigger more questions she couldn't answer.

"And what about Jonny?" Mama asked. "Have you heard from him?"

"I tried calling, but I couldn't reach him. I don't think the call went through. He's in the mountains, after all, so maybe cell reception isn't all that it could be." She didn't mention that she also tried calling him on his satellite phone, where reception was more or less universally accessible. That he didn't answer that line either pinged a danger receptor in her spine, but it wasn't beyond credulity that he would have left it behind as he went out to slaughter God's creatures.

"Do you have a plan to figure out what's going on?" Mama asked.

Venice feigned innocence. "How would I do that?"

Mama made a shooing motion with her hand. "Scat. Go to work and figure out how to stop this nastiness from happening."

"I don't know that I can do that," Venice said.

"Well, you sure as heck can't while you're standin' here, can you? I'll give you a call when I need a ride."

A knock from behind drew Venice's attention to the glass door to the operatory, where Rick Hare, one of the leaders of Digger's security team, was standing on the other side. Venice beckoned for him to enter.

He seemed uncomfortable to be there, and he studiously kept his eyes on Mama's face. "How are you feeling, Mama?" he asked.

Mama's features hardened even more. "What is going on here?"

"Rick is going to stay here until you leave," Venice explained. "I want to have some security with you."

"Oh, that's a terrible thing to do to such a nice man," Mama said. "He's got better things to do than babysit an old woman."

Rick straightened his posture as he said, "Ma'am, under the circumstances, I can't think of a place I'd rather be."

CHAPTER 10

Jonathan advanced on his first target—the man he couldn't see. Ninety-nine-plus percent sure the target was dead, he told himself that now was the time to be most careful. A bullet from that one-tenth of one percent could be just as deadly as a bullet from an active shooter. Worse, even. If he got shot by a dead guy, Boxers would never let him live it down.

The caution paid off. His target was gravely wounded, but he was still alive. He lay at an impossible angle, wedged into a vertical crag between two boulders. His digital camo uniform shirt glistened with blood that leaked at a steady ooze from a hole somewhere in his chest. The man's eyes were open and seemed to be focused. Jonathan thought they showed equal parts fear and anger. The man's breaths came in sharp, quick gasps, each of which brought pink foam to the corners of his mouth.

Jonathan keyed his mic. "I got one still breathing."

Boxers replied with a raspy squelch break.

Jonathan watched the man for another minute or so, just to take in the scene. The target had dropped his rifle well beyond his reach, and his hands were visible and empty. Jonathan saw no sign of a pistol. He did see a portable radio on his belt, though.

It was time to gather intel. Jonathan moved closer to the dying man, shifting his gaze back and forth from the target's eyes to his hands. When he was close enough, Jonathan took a knee next to the dying man's ribs.

"Who are you?" Jonathan asked.

The target answered in Spanish. "You are a dead man."

Jonathan slipped effortlessly into the same language. "Looks to me like you have that backwards, my friend. Who are you?"

"You are dead."

Jonathan decided to roll with that. "Who's going to kill me? It sure as hell isn't going to be you."

The man fell silent, his eyes focused squarely on Jonathan's.

"Look," Jonathan said, changing tacks, still in Spanish. "I can get a doctor for you if you'll answer some questions."

"Go to hell."

"Probably," Jonathan said. "But without medical care, you'll be burned crispy down there for many years before I arrive. Who sent you to do this? Who sent you to commit suicide like this?"

The target spat a wad of blood. "You have no idea who you are dealing with. You started a war you can never win."

"You shot at us, friend," Boxers said in Spanish, startling the crap out of Jonathan, who didn't know that he'd returned. The flow of blood from his ear had slowed, but his neck and collar were soaked with it. "We didn't start anything."

The target never shifted his eyes away from Jonathan. "We know who you are, Mr. Jonathan Grave. We know where you live, and we know who you love." A cough triggered a spasm of pain, and he launched another wad of blood.

Jonathan felt heat rising in his neck and cheeks. He said nothing now, hoping the dying man would continue to boast.

"They are all gone now," the man said. "The little boy and his mother, the girlfriend, all of them. By now, they are all gone."

Jonathan didn't rise to the bait. Instead, he pulled the radio free from the man's belt. Nothing fancy. Just a CB radio that you could pick up for a hundred fifty bucks a pair at a big-box store. He handed it to Boxers, who held up an identical model that he'd apparently lifted from the guy he'd killed.

"If my friends are dead," Jonathan said through the knot of fear that had formed in his stomach, "that means that your friends are better at their jobs than you are."

"If you think this ends anything, you are wrong," the dying man said. "This is only the beginning."

"Which cartel do you work for?" Jonathan asked.

The level of sophistication of this attack reeked to Jonathan of cartel involvement. And it made sense. Tracing all the way back to Jonathan's and Boxers' days in the Unit, they had been embroiled in a continuous running battle with the drug cartels and their suppliers.

His question struck the nerve he was hoping for. He

saw the confirmation in his target's eyes before he had a chance to deny anything.

"You Americans are so stupid," the man said. He launched into a pain-rattled screed about the hubris of Americans' belief that they can stop the flow of commerce at the southern border. Then he shifted to something about powerful men's allegiance only to money.

Jonathan looked up at Boxers. "Holly?"

Big Guy answered with a twitch of his head. *She's dead.*

"You need to do something with that ear."

"I got time."

As the man droned on, Jonathan tried to listen beyond the words, to focus in on the dialect. Just as Bostonian English sounds entirely different from Texan English, Spanish carries nuanced, regional differences. Whereas Mexicans tend to hammer their consonants, this man's language was more vowel-centric to Jonathan's ear. The timbre of his voice was pitched lower than what he'd expect to find from the average Mexican.

The target was still making his speech—albeit in an ever-dwindling tone—when Jonathan shifted his attention to searching the man's pockets. When the guy howled in pain, Jonathan told him to either shut up or die faster. When he was done, all the man's pockets were turned out, and Jonathan's hands were empty.

"He's got nothing useful on him," he said as he stood. He used his phone to take the attacker's picture.

"The good assassins never do," Boxers said. "What are we gonna do with him?"

Jonathan looked down at the guy. "He's not going anywhere. Did you get a picture of the guy you shot?"

"I did. And I got a set of prints on a piece of paper. We're letting this one die, right?"

"Yep. But you don't have to sound so happy about that."

"Buzzards gotta eat, too, boss. Rather him be on their menu than us. By the way, your other guy is very, *very* dead. I got his prints, too, but I don't think facial recognition will be worth a damn."

Getting fingerprints was a good idea—and Jonathan would get them from the shooter after he'd lost more energy—but he didn't harbor high hopes that they would be much use in the short term. Too much detail would be lost in the transfer from a photographic image via email.

"And you're sure about Holly?"

"Yeah," Boxers said. "That really pisses me off."

Jonathan waited for more. Those words were high emotion for Big Guy. "Let me see your ear. Got your med kit?"

Boxers turned and presented his rucksack to Jonathan. "It's the pouch that says *Med Kit*."

Jonathan opened the Velcro closure and withdrew a couple of four-by-fours and a roll of medical adhesive tape. "Take a seat on the rock," he said.

Boxers sat.

The wound wasn't even close to being a serious one. The bullet had caught the fleshy part of Boxers' right ear, carving out a moon-shaped hunk of cartilage. The bleeding had all but stopped, but it was something that needed a serious debriding sooner than later or risk a nasty infection.

"You're going to look like a dog who lost a fight," Jonathan quipped.

"Nah, this is what the winning dog looks like. The losing dog looks like those guys."

Jonathan opened the four-by-four dressings and folded them over the missing flesh.

Boxers flinched at the pain. "You better not be doing that on purpose, Little Man," he growled.

"Hold this in place," Jonathan said.

As Boxers raised his hand, Jonathan took his wrist and directed his fingers to the right spot. "Pinch it tight," he said.

"Kiss my ass," Big Guy said, but he did as he was told. "What do you think about what he said about the folks back home?" he asked. "Gunslinger, Mother Hen, and Roman?"

Jonathan unspooled a five-inch length of tape and tore it off. "It's too early to think about it," he said. "He was either lying, telling the truth, or somewhere in the middle. Not much we can do about it from here, is there? Move your hand."

Jonathan took control of Boxers' ear again. Holding the gauze dressing in place with the fingers of his left hand, he wrapped the tape around the perimeter of the wounded ear.

"Ow, goddammit. Take it easy."

"Keep your ears tucked inside the truck next time," Jonathan said.

When he was done playing doctor, Jonathan stuffed the roll of tape back into the med kit and the paper wrappers of the four-by-fours into his pants pocket.

"I want a lollypop," Boxers said.

"After all that whining? No way." Jonathan stood up to his full height and walked back to his shooter, who had moved on to the next life. He pulled a tiny notebook out of a pocket on his ruck and took a bloody fingerprint sample.

Let's get out of here," Jonathan said, and he started back toward the vehicles. "We never did try to start the Suburban," he said.

"Ten thousand bucks says they disabled it."

"A bet I won't take," Jonathan said. "But let's get our gear. We'll carry out as much as we can, keep from getting hypothermic, and if there's any good thing left that might happen, maybe we'll find the vehicle that these guys drove in.

The interior of the Suburban had been trashed, as Jonathan had expected. The dashboard had been reduced to a mass of shattered plastic and glass, and the entire cowl had been stripped from around the steering column. Predictably (inevitably, perhaps) the satellite phone had been smashed to slivers of plastic and silicone.

Their personal gear had been rummaged through, but the important stuff was still there—the heavy coats and camping gear.

"Talk to me, Boss," Boxers said as he pulled a coat out of the mess. "Who are these guys?"

"From the accent alone, I say Colombian," Jonathan said. "Certainly, that guy wasn't Mexican."

"I was going to say exactly the same thing," Boxers said, though from his tone, Jonathan couldn't tell if he was being truthful or ironic. "What about Holly? Shouldn't we do something with her body?"

That was an unusual question from Big Guy, who generally was practical to the point of annoyance. "We can if it's important to you," Jonathan replied.

Big Guy cast a look back in the direction of her body and then shook his head. "We don't have the tools to bury her," he said.

"And the more we manhandle the body, the more we expose ourselves to legal shit," Jonathan said.

He pulled his map back out of his pocket and spread it open on the hood of the Suburban. "Your turn to talk to *me*, Big Guy," he said. "If you were these guys, where would you have parked?"

Boxers took his time studying the map. "If I'm doing the driving," he said, "I'd want to be far enough away not to attract attention, but close enough to be able to cut out fast when the deed is done." As he spoke, his finger hovered over the sheet, moving in a small but consistent circle. "To know where we parked, they'd have to follow us, right?"

"They could have a drone," Jonathan said. "Followed us that way." Jonathan and Boxers had followed vehicles exactly that way in the past.

"Now you're really thinking like me. Still, it wouldn't make sense for them to park far away. After they did their dirty deeds, they'd want a way out of here. There's only one road."

"Let's take it a step further," Jonathan said. "Ranger Simonsen said that he came looking for us because of the way we were parked off the road. To me, that says that he came up on our truck *before* he had a chance to come up on the killers' truck."

"What's your point?"

"My point is that I think we'll find these asshats' vehicle a little farther up the road. Think about it. If the ranger had come up on them first—"

"That's where his vehicle would be parked."

"Exactly."

Boxers gave the map back to Jonathan and swung his ruck over his shoulders while handing Jonathan's ruck over to him. "What's the next step?"

"Let's find their vehicle and get out of here."

"The bodies?"

"Leave 'em. We'll make a phone call and explain as best we can," Jonathan said as he shrugged into his ruck. "I don't want to belabor any investigation out here. We need to find out who's trying to kill us."

Chapter 11

Victor McCloud did his best to keep busy and to look like he was interested in the goings on with his visiting grandchildren, but his mind never really wandered from the reality of the day. People would die today. They were strangers and he would shed no tears at their deaths, but the darkness of the act weighed on him.

Vic was a businessman, not a murderer—though admittedly, in his line of work, problematic people occasionally paid the ultimate sacrifice in service to the jobs that needed to be done. The fact that his hands would remain clean in the literal sense soothed his conscience. He'd learned that if you never saw the bodies, you could talk yourself into believing that maybe the killings never happened. His friends at the White House called it plausible deniability.

While his grandchildren played out in the front expanse of his ranch, his mind slipped back two weeks to his meeting with White House aide Charlie Aisling. To the meeting when the events of today were first launched.

Charlie Aisling was the man that Victor McCloud had

often wished he could be. Naturally graceful and athletic, he sported a full head of hair even as he approached fifty, and he still carried himself like the Olympic gymnast he once was. He'd gone far, considering that his career had started with a community college education. Somewhere along the way, he'd hooked his wagon to a young politician named Anthony Darmond, and since then, he'd been firmly ensconced at the right hand of power. When Tony Darmond won the White House, Aisling inherited a fine office in the West Wing.

Vic wasn't sure what Aisling's official title was—something amorphous like special counselor to the president—but he knew that his sole purpose for the administration was to make Tony Darmond look good in the eyes of the public. One way to do that was to make sure that the administration and the president's political party had ample amounts of cash to do whatever it was that administrations and political parties did with their undocumented money. Victor McCloud had long ago established himself as a spigot of greenbacks.

The two of them were making the best of pretending that Aisling was even mildly competitive in his pool shooting skills. Vic had rarely seen a player with so miserable a touch with the cue. Having flown the man all the way out to Idaho from Washington, DC, he figured there had to be some element of recreation to the trip that was in reality little more than a discussion that couldn't be made over the phone.

Vic had already deliberately scratched twice to give Aisling a chance of preserving his dignity, but after the clod whiffed an easy tap-in, he decided to end the agony by running the board. The game was eight ball, and Vic brought it to a close in four strokes.

"This is what happens when you have all day to play in your palace," Aisling said. He looked a little relieved that the game was over.

They were playing in the log-walled game room in the main house of Vic's seventeen-hundred-acre Sandstorm Ranch. He'd opened the French doors to the slate patio and the undisturbed vistas of the Rocky Mountains beyond.

"You're absolutely right," Vic said, his voice deliberately loaded with irony. "Doing nothing but playing pool is what bought me all of this."

"Well, on behalf of President Darmond, let me express our continued gratitude at your financial success. Are you going to rack them up again? Give me another chance at humiliation?"

"I'd love to," Vic said. "Gather the balls on your side."

Vic and Aisling worked their respective pockets and dumped the colored pool balls onto the blue felt. Vic grabbed the triangular rack and arranged the balls for the break.

"Do you ever wish you'd just taken the hit and served your time instead of selling your soul to us?" Aisling asked.

Vic froze in his racking duties. "Why would you ask me that? And in that tone?"

Aisling held up his hands in surrender. "I didn't mean offense, Vic. I don't know what I'm here for, but I know you sent an expensive goddamn plane to pick me up. I figure this has something to do with the Big Secret."

"Everything I do with your boss has at least *something* to do with the Big Secret. And both of you would do well to remember that you're as exposed as I am."

"I get your point, but don't kid yourself. Tony Darmond is president of the United States."

"He still serves at the will of the people."

"Yeah, sure he does. Do I get to break?"

"Hell, no. When you win, you break." Vic carried the cue ball to the head of the table and set it down. "It's going to be a very long damn day at the table for you."

The Big Secret started as a favor that quickly turned into a nightmare. Back when Darmond was a mere mortal with distant desires for political office, he spent his days as an up-and-coming assistant United States attorney, specializing in what was then called white collar crime. This was back in the nineties, when Victor McCloud was working to navigate his way to the kind of wealth that made life simple.

Amassing that kind of wealth the old fashioned way took lots of time and required huge risks. Given the distractions of the presidential administration in office at the time, Vic had landed on a shortcut that would put weapons in the hands of the Bosnians at great profit to himself. The gambit had worked perfectly for nearly two years. And then it didn't.

Vic got word through a contact in the FBI that this whip-smart and ambitious young prosecutor named Tony Darmond was looking to pin a hide to his wall and that the hide looked a lot like Victor McCloud. The same FBI contact brought word that Darmond had not yet filed his investigation and was beginning a run at the House of Representatives. He was cash poor but didn't want to be.

"Are you telling me he's hunting for a bribe?" Vic asked at the time.

His contact smirked. "A bribe is something you give to an alderman or a traffic cop. At this level, it's referred to as campaign contributions."

"That's limited to two thousand dollars, isn't it?"

"You really need to speak with Counselor Darmond."

They met in Fort Marcy Park in suburban Northern Virginia—a location that had recently been in the news for other reasons. A member of the administration at the time had killed himself there. Vic should have known from that alone that Tony Darmond was a major leaguer while he, Vic, was still playing varsity.

They sat side by side on a bench, looking out at a walking trail. To a passerby, it might have looked like budding romance. Darmond wore a grey suit with a blue shirt and yellow tie, the fashion trend of ten years before.

"You're in a lot of trouble, Mr. McCloud," the future president said. "Does the name Amid Kodro mean anything to you?"

This was somewhere between hello and nice to meet you. "Is that a pop song?" Vic had asked, hoping to keep things light.

"No, Vic, he's not. May I call you Vic?"

At that point, he could call Vic anything he wanted. "Sure."

"Amid Kodro was a Serbian peace negotiator, and I can prove that one of the rifles you sold to the Bosnians was used in his assassination. That makes you a felon."

Vic felt his insides melt. "I . . . I . . ." A stammer was the best he could do.

"I know that's not what you wanted when you got involved in your scheme to sell guns to America's enemies, but shit does happen sometimes." Darmond paused to draw Vic's attention. "It gets worse," Darmond said.

How could that possibly be true?

"You're a very special kind of felon. If convicted, you could get the death penalty, though these days, life in prison would be more likely. I'll let you decide which of those options is better."

Another pause to allow the gravity of the situation to sink in.

"If that alone were the case, Vic, you could say that you're having the worst day of any of your neighbors, and I wager you would be right. But there's even more."

"Oh, God." This time, he was able to form words and get them clear of his throat.

"Yeah," Darmond said, feigning sympathy. "The nature of the charge is such that it has no statute of limitations. It is the proverbial sword of Damocles, forever hanging over your head. And I own the only pair of scissors that can cut the thread."

"Why are you doing this?"

"Doing what? Giving you an option for your life that doesn't end it outright or condemn it to a concrete room for the next sixty years? I'm doing you a favor here, Vic. I'm giving you a chance to live a normal life."

Vic knew that Darmond wanted him to ask why again, but he also knew that the plot would reveal itself just as clearly if he remained silent and let the man talk.

"Did our mutual friend reveal to you that I am changing my career trajectory?"

"You're running for Congress."

"Yes, I am. And whatever you've heard about the financial needs of a congressional campaign, the truth is way worse. It's astonishing how expensive it is, what with media time and special access."

Vic had learned subsequently that *special access* meant membership in the Star Chamber, the cabal of politicians, past and present, who determine winners and losers. Every now and then, an unanointed player slips through, but it doesn't happen often, and when it does, they last only long enough to be destroyed by the media arm of the power brokerage team.

"How much?" Vic knew he'd been beaten. Might as well cut to the chase.

"How much is your freedom worth to you?"

"I have to live my life, Tony. May I call you Tony?"

"No, you may not. Mr. Darmond will do just fine. I'm not looking to bankrupt you, Vic. That would be short-sighted on my part. Besides, campaign finances are pretty closely regulated. Cheating is possible, but given the intense emotions of politics and the shifting loyalties, I have to be careful."

Vic's shoulder sagged. "Mr. Darmond, this is new territory for me. If you're expecting me to interpret subtext, you're going to be disappointed. You hold all the cards in this game, so tell me what you need to me to do, and I'll do my best."

Darmond made a show of looking down at the space between his feet, his elbows resting on his knees. "Of all the phrases that make me squirm, *do my best* is one of the most troubling. It's so . . . *relative*. And when does one ever reach one's *best* anyway? It's always possible to go one step better, isn't it? No matter what the endeavor is?"

Vic groaned. "Fine. Yes, I suppose. It might not be obvious to you, but it's apparent to me that you're enjoying this conversation far more than I am."

"Vic, let's walk. Sitting for long periods isn't good for you." Darmond stood and walked toward the footpath, clearly confident that Vic would follow.

"Do you know the history of this place?" Darmond asked.

"Only what I've heard in the news."

"That's not history," Darmond said. "That's tawdry current events. This history of Fort Marcy Park is referenced in its name. This fort, such as it is, was erected quickly in the early days of the Civil War to protect Chain Bridge from the Confederates. "

As with many Civil War historical sights, Vic found a sense of peace in the frozen displays of war infrastructure. Copper cannons, corroded green with time, faced out over low berms, threatening sea invaders with mayhem.

"I really don't need a history lesson this afternoon," Vic told the future president. "I need you to tell me what you want from me, and then we'll move on."

"I'll get right to it, then" Darmond said. "I want as much as I can get, but the rules need to be followed."

"What rules?"

"I'm getting to that. Campaign contributions from any one individual or company are set at a maximum of two thousand dollars. To contribute more than that is to expose yourself—and me—to legal action."

"I can write you a two thousand dollar check right now," Vic said. But surely, that wasn't relevant.

"And I will accept it when the time is right," Darmond said. "Are you familiar with the term *bundler*?"

"As in one who bundles things? I know the term but not the context."

"I figured as much," Darmond said. "What about a PAC?"

"Political Action Committee, right?"

"Exactly."

"You want me to start one?" Vic felt a flash of panic. He'd have no idea where to start.

"Oh, heavens no," Darmond said with a derisive chuckle. "I bring it up because they are bundlers in their own right. They develop mailing lists and send out cards and letters requesting contributions—no more than two thousand dollars at a time—for whatever cause they support. PAC money comes to established politicians who already have the backing of their parties. I want you not to be a PAC— because that is a legal entity that has complicated record-keeping requirements. What I want you to do is pull together lots and lots of two thousand dollar checks made out to Elect Anthony Darmond, my campaign entity."

This sounded too easy. "Okay," Vic said dubiously, as he waited for the other shoe. "You want me to lean on my friends, get the checks, and bring them to you."

"Nope," Darmond said. "That would be illegal. I need you to give them to my campaign manager. His name is Charlie Aisling. He'll be in touch."

"And then I'm done? After that we're clear of each other."

Darmond laughed at that, genuinely amused. "I keep

forgetting that you're not from Washington," he said. "There's no such thing as being done, and we'll never be clear of each other. That's why I mentioned that your crime will hang over you forever. No statute of limitations, remember?"

"So, this is an annual event."

"It's not an event, Vic. You need to see that. This is a new normal. This is what you do. We'll start at a hundred grand over the next six months. That feels doable to me."

"In six months?" Vic felt his stomach tighten. "I don't know that many rich people. Not at only two grand a pop."

Darmond cast him a sideward glance. "Do you think for a second that I haven't done my due diligence on you? I know your net worth is approaching ten million dollars. That's a lot of illegal arms sales."

It was actually more like only eight million, but this was not a time to quibble over rounding errors. "That's not my only business," he said. He heard the defensiveness in his tone.

"Oh, of course. I forgot about Horse Spit Transportation, or whatever it is you call it."

"Chaps N Spurs Overland Freight," Vic snapped, and right away, he knew he'd chomped on bait, but he didn't know what it was about.

"Ah, yes," Darmond smarmed. "Moving product to customer. When it absolutely, positively needs to be snorted overnight."

Vic stopped hard. *Jesus, this guy really did his homework.*

Darmond turned with a grin. "Don't look surprised like that. I'm very good at what I do. It's nice knowing a leader of the underground in the war on drugs. Mrs. Reagan would not be happy with you, Victor."

Vic refused to move any farther. "What do you know?"

"Everything," Darmond said. "What I don't know is how you conceal it. I saw a movie a while back that said ground coffee was the best medium to confuse the dogs. Is that true?"

Vic remained silent.

"For what it's worth—if I even have to mention it, given the nature of our conversation—I am off the clock right now. I am not a prosecutor. I'm just a guy talking with a guy."

"You're a thief shaking down a guy," Vic corrected. He was tired of the charade and no longer cared about pissing off this cockroach of a man.

"You've got to be more precise," Darmond said. "I am a man who holds extraordinary power over another man who chose a life of crime."

"And what is this shakedown, if not a crime?"

"They call it politics," Darmond said. "Grow up, for God's sake."

Vic saw the world closing in on him. Suddenly, there wasn't enough air to breathe. This guy owned him, and there was nothing he could do. "So, are you going to hold this over me as a prosecution, too?"

"That's an excellent question," Darmond said. "I'm so glad you asked it. You allow me to display my sensitive side. The business of transporting drugs is of no concern to me. And frankly, it's of no concern to you, either, unless you do something exceedingly stupid. The current administration no longer cares about the drug trade. It's a good thing, too, because there's not a powder-free nose in the entire West Wing. My office saw some activity regarding Chaps N Spurs, but I have just enough clout to quash that investigation before it even started."

Vic's bullshit bell was hammering a full peal. "Why would you do that?"

Darmond started walking again, and Vic followed. "I'd have thought the answer to that question was obvious," he said. "I deal with hundreds of criminals every year. All but a tiny fraction of one percent of them are prosecuted to the fullest extent of the law, and they go to jail. My conviction rate dances right at the one hundred percent mark. But you, Victor McCloud, are one of one. You're an entrepreneur of means whose background speaks of an addiction to the nicer things. I cannot think of a better profile for a committed fundraiser."

Vic felt like a fly on the sticky strip.

"The last thing I want to do is stand between you and earning a living," Darmond said. "If driving drugs from the West Coast to the East Coast and parts in between makes you a rich man, that's a good thing for me, is it not? People are going to snort and shoot what they're going to snort and shoot. From where I sit, with years of practical evidence to lean on, it really doesn't matter what we do. Druggies are willing to kill themselves for the high, and they're willing to kill law enforcement personnel for the freedom to kill themselves. I personally believe that the government would be best to stay out of the way."

"Is that what your campaign literature is going to say?" Vic asked. As soon as the question was past his lips, he regretted it.

"You're trying to be an asshole, Vic, and I appreciate

that, but since you asked, and since I own you, I'll honor you with an answer. No, that's not what my campaign literature will say. In fact, my campaign is going to be all about stopping the scourge of drug trafficking in America."

Vic sensed yet again that he was supposed to have seen a larger message in the words, but it just wasn't there.

"I'm an assistant United States attorney," Darmond expounded. "My entire career has been dedicated to bringing people like you to justice."

Vic stopped again.

"But before you panic," Darmond said, "I'm going to be really honest with you. You know, because I own you. The very last thing I want is for the drug trade to end. If it did, I would lose a talking point."

Vic didn't get it, and apparently, his expression showed it.

"I don't say this with any pride," Darmond explained, "but you need to understand the nature of politics. Politicians are like dogs that chase cars. We have no intention of actually catching what we chase. What would be the point? Once a problem is solved, the public loses interest in it. You get twenty minutes of attention at the celebratory press conference, and then it's gone. People shift to the next issue. We spend years and countless amounts of money developing perceptions of problems into perceptions of crises. No one wants to start that over and over again."

They walked to the end of an ancient parapet, as close as the National Park Service fencing would allow them to go. The view of the Potomac River was stunning.

"Stop looking like you're on the way to a firing squad,"

Darmond said. "You're hearing the wrong words. You're only hearing the parts about where you're breaking the law, when what I really want you to hear is that I don't care if you're breaking the law. In fact, I *encourage* you to continue to break the law. That's my quo to your quid pro."

Vic still didn't get it. He continued to stare.

"Come on, Vic, think." Darmond started walking again. "Think of me as the devil and you are making a deal with me. Here's how it works: you get me two hundred grand a year, and I get DEA and the other alphabets to look the other way on investigations that might involve Chaps N Spurs. Uncle Sam will become officially disinterested in your company."

"You don't have that kind of power," Vic said.

"Don't kid yourself. Who do you think makes the decisions on who gets prosecuted in this country?"

Actually, Vic had no idea.

"U.S. attorneys are political appointees," Darmond explained. "They come and go. They parrot whatever comes out of the mouth of the president, and we all pretend to be interested, but at the end of the day, AUSAs—the career guys—make or break a prosecution."

"And when you get elected to office?" Vic prompted.

"Nothing breeds success like success, Vic. You should know that. After I'm elected to the House, and then on to wherever I go—the White House, I hope—my career colleagues will do everything they can to keep me happy."

As he listened to it all, Vic felt dirty. "So, you're saying that you and your prosecutor colleagues are all corrupt?"

Another laugh. "The phrase is *politically savvy*." He

said it with finger quotes. "You don't need to know the details, but this will work." Darmond let that sink in and then added, "Plus, you have no choice. Now, do you want to hear your end or not?"

Vic knew the rest was coming. He didn't have to wait long.

"Companies are not individuals," Darmond said. "You, Victor McCloud, cannot contribute more than two thousand dollars to my campaign, but if the board of directors of one or more of the companies you own decided to contribute, that would be fine. If you decided to start a foundation of some sort, that foundation could contribute, as well."

Vic felt overwhelmed. "Are you telling me that that is not illegal?"

"Consider the long game here," Darmond pressed. "My goal is the White House. By the time I get there, most of official Washington will owe me big-time. As a practical matter, if you play your cards right and don't do something outrageously stupid, there will essentially be no law that applies to you."

"What about in the meantime?" Vic asked. "You can't just shit out an election victory. It takes a long time, and it may never happen."

Darmond laughed again. It was a sound that Vic had already grown tired of hearing. "You're negotiating as if you have anything but a shit hand. I think that's amusing. If your answer is *no*, I can forward your case to a grand jury tomorrow. Just let me know how you'd like to proceed."

So, Vic made the deal, and Darmond managed to pull all the strings that were necessary for Vic to maximize his fortune. He owned dozens of companies, most of which were legal and all of which were profitable more years than they were not. OTX Security, for example, was born of the aftermath of the 9/11 attacks and had served as a solid cash generator ever since. Chaps N Spurs Overland Freight, though, beat all of the others. It was the rare legitimate shipment that didn't carry with it substantial amounts of product from below the border.

Unfortunately, as Vic had learned over and over, good fortune cannot exist in a vacuum. There's a Newtonian element to business whereby every good bit of business triggers an equal and opposite bit of bad business.

One of the biggest movers of cocaine out of Colombia was the Cinco Muertos cartel—Five Deaths—an increasingly brutal group run by a certified nutjob named Antonio Filho. Vic had met him only twice, and on each occasion, he had left feeling like his insides had turned to ice. Filho had no heart, showed no remorse, and expected nothing but one hundred percent efficiency from his contractors, of which Chaps N Spurs was a significant one. The more the cartel invested, the more efficient—and dependent—Chaps N Spurs became on the revenue.

And the more courageous and demanding Antonio Filho became.

Inevitably, the bloody battles in the northern states of Mexico spilled over the Rio Grande. Starting about five years ago, Filho and his middlemen needed brawn inside the United States, and OTX Security, owned by the man who was already owned by government officials and thugs on both sides of the border, floated to the top as the most obvious provider of services.

The assassination business changed everything for Vic. Never a violent man, he abhorred violence as a business, but he understood the larger deal. He would be either a proprietor of violence or a victim of it. Some choices were easy.

"When are you going to get around to why I'm here?" Aisling asked, leaning over the pool table. He lined up an easy shot to the side pocket and actually made it.

"I want to make a trade," Vic said.

"Of course you do." Aisling never knew enough to make one shot with the next one in mind, so he found his cue ball trapped behind Vic's nine ball, with no hope for sinking anything. Nonetheless, he launched a valiant try on the three ball and got nothing but cushion. Technically, a scratch, but Vic let it go. If they actually enforced every rule for the game, Aisling would be a demoralized mess.

"I was watching the news the other night—"

"Which network?"

"Yours, of course," Vic lied. He didn't watch any of the American alphabets anymore. What was the point? He could peruse Facebook for unsubstantiated angst masquerading as news. He preferred BBC and Al Jazeera for agenda-free reporting. "The lead story dealt with President Darmond's miserable ratings on his management of the southern border. Do you think he would like to seal the deal on a major cartel operation in Brownsville?"

"Texas?"

"That would be the one. If he framed it right, he could put a thumb in the eye of the Texas governor at the same time."

"What've you got?"

"That's where the favor comes in," Vic said. "And before you get all pissy, let's state for the record that I am merely the messenger here. I am told by people in the know that four hundred kilos of cocaine and fentanyl lie ready to be seized in a warehouse, but in order to get it, the president needs to commute a prison sentence."

Aisling looked like he'd been slapped. "The president can't do that."

"Yes, he can," Vic said. "I can understand that he doesn't want to, but he's got all kinds of power over imprisoned people if he wants to flex that muscle."

Aisling laid his cue on the blue felt and wandered over to the tanned leather sofa. "Who is this person?" He helped himself to a seat.

"Nobody," Vic said. "A distant relative of a business associate."

"Does this business associate's name rhyme with Antonio Filho?"

"It's a *business associate*," Vic said. "Four hundred kilos is eight hundred eighty pounds. You're looking at a street value of close to a hundred twenty million dollars." He paused to let his words find their target. "Interested?"

"What kind of commutation are you looking for?"

"Full pardon, if we can get it. A walkaway, no matter what."

"And if the boss says *no way*? Says that you give me the warehouse, or I do the thing?"

The thing, of course, was going public with the Big Secret. "I can't give him what I don't know. My associate knows how to play the game. When he sees the pardon, he'll share the information."

"I need a name," Aisling said. "I mean, if we're talking El Chapo, then no."

"You mean the name of the prisoner?"

"Yes."

"Because I won't give you the name of the associate."

"And I won't ask for it because we all know who it is."

"The prisoner's name is Luciana Lopez."

"Why is Luciana Lopez important to you?"

"She's not. I don't know who she is, beyond being a low-level player in the drug game. But she's important enough to my business associate that he's willing to give President Darmond a victory in the drug war."

"I bet he would," Aisling said. "And in the process, he might just make a hole in the competition for his product."

Vic moved Aisling's cue to the rack and returned to the table to clear the balls. "I have no idea what you're talking about. But I know that the fuse on this is very short. The offer can disappear at any moment."

"All right, then," Aisling said as he stood again and pulled his phone from his pocket. "I will step outside and make a phone call.

As Aisling exited to the yard, Vic's son, Alan, entered from the hallway. "Who is that?" he asked.

Vic felt heat rising in his cheeks. "Have you been eavesdropping?" His tone was all accusation.

"Of course not," Alan said. "But should I? Isn't that guy a Washington bigwig?"

"He is, and no, you should not."

"But Pops—"

"Not now," Vic said. "Just no. Please leave me alone."

"Is the White House trying to pressure you again?"

Victor pointed to the door through which Alan had just entered. "Be sure the door is latched when you close it."

CHAPTER 12

Renaldo Vega pulled his horse to a stop when the distant woods erupted in gunfire. It was a faint rumble from far away—so subtle that it might go unnoticed for what he knew it to be. It was impossible to translate sounds into distances out here in the mountains, but he knew it had to be at least a mile.

So, Grave had engaged his colleagues in a firefight. Knowing the others—and having more than a passing familiarity with the likes of Jonathan Grave—he couldn't imagine that the results of the conflict would be anything short of all-or-nothing. The entirety of one team of combatants would be dead.

He eased the horse forward at a slow walk. Whatever the outcome of the battle, it was bound to be over by the time he arrived on the scene, and the last thing he wanted was to wander into the middle of an ongoing bloodbath.

Given that the others in his team had been forewarned, it was hard for Renaldo to conceive of a circumstance where Grave and Brian the Giant could emerge victorious, but he would have thought the same thing earlier today when he'd missed the shot that had started it all.

The firing ceased for what felt like several minutes, leading Renaldo to believe that maybe the fight had ended. But then it sparked back up. Not like before, with the sustained fire, but just a few sporadic shots.

Then the guns fell silent again.

Renaldo absently stroked the radio on his belt. If Grave and his team had lost the battle, the others would have radioed him of the success, wouldn't they? That seemed to him like the sensible thing to do.

Yet, the radio remained silent.

In his heart, Renaldo knew what that really meant for him.

"It feels like a bad sign that they know our names," Boxers said as they walked away from their trashed Suburban and headed up the roadway, keeping their eyes open for signs of the bad guys' vehicle.

"Yes, it does," Jonathan agreed.

"We both think they sounded Colombian," Boxers said. "We've pissed off a lot of people in Colombia. Narrowing the list could be a challenge."

"It's pretty clear to me that this is the work of the cartels," Jonathan said.

"*Pretty* clear? This has cartel written all over it."

"I don't disagree," Jonathan said, "but there shouldn't be much left of the cartels we've gone against. I hear that last guy whose ass we kicked got cut up into little pieces and mailed all over Mexico."

"Come on, Dig, we barely made a dent. The cartels aren't snakes, where you can cut their heads off and kill them. They're worms. You cut off their heads and they grow a new one."

Jonathan craned his neck to look up at his friend. "That's pretty good. Did you think of that all by yourself?"

Boxers flipped him off.

"I'm thinking of that thing with Roman," Jonathan said. "It particularly bothers me that Pedro back there mentioned the boy."

"Cuts awfully close to home," Boxers said.

Jonathan looked up at Big Guy. "We never got a good answer for why the Cortez cartel was shipping him off to Colombia when we got there."

"You think this is related to that?"

"Yes," Jonathan said. "You know my thoughts on co-incidences. What I don't know is *how* they're linked. Or *why*. The Cortezes snatched up him and Ciara Kelly. Why then palm Roman off to the Colombians?"

"I thought we decided it was sex trafficking," Boxers said.

"But *this* isn't about sex trafficking," Jonathan said. "This was a hit, pure and simple. Revenge. Retribution."

"More than that," Boxers added, "It's risky as shit to try to hit us on our own turf, in the USA."

"That means intel capability," Jonathan said. "They had to know that we were in Montana and out of here. And then manage the logistics of coming across the border."

"Well, *that's* not what it used to be," Boxers scoffed. "I mean, how hard can it be to wade across the Rio Grande and give the feds the finger?"

Jonathan let that go. "The point is that this all has to

be about something loftier than denying the cartels a couple of sex workers."

"We *did* sink their navy," Boxers reminded. The bad guys had been in the process of loading Roman onto a narco-sub when the team intervened in his kidnapping.

"True enough," Jonathan said. "And maybe that pissed them off to the point of doing all of this, but I don't buy it."

"Why not? They're crazy."

"Crazy, maybe, but they're also savvy businessmen," Jonathan said. "The Colombians in particular run their businesses like corporations. That means you don't take unnecessary risks."

"Unless the payoff is worth it," Boxers said.

"Or, you're pissed off enough not to care."

They walked in silence for thirty seconds or so before Boxers said, "What does any of this have to do with Roman?"

Jonathan detected an odd tone. "You have a theory?"

"Maybe. I keep thinking that he's the single new variable to this equation. I mean, we've been doing this shit for a long time, pissing people off every day. Now, all of a sudden, we've got Colombians invading America to take us out."

He stopped talking, and Jonathan shot him a look. Surely, there was more to come.

"Roman gave up our names," Boxers said. "That's the new bit."

Jonathan recoiled. "You can't hold that against him. Jesus, he's just a kid."

"And a terrified one at that," Boxers said. "So, no, of course I don't hold it against him. But the fact remains."

Jonathan didn't want Big Guy to be right on this but

feared that he was. Anonymity had been a secret to their survival for all these years. Invisible to every fingerprint and facial recognition database, they operated as ghosts. Perhaps that was the reason why this attack happened now. Perhaps that important bit of data had been enough to embolden their enemies.

So, why the Colombians? It had been ages since they'd blown stuff up in South America. "Roman revealed our identities to the Cortezes," Jonathan said, thinking aloud. He ran through the details of that night on the shore of the Pacific. If the people they'd just killed had been Mexicans, this would make more sense.

Then he saw it. He pulled to a stop, nearly causing a collision with Boxers. "They split the kids up," Jonathan said.

"Did we just change subjects?" Boxers asked. He shifted his rifle to better rest his hands.

"That night at the shore," Jonathan said. "With the submarine and all that. Roman and his girlfriend Ciara were split up. When we got there, Ciara was being taken to a car, while Roman was being taken out to sea. Why the separation?"

"I have no idea."

"Well, neither do I," Jonathan confessed. "But it's a data point. An important one, I think."

They started walking again.

"That's the Colombian connection," Jonathan went on, more mumbling thoughts than making a point. "In the same series of events when Roman revealed our names, a Mexican cartel leader splits the kids up, with one heading out to sea. Somehow, and for some reason, the Cortez team must have shared information with a Colombian team."

"And the team sent a submarine?"

The pieces were beginning to fall into place for Jonathan now. "No, I don't think they sent the submarine for Roman. I think that was serendipity. Roman happened to be there on a day when the Cortezes were receiving their shipment from down south. Remember all that shit on the shore?"

"I do," Boxers said. "So, what did they want with Roman?"

Bingo. Jonathan saw the answer now, fully formed and perfectly logical. "They were kidnapping him to hurt us."

Boxers' answer came in the form of a deep scowl.

"Think about it," Jonathan said, becoming more animated. "Armed with our names, the bad guys somehow connected the dots to stuff we have done to them in the past. They were going to leverage Roman somehow to get back to us."

"Whoa, cowboy," Boxers said. "That's a lot of concluding in the absence of evidence."

"The duck theory," Jonathan said. "What it walks like and quacks like it almost certainly is."

"Well, shit," Boxers said. "That means the folks back home really are in danger."

"Yes, it does. It also means we need to get home."

A few more seconds passed as they walked on up the road.

"I don't know, though," Boxers said. "We haven't gotten crosswise with the Colombians in a long time."

"Those guys' memories are long," Jonathan said. "I

imagine that the supply chain is the detail that links the Cortez cartel with whoever the Colombians are."

"You mean, Cortez buys his poison from Submarine Guy?"

"Exactly." Another piece fell into place, and Jonathan stopped again, this time causing a real collision.

"Goddammit, Dig, would you stop doing that?"

"Doesn't this remind you of a similar pattern a while ago? During our last trip to Colombia, I believe?"

Boxers looked confused, knitting his forehead into a wrinkle. Then his eyes got big and he snapped his fingers. "Evan Somebody."

"Guinn," Jonathan said. "Evan Guinn. About Roman's age. Kidnapped and taken south to Colombia."

"Yeah," Boxers said, the memory clarifying in his eyes. "They took him from RezHouse. Shot the place up."

Jonathan thought that was an exaggeration, but he let it go. In reality, the kidnappers didn't *shoot the place up* so much as they shot a dormitory staffer. "And we made them pay a high price."

In rescuing Even Guinn from the coca fields, they'd leveled a good bit of the Colombian jungle.

"Nobody was left there, either," Boxers said.

"There's always somebody left," Jonathan said. "Everybody's got a boss, a benefactor, or an important client."

Less than ten minutes into their walk up the mountain road, Boxers was first to notice the tire impressions through the gravel shoulder into the cover of trees. How many reasons could there be for that?

The tracks turned into a deer trail—or maybe a fire road. Wide enough for a vehicle, but barely. Twenty-five yards in, they wandered up on the ass end of a horse trailer.

The tailgate was down, and there were no horses to be found. Though judging from the stench of horse shit, there'd been some here recently.

"Wrong truck?" Boxers asked.

"Maybe." On the far side of the trailer, the hitch was still attached to a navy blue Toyota Sequoia.

One peek through the windows proved that this was, indeed, the shooters' vehicle. "Look at all the toys," Boxers said. "Let's go shopping."

"You run the aisles," Jonathan said. "I'm going to check the glove box. Let's perform a little due diligence before we drive off in a truck that doesn't belong to us."

The Sequoia carried Wyoming tags, and according to the documents Jonathan found in the glove box, it was owned by Teton Luxury Car Rental in Jackson Hole. The name on the contract was Leonard V. Franklin, of Owings Mills, Maryland, but they'd be morons to use their real names. Crooks could be stupid, but only to a point.

"Hey, Boss," Boxers said. "Lots of good stuff back here. We've got ammo—mostly five-five-six but some three-oh-eight—that we can add to our pockets. And . . . look at this!" Boxers lifted a pair of night vision goggles out of a canvas bag and held them up as if a trophy. "We've got NVGs." He unzipped a second bag and withdrew a second pair. "You were right. These assholes were serious about their mission."

Jonathan came around to join him at the cargo bed. The NVGs were old-school two-tube arrays, as opposed to the more modern four-tube arrays that they'd been using for years, but ten years ago, this model was close to state-of-the-art gear.

They found some cold weather gear, some surplus

MREs—meals ready to eat—spare batteries for their radios, and a couple of knives—an old-school folding Buck in one bag and a CRKT straight blade in the other. If nothing else, a few spare bullets and the NVGs made for a good haul.

Then Jonathan found a map that had been folded and shoved into one of the outer pockets. It was a topo map more or less identical to the one he was carrying. He spread it out on the floor of the cargo bay and took in the details.

Jonathan thumped a circle on the map with his finger. "Recognize that?"

"That's Holly Looney's place."

"That's exactly what that is."

Boxers stood to his full height. "What do you think that means? She was somehow part of their plot?"

Jonathan made a face. "I guess it could, but that's not where my head went. I figure that they had also identified it as the only source of shelter out here. If the shooter failed—as he did—and we didn't come back for the truck, I figure they knew that was our only option for shelter."

Boxers gave a low whistle. "They really planned for this thing."

"And it's damn lucky we didn't hunker down at that cabin," Jonathan added. "It's a real tragedy that Holly died in the crossfire, but we'd all have been toast if we'd stuck around there."

"Well, you guessed they'd have NVGs, and sure enough, they did."

Boxers buttoned up the back of the Toyota and detached the horse trailer from the hitch while Jonathan walked to the shotgun seat and got in. Big Guy then slid in behind the steering wheel and asked, "Where are we going?"

"Farther up the mountain," Jonathan said. "Put some distance between us and them and high enough that maybe I can get a cell signal."

The Sequoia started right away, and a mile later, Jonathan's phone showed signs of life. "I've got two bars," he said. "Pull over."

Gravel crunched as Boxers piloted the Sequoia onto the shoulder. "Gonna call Mother Hen?"

"I'm going to start with Gunslinger," Jonathan said. "If bad things have happened, I'll get a calmer recitation."

Gail answered on the fourth ring. "Jesus, Dig, where have you been?"

"Everything okay there?" he asked.

Jonathan put the call on the speaker while Gunslinger ran through the details of her gunfight in the street.

"Holy shit, Slinger. Is everybody okay?"

"The good guys are, yes. Mother Hen and I both." A long-standing rule among Jonathan and his colleagues mandated the use of call signs on any communication over any airwaves. It was vast bit of overkill, but it made him feel better.

"What about Mother Hen's chick?" Jonathan asked. Roman didn't have a call sign.

"What about him?"

"What's his status?"

"We had them lock down the school," Gail said, "Plus, he's in the Zulu Room." Then her tone changed. "How do you already know about this?"

"I think we're under attack," he said. Then he gave an overview of their day so far.

"Oh, my God, Scorpion," Gail said.

"Big Guy and I are both fine, but there's a pile of bodies up here on the mountain that we're gonna need Wolverine's help to explain." Known to the rest of the world as Irene Rivers, Wolverine had worked with Jonathan and Boxers even before she'd been elevated to her current role as director of the FBI.

"I'll pass that along to Our Special Friend," Gail said. Jonathan knew she meant Father Dom, who, for complicated reasons, was the go-between for Jonathan and Irene Rivers when they needed to meet or speak.

"It won't be for a while," Jonathan said. "Our cell signal is shit."

"Who do you think is doing this, Scorpion?"

"I don't have a name," Jonathan said. "And let's face it, the list of potential candidates is pretty long."

"Are you coming back home?" Gail asked.

"Not yet."

That drew an odd look from Boxers. *We're not?*

Jonathan explained, "The bad guys' vehicle is a rental. A Toyota. We have both the vehicle and the paperwork. I need Mother Hen to work some of her magic to figure out where it came from. I also have some fingerprints to send to get them analyzed. This attack was organized, planned, and multifocused. All of that tells me that it's got legs. These guys are going to keep coming unless we stop them."

"Even if we don't know who they are?" Gail asked.

"That's where Mother Hen comes in," Jonathan said.

Gail fell silent long enough for Jonathan to wonder if they'd been disconnected. "Slinger?"

"I'm here," she said. "I'm weighing whether or not to tell you this next part."

"Now that you've said that much, I'd say there's not a lot of choice anymore."

Gail said, "It's just that Mother Hen is pretty distracted."

He could hear the big breath she took.

"People came at Mama Alexander, too," Gail said. "They pushed her off the road."

Something churned in Jonathan's gut. A combination of ice and acid.

"She's okay, though," Gail added quickly.

"What does *okay* mean?"

"Bump on the head. Maybe a broken ankle. They're going to release her from the hospital. That's where Mother Hen is now."

"With what kind of security?" Jonathan asked.

"Some of our own," Gail said. "Some local police, too. Doug Kramer is going to drive Mama home in his buggy."

In recent years, Jonathan had lost a lot of faith in the capabilities of the Fisherman's Cove Police Department, but Doug was a dear friend who'd do anything for Mama.

"What do we know about the people who attacked her?" Boxers asked.

"We don't know anything about anybody," Gail said. "With the police involved, they're going to be in charge of the investigation. Doug said that likely means no one will share anything with us."

"So, are Mama's attackers still out there?" Jonathan asked.

"As far as I know," Gail said. "One bit of good news is that Mother Hen has a fingerprint sample from the guy that tried to kill us. That's something. Not a lot, but better than nothing."

"We'll take what we can get. I'm sorry we won't be around to help with buttoning down everything there at the home front, but it doesn't make sense to go all the way there when there's a hot op ongoing here. This rental truck is from Jackson Hole. Teton Luxury Car Rental. I'll take pix of everything and send them on to you, but that feels significant to me. That's a couple hundred miles from here and not an easy drive. There are closer airports where they could have rented cars. Let's see if we can find out why they might do that."

After Jonathan clicked off, Boxers dropped the transmission into gear and pulled free of their parking place. "You okay, Boss?"

"Under the circumstances, I think *okay* is exactly the wrong word."

"The part about Mama?" Boxers asked.

Jonathan didn't trust his voice.

"Sounds like she wasn't badly hurt," Big Guy said.

Jonathan kept his hands on his thighs, fearful that they might be trembling. He felt the heat in his face, and he felt a level of anger brewing in his gut that rarely appeared, but when it did, it was always destructive.

"We'll get 'em, Dig," Boxers said. His tone was unnaturally soothing.

"They attacked *Mama*, Box. Who would do that?"

It was Boxers' turn to fall silent.

"I mean, honest to God," Jonathan said. "Somebody's got to die for that. Right?"

"You know I'd be happy to help," Boxers said, "but you're scaring me a little now. You've said yourself that we're not assassins. That's not what we do."

Big Guy was right. Jonathan *knew* he was right. If there was one overarching lesson that his years as a door kicker had taught him, it was that there was no room for anger in an op that might lead to violence. Anger clouded decision-making, clouded even the ability to think clearly.

"This will pass," Jonathan said. "I know you're right. Killing is not what we're about."

They drove in silence for fifteen or twenty seconds before Boxers said, "Doesn't mean we can't hurt 'em real bad, though."

CHAPTER 13

Gail was outside waiting for Venice and Mama when they came home. The gates to the entire RezHouse compound—including the mansion—were closed and manned by armed security personnel. Venice's Blazer got there first, with Chief Kramer and Mama close behind. Both vehicles waited while the heavy gates swung open, and then they pulled through. As soon as the vehicles cleared, the guards returned to their positions.

As Venice pulled around the sweeping driveway, Gail hurried to intercept her.

"What's wrong?" Venice asked as she got out of the car. "Please tell me this horrible day hasn't gotten any worse."

"Can't do that, I'm afraid," Gail said. It took about forty-five seconds to pass along the short version of what Jonathan had shared with her. She concluded with, "He's sending you a bunch of data, all of which needs to be analyzed. He's staying out West until he's sure that's not where this whole thing is centered."

Venice closed her eyes and looked toward the sky. "Lord, bring us through this unharmed," she said. "I've heard that Roman is safely back here in the mansion, in the Zulu Room. The school is on lockdown, too."

"What are we telling everyone?" Gail asked. "What's the official reason for locking down the school?"

Venice looked confused.

"Are we telling people about the attacks?" Gail clarified.

"No," Venice said. "For the moment, we won't tell them anything. This could just be a drill for all they know."

"That's not going to fly for long," Gail said. "The place looks like we went to war. Texts are going to fly. People are going to want to have answers."

"The answers can wait till we get Mama inside and stabilized," Venice said. "One thing at a time."

She started to walk away. Over at his vehicle, Chief Kramer was helping Mama Alexander out of the backseat. She wore an orthopedic boot on her right foot and was doing her best to navigate a cane.

"One more thing," Gail said. "We need to get Dom to set up contact with Wolverine as soon as possible."

"Do what you need to do," Venice said. And she was gone.

The bizarre urgency of the atmosphere here on the campus unsettled Gail. It wasn't just the shooting. She'd been shot at before, and she'd shot back before. She'd even endured violence that was far too close to home, but there was something about the scope of these attacks—and the fact that they included Mama on the hit list—that spoke of something far more pernicious than any threats they'd faced in the past.

The scope of the operation—with Jonathan targeted in Montana, for God's sake, more or less at the same moment when the attacks happened in Virginia—spoke of a level of organization that frightened her.

Gail knew that she would need to participate in the debriefings in the mansion along with Mama Alexander, but she needed to take care of her phone call first.

Dom D'Angelo answered on the first ring. "There's a bad rhythm to the movement over there," he said, clearly knowing he was speaking to Gail. "You calling to clue me in?"

"Not quite," she replied. "I can fill you in on the details later, but for now, Wolverine needs some spiritual counseling."

"Is this for you or for the boys?" Dom asked.

"For the boys, I'm afraid. They're under attack."

"I'm on it," Dom said. He clicked off.

The sights at the ambush site disgusted Renaldo. He'd even given his men advance warning. He slung his rifle across his back and dismounted.

A quick glance at the Dodge pickup told him everything he needed to know about what had transpired. He had no idea who the lady driver was, but the through-and-through belly wound lined up with the bullet hole in the driver's side door. The bullet though the engine block told of misplaced priorities. It makes sense to disable your enemy's transportation, but in this case, they had clear shots of the two targets in the bed of the truck.

The lady clearly provided cover for the other two after she'd been wounded. A blood trail marked her path across the front seat and out onto the ground, and the sheer number of spent shell casings around her body spoke of a withering fusillade.

In his mind, he could witness the two morons from the ambush team cowering in their hidey-holes while Grave and his friend moved into the woods to gain advantage on them.

Renaldo was in no hurry at this point. Grave's head start was too great for him to close on foot, or even on horseback. He walked the scene of the shoot-out to learn what went wrong for his team and what went right for Grave. Renaldo had heard that Jonathan Grave was a skilled fighter, but even with that forewarning, he feared he'd underappreciated his adversary.

One can learn much from the way people handle themselves under fire. For those who have not endured return fire—which was the case with most of the cartel assassins because they were smart and never gave a chance for their adversary to shoot back—the instinct is to hide and hope for the best. For people like Renaldo, however—and clearly, Jonathan Grave—those instincts evolved to survival via aggression. You learn to stay behind cover only through the moment when an opportunity presents itself to bring the fight to the other side.

Perhaps it's the moment when your opponent is reloading or when he is on the move.

Covering fire like the heroic lady driver threw out was to be feared only so far as all strokes of bad luck should be feared. Covering fire is unaimed, and therefore it is inaccurate. To be sure, randomly fired bullets kill just as thoroughly as aimed ones, but in that circumstance, the shooter is the party at a disadvantage because he has given away his position.

When his magazine runs dry and he has to change out, he is vulnerable.

A glance at his two team members in their rock fortresses told him that they'd been shot from behind while watching the area where the lady shooter was likely already dead. He noted that their pockets had been turned out. It was the professional thing for them to do, but Renaldo knew that the search would reveal nothing.

Renaldo wandered up the slight slope toward what he figured the shooter's place to be. It took a few minutes, but when he found five spent shell casings in the weeds, it was easy to see the cover from which they were expelled.

He was impressed. Whether Grave was the shooter or it was his giant friend, he'd been able to maneuver effectively and to good purpose.

A horse whinnied and huffed somewhere in the near distance, and Renaldo followed the sound. That's where he found the body of their third team member, equally as dead as the others, his pockets likewise turned out.

With Grave's vehicle disabled and the pickup they came in shot dead, Renaldo figured their next move would to be to find transportation. If they were smart, they'd focus on taking the vehicle that brought in Renaldo and his team. If they found it, they would have lots of additional and deadly equipment.

Yet another troubling development to keep in mind.

Renaldo lifted his phone from his pocket and thumbed it to life. He opened the appropriate app and saw exactly what he'd expected. Not only had they found the Toyota Sequoia, but they had already hit the road in it.

He smiled.

Renaldo knew the types of men he was working with, and he understood the vulnerability of being one of the two who went off on horseback while the other two stayed near the getaway vehicle. If the operation got difficult or if the team got scared, it would be too easy for them to drive off and leave Renaldo stranded.

That's why Renaldo had dropped a GPS transmitter into the map pocket in the backseat. To leave him stranded would be to sign their own death warrants.

Now, it would bring him to Jonathan Grave. If Renaldo understood his prey as well as he believed, Jonathan Grave would not return to his home in Virginia until business was settled here.

Now, Renaldo needed a vehicle of his own, an easy chore to accomplish.

He strolled back to his horse, mounted it, and pressed his heels into the beast's flanks to get her to move.

CHAPTER 14

R oman felt someone squeeze his shoulder, and he jumped when he saw Moses standing next to the sofa where he'd dozed off. He didn't realize that he'd fallen asleep.

"Didn't mean to startle you," Moses said. "But you've got to get up. Everybody's back. They want you downstairs."

"Do we know what's happening yet?"

"They're right downstairs," Moses repeated. "In the front room, I believe."

Roman wanted to ask why they could sit in front of windows when he had to rot in a prison cell, but he let it go. For sure, Moses wouldn't answer him.

Roman grabbed his backpack and his phone and headed down the stairs. There'd always been a security station inside the front door, on the opposite side of the foyer from the living room, but usually, the security guards were invisible. And when visible, they looked like ordinary guys and ladies in blue-on-blue uniforms. Today, though, they all looked very serious, and they were dressed for war with vests and rifles and tons of extra ammunition. When he smiled and waved *hi*, they mostly looked away, clearly uncomfortable.

Mom and Gail and Chief Kramer had pulled chairs closer to Mama, whose left eye was swollen nearly shut and whose booted foot they'd propped up on the coffee table atop a pillow. She looked like someone had punched her.

As Roman appeared in the doorway, his mom caught his eye and shook her head *no*—more of a twitch, really. It was his cue to remain quiet while the adults talked.

Mama's face brightened at the sight of her grandson. "Romy, honey, you come right on in here and sit with Mama."

Roman hated that version of his name when it came from anyone else, but it was fine when Mama used it. "What happened to you?"

"Mama, please let the chief do his job," his mom said.

"I don't mind him being here if you don't," Kramer said.

"They're my injuries, and it's my decision." Mama patted the sofa again. "Right here."

"What *happened*?" Roman asked again.

"A bit of a bump with the car is all," Mama replied.

"She was in a pretty serious car wreck," Kramer corrected.

"It was nothing," Mama said. She patted the sofa one more time.

"I don't want to hurt you," Roman said. He was small for his age, but he still took up a whole seat on a sofa. "I'll sit over here on the chair."

"You can't hurt me," Mama said.

Roman recognized this talking circle for what it was,

and he disengaged. He walked to the yellow wing-back chair that he never liked very much and sat down. He started to bring his legs under him, but realized he was still wearing his tennis shoes and crossed his legs, instead.

"You were telling me about people getting out of the car," Chief Kramer said.

"Right," Mama said. "I was upside down and—"

Holy shit! Roman nearly blurted it out loud. He uncrossed his legs and leaned in closer.

"—I was worried that I might be in trouble. The car that ran me off the road stopped a little ways further up."

"They ran you off the road?" Roman blurted. This time, he couldn't control the words.

"I'll catch you up later," his mom said. "For now, please just sit quietly and listen."

Chief Kramer turned in his chair to look at Roman. "I agree with your mom," he said. "I really need to keep this conversation on track."

As scoldings went, that was far gentler than others he'd had.

"Go ahead, Mama," Kramer said. "The people were getting out of their car."

"Two or three of them," she went on. "Men, I think. I'm pretty sure, but my glasses had been knocked off, and, well . . ."

"What can you tell me about them?"

"I just told you," Mama said. A touch of annoyance had invaded her tone. "I'd lost my glasses."

"How were they dressed?"

"Lord in heaven, Douglas, how many times do I need to say it?"

"There's always some detail," Kramer pressed. "Were they wearing coats?"

"Well, of course they were," Mama said. "It was cold outside."

"What color?"

"I don't know. Green, maybe? Blue? Who notices such things?"

She sure as hell notices when I'm wearing the same shirt as yesterday, Roman thought.

"Please do your best," Kramer continued. "Were the coats short? Long? Any logos on them? Were they cloth or leather?"

"I do not know," Mama said. "And if you let me finish, I think you'll understand why."

Kramer held up his hands. "Okay, sorry."

"Honest to goodness, Douglas Kramer, you are too good at interrupting. I swear—"

"Mama," Venice said. "You were telling us why you didn't know—"

"Laws, Venny, you too?"

Roman could see the anger burning behind his mom's eyes, and he kind of enjoyed it. Maybe now she'd understand why he got so frustrated whenever he was trying to tell her a story.

Mama took a few seconds to gather herself. "They didn't get out of the car all at once and come running to me or anything. They sort of oozed out of the car, know what I mean? They got out, took their time, and wandered my way. They—a blue vest!"

She shouted that last part, making Roman jump.

"One of them was wearing a blue vest. Not like a

cowboy wears or one you'd wear with a suit. This one was blue and puffy. Probably stuffed with down filling, if I was to guess. And blue jeans."

Chief Kramer looked like he wanted to ask something else, but he didn't. Probably a good idea.

"So, anyway, they looked like they were standing around talking about what they'd done. I called after them because I was hurt and I couldn't reach my glasses, but they didn't come a-runnin'. When they did come, they sort of walked my way."

"Sorry to interrupt, but I have to," Chief Kramer said. "I need to see the picture. How long did they stand and talk before they came over to you?"

"Oh, laws, it's hard to know," Mama said. "It felt like a long time."

"A minute?"

"Oh, it felt like an hour, but it probably wasn't a whole minute. Maybe half a one."

"That's still a long time after an accident like that," Gail said.

"So, they finally started your way," Kramer reminded.

"Right," Mama said. "That's exactly what they did. But then I heard the sound of another car approaching. I couldn't see the car but I could hear the engine, and then I heard the tires crunching in the gravel. The men that hit me stopped right away at that and then turned and went back to their car."

"Did they run?"

"No, they didn't run, but they didn't dawdle, either. I don't think they wanted to mix with the people in the other car."

"That was your angel, as you call her?" Kramer asked.

"Yes, exactly. My angel. She and her friend called the ambulance, and here I am. All things considered, the day could have gone a lot worse."

"Ever the optimist," Venice said. "There's no way that was anything but a bad day."

"I'm here, ain't I?" Mama grinned as she winked at Roman with her good eye. "Here to see my favorite boy."

"I always thought Digger was your favorite boy," Gail teased.

"Right now, he's on my poop list," Mama said. "That boy should be here instead of terrorizing God's creatures out wherever he is."

"Montana," Roman said. But he thought she actually knew that. She liked to sandbag people. That's what she called it.

"He'll be back when he can," Gail said. "He's aware of what happened, and they'll make the best time that they can."

"Do you have anything else for me?" Chief Kramer asked.

"I'm a little tired," Mama said. "If I think of anything more, I know where to find you."

The chief stood, and Roman stood with him. It's what he had been trained to do.

"Anybody else have any details they want to share?"

Roman did. He wanted to share everything about his weird conversation with Mateo, but he sensed that this was the wrong time. His mom had made it clear many times that when strange things happened, he was to tell her first. You can call the police when there's an emergency, but when there's a story to tell or details to share, that stayed inside the family.

"All right, then," the chief said. "We'll keep an eye out for the people who did this to you, Mama. You're sure you can't remember the kind of car it was?"

"I know it was an SUV," Mama said, "but I don't know one kind from the other. It looked kind of new, if that helps."

"No color there, either?"

"Douglas, are we going to have every conversation two or three times from now on?" Mama said. She had her I'm-disappointed-in-you look in her face.

"No, ma'am, we won't," Kramer said. "But whatever you remember, you be sure to tell me as soon as you remember it. Call me at home and wake me up if you have to."

"I promise I will do just that, Douglas."

With that, Chief Kramer headed for the door. He was almost to the hallway when he turned. "Gail and Venice, we need to discuss that other thing, too."

Roman saw his mom's eyes flash. That was a look that you never wanted to be on the wrong side of. There was a secret, and the chief had said too much. If there was a constant in this house, it was secrets that always had to be kept.

The kinds of secrets that cause people to sink submarines off the coast of Mexico.

After the chief was gone, Roman took his place in the chair closer to Mama. "How are you *really* feeling?"

Mama patted Roman's knee. "Apparently, better than

I look." She shifted on the sofa and moved her feet to the floor.

Roman jumped up to help her. "Wait, where are you going?"

"I'm going to my room," Mama said. "Thought I'd save your mother and Gail the bother of convincing me to leave."

Roman shot a look to his mom, who did not disagree.

"It's okay, Romy," Mama said. "I know there's things around here that can't be spoken of. It used to bother me, but I have a very good idea that it's those very same things that brought you home from the hands of some very bad people."

"You know about that?"

"Not really," Mama said. "Just a little more than I want to. As for today, and whatever that means, I have every confidence that Jonny and your mother and Gail and Big Brian will make everything okay again."

It took a second or two to realize that Big Brian was really Mr. Boxers. Mama didn't think much of call signs and nicknames.

Gail and Venice moved to either side of Mama and helped her rise to her feet, where she wobbled a bit as she found her balance with her cane. Roman darted in before she could fall, but it came out all right.

"You know I don't like to use the elevator," Mama said.

"Well, that's a shame," Venice said. "Because I'm not dragging you up the stairs, and you can't make the climb. That leaves the elevator."

Mama had a thing about a lot of things, and one of them dealt with enclosed spaces. She hated them. Elevators qualified. She didn't even like for other members of the family to use them, ostensibly because the exercise from the stairs was good for you. Roman figured the truth of the matter to have something to do with her love of being bossy.

"You wait here, Roman," his mom said. "We'll only be a couple of minutes."

"Then will you tell me what is going on?" Roman asked. He didn't get a response.

This whole thing was beginning to freak him out. Left alone now in the front parlor, he felt exposed and moved away from the window. Part of him missed the security of the Zulu Room, but he'd never give anyone the satisfaction of telling them that.

So, was this what all of the panic was about? The fact that Mama got into a car wreck? It had to be more than that, didn't it?

His heart rate doubled as he thought through the possibilities. Ever since he had been kidnapped, he'd been borderline scared pretty much all the time. He heard more noises than he used to, and he paid closer attention to people who were lurking near him. He wanted to be braver than he was—at least as brave as he pretended to be when he was around others.

Mr. Jonathan had told him that half of being courageous was owning the fear that you actually felt. God gives you fear for a reason. It tells you to be hypervigilant and to be ready to react. It tells you that you have to make choices quickly and decisively. Roman had seen for himself how quickly normal can go to holy-shit nutso. The time to run away or engage in a fight arrives and evaporates in the space of an eye blink.

So, here he was, sitting by himself, not having any idea

of what was going on, while everybody around him acted like they were in a war zone.

It took nearly ten minutes for Gail and his mom to return to the parlor. Roman heard their footsteps in the hall and made sure to be standing near the door when they entered.

"Dammit, Mom, what's going on?"

"Watch your mouth," she said. As if a little cussing mattered.

"Did Mama's crash happen on purpose?" Roman asked. "Is that what y'all were talking about when I came down? Is somebody trying to kill her?"

Gail and his mom looked down at the floor, almost as if they'd rehearsed it. Their body dynamics doubled his sense of unease.

"We need to sit down," Venice said.

"I've been sitting down."

"Don't go all adolescent," Gail said—something she normally never would have said. "We don't have time for picking arguments."

Roman sat on the sofa where Mama had been. This time he did draw his feet under him. *Let's see who picks arguments now,* he thought.

When no one said anything about getting the sofa dirty, his heart rate picked up yet again. This shit was serious.

His mom started. "We pulled you out of school because someone tried to kill Gail and me this afternoon."

Roman felt the blood drain from his face, and he sat back in the sofa's cushion. He tried to articulate a question, but his mouth wouldn't work.

"We were shopping at Ike's store . . ." For the next three

minutes, Venice spun out the story of the shoot-out on the roadway and of Gail's victory.

"Are you okay?" Roman asked. "Both of you?"

"Okay *and* lucky," Venice said, and to Gail she added, "If you hadn't noticed the car—"

"What might have been doesn't matter," Gail said. "But you're right. *Very* lucky."

"You're sure that the guy is dead?" Roman asked.

"Very sure," Gail said.

"Are you okay hearing this?" his mom asked. "I figured you were old enough."

"Mom, I *lived* something like this," Roman said. "So, is this the *other thing* that you didn't want Chief Kramer to talk about?"

"Mama doesn't know about the shooting," Venice said.

"Shouldn't she?" Roman asked.

Venice gave him a tired smile. "Mama is a lot smarter and a lot savvier than she lets on," she said. "There are things she doesn't *want* to know. Her life is hectic enough knowing that she's in charge of the well-being of so many children in Resurrection House. The burdens they hand off to her would buckle most people's knees. She knows that Mr. Jonathan and the rest of us get involved with dangerous things, but she doesn't want to know the details. And why would she? She can't do anything about them."

"When do I get to know?"

"Not today," his mom said.

"There's more," Gail said to Roman.

"More what?"

"Some people attacked Digger and Boxers while they were on their hunting trip."

There was that dizzy feeling again. *Holy shit, how huge is this?*

"They're both fine," Gail added quickly.

"But not the people who attacked them, I bet," Roman said through a smile.

"There's no humor in any of this," Venice scolded.

"Yes, there is," Roman said. "The good guys are alive, and the bad guys are dead. That's sure what Mr. Jonathan would say. Mr. Boxers, too."

"Only a lot more colorfully," Gail said.

"So, if you're wondering why we pulled you out of school and locked everything down, now you know."

"I have something, too," Roman said. He felt happy to be able to contribute to the conversation. He relayed the cryptic encounter out in the courtyard with Mateo. "I don't know what he was talking about exactly, but it's got to be tied to this, right?"

It was his mom's turn to look like she might pass out. "He said specifically that you were in danger?"

Roman started to say *yes*, but he stopped himself. The details would matter. "He told me that I needed to stay inside the RezHouse compound for the next few days."

"He didn't tell you why? You didn't ask?"

"Of course I *asked*," Roman said. He started to say more but cut himself off. Mateo was his friend, and he owed him loyalty. Mateo had protected him and greased the pathway for him to find some level of acceptance among the other students.

"What's wrong?" his mom asked. "Why did you stop talking?"

Roman didn't know what to say.

Gail said, "Roman, I don't know what you're thinking,

but consider that if he advised you to stay inside, then he likely knows something about why Mama Alexander was attacked. Let alone your mother and me."

And Mr. Jonathan, Roman didn't say. Those guys had risked a lot to save his ass, and now they were under attack, too.

"I asked, but he refused to answer. He said that he wasn't supposed to say anything to me at all. He said something about people trying to kill *him* if they found out that he'd talked to me."

"He didn't say who those people were?"

"Nothing he said made a lot of sense," Roman said. "And before we could really settle anything, Moses showed up and made me come back here."

Venice and Gail looked at each other, as if to read each other's minds. Finally, his mom said, "Okay, Roman. Thanks for that. You can—"

"No," he said.

"No what?"

"No, I'm not being pushed off again. I'm not going to hide in the Zulu Room while you guys pretend I don't already know as much as I do about what you do."

Venice shook her head aggressively. "No, Roman, we are not having this conversation now."

"Yes, we are, Mom," he said. "Unless you're prepared to have Moses come in here and tie me up, yes, we're having this conversation."

Roman rose to his feet and thrust his hands into his carefully coiffed 'fro. "You've never asked me about the details from Mexico," he said. "Did you know that? Maybe this isn't the time for that, either, but the details involve a lot of shooting, people dying, and me watching a guy get beaten to death with a sledgehammer."

His mom looked away, even as Gail put a hand on her arm.

"That's some pretty heavy shit, Mom. And don't you dare tell me to watch my mouth. If I can go through that and not end up in a corner blowing spit bubbles all day, then I think you have to agree that I'm more *mature* than you'd like me to be."

He saw that his words were hurting his mother, and while he knew that should make him feel bad, it actually made him feel *good*.

"Mom, this is the shit that's been going through my mind ever since I got back. I tell Father Dom, and he swears that he doesn't tell you, so I'm telling you now."

The thoughts were coming too fast for him to manage them. He felt as if they were all jamming up behind his tongue.

"Have you ever seen Mr. Jonathan and Mr. Boxers when they're mad? Have you ever seen the way they shoot people and blow them up and set them on fire?"

"Yes." That came from Gail, and it startled him. "I *have* seen it, Roman. And you know what? A lot of people are still alive who would otherwise be dead if we didn't do those things."

Roman hadn't expected that. "You, too?"

"Yes, me, too." She took her hand off of Venice's arm and stood to face him.

"Please don't," Venice said.

"It's time," Gail said. "You're his mom, but I'm neck deep in all of this. Do you really want to know, Roman?

Are you really sure that you want details? Because I'm telling you that the details come with very real consequences and risks. If you're not prepared for that, then this is your time to pull back your request and head back to the Zulu Room."

Suddenly, Roman wasn't sure that he *did* want to hear. The heaviness of her tone told him that bad stuff was coming, and maybe he didn't want to know the whole truth.

But he'd already lived it, hadn't he? He'd already seen things that kept him awake every night, and he already knew that they'd left more than a few bodies unburied on that beach.

"Yes, I want to know."

"Then sit down," Gail said.

Roman sat.

"Boxers is going to be furious that you're doing this," Venice said.

"He'll get over it," Gail said. "The moment had to come." She sat down, too, and focused her attention on Roman. "But before I start, I need you to make the most important promise you've ever made. And that is to never speak of anything you're about to hear. Not to anyone. Ever. My life hangs in the balance, as do those of your mother, Digger, and Boxers. And I'm not exaggerating. This is *that* important. Will you make that promise?"

Roman nodded emphatically.

"You need to say it."

"I promise."

"And there's one more life that will lie in the balance," Gail went on. "That would be yours. There comes a point where you know something or you don't, and the act of knowing is itself a crime. A serious one. Walk away now, or there's no going back."

Roman swallowed hard. "I already know that you kill people," he said. "I already haven't told anybody about the Mexico stuff."

Gail settled herself with a deep sigh. "Okay," she said. "Here we go. First of all, we don't *kill people*. We are not assassins. In fact, we are the very opposite of that."

CHAPTER 15

Gail unspun the story over the course of forty-five minutes. Roman seemed totally engaged, though he asked few questions, and he seemed oddly unsurprised. She tried to speak in direct terms as she described an overview of their covert activities. She told Roman that Digger and Boxers used to be elite Special Forces operators and that when they separated from the Army, they saw a need for the services of freelance hostage rescuers.

"I used to be part of the FBI's Hostage Rescue Team," she said. "You might be surprised to learn that when the HRT is called in after people are kidnapped, their mission isn't actually to rescue the hostages."

Roman's eyebrows knitted in confusion.

"Their mission is to make sure that the perpetrators are caught and punished," Gail explained. "Certainly, they want to get the hostages to safety, but that is not the primary goal. In fact, when I was on the team, we used to call a hostage situation a homicide in slow motion." She used finger quotes.

Roman clearly still did not understand.

"I'll explain it by way of comparison," Gail said.

"When *we* take on a mission, our *sole* objective is to bring the hostage home."

"I don't understand the difference," Roman said.

"This is where the secrets become most important," Gail said. "We don't work with warrants, and we don't arrest bad guys. We just bring the hostages home."

"What happens to the kidnappers?"

Gail waited for him to catch up in his head.

"You *kill* them?" That was his first sign of surprise.

"We give them a chance to surrender. Often, they choose not to."

Roman's scowl creased even deeper. "Isn't that murder?"

Gail felt ready for this one. "That scene on the beach in Mexico," she said. "I've heard details from both Digger and Big Guy. We both have. When they shot the people who were trying to load you onto a submarine, did that feel like *murder* to you? Or did it feel like heroism?"

"Well, not murder," he said.

"And there's your answer."

Roman looked over to his mother. "You do these things, too?"

"I'm the back-office gal," Venice said. "I'm the computer geek who makes the rest of it a little easier."

"She makes it a *lot* easier," Gail said. "We call her Mother Hen."

His eyes flashed recognition.

"That's my radio call sign," Venice said.

"What's yours?" he asked Gail.

"That's one thing you don't need to know." Gail had never been comfortable with Gunslinger as her call sign. She didn't like what it implied, and in this circumstance, it wasn't something she wanted Roman to know.

"So, that's it," Gail said with a soft clap of her hands. "That's what we do, and that's what Mama Alexander *suspects* we do but doesn't want to know."

"How do you get away with everything?"

"That, young man, is beyond your pay grade," Venice said.

"So, you're sort of like Batman?" Roman asked.

Gail rolled her eyes. A fourteen-year-old was still a fourteen-year-old. "If you discount for the fact that Batman isn't real, then yes."

The question seemed to bother Venice. "Listen to me, Roman," she said. "I'm not sure how you're processing all of this, but I cannot emphasize enough how important secrecy is."

"I get it," he said.

"This isn't a comic book. The ramifications are very real. Very deadly."

"I get it!"

Gail said, "Roman, stop it."

"Stop what?"

"Whatever you think you're doing with this teen angst bullshit that is frankly wearing on my nerves. Everything we do—everything you've heard and much more—is bigger than you trying to get along with your mother—who, by the way, is a pretty tremendous person who loves you very much. This is about trusting each other with our lives."

He looked startled.

"I'll put it right out there," Gail said. "At this moment in time, you are the weakest link we've ever had in our security chain. You're young, and young people like to impress other young people. You're going to meet a girl someday, and you're going to think how you can impress her with stories of the cool stuff your family does. You can never do that."

"I've already told you—"

"I'm not finished yet," she snapped. "This is not a conversation now. This is all lecture. Your mother is a key part of this team—hell, she's *the* key to this team. Now that you're in the know, that makes you a part of this team, and when she says jump, you ask how high. Am I making myself clear?"

His jaw set. "Yes."

"You've got your angry face on," Gail went on. "Lose it. This is a very dangerous business, and you're now a part of it. This is *not* Batman. This is *not* a game in any form or function. I decided to tell you what you've heard because you were a witness to it on the other end. You had a right to know how Jonathan and Boxers ended up at your side. Now, you have a responsibility to understand how indispensable your mother was in all of that."

"You, too, Gail," Venice said.

Gail waved her off. "This is a lot, Roman. I know it's a whole lot to process, but there you go."

His features softened. She was getting through.

"Don't let me down," she said.

"I won't."

"And for damn sure don't let Boxers down," Gail said with a smile.

The very thought seemed to frighten him. And for good reason.

"That's enough of all that," Venice said. "Our family is under attack. The guys who came after Mama are still out there."

"And more importantly," Gail said, "Roman knows someone who knows what is happening. Tell us every conversation you've had with . . . what's his name?"

"Mateo," Roman said. "We talk all the time."

"About what?" Venice asked.

Gail saw his armor come up. "Not everything," she said. "We don't need to know about boy stuff or girl stuff, or about which teachers are good and which are bad. What family stuff have you talked about?"

He shot a look at his mom.

"Not relationship stuff either, Roman," Gail said. "Jesus. We've told you about the attacks today. Can you think of any way that Mateo would know that Digger and Boxers would be in Montana today?"

Roman considered the question. "I don't see how. I mean, don't take offense, but I don't talk about you guys a whole lot. I mean, how could I? Everything is off limits to strangers. It's been like that forever."

Venice stood. "We need to go upstairs." Without further explanation, she led the way out of the room.

Gail and Roman followed her up two flights to what Gail knew to be the Little War Room and Roman knew to be the office he was never to enter. From there, Venice could work nearly all of the computer magic that she could from the real War Room in the offices of Security Solutions. A world-class hacker in her own right, she had access to databases and decryption software that had once inspired the director of the FBI to offer her whatever job she wanted, if only to get access to her brain and her skills.

The smaller office had all of the essentials for doing what needed to be done, but none of the bells and whistles that they enjoyed in the firehouse office. For example, whereas the War Room down the street featured a 106-inch projection screen on which she could share her screen with others in the room, here she would have to spin her computer around for others to see.

She settled into her Aeron chair, pulled herself into the desk, and toggled her computer to life. "What is Mateo's last name?" she asked.

"Lopez," Roman said.

Venice scowled as she typed.

"You can get school records from here?" Roman asked.

"She can get nuclear launch codes from here if she set her mind to it," Gail said with a grin.

Venice said, "According to the records, Mateo first came to Resurrection House two years ago." She typed some more. "His mother and father are both doing federal time on drug distribution charges."

More typing. As Roman moved around to see her screen, she snapped her fingers and pointed to the padded visitor's chairs along the front edge of her desk. "Nope," she said. "This you don't get to see. Have a seat."

Gail figured that Venice was accessing an FBI database or maybe one from the DEA that would give her more details on the nature of the parents' crimes. It was the nature of RezHouse that students had complicated backgrounds, most of which were kept hidden from prying eyes.

Venice, it seemed, had the skeleton key to everything.

When she finished typing, Venice leaned in closer to her screen. "Whoa," she said. "Pretty serious stuff. Life sentence for his father, Marco." She typed some more. "Twenty-seven years for his mother, Luciana."

Gail saw Roman grow uncomfortable. "You okay?"

He squirmed in his seat. "We're not supposed to know about this stuff. Kinda makes me feel dirty."

"Never forget that we're on the side of the angels," Gail said. "What we do, we do for the right reasons." She had to believe that or sleep would never come. Sometimes, it still didn't.

Roman bolted upright in his chair. "There *is* something," he blurted. "A few nights ago—well, probably two weeks ago—Mateo had to come to the mansion to meet a visitor. I don't know who it was, but it was late—like, eight or eight-thirty. We were talking in his room when the house mother told him about it."

"Did the visitor have a name?" Venice asked.

"She probably said it, but I didn't pay attention. I know I didn't recognize it."

Venice started typing again. "Two weeks ago?"

"Something like that. Maybe a little sooner, maybe a little later."

"Let me see if I can access the visitor logs," Venice said, but in a singsong-y tone that Gail had come to recognize was her talking to herself when she was concentrating. Clearly scrolling through a list of some sort, she kept mumbling "no . . . no . . . no . . ."

Finally, Venice knocked her desk with a single knuckle. "It was eighteen days ago," she said. "So you were close. Russell Greenberg, attorney at law. He visited Mateo Lopez at eight thirty-seven and stayed till nine twenty-nine." She rocked her head up to look at Roman. "That name sound familiar?"

The boy clearly wanted to give the answer that everyone wanted to hear, but instead, he said, "It could have been."

Gail considered that bit of honesty to be an encouraging sign. Wild guesses could derail the investigation, and the clock was ticking.

"What did he tell you after he got back to the dorm?"

"Nothing. By then, I'd gone back to my room. Lights out is at ten."

Venice's fingers clacked some more on the keys. "Russell Greenberg . . . Russell Greenberg. Why does that name sound so familiar?"

She thumped the desk again. "Because I just read it in the record. Russell Greenberg is the attorney for Luciana Lopez, Mateo's mother."

"Why would he be visiting Mateo?" Gail asked.

"And why so late at night?" Venice added. "I have no idea. Roman?"

"What?"

"Any thoughts? Has Mateo talked about anything important in his mom's legal case?"

"That's what I told you. We don't discuss that stuff. In fact, I don't think we're *allowed* to talk about that stuff. But one thing for sure is that if you do, that's a good way to get your ass beat."

"I guess that makes sense," Gail said. "If the kids are going to have a shot at a new life, they can't constantly be dragged back into their old one."

"But you know what?" Roman said. "Mateo was different after that."

Venice leaned forward, her forearms on her desk. "What does that mean?"

"Well, I don't know if this is because of that meeting or not, but starting a few weeks ago, Mateo's seemed, I don't know, sad, maybe? I thought he might have been angry with me, but I couldn't figure out why."

"Did you finally?" Gail asked.

"No. It's not like that. Guys don't just ask each other if they're angry. He was just, well, *different*. Normally, we'd hang out together and shoot the sh . . . talk in the dorm at night, but then, starting a couple of weeks ago, it was . . . *different*."

"You keep using that word," Venice said. "*Different*. Different how?"

"You know how you just *know* when something's wrong?" Roman asked. His frustration was showing. "It was like that. The way he looked at me. Or didn't. We didn't fight or anything, he was just . . . well, you know."

They fell silent for a few seconds.

Gail said, "Given the timing, I think we have to assume that the meeting with the lawyer and Mateo's *different-ness* have to be related. Now, we just have to figure how."

"Do you all lock your doors when you're not in your rooms?" Venice asked.

"I don't know about everybody," Roman said, "but I don't. I don't even have a key."

Gail recoiled at the thought. "Really? Why would that be?"

Venice explained, "Can you imagine how many hours would be lost every week to chasing down lost keys? Also, during the design, we decided to eliminate issues of kids locking themselves into their rooms."

"Is theft a problem?" Gail asked.

"You remember who the students are, right?" Roman asked. "Kind of a rough crowd, if you know what I mean. Anyway, I haven't heard of any theft problems."

"What about your computer?" Venice asked. "Is that with you all the time?"

Roman answered by hefting his backpack. "Right here."

"But it can't be with you when you shower or go to the bathroom," Venice observed. She made a beckoning motion with her fingers. "Let me see your machine."

A look of genuine horror enveloped Roman's features. "No way."

Venice rolled her eyes. "Oh, for God's sake. I don't want to read your emails or see your browser history. I want to see if there's any software on it that you don't know about."

"How do you know what software I want?" he asked. He pulled the backpack closer.

"Roman, think about it," Gail said. "Mateo seems to be the pivot point here, and you're good friends with him. Killers out there know things that they shouldn't know, and your computer is sometimes left alone in an unlocked room. Connect the dots."

Roman eyes showed panic.

"I swear to you," Venice said. "I'm going to look for code that doesn't belong and nothing else. I promise you that I will respect your privacy. This is bigger than that."

Gail could tell that the boy wanted to say *no* but that he couldn't muster the words. Moving like a condemned prisoner on the way to the death chamber, he unzipped the top of his backpack, reached in, and withdrew the sleek laptop. He handed it to his mother.

"Thank you," she said. "This could take a few minutes, if you want to do something else for a while."

"No, I'm good," he said.

It took her less than five minutes. "Here it is," she proclaimed. "It's a Trojan horse that infected your system . . ." Her scowl returned as she leaned into the screen to read in more detail. "Yep, fifteen days ago." She tapped and scrolled for another minute or more. "Wow, it's everywhere."

"I've got the antivirus software that you gave me," Roman said.

"That'll protect you from links you click on, but it won't necessarily protect you from a direct attack."

"What does that mean?"

"The way I mean it is a case where someone physically infects your computer from a thumb drive or other external drive. Have you used a promotional drive or some such? A freebie that someone gave you?"

"No." Roman's answer was instant and definitive. "I wouldn't do that."

"Doesn't matter how it got there, I guess."

"Can we get it off?" Roman asked.

"I imagine we can," Venice said, "but I'm pretty sure we don't want to. Not yet anyway. Maybe we can draw the hacker out into the open."

"How do we do that?" Gail asked.

"I don't know yet."

"Ticktock," Gail said, pointing to the spot on her wrist where a watch would be if she wore one.

Venice handed the computer back to Roman. "I need

you to pull up your emails from the past few weeks," she said. "I don't need to see them. I want you to pull them up and tell me what you've got on there that might lead a spy to know that Digger and Boxers were hunting in Montana."

"It's on my calendar," Roman said. "I keep everybody's schedules on my calendar."

"Why would you do that?" Gail asked.

"Why wouldn't I? When Mr. Jonathan is out of town, things are always more stressful. Plus, this time, I thought it was really cool that he was hunting in Montana. I sent him an email asking what gun he was going to use. You know, just to know."

"I think we're on it," Gail said. "You need to apply for a permit to hunt, and I think the permits are public information."

Venice nodded vigorously. "That's all they need."

"But who's *they*?" Roman asked.

"*They* are who we need to figure out," Venice said.

"The world's a big place," Gail said.

"Wait a second," Roman said. "You both think that Mateo is a link in all of this, right? And his parents are in jail for dealing drugs. Mr. Jonathan and Mr. Boxers rescued me from drug guys in Mexico. Isn't that enough?"

"No," Venice said. "I mean, it's a start, but we need to be sure. If we're going to eliminate this threat, then we need to know for sure who the person is who's making the threat."

"Can't we just put a virus or whatever into Mateo's computer?" Roman asked.

Venice and Gail exchanged looks.

"How would we get it there?" Gail asked.

"Same way I got it," Roman said. "Mateo doesn't take his computer into the shower, either."

"I don't know," Venice said. "I guess we could ask one of the security team to sneak into the room—"

"I'll do it," Roman said. "Let me move back into the dorm, and I'll take care of it. I mean, if you can copy the virus or whatever and put it on a stick, I can wait for Mateo to walk away and stick it into his USB drive. Is it that easy?"

"It's exactly that easy," Venice said. "But we can't stop there."

CHAPTER 16

Diego Ruiz had spent decades building the career that had earned him the director's chair for the Montana Fish, Wildlife and Parks Department. It was rare throughout the world for a political position to be granted to someone who had done many of the jobs for which his deputies and their deputies were now responsible, and he felt pride for the respect that his people projected his way. He was one of them, and they knew it.

But he was also a bureaucrat and now a politician—a member of the class of worker for whom he generally had no respect. As he sat in the governor's office, having just finished his report on the state of his department, he found it difficult to stay awake through the droning recitations of facts and feelings that were in all cases engineered to reflect the desires and prejudices of Governor Larry Baker, a carpetbagger from Michigan who now ruled the state in large measure because President Tony Darmond's election machine had twisted partial truths about his opponent into outright lies that had caught fire on social media.

"You can't change politics," his wife, Rosario, had told

him just this morning. "All you can do is fight for what you know to be right and protect the people who count on you to protect their jobs."

She was right, of course. Listening to Harvey Strong, state director of transportation, report the status of line painting projects was a small price to pay for his much larger role of managing the wildlife of the state and enforcing the rules associated with hunting and fishing. Harvey had listened patiently to Diego's own recitation only seventeen minutes ago, so Diego owed him the courtesy, at the very least.

The seating arrangement in the governor's conference room was identical to every other high-level meeting that Diego had ever attended. The governor sat in the middle of one side of the long conference table, and the department directors manned the rest of the table, their distance from the governor testament to how politically connected they were to the people who mattered. Diego could not be a lot farther away, but at least he was still on the governor's side of the table.

The directors' chiefs of staff sat behind their respective bosses in padded straight-backed chairs along the walls, flanked by their own minions. In Diego's case, it was Mary Bauer's responsibility to see to it that every document he needed magically appeared in his hand the instant before he knew that he needed it. She was very good at that, which was why she'd been *somebody's* chief of staff for the past six years, the last three of them for Diego.

He sensed commotion along the wall behind him, a buzzing of interest, but he fought the urge to turn and inquire. If it was important, they'd—

A hand touched his shoulder, and a mouth appeared

near his ear. He recognized Mary Bauer's perfume, though he had no idea what it might be. Something floral, he figured. Maybe with cinnamon overtones. Or maybe not.

"Excuse me, Mr. Ruiz," she whispered. "You need to step out into the hall."

Diego raised his forefinger an inch or two above the desk, silently commanding that Mary wait.

"It's important, sir," she whispered.

Diego cast a glimpse down the long row of directors, most of whom were more talented at feigning interest than he was. It was rude to duck out on the governor under any circumstances. Mary was the ultimate political player, though, and if she said something was important, then it was exactly that.

As he stood, he caught the eye of Harlan Estrella, the governor's chief of staff, who acknowledged him with a nod that Diego interpreted as permission to step away from the table.

Once he was in the thickly carpeted hallway and the door was closed, Diego said, "I'd like to thank you for the parole, but this had better be important."

"It is, sir, I promise." Mary started leading the way down the hall, away from the governor's inner office but still inside the office suite.

"What is it?"

"A phone call, sir."

Diego pulled up short. "Tell me you're joking."

Mary had never stopped, so Diego needed to hurry to catch up as she said, "I am very much not joking, and before you ask me what is going on, I'll tell you up front that I don't know."

"But you said—"

"I'm reporting on what I've been told, sir, not on what I know. And what I've been told comes from the special agent in charge of the FBI's field office in Salt Lake City. He told me to grab you out of whatever you are doing to take a phone call that will come in, in—" She checked her watch. "In four minutes."

"Who is going to call?"

"I don't know, sir."

"Did the SAC know?"

"He said he didn't," Mary said. Was it possible that she was speeding up? "But I have not done independent study to verify that." She threw him a crooked smile to sell the snarkiness. When you looked too closely, everything about Mary's physicality was at least a little crooked, from her nose to her teeth to the way she carried herself, listing ever so slightly to the left as she walked. Somehow, the imperfections melded together in Diego's mind as a very attractive young lady, in a farm-raised sort of way.

Mary stopped in front of what Diego would have assumed to be a closet door but turned out to be a small conference room, complete with a tiny desk and an ancient office chair.

"Is this a SCIF?" he asked. Pronounced "skiff," he referred to a sensitive compartmentalized information facility—a place where classified information could be discussed without fear of being overheard. In this case, where there might have been a telephone, there was a video screen, camera, and microphone.

"That's exactly what it is," Mary said. "Have at it, sir. I'll be right here outside the door if you need anything."

"You seriously have no idea what this is about?"

"Got me, sir, I know every detail. I'm lying to you because that is so what I do." The smile flashed again.

"No one loves a smart-ass," Diego said as he crossed the threshold.

"Yet here you are, sir." Mary closed the door behind him.

With one minute to go before the call was to start, the screen popped to life, displaying the famous logo of the Federal Bureau of Investigation, an organization for which Diego had lost a great deal of respect over the course of the past few years. Between laboratory cover-ups and politically motivated investigations, he thought they'd lost a considerable step in their professionalism.

The screen clicked again, displaying Diego's live image on the lower right-hand corner of the screen. It wasn't very big, but it was enough for him to see that he needed to straighten out a few unruly hairs over his left ear. No, make that his right ear—it just looked to be on his left in the displayed image.

When the screen jumped the next time, the image of the FBI shield was replaced by the live image of Irene Rivers, the face of the most famous woman in American law enforcement.

"Good afternoon, Director Ruiz," she said. "I'm Irene Rivers, director of the FBI. How is your day going so far, sir?"

Diego wasn't one to become starstruck over anyone. He'd met more movie stars than he could count as they'd passed through his state to either hunt or shoot a film, and he never thought much of them, one way or the other. But

Director Rivers was another story. Her rise through the ranks of street agents to sit in the big chair was legendary.

"Good afternoon," he said. "And today has been a day of meetings, so I don't know how to answer that last part." He'd meant it as a lighthearted comment, but he could see that it failed to hit the mark.

"Well, sir, I'm sorry to tell you that I'm going to make even the best day a bad one," Rivers said. "One of your rangers was shot and killed today, Director. May I call you Diego? Please call me Irene."

The way she presented the information seemed at once perfunctory and caring. She kept her eyes focused squarely on her camera's lens, with the effect that she was speaking directly to him.

"I'm sorry to be so blunt," she said, "but in my experience, there really is no soft way to present terrible news."

Countless questions flooded Diego's brain, but he remained quiet. Irene was still talking, and he wanted to give her a chance to finish.

Irene looked down for the first time, but her gaze came right back. "The ranger's name was Peter Simonsen. My office is already sending you the coordinates where you'll be able to find his body. We don't know who the bad guys are, but he was shot down at some distance by an unknown assailant, whose body may or not be found on the far side of the valley where this happened."

Diego had had enough. He held up his hand for silence. "How do you know all of this?" he asked. "And as importantly, why is the director of the FBI taking time out of your day to tell me directly? As I understand it, the

SAC of the Salt Lake City field office is the one who arranged this."

"I'm sure he is," Irene confirmed. "And he doesn't know any of this because I haven't yet told him."

"So, how do *you* know?"

Irene's features scrunched up a bit, as if enduring a brief gas pain. "I can't get into that," she said. "Suffice it to say that I have been in contact with a very reliable witness who relayed all of this to me. Now, I understand that you want to move quickly to take care of matters, but before you sign off, I need to fill you in on a few details. First, I'd like your word that this next part I'm about to tell you will stay just between the two of us for at least twenty-four hours. Forty-eight hours would be even better."

"That's a hard commitment to make, ma'am, before I know what I'm dealing with."

Irene weighed his words and then nodded. "That's fair," she said. "But understand that early dissemination may well cost people their lives. Maybe that will help you decide. Anyway, here it is: When you go to the scene of Ranger Simonsen's murder, you're going to find other bodies in the general vicinity."

Diego reared back in his chair. "Other bodies? How many?"

"Truthfully, I don't have an answer for that," Irene said. "At least four that I'm aware of."

Diego listened with deepening interest and horror as Director Rivers told of two of her agents who were ambushed and had to fight their way out of the forest.

When she was done, Diego tried to recap what he'd

heard. "Are you telling me that my dead ranger was not the assassins' intended target?"

"That appears to be the case, yes," she said. "I don't know anything definitively yet, but the smart money says that Ranger Simonsen, tragically, was in the wrong place at the wrong time."

"And these other bodies you told me about," Diego said. "Those are all members of some hit squad?"

"All but one of them," Irene clarified. "You'll find the body of one Holly Looney near the cab of a shot-up truck. She was likewise killed by the attackers."

"What kind of assassins are these?" Diego asked. His head spun with the absurdity and awfulness of everything he'd just heard. "They can only shoot what they don't want to hit?"

"I don't have those details," Director Rivers said. "This is an evolving investigation."

"So, this has federal jurisdiction?" Diego asked. "The FBI is taking lead?"

"I don't get involved with that level of detail," Irene said. "I don't mean that as a kiss-off, it's just the way of things. I don't make assignments at the field office level."

"Yet you take time out of your day to call me directly, rather than working through that field office." Something stank about all of this. Diego couldn't get the equation to work in his head.

"This is not what you want to hear," Irene said, "but there are elements at work that I cannot share with you."

"*Can*not or *will* not?"

Irene chuckled. "I'm director of the FBI, Diego. At my level, *cannot* and *will not* don't have a lot of distinction.

Suffice it to say that the agents involved in this are unique. Their jobs . . ." She scowled as she searched for the right words. "Let's leave it at this: their jobs fall outside the normal scope of what federal agents do."

As Diego replayed the conversation in his head, he realized that in many ways, he was more confused now than when they'd first started talking. "Pushing aside all the cloak and dagger crap, I'm not sure what you want me to do with this information."

Irene seemed prepared for this one. She folded her arms. "First of all, I want you to take care of your fallen hero. Then, I want you to do whatever you do with a murder case in your part of the world."

"But why did you even call?"

"A couple of reasons," Irene said. "First of all, I didn't want Ranger Simonsen's body to go unfound and fall prey to predators. And second, I want to aid in your investigation. What you're going to find out there will be very confusing, or so I'm told. By telling you about my two agents, I want to fill in some pretty big blanks. Trust me when I tell you that with the exception of Ranger Simonsen and Ms. Looney, all of the decedents were bad guys. The aggressors. The men who killed those aggressors are the good guys."

"Are you telling me to lay off any investigation into who your good guys are?" Diego asked. Finally, this made at least a little sense to him.

"That's exactly correct," she said. "But I can't tell you to do anything, Director Ruiz. Your department is your department, and I trust you to decide what the best course of action is in every circumstance."

Diego's bullshit bell was pounding.

"That said, I'll trust you to understand that it takes more than just a tiny issue to make me stop my day and have a conversation like this. Whatever discretion you are willing to offer will be greatly appreciated."

CHAPTER 17

When Gail finished reciting the plan, Roman was ready to go. "I'll do it," he said.

"No, you won't," his mom objected. "It's too dangerous."

"We live in friggin' Fort Knox, Mom," Roman said. "You said yourself that there are killers out there on the street. Are we just going to hide here in the house?"

Venice looked to Gail, who shook her head vigorously. "It's what we have to do. What we have to try, anyway."

"You said I'm part of the team, Mom. And I don't see where anything can go wrong."

"Oh, be careful with those words," Gail warned. "There's *always* something that can go wrong. And when it does, it will be at the worst possible moment."

Roman laughed, but then saw that the others weren't.

"Don't get cocky," Venice warned. Then, to Gail: "Are you sure there's not another way?"

She answered with raised eyebrows.

Venice didn't like it, but she settled herself with a sigh and pressed a speed-dial number on her phone. She put the phone on speaker.

On the third ring, the line clicked open. "Father Dom speaking."

"Hi, Dom," Venice said. "You're on speaker with Gail and Roman in the room. Has Mama filled you in on today's excitement?"

"You said Roman's in the room?" Dom said. His tone showed equal parts surprise and hesitancy.

"It's a long story," Venice said, "but he knows pretty much everything. More than I'd like him to, but these are interesting times."

"Mama gave me the overview," he said. "Are you two all right?"

"We're fine," Venice said. "I need a favor."

"Was Roman involved in the attacks?"

"Can we discuss the background later, Father?" Gail said. "We're feeling some serious time pressure here."

"Of course," Dom said. "Tell me what you need."

Venice explained, "We need you to have a serious talk with a RezHouse student named Mateo Lopez."

"About what?"

"That's entirely up to you," she said. "Fifteen minutes should handle it."

Roman was shocked by the fact that Father Dom had asked so few questions. The whole conversation lasted less than five minutes. It was almost as if Dom knew enough to know what he didn't want to know.

"Tell me again what you need to do," Venice said as she handed him a flash drive.

"I stick this into his USB drive and wait," Roman said.

"How will you know that the program is loaded?"

"The light will change from red to green. It shouldn't take more than a minute." He turned the tiny drive over between his thumb and forefinger. "I've never seen a thumb drive like this."

"Because the drives I make are not available on the open market," Venice said. Roman heard uncharacteristic arrogance in his mom's tone.

"And I don't have to boot up his computer?" Roman asked. He started to work his way around to her side again. This time, she didn't stop him.

"No, you don't. If his laptop hasn't gone to sleep yet, the program will load faster, but it will also load while the machine is sleeping."

"I don't get how you know how to do stuff like this," Roman said.

His mom didn't answer. Instead, she tapped on her keyboard. The image on her screen shifted from meaningless lines of code to an image of a door-lined hallway. Roman recognized the divot in the drywall between the third and fourth doors on the left, a souvenir from a wrestling match between him and Michael Stanns that started out as play and ended up turning serious. If anyone in authority has witnessed the scuffle, they'd said nothing to him about it.

Only the angle was wrong. The security camera was on the other end of the hallway. In fact, he could see it in the image.

"What camera is that?" he asked.

"Not every exit sign is just an exit sign," Venice said. "Which room belongs to Mateo?"

Roman leaned closer to the screen. "Third on the right."

After thirty seconds or so, the house mother on duty

entered the frame from the bottom and strode to Mateo's door. When she knocked, Roman was surprised that he could hear the raps through the speakers on the computer.

"You've got sound, too?"

"Clearly," Venice said. She seemed to be growing uncomfortable.

The house mother was about to knock a second time when the door opened a crack.

"Hi," Mateo said. "Is something wrong?"

"I don't know," the house mother said. "Father Dom called. He'd like to speak to you in the mansion."

"I didn't do anything wrong," Mateo said. Though his tone indicated that he might have.

"That's good to know," the house mother said. "The father said he needed to see you as soon as possible."

The next words were unintelligible, but a few seconds later, Mateo exited his doorway, still pulling a sweatshirt over his head.

"It's a big deal when Father Dom wants to talk to you," Roman observed.

"You need to get going," Gail said.

"And you want me to spend the night in the dorm, right?" Roman asked.

Gail took this one. "For this to work, I think you have to."

With that, he reslung his backpack and was off.

He exited through mansion's kitchen, a massive expanse across the back of the building. For as long as Roman could remember, this was Mama's domain. The kitchen was the place for both hugs and lectures, often administered while assembling the elements for something yummy. Everything Mama cooked was yummy, so that part was easy.

* * *

It wasn't until the air hit him that Roman remembered that he'd left his jacket inside the Zulu Room. Going back for it was not an option.

At one point, apparently, the mansion and RezHouse were one and the same, just one building. The top two floors were dormitories, and the classrooms were all located on the first floor. Over the years, as the student population grew, the school built the academic buildings out back, with the mansion converting to all dormitories, except for the section on the third floor where Mama and Venice lived. By the time Roman could remember, the separate dormitory structures had been built, and the mansion was strictly administration, security, and home for the Alexander family on the upper floors. The first floor hosted galas and fundraisers all the time. Roman had always assumed that the money raised went to Resurrection House, but now that he thought about it, he really had no idea.

The gated, secured area of RezHouse, including the mansion and all the rest, spanned a big area. Roman wasn't good with distances, but he'd guess ten acres. Certainly, it was the largest plot of land in Fisherman's Cove. Not so wide on the Church Street side, it stretched forever out back, and it featured hardwoods, pine barrens, a stream, and a bog that the kids called the Mosquito Pit, and for good reason.

The walk from the kitchen to his dormitory building was not an approved one, meaning that you couldn't just follow a walkway to get from one to the other. You had to work your way through the woods, pushing branches out of your way and doing your best to ignore the sticker bushes that could penetrate steel, let alone denim.

As he wound his way through the undergrowth, he tried to be quiet but then realized that there was no reason to. This wasn't forbidden territory. Still, as he approached the spot where the woods transitioned to open space and from there to the real pathway from the dorms to the mansion, he stood straighter and stepped out into the open.

He'd taken fewer than a dozen steps when he heard a familiar voice. "Yo, Roman!"

Mateo Lopez was walking across the lawn from the side entrance to the dormitory building. It was a route that took longer to walk but bypassed a lot of the bullshit security steps that took you out the main entrance.

"What's happening?" Mateo asked. "I thought you were under house arrest."

Mr. Jonathan had told Roman a long time ago that he had shitty poker face—that his emotions showed in his eyes. Those were the words that coursed through his head now. "Oh, hi," he said. *What a stupid answer.* "They let me out."

"What's going on?"

Mateo hadn't been this friendly—this *conversational*—in weeks. Even in these few seconds, Roman saw the difference. His Spidey sense started pinging.

"Some kind of threat," Roman said. He cringed at the vagueness of his words.

The good news was that Mateo didn't have a good poker face, either. "To you?"

"I guess. Whatever it was, they're okay with me going back to the dorm."

"Was your mother there?" Mateo asked.

There it is, Roman thought. Mateo knew there would

be attacks on his mom and Gail. "No," he lied. "They're still out. The guard just took me back, made me hang out for a while, and then let me go."

Mateo's eyes narrowed. Was he buying what Roman was selling?

"Where are *you* going?" Roman asked, hoping to change the subject.

"Father Dom wants to talk to me about something."

Roman nodded thoughtfully. "Ah," he said.

"Don't you want to know what he wants to talk to me about?" Mateo asked.

Shit, shit, shit. He knows I know something. "Sure. But I figured with it being Father Dom, it was probably none of my business."

Mateo's frown brightened to a grin. "The answer is, I don't know. You gonna be in your room when I get back?"

"Don't know where else I'd be."

"Oh, my God, they ran into each other on the lawn," Venice said, pointing at the screen. "They're talking."

"I don't suppose you have microphones buried in the grass?" Gail quipped. Truth be told, she was not comfortable with the level of surveillance Digger had allowed Venice to install throughout the campus. Security was one thing, but kids needed privacy, too.

The irony eluded Venice completely. "It's not feasible out on the quad like that. We should have waited till we saw Mateo leaving before we let Roman go out."

"He'll be fine," Gail said. What else could she say? "They're going to be together later. That's the plan."

"But the program will be installed then. And we'll

know what they're talking about." She shot a desperate look to Gail. "Are we making a mistake letting him do this?"

"He'll be fine," Gail repeated.

The boys chatted for only a minute or so, then fist bumped and parted company.

Gail let go of breath she didn't know she'd been holding. Now she could actually believe what she'd said she believed about Roman's safety.

They watched until Roman approached the top of the screen, and then Venice toggled to a different angle. In this view, Roman crossed from left to right.

"Are all of the cameras hidden?" Gail asked.

"The effective ones are," Venice replied. "Kids are smart. They avoid the cameras they can see." She shifted in her chair. "It's not voyeurism, you know."

Gail raised her hands, as if surrendering. "I never said it was."

"You know the background of the students," Venice said.

"I do. Why are you being defensive?"

"Because I'm good at reading body language."

As Roman exited the screen, another click showed him from an elevated angle entering a scrum of other students in the lobby of the dorm. The school was still on lockdown, but that didn't prevent the students from milling around inside the residence halls. Now that the level of lockdown had been reduced, they could even wander around the campus. Anything beyond the fences, though, was off limits.

"It looks like classes changed," Gail observed.

"Kids gotta roam," Venice said. "Classes are over for the day."

Gail noticed that none of the other kids greeted Roman as he wended his way through the crowd. She didn't know what to make of that, but it was an interesting observation.

It ended up being a longer walk back to the dorm than Gail had anticipated. That explained the miscalculation that allowed Roman and Mateo to run into each other.

Roman was still climbing the steps to the second floor when Venice's phone buzzed. She answered on speaker. "Hi, Dom."

"You sounded like time was of the essence in whatever's going on. I just wanted you to know that Mateo Lopez still hasn't shown up."

"Oh, shit." Gail and Venice said it together.

Venice disconnected the call and hammered her keyboard, changing the view away from Roman and scouring the campus, instead. In just the past couple of minutes, the campus lawn had changed from abandoned to swarming like a pierced anthill.

"Do you remember what Mateo was wearing?" Venice asked.

"No, I don't," Gail said. "I do remember that he wasn't wearing a backpack, though."

"What isn't there doesn't help."

"Sure it does," Gail argued. "Pretty much everybody else *is* wearing a backpack." She leaned in closer to the screen. "This thing doesn't have a zoom lens, does it?"

"No. I can make the image bigger on the screen, but when I do, it sacrifices clarity." Venice demonstrated, and the images turned grainy. "I don't think it's worth the tradeoff."

"Maybe we should narrow the focus," Gail said. "We're looking for timing, right? I mean, if Mateo blew off his meeting with Dom entirely and is hanging out with a girlfriend under a tree, we don't care, right? We only have to worry if he's coming back toward the dorm."

Venice smiled. "So, focus on the approaches to the doors and the doors themselves," she said. A few keystrokes later, her screen divided into six panels. There were fewer kids than before, but they were still complicated views. Most of the students they saw were laughing and engaged in conversation, all of them clearly oblivious to the unblinking eye that was watching them.

"There!" Gail said, pointing to the lower right-hand corner on the lower left-hand image. "I think I saw him. He's out of the frame now, though."

"Did he exit the bottom or the side?" Venice asked.

"Side, I guess, but that's a tough call."

Venice made a V with her fingers and pointed. "That would put him in one of these two screens."

Two seconds later, Gail said, "Got him. He's heading for the stairs."

"Oh, no, no, no," Venice said. More tapping wiped Mateo away and brought up the now-familiar image of Roman's hall. The image showed nothing but closed doors.

"Is he already inside?" Gail asked.

As if to answer her question, Roman appeared at the top of the screen, emerging from the boys' restroom.

"Oh, God," Venice moaned. "He hasn't started yet."

"Call him," Gail said. "Tell him to hurry. Better yet, tell him to abort."

Venice pressed a speed-dial number on her phone, and they waited.

Roman hated the fact that his nerves and his bladder were directly connected. He knew he was supposed to be in a hurry—and he really was—but pissing all over Mateo's floor wouldn't help anything. Now, he could take his time and do things right.

When you don't want to get caught doing something bad, Mr. Boxers had told him once, *don't look like you're doing something bad.* He called it the Big Bluff.

Roman stood tall and tried his best to walk normally as he closed the distance to his door and then turned at the last second to duck into Mateo's room, instead. As anticipated, the door was unlocked. It opened without resistance or even making a sound. Roman tossed off a two-fingered salute to the exit sign that he now knew housed a camera and slipped inside, closing the door behind him.

The house mothers were sticklers about neatness, routinely performing room inspections, but Mateo's room was always beyond tidy. It was actually neat. Whereas Roman never tied his shoes a second time unless the laces snagged on something—instead choosing to kick them on and off with the bows in place—Mateo's shoes were neatly lined against the bottom wall of the cabinet that served as his closet, the laces carefully arranged to stream down the center of the instep.

The room even smelled clean. Roman had no idea how he accomplished that.

Mateo's laptop sat at the center of his desk, the top closed, its surface shiny. Did he actually polish the case of his laptop? Could you even do that and not ruin something?

Roman's heart jumped when he shoved his hand into the front pocket of his jeans for the flash drive and he couldn't find it. "Shit."

No, wait, it had to be there. Where else could it go?

He moved his hands to the outside of the pants and patted himself down. It had—

There it was. It had wedged itself into the far corner of the stitching.

Roman wished that he was better with computers than he was. He could play the crap out of pretty much any video game, but when it came to the actual functioning of the machine or interpreting the codes that ran the software, he might as well have been born in the eighties. Inserting a drive into a USB port wasn't an advanced skill, but as Roman examined Mateo's laptop, he saw that there was only one port, and that was already taken by something that had a thicker cord than you usually see attached to USB ports.

He could unplug it, but if he did that, might that do something that would tell Mateo that he'd been there?

Roman traced the cord through a hole in the top of the desk down to a box that was brimming with other flash drives and memory sticks. A splitter.

Dropping to his hands and knees, Roman crawled under the desk, into the box where Mateo's legs would go, and reached for the splitter. It was dark and shadowy down there, and he couldn't quite see what he was doing.

"This is stupid," he mumbled, and he sat back up on the floor to get access to his pocket and his phone. He could use the flashlight on his phone to—

He'd missed a call from his mom. Why hadn't it gone through? he wondered. Then he saw that he'd turned it to silent. He did that a lot on his way to bed, and sometimes he forgot to reset it in the morning. He pulled down the menu and switched it to vibrate. If it rang now, while he was in the midst of this, the sound would cause him to shit himself for sure.

He'd call her in a couple of minutes. He needed to get this thing done, get back in his room, and then wait for the next phase of his first covert operation. That's what they called it, right?

He pressed the flashlight icon on the phone and climbed back under to go to work.

The splitter featured six USB ports, and of them, four were already taken. His mom had told him to put the flash drive in the *computer*, not in a thing that was connected to the computer. He hoped he wasn't screwing this all up.

His phone buzzed in his hand. It was a double-buzz actually, indicating that he had a text message.

It was hard to deny the urge to look at the screen, but the whole world would open up for him after he inserted the drive into the slot.

And of course, it was upside down.

The phone double-buzzed again.

"Yeah, yeah, yeah," he muttered. "A little patience."

He finally matched the flash drive to the slot, and he

pressed it into place. Instantly, he was rewarded with a little red LED light.

His phone double-buzzed again.

"God *dammit*, Mom." He sat up again and looked at the screen.

Mateo never came to Fr Dom. He's back in the dorm. Get out. Abort.

"Oh, holy shit," Roman breathed.

Time stamped fifteen seconds later:

"Answer up. He's on your floor.

Just now:

Roman, he's at the door for God's sake!

CHAPTER 18

Renaldo Vega didn't much like horses. They were stupid animals, as far as he was concerned, and they smelled like . . . well, like horses. Years ago, he'd taken a bullet through his iliac crest on the left side, and his pelvis on that side hadn't been quite right ever since. It wasn't a debilitating wound—after it healed—but it ached in certain weather conditions, and it transformed into an internal lightning storm after he'd sat in a saddle for more than an hour or two.

Today had pushed him over the edge.

He was ready for a twenty-first century mode of transportation.

The only roadway this far into the mountains was narrow in the extreme, perhaps twenty feet across. It was paved, but Mother Nature was cruel to asphalt in this part of the world. Renaldo was certain that dirt bikers enjoyed the bumps and divots, and the horse didn't care one way or the other.

Motor vehicles, though, weren't so forgiving, and he could imagine lots of cursing on the part of drivers as they bounced around the interiors of their cabs.

For Renaldo, the bounciest of vehicles was vastly preferred over the prolonged agony of straddling this beast.

He needed to choose the spot for this next part carefully. He wanted the roadway to be narrow, but he didn't want the spot to be near a curve in case the oncoming vehicle would take the curve too quickly and wreck. He figured he had one good shot at this, and if the result was a vehicle that couldn't be driven, then what was the point?

According to his GPS tracker, the Sequoia had pulled over somewhere and hadn't moved in nearly twenty minutes. Were they waiting for something? Or had they abandoned the vehicle?

He'd know soon enough, he supposed.

He reined his horse to a stop at a spot where he figured there must be seventy yards of straightaway, plenty of time to stop if the driver wasn't going crazy-fast. He dismounted, then stood at the beast's head, reins clutched in his fist.

There were only a few ways for this plan to end. He wanted to be free to dodge to the left or the right to avoid getting run over if things went wrong.

Given the violence of the day, the air seemed unnaturally calm and quiet. Soothing.

He heard the sound of an approaching engine after about ten minutes of standing sentry in the middle of the road. The horse had already shat and pissed in that time, and he had to shift his stance twice to keep his shoes out of the river of horse urine.

Yeah, he hated horses. He pulled his Glock 23 from its holster on his right hip.

Ahead, coming from the west, a milky green Ford

Explorer turned the corner doing about thirty-five. Renaldo watched the driver's eyes grow to the size of saucers as he stood on the brakes.

The action spooked the horse, which tried to run, but Renaldo kept him at bay with a hard pull on the reins.

The Explorer skidded till it was crosswise in the road, its nose facing south.

Renaldo could hear the startled screams of the occupants, even through the closed windows. The driver transitioned quickly from frightened to angry. Within a few seconds after skidding to a stop, the driver threw open his door and climbed out. Maybe thirty-five and fit, he wore his jet black hair pulled back in a man bun and wore the clothes of the kind of cowboy one saw at ski resorts. The guy had money and he had attitude.

As the driver stepped away from his door, Renaldo let go of the reins and made note of the pretty blond wife in the front seat and the two children in the backseat. The boy appeared to be about ten, the girl older at twelve or thirteen.

"Jesus God," the driver said. "What the hell are you doing?"

"Come on, Aiden," the wife said. "Don't get out of the car."

Too late for that. Aiden wanted a fight. "You could have killed—"

Renaldo raised the pistol and fired a .40-caliber hollow point through the bridge of Aiden's nose, launching a spray of brain into the air. The man dropped and didn't matter anymore.

The horse didn't like the noise. It reared back and

bolted a few steps, but then stopped. Perhaps it had been trained for this kind of noise.

Stepping over Aiden's body, Renaldo walked to the open door and looked inside. The kids were squirming in the backseat to pull free of their seatbelts to get a look at what just happened, but the wife looked stunned. Terrified.

"Hello, everyone," Renaldo said. He knew that his accent was strong, so speaking English always made him uncomfortable. "Children, please stay in your seats." He reached across the steering column and pushed the button that killed the engine. "Missus, I'm going to come over to your side. When I do, please step out of the car. Tell your *hijos* to do the same from the door on your side."

"What are you going to do?" she asked.

"What's your name?" Renaldo asked.

"Um, Lara."

He tried to form a friendly smile. "Lara, this will all end soon, I promise you."

"You can have anything," she said. "Please don't hurt the rest of us."

That was the children's clue to start panicking. "Mommy, what's happening?" the girl asked. The boy just gaped and started to cry.

"Come out the other doors," he said, "and no one needs to get hurt."

"Did you kill Daddy?"

Lara said, "Do as he says, Amy. You too, Michael. Get out of the car. Both of you, on my side."

Renaldo waited till the doors were open before he said, "Thank you, Lara," and he moved around the front of the vehicle to their side. When he glanced down, he felt sorry that the children might see so much of their father's brains on the pavement.

"All right, Lara," Renaldo said when they were all outside and gathered near the edge of the road. "I need your cell phone and your wallet."

"We don't have much cash on us," she said. In his experience, people always told the truth when they were this frightened. Such a shame that he didn't give a shit about how much cash they had.

"That's not what I said." He kept his voice calm. Soothing, almost. "Your phone and your wallet."

"Did you kill Daddy?" Amy asked again.

"Yes, I did," he said. "And I will do the same for all of you if you don't listen carefully and do exactly what I say.

Michael seemed oblivious to the fact that he'd wet himself. Such things happened.

Lara fished her cell phone out of the front pocket of her jeans and held it out for him. "My wallet is in my purse. It's still in the car."

"Just put the phone on the ground," he said.

She stooped and did just that.

"What about your children? Do they have phones?"

Lara nodded quickly, a twitch, really.

"Michael, where is your phone?" Renaldo asked.

"They're both in the truck," Amy said. "In the back. On the seat."

"I see," Renaldo said. "All of you do me a favor and turn out your pockets."

All of them might have dressed from the same catalogue of expensive denim. Two quarters fell free from the liner of Michael's left pocket as he turned it inside out, and his eyes grew wide. It was the same expression as his father's as he skidded the Explorer.

"I-I'm sorry," the boy said. "I didn't know it was there. I really didn't." He started to cry again.

"Please stop doing that," Renaldo asked. "It's annoying. I don't care about the fifty cents." He turned his attention to Lara. "Where are you on your way to?"

"Salt Lake City," she said.

"Do you have a hotel room there?"

She did that twitching nod again.

"You're not lying to me, are you?"

"N-no, sir, I'm not."

Renaldo smiled. "Sir," he said. "That's a nice touch. I believe you." Then he shot her above her right eye. She died before her legs had a chance to buckle.

"Mommy!" Amy yelled, and she rushed toward her mother's body.

Renaldo killed her before she'd taken two steps.

Michael was the smart one. He chose to run the other way. He was fast, too. But he didn't know about the importance of zigzagging. Renaldo adopted a two-handed stance, settled the front sight at a spot directly between the boy's shoulder blades, and pressed the trigger.

Roman banged his head on the center drawer of the desk as he shot out of the leg well and scrabbled to his feet. The effort caused Mateo's desk chair to roll away and pivot ninety degrees.

Roman had no time to think, no time to hide. No time to set things straight.

As the doorknob turned, Roman planted himself in Mateo's chair and brought his phone up. For good measure, he deleted his mom's messages.

Mateo jumped when he saw Roman at the desk. "What the hell are you doing here?" he demanded from the doorway. He took two steps into the room and closed the door behind him.

The look in his friend's eyes frightened Roman. Mateo was ready for a fight.

"I'm waiting for you," Roman said.

"Waiting for me to do what?"

"Come back. We said we'd talk."

Mateo walked to his desk and pulled Roman from the chair by the fabric of his shirt collar. "What did you take?"

"Nothing! Why would I take anything?"

"Because you're here!" Mateo was nearly shouting. "And I wasn't! This is my room!"

"I hang out here all the time," Roman said. He prayed that Mateo did not hear the nervous catch in his voice.

"Don't bullshit me, Roman. I swear to God, I'm the last one you want to lie to."

"I'm not bullshitting, and I'm not lying," Roman lied. He thought he might be getting better at it. He wrenched himself out of Mateo's grasp. "And screw you." He stormed across the room, pulled open the door, and said, "You looked like you needed to talk. You looked scared when you talked to me before the lockdown. I thought I'd see if you're okay. I'm sorry." He crossed the hallway to his own room, threw his door open, then slammed it shut.

Then he breathed for the first time in what felt like an hour.

"Jesus Christ," he whispered as he plopped his butt on his bed. That was stupid-close. He placed his hand on his chest, as if that might slow his hammering heart.

His phone double-buzzed.

Saw you run out of the room. Everything okay?

He typed with his thumbs:

JEEZE MOM STOP! I AM FINE! JUST STOP!

As soon as he hit send, he realized that the caps were a bit much. She was just checking on him, after all. And it had to look very scary from—

Someone knocked on his door. Not gentle, but not urgent.

"Yeah, come in," Roman said. He was not surprised to see Mateo standing on the other side. He looked . . . odd.

"Sorry, *hijo*," he said. "I should not have laid hands on you."

"That's okay," Roman said.

"No, it's not okay. Thank you for not kicking my ass." Call it paranoia, but something wasn't quite right in his delivery. Mateo never apologized to anybody for anything.

"I didn't steal any of your shit," Roman said.

"I know. You startled me. It's been a shit day."

Roman let the words hang, unanswered.

"But you lied to me, *hijo*," Mateo said. "I *know* you lied to me."

Roman's stomach knotted. As much as he knew that he sucked at not telling the truth, he knew that he sucked ten times as much at denying that he'd lied when he had.

"You said that nothing happened," Mateo said. "You said that you didn't see your mom when you went back to the mansion, but her car is parked right there."

Roman couldn't form words to respond. This was not how his script was supposed to go, but he saw an opportunity to get the information he needed, anyway.

"What actually happened when you went back to the mansion?" Mateo asked.

"What were you warning me about?" Roman asked in reply. "You said we were in danger. What did you *think* was going to happen?"

Mateo walked to Roman's desk chair and sat down. "I can't tell you that," he said.

"Why not?"

"I can't tell you why not, either."

"Did you know that people were going to try to kill my mother and her friend today?"

Mateo wouldn't make eye contact. "No."

"Now who's lying?"

When Mateo's gaze rocked back up, his eyes were hot with anger. "Be careful, Roman."

"Or what? Are you going to have people jump out and try to shoot me down on the street?"

"I'm not doing any of this stuff."

"Then who is?"

"I can't tell you!"

It was time to go for the line he'd been coached on. "Okay, whoever it is, do you think they know that everybody they sent to kill people is dead?"

Mateo recoiled from the question. "What do you mean?"

"I mean that they're all dead. The people who tried to kill my mom and my grandmother. The people who tried to kill Mr. Jonathan—the guy who finances this place and gives you a place to live—are all dead. All the people they were trying to kill are still alive. Apparently, the killers are not very good at what they do."

The surprise in Mateo's face seemed genuine.

"So, what's the thing that's supposed to happen to me?" Roman asked.

Mateo pivoted. "Why were you really in my room?"

This was where the little bit of training and rehearsal kicked in. "To have this conversation," Roman said. "I thought about starting it by kicking you in the balls as you came through the door, but then I got control of my temper."

"I was trying to help you," Mateo said.

"But not my mom or Mama Alexander or the others? Just to hell with them, right? You *knew* people were coming for them."

"It's not like that." Mateo had tears in his eyes. He swiped them away with his palms and stood, then started for the door. "Anyway, I'm sorry. And I'm glad everybody's okay."

"Why did that lawyer visit you a couple of weeks ago?" Roman asked. This was not part of the script, but he wanted to know.

The question caused a hitch in Mateo's stride, but he recovered in less than a second. "I don't know what you're talking about."

Roman thought about challenging the lie but knew instinctively that it would launch a dick-knocking who-are-you-calling-a-liar fight. Instead, he said, "Every visitor has to leave his name when they come and want to talk to one of us. They also have to give a reason. You're not denying that you had that visitor a few weeks ago, right?

The one that came when we were shooting the shit in your room?"

Turned out that Mateo wasn't a great liar, either. His eyes got red, and his body language said that he wanted to bolt out of the room but realized that wouldn't help anything. "What are you doing, *hijo*?"

Roman recognized the pivot for what it was and stayed quiet. He'd already done everything he'd needed to do per the plan hatched in the mansion.

"This is a very dangerous game you're playing," Mateo said.

"I didn't even know there *was* a game until you warned me about it," Roman said. "People tried to *kill* my mother and grandmother today. Yeah, I think I know the game is dangerous. And you're not answering my goddamn question!"

Mateo seemed startled by the shouting at the end. Still standing at the door, his hand on the knob, he looked to be at a loss for words.

"Your visitor said his name was Russell Greenberg," Roman said.

The words hit Mateo with the force of arrows launched by a bow. They literally rocked him back. He considered bolting again. That was clear from the look he threw over his shoulder to his room across the hall. In the end, though, he opted to stay. He pushed Roman's door closed and sat down on the bed next to him.

"Russell Greenberg is my mother's lawyer," he said, mostly to the floor. "When they told me he was here, I thought for sure something bad had happened to her in prison." He rocked his eyes up at the mention of the P-word, as if to test Roman's reaction.

Roman worked hard to show nothing.

"We've never talked about it, but both my parents were druggies, and they did bad stuff, and they'll both die in prison sooner or later. I guess I'd care, but I'm really not sure. That sounds really awful, doesn't it?"

"I don't know how to answer that," Roman said.

Mateo gave a rueful chuckle. "I guess that's why we never talk about this stuff. You're lucky you don't have to worry about any of that. Must be nice to have all of that money. It's a shame you have to slum it out here with us."

"I'm not slumming anything," Roman said. He didn't know why he found that insulting, but he did. "You don't know anything about me."

Mateo shifted his position to look more directly at Roman. "Yes, I do," he said. "I know a lot more about you that you think I do. More than I should. That's what the meeting with Russell Greenberg was all about. He wanted me to find out everything I could about you and your family. And especially about Mr. Jonathan Grave."

"Why?"

"He wanted to know *everything*. He said that if I did that, my mother's prison sentence would be cut back."

Roman rattled his head, as if to make loose pieces fall into place. "What does one have to do with the other?"

"I don't know. He might have been lying to me for all I know. That's what lawyers do, right?"

"If you say so." Roman had no experience with lawyers, one way or the other.

"But if there was a chance that it could help my mother's case, I had to try, right? Wasn't that my only choice?"

"They tried to kill my family."

"I didn't know they were going to do that. I don't even know who *they* are."

"Were," Roman corrected, then felt bad about piling on. "You knew they were going to do something bad. You had to or else you wouldn't have warned me to stay on campus."

Mateo stood abruptly, fast enough to startle Roman. "It was the stuff they were asking for," he said. "They wanted to know where people lived, where they liked to go, what they liked to do. Once they found out that Mr. Jonathan was going on that hunt, they got, like, really excited."

"How did you know that Mr. Jonathan was going on a hunting trip?"

There was that hitch again, Mateo's tell. "We talked about it," he said.

"No, we didn't. I would never talk about what Mr. Jonathan does."

"You must have! How else—"

"You put spyware on my computer," Roman said. His words once again seemed to hit with physical force. He waited for Mateo to say something, then filled the silence with, "Are you saying you didn't?"

Tears formed in Mateo's eyes. "I'm sorry," he said. "I didn't have any choice. I had to help my mother."

"By helping to kill mine?" The words hung in the air, and the atmosphere between them thickened. "You should go," Roman said.

"Oh, come on, Roman, I'm really—"

"Just go."

Mateo didn't want to. He clearly wanted to talk things through more, but for all Roman knew, that was just more manipulation.

Roman stared at his friend's back as he exited the room. When the door closed again, Roman took out his phone and called his mom. She was going to shit when she heard the details he'd collected. The connection clicked after four rings.

"Hi, sweetie," she said. "Are you safe?"

"Yes, and I just talked with Mateo. I planted the seeds."

"What does that mean?"

"I got the virus installed, and I told him that the people who attacked you and Mr. Jonathan are all dead."

"How did he react?"

Roman could still see the expression. "He looked scared. No, he looked *shaken*."

"What about the thumb drive?" his mom asked. "Did you get that back?"

"I barely got it inserted," Roman said. "But it's in a splitter under his desk. I don't think he'll see it."

His mother didn't say anything.

"Are you there?"

"Right here. I'm trying to figure out how exposed the thumb drive might leave you."

"He already knows that I know," Roman said. "He can't undo the Trojan horse you put in, can he?"

Another long silence. "You just be very careful," his mom said.

"I will."

"And Roman? Nice job. Now I have to get back to helping Mr. Jonathan. We'll talk later."

Then she clicked off.

CHAPTER 19

Venice and Gail moved from the mansion back down the street to the offices of Security Solutions, under an armed escort the whole way that was far more conspicuous than Gail would have liked.

Located across the street from the Fisherman's Cove Marina, Security Solutions occupied the third floor of the same converted firehouse whose first two floors served as Digger's home. Always locked down pretty tightly, it now was under the same wartime precautions as the mansion and the school. Gail had no idea what Jonathan doled out for the physical and electronic security, but it had to be astronomical.

Venice and Gail sat at the teak conference table in the War Room, researching their available leads. They'd split up the work between them, with Gail taking on the fingerprint samples they had available, while Venice pursued the evidence provided by the rented Sequoia.

The prints from the shooter Gail killed were by far the best of the three sets they'd been able to obtain. They revealed the dead man to be Eric Lonergan, age thirty-seven, of no current fixed address. He had a sealed juvie file and that led to a stint in the regular Army, where he served for six years and rose to the rank of E5, sergeant. That was not bad, from what Jonathan had told her. It said that he'd gotten his act together at least a little.

He received a leg wound in Iraq that booted him from the service, at which point the easy part of tracking him disappeared.

By working inside the War Room, Gail had access to the decryption software and work-around hacks that Venice had amassed over the years, largely with the help of her now-deceased lover, Derek Halstrom, who had been tragically killed in a shoot-out not long ago. He'd been a hacker of nearly equal talent to Venice, and he'd worked for the National Security Agency, from which he'd . . . *borrowed* technology that even the FBI did not possess.

Eric Lonergan's military records gave Gail access to his Social Security number, and with that, she was able to tap into his tax returns. After his separation from Uncle Sam, he worked for a big-box sporting goods store for a while, and then he went to work for Oak View Armory in Kansas, where he stayed for a little over three years.

Gail pulled up the file on Oak View Armory and saw that it was more than your standard gun shop. It was part of a burgeoning trend in the shooter world, a "guntry club" where expensive dues bought a membership with access to an elaborate assortment of shooting ranges that catered to pistols, shotguns, carbines, and long-range rifles. It sounded great, actually, and Gail wished that she lived closer.

A deeper dive into the website revealed that Eric Lonergan was a "range master emeritus," which Gail took to mean he had been the top shooter for a while. It was interesting, she thought, because in her brief review of his Army records, she didn't see anything about remarkable marksmanship skills. Perhaps he was self-taught?

Gail returned to Lonergan's tax records. After leaving Oak View Armory, he went to work for OTX Security LLC, headquartered at a post office box in Twin Falls, Idaho—about a two-hour drive from Salt Lake City International Airport.

"Hey, Ven, does Twin Falls, Idaho, show up in the GPS routing you've got?"

Venice scoured whatever was on her screen. "Not Twin Falls, proper, no. But the car spent quite some time near Hailey, Idaho, which isn't far away."

"How much time?"

Venice scoured more closely. "Looks like three days. Why?"

"The guy I shot worked for a company that's headquartered out that way. That smells significant to me."

Gail switched to the fingerprints that Jonathan had sent in on his phone. Of the two, one was too smeared to be of any use, but the second one belonged to an Alroy Montoya, whose prints were readily available because he was on a terror watch list. Such was the problem with a southern border that provided for hot and cold running illegals.

"Do you have the car rental agreement up and handy?" Gail asked.

Venice clacked a few keys. "Yep."

"Did they list an incoming flight number on the rental application?"

"They listed a flight from El Paso, but that doesn't

necessarily mean anything. I can't imagine that the rental agent verifies the incoming flight info."

Gail agreed that was probably the case, but if nothing else, might listing El Paso, even if they were lying, have indicated their mindset? Under the circumstances, *might* wasn't terribly relevant, but at this stage, you grabbed at anything that might be significant.

Alroy Montoya was a bad dude, wanted for the murder of two Border Patrol agents and for the torture killing of a fourteen-year-old high school student in New Orleans whose father was a bigwig in the Sinaloa cartel in Mexico. And those were just the charges on this side of the border. His international rap sheet scrolled longer than a full screen on Gail's computer. From what she could tell, Montoya had been a freelance killer, offering up violence to whoever wanted to pay him.

But he had no ties to Idaho that she could see. In a perfect world, she'd find that he'd worked for OTX Security like the other guy, and they'd have a straight line. Alas, the world was never that perfect.

"Okay, Slinger," Venice said. "Take a look at the big screen."

As Gail watched, the lights in the War Room dimmed and the projector came to life. In thirty seconds, the 106-inch screen displayed what appeared to be topographical map of the Western states.

"I've animated it," Venice said. "This is the route that the rental car took when it left Salt Lake City airport five days ago."

The image on the screen looked like any commercial satellite mapping program, and it zoomed down to about the five-hundred-foot level, where the rental car lot was plainly visible. A yellow line started to trace away from the lot and then out onto the roadway.

"You did this while you were sitting there?" Gail asked. Venice's computer skills never failed to impress.

"I wasn't just sitting here," Venice said with feigned insult. "I was doing this."

"There's no little car image?" Gail teased. "You know, with the rich guy from Monopoly waving his hand at us?"

"Wait for the polished version," Venice said.

As the line moved, the image pulled away to show more perspective. Then it zoomed in again on what appeared to be a strip mall.

"We've gone about twenty-three miles in those five seconds," Venice explained. "This was their first stop— at an ATM."

The screen jumped, and the image became a street view of the strip mall, on the far right-hand side of which was a tiny branch of what Gail thought she read as Teton Savings Bank, but the sign was partially blocked.

"This took a little time," Venice continued. "I had to search through a lot of camera footage, but it helped to know the time and date. After a bit a scrolling, I landed on this."

The image changed to that of a man in his thirties, shot from that awkward angle typical of ATM security cameras—lots of chin and nose but not a lot of eyes and forehead.

Venice said, "To me, this looks like one of the death photos that Digger sent us. I'm running it through high-level facial recognition as we speak, so maybe we'll catch a break there."

"I agree," Gail said, but she saw something else of

interest. She rose from her chair and walked closer to the screen, taking care to stay out of her own shadow. "Can you zoom in on that upper left corner? Get a better look at the car in the background?"

"I can magnify the image," Venice said as she did just that. "But at the expense of quality." As she zoomed in on the vehicle, the image got grainy.

"Does that look like a Toyota Sequoia to you?" Gail asked.

"Oh, Lord, I have no idea," Venice said. She typed, and a Toyota ad popped onto the screen. "I guess it could be. The SUVs these days all look alike to me."

She had a point, but Gail felt good that the vehicle in the picture was, indeed, the one they were looking for.

Venice explained, "This guy withdrew five hundred dollars from a preloaded cash card, the limit allowed by this bank."

"How do you know that?" Gail asked.

"I know it was a gift card because it's obvious from the metadata, and if I looked it up on the internet, I'm sure that I'd find what the withdrawal limits are." A smile bloomed. "As it turns out, though, I won't have to do that."

Gail retook her seat at the table as the map reappeared, and the ground dropped away. The yellow line started moving again, but this time for just a few inches on the image. A new strip mall appeared.

Venice explained, "Only eleven miles from the Teton branch, is the Cattleman Savings and Loan. All of these are part of the Vista ATM network, so much of the connective tissue for this search was already in place."

The same face as before appeared in the security camera shot.

"Here, he could only withdraw three hundred dollars," Venice said. "And that definitely looks like the Toyota Sequoia in the background."

"Were there more stops for money?" Gail asked.

"Two more," Venice said. The yellow line took them fifteen miles farther northwest to Cactus National Bank, where they were able to pull out another five hundred, with a final five hundred from Industry Savings and Loan, just this side of the Idaho border.

"Idaho is suddenly looking pretty important to this," Gail observed.

In each case, the security photo showed the same face with the same frown as he ordered up the money. At Cactus National, the car was not in the frame at all, but at Industry Savings and Loan, they got their money shot. The guy with the cash card was apparently the driver, and at Industry, he'd parked with the passenger side closest to the machine, and they got a good enough shot of the man in the shotgun seat for Gail to proclaim him to be Alroy Montoya.

"That's our guy!" Gail said, pointing.

"So, at least we know we have the right vehicle," Venice said. "Once our boys got their eighteen hundred bucks, they drove another four hours. I'll speed up the time frame."

The ground fell away again, and the yellow line streaked northward, over the border into Idaho. "Where did you say your guy's security company was headquartered?" Venice asked.

"Hailey, Idaho."

"That's what I thought. The tracking line is passing through there right . . . now."

The animation paused, and a satellite view of Hailey replaced it. About a mile wide—the entire width of the valley where it resided—and five miles long, Hailey consisted of lots of gridded streets lined with charming homes and businesses. Although clearly not built specifically for tourists, à la Colorado's Aspen or Vail, Gail imagined that this burg attracted its fair share of tourist dollars, especially in the wintertime.

The picture changed to a sprawling red brick building with blue awnings. "Since the office address is a post office box, I thought I'd show you the post office."

"Fascinating," Gail said. *Not.* "Let's move on." The post office building went away, and the map returned. The yellow line plowed through Ketchum and beyond, until finally coming to rest squarely in the middle of nowhere. "Welcome to the outskirts of Stanley, Idaho."

"There's nothing there," Gail said. The yellow line had stopped in the middle of the mountains, seven miles from the actual town of Stanley, which itself wasn't big enough to warrant images from the mapping software's "street view" feature.

"Clearly, there is," Venice said. "Because our boys spent nearly three days there before they headed off to Montana."

"Just there?" Gail asked. "They didn't move around?"

"Yes, they did move around," Venice said. The screen reanimated, and the yellow line formed a kind of star pattern as it reached out into Stanley, with stops in Ketchum and its environs.

"Looks like they might have been running errands," Gail said.

"I agree. And remember, those short trips you're

seeing in fast motion actually took place over the three days they were there. The key to remember, I think, is that they always come back to this spot on the mountain." She zoomed in tighter on that spot. "You can see that there are a few structures there, but I can't get any useable detail from the commercial satellites over the U.S., and we don't do much surveillance over Idaho. Texas, Arizona, New Mexico, yes, but not so much in the landlocked states."

"I know you're not giving up," Gail said.

"Oh, heavens no. I'm just beginning, in fact. I should be able to track down the places they traveled to, particularly in town."

"Finding out what they bought might be a little more challenging," Gail said. "Assuming that's what all the cash was for."

Venice went back to her computer and started typing. "I'm going to reach out to Scorpion and Big Guy and get them heading to Idaho. I'll send the directions to their GPS."

CHAPTER 20

"Stanley, Idaho," Boxers repeated as he heard the directions from Mother Hen. "That's really a place?" He dropped the Toyota into gear and started heading west.

"It's a spot on the map," Venice explained, "and it's reasonably near Twin Falls, Idaho, which is the headquarters of OTX Security, the occasional employer of at least one of the men who tried to kill Gail, Mama, and me today. I've sent you the GPS coordinates of the spot where your assassins stopped on their way up from the southern border on their way to kill you."

Jonathan looked across the console at Boxers. "That sounds like a strong link to me."

"That's what we were thinking here, too," Venice said. She explained about the lengthy route to pick up cash along the way from the Salt Lake City airport to Stanley, Idaho.

"Quite a bit has happened in the last twenty or thirty minutes that you need to know about," Venice continued. "As I told you, we were able to identify Alroy Montoya from the fingerprints you sent, but the other shooters' prints you sent in weren't of high enough quality to get an identification. But we got lucky with facial recognition software. The man withdrawing the cash is Benedicto Jimenez, another Interpol wanna-have. Drugs, murder, the standard fare."

"We must be doing something right," Boxers said. "Whoever these asshats are, they hate us enough to send their first string to take us out."

"There's more," Venice said. "You didn't get them all. There's still one killer out there in your part of the world. At least one. When I took a closer look at the security camera footage from the third bank, I can see three more heads in the Sequoia, for a total of four. You confirmed only three kills."

"Three kills plus the guy who took the first shot," Jonathan clarified.

"He may or may not be alive," Boxers said. He aimed a silent snarl at Jonathan. "Somebody didn't want to check on the body."

"If he's alive, it's because Big Guy's aim sucked," Jonathan said. "Assuming he's still walking among the living, do we have any information on him this fourth guy?"

"Not even a good image," Venice said. "Just a silhouette in the backseat."

"So, what did they do with all the money they picked up?" Jonathan asked.

"They did a fair amount of shopping," Venice replied. "They stopped at a grocery in Hailey and a place called Gibson's Grab-n-Go in Stanley."

"Did they use a credit card?" Boxers asked. "Is that how you know the stores?"

"Negative," Venice said. "The mapping software doesn't

show street views of these little towns, but I could track where they went, and then I cross referenced against tax records. I suppose the businesses could have changed, but why assume that? But no, they did not create a credit record from any of those locations."

"Thus, the cash," Jonathan said.

"Exactly."

"Did you pick up any images from security cameras to see what they might have bought?" Boxers asked.

"If these stores have cameras, they're not tied to any network I can access," Venice said.

"Okay, let's shift gears," Jonathan said. "What do we know about the place our shooters were visiting in . . . Where is it?"

"Stanley, Idaho," Venice said. "Assuming the satellite didn't malfunction, there are two choices for the location where they've been holding up. It's either in the middle of nowhere—as in, camping—or they have been guests at a seventeen-hundred-acre ranch."

Boxers gave a low whistle.

"Who owns the ranch?"

"According to tax records, it's owned by Big Herd Holding Company, headquartered in . . . wait for it . . . Twin Falls, Idaho."

"I hear the ominous organ chord in your voice," Jonathan said. "But keep in mind that as communities get smaller, coincidences become more common."

"Think what you like, Boss," Venice said. "But there's more."

There always seemed to be more when Venice was doling out information.

She continued, "The land records list the ranch there—

the Sandstorm Ranch—as belonging to Big Herd Holding for only ten years. Before that, it was a bunch of little ranches that all got bought up and combined into one behemoth."

"Actually, as ranches go, seventeen hundred acres isn't that big," Boxers said.

"Well, it is for Stanley," Venice said. She didn't like being interrupted in general and kind of hated being interrupted with a correction.

"Go on," Jonathan said.

"I looked into Big Herd Holding," she continued, "and I learned that the primary shareholder is a Nevada transplant named Victor McCloud, who also has an ownership share in a number of other companies. Among them are Chaps N Spurs Overland Freight, whose territory is most of the Western states, running north-south routes from Texas to Canada and all parts in between."

Jonathan's mind shot right to the obvious connection with the southern border. "You think he's a smuggler?"

"I don't think one way or the other," Venice said. "I don't have data to draw a conclusion, but how are those small-town coincidences feeling to you now?"

"Admittedly less random," Jonathan said. "You use the phrase *shareholder*. Who are the other owners?"

"I'm still working on that," Venice said. "But I've saved the best for last."

"Of course you have," Boxers grumbled.

"Where do you suppose Victor McCloud got his original stake of cash to start all of this?"

Jonathan hated it when she played this game. He held up a finger for Boxers to remain silent. Sooner or later, she'd do the reveal without prompting.

She said, "Fine, don't let me have my moment in the bright light. In 2002, Victor McCloud established OTX Security."

Now, there was a coincidence that couldn't be a coincidence at all.

"I'm confused," Boxers said. "What links Idaho and Montana to Fisherman's Cove and the attacks there?"

A familiar voice popped into the conversation from Venice's side. "The nexus appears to be drugs," said Gail.

"Gunslinger just entered the War Room," Venice explained.

"I've been chatting with Roman," Gail said. "And he told me—"

"Whoa," Jonathan said. "Wait. Roman's involved with this?"

"He was warned of the attack on Mother Hen and me," Gail explained. "We've decided that one of his classmates has been pressured by people in the cartels to spy on us."

"Us?" Boxers asked. Jonathan saw the redness rising in Big Guy's face. Operational secrecy was a passion of his—a fetish, almost.

"All of us," Gail said. She described the details of the boys' conversation in the dormitory. "But Roman was a trooper. He successfully loaded spyware onto his friend's laptop. We'll know everything he does."

"Let's not get ahead of ourselves," Big Guy said. "You've brought a little boy into the inner circle? He knows what we do?"

"You traveled to Mexico to kill his kidnappers and sink a submarine," Venice said. "I'd say he had a pretty good head start before we told him anything. And no, he does not know all the details, and nor does he need to."

Boxers looked to Jonathan. "This is a big problem," he said.

"Not for today, it's not," Jonathan said. It was a hell of a burden to put on a kid, but Jonathan didn't worry about his spilling the proverbial beans. Everything he knew or loved would be destroyed if he did.

Jonathan pivoted back to the boys' conversation. "How does spying on us get his mother a shorter prison sentence?"

"That's not clear," Gail said. "I pressed Roman on it, and he indicated that it wasn't clear to the other boy, either."

"This other boy have a name?" Big Guy asked.

"Mateo Lopez," Venice said. "I have verified that both his parents are serving long prison sentences on drug charges. His father has a murder charge that will keep him in a cell forever, but there's a chance that his mother— her name is Luciana—could get out before the end of her sentence. Good behavior, that sort of thing."

"And this offer came via his mother's attorney, is that what you said?"

"That's right," Gail said. "But I don't think that's the important link. What we need to focus on is the inferred influence."

Boxers piloted the Sequoia onto a large road and picked up speed. Jonathan hoped that meant that the cell signal would remain strong. This felt like it was going to be a long conversation. Hell, it was already a long conversation.

"I know you, Gunslinger," Jonathan commented. "You don't say stuff like that unless you have an idea."

"Not an idea as much as an observation. Remember, I

sat at a table behind the bar for a good bit of time. Luciana Lopez is in federal prison, serving a federal rap. You know as well as I do how jealously the feds guard their convictions. To even suggest having enough clout to commute or even reduce a sentence requires a good bit of horsepower."

"The lawyer could have been bluffing," Venice said.

"We call that lying," Boxers said. "Damn scum suckers."

"Big Guy got cranky," Jonathan said. "But he could have a point."

The line fell silent, leading Jonathan to wonder if the call had been dropped. "Mother Hen?"

"She's typing," Gail said. "Seems she got smacked with inspiration."

"We've got a finite battery life on the phone," Jonathan said. "Should we try back later?"

"No, you don't have to try back later," Venice said in a mocking tone. "Your comments triggered something in my head. Coincidence and all that. If Victor McCloud and OTX Security are the nexus to everything, I thought I might do an additional search on him. For what it's worth, he is a major contributor to President Darmond and his party. Major enough that he had to be named in FEC declarations."

"So the president of the United States is trying to kill us," Boxers said. "Is that what you're saying?"

"Sometimes, I wouldn't blame him if he were," Venice said, "but no, that's not what I'm saying. Your question dealt with clout. Access is another word for clout, and a bundler like Victor McCloud—to the tune of millions of dollars over the years—would have plenty of access. Do with that information what you will."

It was Jonathan's turn to fall silent. He felt like they were headed in the right direction, but he had no idea what that direction might be. Surely, the president of the United States was not interested in killing Jonathan and his team—hell, if anything, the president owed the team a big kiss on the forehead, even if Jonathan couldn't stand the son of a bitch—but that didn't mean his underlings didn't think bad thoughts and hold grudges.

But what the hell did Mama do to hurt anyone?

"The cartel connection is the one to track down," Jonathan said. "It's the only one that makes sense. Think of the characters who are involved and think of the stakes. This one involves Mama Alexander and Roman. The dots all seem to connect to south of the border, and there's no limit to the cartels' bloodlust or their willingness to hurt innocents in retribution."

"Might you be going too fast?" Gail asked. "The world is full of really bad people who have reason to hurt you and yours."

"You're right," Jonathan agreed. "And if the links of this case traced back to the Chechens or the Russians or any of the 'Stans, then I think you'd have a point. But that's not where the bread crumbs are leading from any of this."

"What about the mother?" Boxers asked.

"Whose mother?" They all asked it together.

"Roman's school mate's mother," Big Guy said. "If reducing her sentence is really the pressure point to all of this, then she must be something special. Might be, anyway."

Jonathan thought Boxers had raised a very good point. "Mother Hen?"

"I've looked at her record," Venice said. "I'd be hard-pressed to find anything there that I'd call *special*." She cleared her throat and began reciting from something. "Luciana Lopez was arrested nearly four years ago along with her husband, Marco Lopez, on . . . Oh, geeze, do you want me to read the whole list? It's a thirty-five page indictment. They were convicted on all charges."

Jonathan saw no need to go through all that. No one would vote them parents of the year, that's for sure. "Just out of curiosity, does . . . what's the son's name again?"

"Mateo Lopez."

"Does Mateo Lopez have any siblings?"

He heard some typing in the background. "An older sister," Venice said. "Maria. She's married now, though. Last name . . ." Venice laughed. "Not what I was expecting. O'Mally. Maria O'Mally."

"It has a lyrical sound to it, though," Gail said.

Something clicked in Jonathan's head. "Whoa, wait a second," he said. "What was Luciana Lopez's maiden name?"

"Oh, Lord, Scorpion," Venice groaned. "You got me. I hadn't looked that up. Give me a few." More clacking.

Latins of all stripes and nationalities had long had a history of strong family ties. He didn't know if it meant anything, but if Luciana Perez was unremarkable, then maybe—

"Filho," Venice said. "Her maiden name was Filho." She spelled it.

Jonathan and Boxers exchanged looks of horror.

"Let me guess," Jonathan said. "She's Colombian."

"Good guess."

"Not a guess," Big Guy said. "This shit finally makes sense."

"Not to all of us," Gail said.

"Remember the boy that was kidnapped a while back when Mr. Stewart was shot?" Jonathan prompted.

"Of course," Venice said. "That was awful. Evan Guinn was the boy's name."

"Right," Jonathan said. "And remember the coca fields we burned down to the roots?"

"Yeaaah . . ." The way Venice drew out the word, Jonathan could feel her growing sense of dread.

"Care to guess who ultimately owned those fields?"

"Are you kidding me?" Venice asked.

"Antonio Filho," Boxers said.

"That name's been important more recently than that," Gail observed.

"Yes, it has," Jonathan confirmed. "We thought he might be the guy whose navy we sunk when we rescued Roman."

They all fell silent.

"That gives him motive for trying to kill everybody," Gail said, finally. "But a big chunk is missing."

"A huge chunk," Jonathan confirmed. "We've got a few hours of driving ahead of us, and you've got a lot of research to do."

"Where are you driving to?" Gail asked.

"At first, I didn't know," Jonathan said. "But now it seems prudent to have a nice conversation with Victor McCloud, don't you think?"

"No, no, no," Venice said. "Time out, Scorpion. Did you hear the part about seventeen hundred acres? This guy's a gajillionaire. He might have advanced security. You can't just go barging in there."

"This shit is going to stop," Jonathan snapped. "And it's going to stop tonight. I want as much information as you can give me on the various stops this rental car made when it was wandering around Twin Falls, Hailey, and Stanley. I want business data and owners' names and addresses."

"What are you planning to do?" Gail asked.

"I'm going to learn as much as I can about the man we presume to be our enemy."

CHAPTER 21

Diego Ruiz tried to concentrate on the paperwork that Mary Bauer, his chief of staff, had brought for him to review on the flight to the crime scene, but he couldn't get his mind to focus. Murders didn't happen much in Montana. They were unheard of in his slice of the bureaucracy. Sure, there were the occasional drunken disputes that went too far and ended up with hunters plinking at each other with fatal results, but he considered incidents like that to be stupidity, not murder.

These killings, as first reported by Director Rivers and subsequently substantiated by rangers on the ground and by state police officers, were beyond comprehension. A quadruple shooting? How could that happen? What the hell was going on in his state?

Governor Baker was beyond pissed off when Diego told him of the situation—and apoplectic when he found out that the FBI knew about it before he did. The governor had wanted to fly straight out to the site himself, but Diego had been able to talk him down from that idea. It was too early, he said, to bring that kind of horsepower onto a crime scene.

As usual, Baker was focused on the optics of the situation—the political fallout if he did versus didn't show up—while Diego understood that the law enforcement community would need at least a little time to grieve in private over the loss of one of their own. Larry Baker didn't take a crap without a camera crew in tow, and Diego's people most definitely would not want cameras and reporters ruing the solemnity of the moment.

"Sir, have you thought about your remarks when you land?" Mary Bauer asked him. A former rodeo rider and barrel racer, Mary's inner rancher showed through the thin veneer of political hackery. Aged somewhere between forty and sixty, she walked with a permanent limp on her left side, thanks to a loose saddle cinch during her last race, and the limp affected how she sat, as well. She never looked comfortable, but she always looked thoroughly dialed into every moment of her workday. Her instincts about people and situations were always spot-on, and he relied on her every bit as much as she relied on the knee brace that kept her leg from folding under her.

"I'm not going to be making remarks," Diego said. "Not formal ones, anyway. This is a fact-finding trip, pure and simple."

"All respect, sir, there is nothing pure nor simple about the number of bodies that we're going to find stacked down there when we land."

As the helicopter made its final approach to the clearing where a reception party had been set up, the attitude in the cabin changed, as if flipping a switch. All lightness evaporated. The seriousness of purpose subsumed everything. A fire truck stood on standby to stave off a forest fire in case the chopper crashed, and six or seven police cars formed a circle, in addition to the ranger vehicle that would take them to the site of the shootings.

Diego was old-school about waiting for the rotor disc to stop turning before he stepped out. As they waited for the wind-down to finish, Diego wondered why so many police vehicles surrounded their landing zone.

"You're all set, sir," the pilot called back to them.

Diego pulled the latch on the back half of the clamshell door and pushed it open. It hadn't moved more than a few inches when Pete Simonsen's supervisor, Mike Elmore, pulled it open all the way.

In a social situation, Diego would have let Mary lead the party out of the chopper, but this was business, and the unwritten rules of the game were that the senior person always went first.

Elmore was equal parts professional ranger and Marlboro Man. He was always serious about his work and his life, and his weathered face was particularly grim as he offered his hand to his boss. "I got unpleasant stuff to say to you, Diego," Elmore said. "You want to do it here or go someplace private?"

"You've got a vehicle for us, I presume?" Diego asked. He kept his tone light. Elmore had every right to be mad, and mad people had every right to pop off. To a point.

As they walked toward a Suburban with the markings of the Montana Fish, Wildlife and Parks Department, a Montana state trooper angled toward them. He was still fifteen feet away when he called, "You are Mr. Ruiz, I presume?"

"Not yet, Patrick," Elmore said. "I get him first."

Diego jerked to a stop, causing the others to do the same and Mary to nearly run him over from behind.

"Okay, let's have it. Right here, right now. It's been a long day for all of us—okay, probably longer for you—but what's going on?"

"There have been more murders," the Montana cop said.

"We haven't met," Diego said. He extended his hand. "Diego Ruiz."

"I know who you are," the cop said. "We've established that. I'm Patrick Sullivan, Montana State Police. A family of four—two children included—was murdered on the highway out near where your ranger's killers were found. That's a lot of goddamn blood on the ground, Mr. Ruiz, and I understand that you are keeping the identities of our only witnesses a secret."

"That's not reasonable, Diego," Elmore said, piling on. "You can't tie our hands this way. Not and expect us to do our jobs."

The murdered family was news to Diego. He turned to Mary. "Did we know about additional killings?"

"No, sir."

"We just found out ourselves within the last fifteen, twenty minutes," Sullivan said. "It appears to have been a carjacking."

"Why do you say that?"

"They were dead on the street, but there was no vehicle nearby."

"Who were they?" Diego asked.

"We're still working on that," Sullivan replied. "The killer took all their identification and phones. We're hoping we can find them via their fingerprints. We're working on that now."

"Can you tell how long ago they were killed?" Diego asked.

"Not with any degree of accuracy. Not yet. It's been a while, though. The blood on the street had dried. Rigor had set in pretty solidly on the boy, was advancing on both parents. I give it two to three hours."

Diego put his briefcase down on the grass. "That's a long time to go undiscovered, isn't it?"

"It's a pretty remote area," Sullivan explained. "I'd be surprised if there were two dozen cars a day out that way."

"How far away are we from all of this?" Diego asked. "Distance wise, I mean?"

"Ten miles, give or take, from the site where Ranger Simonsen was killed," Elmore said.

"Four or five from the others," Sullivan said.

Diego pointed with his forehead at Sullivan. "Let's go to yours."

"Excuse me, Diego," Elmore said, reaching out to grab his boss's arm. "Are you sure that's a good idea? That's not the right message for the guys."

"I'm not interested in the messages I send to the guys," Diego said. "I'm interested in bringing justice to Ranger Simonsen's memory and vengeance to the people who took his life. You're welcome to come along, Mike."

"I've got to see to Pete," Elmore said. "Ranger Simonsen."

"I understand," Diego said. He turned to the cop. "Please take me where I need to go."

Out in this part of the country, every vehicle was large, and Trooper Sullivan's was no exception. The GMC Yukon sat higher than most, and most were damn high to begin with. Thank God for the pop-out step, or Diego would have had to crawl through the back door on his hands and knees. He grunted as he climbed aboard, as did Mary before Sullivan followed them. Up front, a young trooper was behind the wheel, ready to serve as driver.

The interior of the vehicle had been modified to accommodate the trappings of a mobile command post. In addition to fold-down jump seats for passengers, there were three workstations, each with a computer terminal and high-end communication gear.

"Are you in charge of this operation?" Diego asked as he took one of the jump seats. Mary Bauer took the other, while Sullivan sat at one of the workstations.

"For now," Sullivan said. "Though this kind of incident attracts lots of attention." He crossed his legs and set one elbow on the desk. "Look, Mr. Ruiz—"

"Call me Diego."

"Fine. Diego. What is this about you knowing who our killers are but not being able to tell anyone?"

"Before I get to that," Diego said, "and I promise I will, tell me details about the crime scene with the family."

"I did," Sullivan said. "Two dead adults, two dead kids, all in the street, all shot with what I consider a kind of expertise."

Diego cocked his head at the choice of words. "What does that mean? *A kind of expertise?*"

"Add coldness to it," Sullivan said. "Mom and dad were both shot at contact distance, one bullet each to the head. The girl was also shot in the head, but at greater distance. The boy apparently tried to run away, and he was taken with a shot between the shoulder blades. None of those shots are difficult to make, but they take a certain homicidal mindset, if you know what I mean."

"I know exactly what you mean," Diego said. In his mind, he tried to balance the actions described to him by Director Rivers and the callousness of these killings. "Is it your theory that the killer just hung out in the middle of the road and waited for a random victim? How did the killer even get there?"

"We found a horse nearby," Sullivan said. "Wandering and munching. He was saddled and shod. The freeze brand on his shoulder matched the one on another horse we found near the quadruple murder in the woods. Jesus, Diego. I've only investigated thirteen murders in my entire career, and now I've got eight more. So, now it's your turn. Tell me about these killers."

"You're mischaracterizing them," Diego said. "At least that's what I have been told from the very highest levels."

"What does *very highest levels* mean?"

"Exactly what it sounds like," Diego said. "And beyond that, I can't tell you anything. Not about the source, anyway, and if that is your focus, then we won't get very far in this discussion." He relayed the story of unnamed FBI agents who were fired on and who brought justice to the people who did the shooting.

"Holly Looney was not killed by those agents," Diego concluded. "That's what I'm told, and I'm sure you will do an independent investigation on that. I think you will also find that the dead men in camouflage were killed by weapons that are not present at the kill site."

Sullivan mulled over what he'd been told and seemed resigned to not knowing everything he wanted to know. "Why is this a federal case at all?" he asked.

"Apparently, it's not," Diego said. "Have you been contacted by the feds to take over any elements?"

"No, but you said the shooters—the good guy shooters, if you'd like—are FBI agents."

"That's what I was told."

"By the unnamed highest authority."

"Yes."

Sullivan took off his Smoky Bear hat and placed it crown-down on the desk. "Just when you think you've seen everything, right?"

The Yukon slowed and stopped. "We're here," the driver said.

Sullivan led the way back outside. Dusk was approaching fast, and the temperature had dropped considerably, just during the drive. A trailer-mounted generator had been pulled in, and troopers were in the process of extending light poles to illuminate the scene. The bodies of the dead family still lay where they had fallen, but they had been covered with blue tarps.

"Do you want to look at the bodies?" Sullivan asked.

"I see more than I care to already. If there's not a specific reason to get closer, I'm fine with staying back." He looked back at his chief of staff. "You okay, Mary?"

"I've seen nasty before," she said. "Don't worry about me."

"Let me show you something interesting," Sullivan said. "I think this helps explain what might have happened out here."

Diego pulled his leather jacket tighter as he followed the trooper around the active part of the crime scene and farther up the road, where a second generator was being set up.

"Is this where the big shoot-out happened?" Diego asked.

"Not quite, but close," Sullivan said. "I think I know *why* the family was killed."

Sullivan led them to the edge of the roadway, and then stopped. "See the tire tracks?" he asked.

Once he was looking for them, Diego clearly saw the imprints of tires in the gravel as they disappeared into the tree line."

"Somebody drive off the road?" Diego asked.

"Yes. But not the way you're thinking about it." Twenty yards in, they encountered the ass end of a horse trailer, whose ramp was still down. Crime scene technicians were doing what they do.

Sullivan explained, "I don't want to walk all the way up there, but there quite obviously used to be a vehicle attached to this thing. That vehicle is now gone, and I've got a lot of dead people on my hands."

Diego knew that he should be seeing a bigger picture, but it wasn't coming to him. "I'm not sure I follow."

Sullivan said, "I think it's clear—clear to me, anyway— that your good guy shooters stole the bad guy shooters' truck after they killed them. That left the killer on horseback without wheels."

"So, he hijacked the family of four and took their car."

"Or truck or whatever," Sullivan said. "That's a scenario that comes together very well in my head."

"Where are the horses now?" Mary asked.

"Tied up somewhere nearby," Sullivan said.

"You said they were freeze branded," she said.

"That's right." Freeze branding accomplished the same goal as traditional branding, but absent the flames and scarring. When a super-cooled branding iron was placed on the animal's hair, the chill changed the chemistry of the hair, turning it white in perpetuity.

"Do you have a picture of the brand?"

Sullivan pulled it up on his phone and then complied with Diego's and Mary's requests to text the image to them.

"Same brand on both horses?" Diego asked.

"Yessir."

"Those are traceable, aren't they?"

Mary said, "If a rancher cares enough about his herd to brand them, then he's registered the brand somewhere. The trick is knowing where to look."

Sullivan offered, "Assuming the license plate on the trailer is legit, it comes from Utah. That might help."

Mary got close enough to the trailer to earn a rebuke from one of the techs. "Okay," she said to the tech. "If you don't want me to get closer, do me a favor and shine your light up there into the opening. Into the area where the horses go."

The tech did as he was asked, shining the beam from one corner to the next.

"What are we learning, Mary?" Diego asked.

She said, "The license plate isn't going to help. I mean, I guess it can't hurt to follow it up, but you're not going to get useful results. This thing is a rental. I'd bet a year's salary on it. Maybe stolen, but that would be easy enough to check, right, Trooper Sullivan?"

"It's easy to check for reports of stolen horse trailers," Sullivan replied, "but what makes you so sure it's rented or stolen?"

"The condition of it," she said. "Look how beat up it

is on the inside. There's shit stains and piss stains that are as old as the trailer itself. That freeze brand is pretty elaborate, and those can be expensive to design." She shifted her attention to Sullivan. "Are the horses in pretty good shape? Well cared for?"

"They seem to be," Sullivan said. "I'm no vet, but I've been around horses my whole life."

"Can I see them?"

"One of them, anyway." Sullivan pointed back to the area where the bodies lay covered. "She's over there."

The walk took less than two minutes. A jet black saddled mare stood contentedly next to the tree she'd been tied to.

Mary patted the beast's nose and said something that Diego didn't catch. She ran her hand across the mare's shoulder. "I've been a rancher, a rancher's kid, and a rancher's grandkid," she said. "This is a strong horse. Well cared for. The tack is real quality. Not only are we likely to find that these horses come from a ranch, I'm willing to bet that the ranch is bigger than little. The owner has money."

Sullivan and Diego both waited for more.

"I don't know who he is," Mary said with a chuckle. "If that's what you're waiting for."

"So, what's the connection?" Sullivan asked. "These guys do not look like ranch hands to me."

"They were professional killers," Diego said. "I thought I told you that already."

"Hired to kill FBI agents?" Sullivan asked.

"That's what we're being asked to believe," Diego confirmed.

"Sounds like you're not buying it," Sullivan said.

"It *should* sound like I don't *care*. What I do care about is the same thing that you care about. That these guys killed my ranger and a bunch of innocents."

"And that one of them is still out there," Sullivan said.

"If we can figure out what kind of car or truck the dead family was driving, you could set up roadblocks, couldn't you?" Mary asked.

"Even in the days of full staffing, that would be difficult," Sullivan said. "Even if we knew what we were looking for, which we don't. Not yet, anyway. Now, though, in these days of reduced funding and bureaucratic hand-tying, we've bled so much personnel that we're lucky we can respond to emergency calls. This operation right here has stripped the area clean of cops."

"Do you mind if I do a little detective work? Mary asked.

Sullivan's eyes narrowed. "What do you have in mind?"

She pointed back toward the Yukon they'd arrived in. "If I can have access to one of those computers for a few minutes, I think I could trace down that brand. It'd give you a place to start, anyway."

CHAPTER 22

Gail's office sat outside the Cave in the Fishbowl—the large area on the third floor of the firehouse that served as the offices for Security Solutions. More a cubical with a door than a proper office, it gave her the level of privacy she needed for most duties of the day, but if she needed to deal with personnel or confidential matters, she would step into the conference room.

Her official job at the company was to run the overt side of the business, making sure that their team of investigators stayed on track with their assignments and that their clients were happy.

Word traveled quickly in a town the size of Fisherman's Cove, so everyone knew about her shoot-out earlier in the day. All were concerned, and the more senior investigators—drawn mostly from the ranks of medically discharged veterans, Jonathan's preferred source for job candidates—vowed to provide her with protection whenever and wherever she needed it.

A few of the millennial hires, on the other hand, were frightened about their own safety. Was this an attack on

Gail and Venice (the answer they wanted to hear) or an attack on the company in general? Gail assured them that if anyone was likely to die, it was herself. That seemed to make them happy.

Gail was neck-deep in a report from an investigation ordered by one Fortune 500 company into the roots of another Fortune 500 company's overhead rates. The overriding question being, how was the company under investigation able to so consistently undercut the bids of Security Solutions' client?

Jonathan had started Security Solutions primarily as a cover for the covert rescue operations that he preferred, but his commitment to using questionable means to deliver excellent results had earned the company the kind of reputation that justified outrageous hourly rates.

In the report that Gail was reviewing, she couldn't see how the evidence presented could justify the investigator's conclusions. Even when dealing with some of the most famous CEOs on the planet—Jonathan would not allow the company to deal with underlings—it was important to assume an eighth-grade reading level for a client.

Gail preferred manual editing with a red pencil over the editing functions on the computer screen. She spent enough time staring into a light bulb, thank you very much. There was something satisfying about handling paper and holding a writing instrument in her fingers.

She'd just begun to see the logical thread beginning to emerge from the narrative when commotion in the Fishbowl pulled her attention away.

"You can't be here!" She recognized the voice of Charlie Keeling, the on-duty guard stationed at the security door leading to the Cave, the superconfidential offices of the covert side of the business.

"I want to see my mother! I have information that she needs to see. She won't answer my texts or phone calls!"

Oh, Lord, Gail thought. She wasn't sure how much more adolescent angst she could handle.

She pushed away from her desk and pulled her door open. Looking across the sea of cubicles, she saw a dozen people standing at their desks to get a look at what was going on.

"You can't keep me away from seeing my own mother!" Roman proclaimed.

"I'm sorry, but that's exactly what my job is," Charlie replied. He looked vaguely amused, but also uncomfortable at the attention.

Roman tried to move past the guard to get to the door, and something changed in Charlie's demeanor. He moved to block the boy, but he was *this close* to putting his hands on the kid. Not that it wouldn't have been justified, but it would have been ugly.

"Roman!" Gail shouted from her door. She started toward the scuffle. "Stop that right now."

"But Mom won't—"

The security door opened up to reveal a *very* pissed off Venice.

"Why won't you answer my texts?" Roman demanded. "They're important!"

Venice's jaw set tight, her lips a thin line. She grabbed the front of her son's shirt, pulled him across the threshold, and disappeared into the Cave.

Charlie was about to close the security door when Gail

approached. "Not yet," she said. Then, before crossing the threshold herself, she turned back to the staring faces in the Fishbowl. "Sorry, everyone. He's fourteen. That should explain everything."

Her comment drew the laughter she was hoping for, but she knew there would be consequences sooner rather than later. It was a chafing point, particularly among the younger employees, that secret things happened behind closed doors. The fact that a kid would have access to a view that was denied to them was sure to raise discontent.

By the time Gail crossed into the Cave, Venice was marching Roman past the War Room and into her office. Gail followed.

"You said I was part of the team!" Roman nearly shouted as they disappeared into Venice's space.

The offices back here reflected the personalities of their occupants. Ironically, Boxers' office was the smallest of the three because he rarely spent time in it. Jonathan's was the largest by far, and it sported a fireplace, a view of the marina, and a decorating aesthetic that leaned toward the leather and dark wood of an exclusive club room.

Venice's tastes tilted heavily into chrome-and-glass modern. Very functional but also very stylish. When Gail entered, Venice was directing Roman to one of the leather-sling desk chairs at the front of her desk, while she took the other one.

Gail didn't ask permission before she helped herself to a rarely used hardback chair in the far corner.

Roman looked confused by the surroundings.

Venice said, "Before we talk about what's on your

mind, you need to know that there are rules that everyone needs to follow around here."

Roman rolled his eyes.

"Don't you do that," Venice said.

Gail didn't have the patience for witnessing another family quarrel. "I witnessed every word of that disgusting scene out there," she said.

"I have more information with Mateo. I've been trying to get it to Mom, but she keeps ignoring my texts."

"Well, you know what, Roman?" Venice said. "I've been trying to get people to answer my phone calls, too. Sometimes, the world is busy and we all have to wait our turn."

"Even if Mateo contacted his uncle about the people who tried to kill you screwing it up?" He fired the question like a missile.

It was not what Gail had been expecting.

"The point remains," Venice said.

Gail said, "Roman, remember what we talked about before regarding the secrets of what goes on in here? The people out in the Fishbowl don't know what we do in here. *Nobody* knows what we do in here. It needs to stay that way. Do you understand?"

"Yes, I understand." Then, to his mother: "Why didn't you answer my texts and emails?"

"Because we all have many things to do, and each of them can be done only one at a time," Venice said. "Now, what do you have?"

"Pull up the spyware on Mateo's computer," Roman said. "I've been watching it to see what he would do after we had our talk."

Venice moved to her chair behind her desk and the

others followed, gathering behind her. She went through the login procedure, and there they were, a flurry of emails, all in Spanish, that spanned less than a half hour. They were over an hour old.

"Wouldn't it be easier to do this in the conference room we just passed?" Roman asked.

"You're not that deep a part of the team yet," Gail said. The War Room had too much proprietary technology to trust any of it to a smart fourteen-year-old.

"I presume that MachoMan is Mateo?" Venice said.

"Right. And XTXX4 is his uncle. At least that's what I think."

Gail was impressed that he was weighting his conclusion with what he knew to be true and what he only suspected.

Venice famously hated reading email strings from the bottom up, so she flipped it on her screen to read from top to bottom. Then she highlighted the whole thing and ran it through a translation software.

MachoMan: "uncle a are you there?"
XTXX4: "Boy, I told you not to contact me this way."
MachoMan: "it is important. everything went wrong. Everybody here is still okay but the people you sent are not."
XTXX4: "Are not what?"
MachoMan: "ok. they are not ok they are dead"

Venice noted that nearly two minutes passed with the uncle saying nothing. "You think he's consulting his friends in that time?" she asked.

No one answered her. It was a rhetorical question,
anyway.

XTXX4: "Where do you get your information on
this?"
MachoMan: "i saw the targets still alive they say they
killed the killers."
XTXX4: "Erase this email immediately. Do not contact
me about this ever again."

"Is Uncle A who I think it is?" Gail asked. She knew
that Venice would understand the connection to
Antonio Filho.
"Coincidences don't happen, remember?" she said.
"What are you talking about?" Roman asked.
"Did Mateo ever tell you the name of his uncle?"
Venice asked.
"No. I never asked."
"That's okay," Venice said. "I think I can figure this out."
Then she went into what Digger called Venice Land,
where her fingers started flying across the keyboard and
the content on her screen became an indecipherable col-
lection of letters, numbers, and punctuation.
"Are you typing code?" Roman asked. He seemed gen-
uinely shocked.
Gail beckoned him to join her back in the visitors'
chairs. "I told you before that your mother has some wild
talents. This is her in action. Don't try to interrupt her
because she won't hear you."
"I didn't know she was into computers that much,"
Roman said.
"*Into computers* doesn't touch it," Gail said. She in-

haled deeply and let it go as a silent whistle. This scenario was all wrong, and she knew it. Roman was too young to know the ins and outs of any of their investigative protocols, let alone the details of the covert side, but that genie was already out of the bottle.

This moment became inevitable the instant Digger plucked Roman and his girlfriend out of harm's way in Mexico.

"Roman, I need you to listen carefully to me." She turned in her chair and took his hand in hers. "The floodgates have opened on things that you should not know."

"We've already talked about that," Roman said.

"Yet there you were, pounding on the door. That is totally unacceptable."

"Okay." His frustration was showing. He didn't like being spoken to this way.

"Roman, this is really important. I want you to listen carefully and then work very hard to pretend you never heard any of it. Just lose all the attitude and listen."

She waited for an annoyed response but was pleased that it didn't come.

"Imagine that you found out that the people closest to you were spies and that the work they did was critically important for America, but that that same work put them in serious danger every day."

"Mom's a spy?"

"No, she's not a spy. It's kind of like that, but not that exactly. Mr. Jonathan and Mr. Boxers and your mom and I often are hired to do things that technically are illegal, but still necessary. If our secrets leak out—as they have in this case, to be perfectly honest—violence is likely to follow."

"Is that what happened today?"

"Yes." She squeezed his hand harder. "And this is the hard part to tell you, and it's going to be even harder for you to hear. Your mom and I were almost shot today because you told the people in Mexico about Mr. Jonathan. I don't know what you said, and the words are not important, but if you're going to be in on the big secret, you need to be all the way in. You need to know that actions have consequences."

"What else could I have done?" Roman asked. His voice was raised, but Venice seemed still to be totally absorbed in her virtual world.

"Settle down," Gail said. "This isn't about casting blame or saying that anything is anybody's fault. There probably wasn't anything you could have done differently, but you need to own the fact that whatever words you spoke have had the effect of putting everyone in serious danger."

He looked horrified. Appropriately so, Gail thought.

"I told you this would be hard to hear," she went on. "You have nothing to apologize for. What happened, happened, and we're working very hard to mitigate the damage. I know you like the idea of being on the inside of the secret, but this is the burden that comes with it.

"If your parents—your mom, in this case—*were* a part of a spy network, it would fall upon you to limit what you say to people and monitor your actions to make sure not to attract undue attention. That's the situation here. And it will always be the situation here."

"But what if—"

Gail held up her palm for silence. "Keeping important

secrets is more than keeping your mouth shut and not telling people things. It's *much* more than that."

Roman's demeanor had changed. He seemed to sense the gravity of what he was hearing. "I don't think I understand."

Gail knew she wasn't doing a very good job of explaining. "Maybe this will help. When you got kidnapped, I guess you know that you were changed forever, right?"

He nodded. His eyes reddened.

"That was a very traumatic event with an equally traumatic end, although the end was ultimately a happy one."

"Mr. Jonathan and Mr. Boxers killed people."

"I know."

"I mean, they just killed. It didn't bother them or anything."

"Mr. Jonathan and Mr. Boxers were both very elite soldiers," Gail explained. "The jobs they did then and, as you've seen, the jobs they do now put them into conflict with some very bad people. Can you think of a better way for them to have settled the situation on the coast?"

He looked down, shook his head.

"They have nothing to apologize for, either," Gail said. "None of us do."

"Have you killed people, too?"

"None of us have anything to apologize for," Gail repeated. She left it to him to draw his own conclusions.

They fell silent as Venice's fingers on the keyboard provided percussion.

"This is a lot, I know," Gail said. "You have some very adult responsibilities on your shoulders now. I don't know if it's unfair, but I know it's more of a burden than you wanted. It's certainly more than you should have, but there you go."

"I got it!" Venice proclaimed.

Gail felt genuine relief to be able to talk about something else. She let go of Roman's hand, and together they rose and resumed their places behind Venice.

"I was able to use the metadata to track Uncle A's email address back to its source. XTXX4 lives in a tiny village in the hinterlands of . . . wait for it . . ."

"Colombia," Gail said.

"Bingo," Venice said.

Venice's phone dinged, and the sound seemed to startle her. "You two go around to the other side of the desk. Let me read this."

Roman complied without argument, and together he and Gail watched as Venice read whatever had popped up on her screen.

"Bad news?" Roman asked. Clearly, it was.

"I need you both to leave me alone for bit," Venice said. "Roman, please go back to your dormitory." She made a point of smiling. "And thank you for the update. You're right, that was very important information."

To Gail's ear, the compliment sounded patronizing, but Roman didn't seem to take it that way. She let the boy leave and turned back to Venice. "What is it?"

"I just got an update from ICIS," Venice said. The Interstate Crime Information System was a post-9/11 construct that allowed law enforcement agencies to track investigations in real time. When the system caught similarities between crime scenarios, it would alert investigators. Not available to civilians, the ICIS network—which used to be pronounced "EYE-sis" before the Islamic State assholes claimed the acronym for their own—had been one of Venice's first important hacks.

"I need to reach out to Digger right away."

Gail's phone rang. She glanced at the caller ID and frowned when she saw it was Chief Kramer. "I need to take this," she said. She pressed the connect button and brought the phone to her ear. "Hi, Doug. I thought we'd covered everything—"

"This is new," he said. "Your house is on fire, Gail."

CHAPTER 23

Jonathan answered on the first ring. "Go ahead, Mother Hen. You're on speaker. What've you got?"

"One of the shooters you dealt with out there is still alive," Venice said. "He killed a family of four to steal their car."

"How do you know this?"

"I've been monitoring ICIS," she said. "The family isn't yet identified, but the Montana State Police and the Fish, Wildlife and Parks Department have been making inquiries into the trailer that they found at the scene of the shooting. That's likely to bring them to the vehicle you're driving."

"Well, shit," Jonathan said. "What's this about the trailer?"

"Apparently, the police think that the horse trailer was a rental," Venice explained. "The good news is that one of the stops our friends made while they were driving around town was to an equipment rental place. The good news there is I have business and home addresses for the owners, in case you want to chat with them."

"I doubt they showed much of their hand," Jonathan said. "But it's worth reaching out to them."

"And when we're done, I can shop the neighborhood for a new vehicle," Boxers said.

"That's great work, Mother Hen," Jonathan said.

"There's more." Venice told him about the conversation with Roman and the emails involving Uncle A. "I think we're about eighty percent—maybe ninety—that this is the work of Antonio Filho."

"Have you figured out the McCloud connection yet?" Jonathan asked.

"Not yet," Venice said. "But it's on my list."

"Dig deep," Jonathan said. "Find out which politicians he supports and why he would be willing to extend himself this far for the benefit of a drug dealer. If we take Roman's friend at his word and McCloud is our man, he's got some serious clout."

"There's one more thing," Venice said.

"Oh, good God."

"This one's big. Gunslinger just got word that her house is on fire."

"Oh, my God," Jonathan said. "What happened?"

"We don't know yet. She just left to check it out."

Jonathan's heart skipped a beat. "No!" he said. "Call her back."

"Her house is burning," Venice repeated. "She's not going to not go there to see it."

"Don't you get it?" Jonathan asked. "This could be a ruse to pull her out of the security of the office and the RezHouse compound. This could be a way to get to her."

"She didn't go alone," Venice said. "Chief Kramer came and got her."

That took some of the wind out of his sails. Settled him some. "Keep on top of her."

"I can only do so much at the same time, Scorpion. What is your next step, by the way?"

"Send the addresses for this rental place for the trailer." Jonathan said. "I'll start there, and then I believe we're going to knock on Victor McCloud's door and get to know him."

CHAPTER 24

Doug Kramer's buggy was still two blocks away when Gail first caught sight of the orange glow in the distance, punctuated by pulsating strobes and sweeping light streams from the fire department vehicles that had only just begun to stream water. As he approached, he added his blue strobes to the red-and-white display of the fire vehicles. Firefighters scrambled from their trucks to the hose beds, dragging lines across the street and up her lawn.

Gail's house was just another like so many along Water Street, facing the river and fronted by sixty feet of lawn. Doug Kramer had barely pulled to a stop when she opened her door and climbed out into the chilly night.

"Wait for me," Doug said as he climbed out of the driver's door. "I don't want you wandering far. This could be a ruse to pull you out."

Gail had already thought of that but decided that for the moment, she didn't care. If the bad guys were stupid enough to take a shot at her in front of all these people, then at least they'd get caught and she wouldn't have died in vain. "Keep up," she said to Kramer.

As she approached her house, still twenty-five yards away, a *very* young man wearing yellow turnout gear and a red helmet moved to intercept her, his arms outspread. "I'm sorry, ma'am, you have to stay back."

"That's my house," she said.

"I'm sorry, but I can't let you get any closer."

"Fair enough," she said, and she pushed past him.

"Hey, I said—"

"I heard you. You can't let me, but I never asked permission."

As she took her next steps, she heard the kid moving closer and she whirled on him. "I'm happy to fight you," she said. "It's a bad night and getting worse. What happens next is all on you."

Chief Kramer stepped in. "Okay, stop," he said. "She's with me," he said to the young firefighter, who she thought looked a little relieved.

As they moved closer to the house, Kramer said to Gail, "Oh, shit, this looks bad." One pumper was nosed into a hydrant, connected by a water-charged soft sleeve to the steamer outlet. Hoses ran from that pumper, which looked like a sow servicing her piglets, to two other fire trucks whose crews had pulled the hand lines from their beds and were in the process of deploying them to the fire.

As Gail got close enough, she could see that one crew had thrown ladders to the roof of the front porch, while another was humping hose around to the black side—the rear side—of her house.

Fire was blowing out of the front windows, on either side of the front door. Those were her living room and dining room. On an impulse, she took off at a run, following the crew that was crossing to the back. On her way, she passed the exterior side wall of her living room on her left, the heat from which caused her to arc away a few steps, and then the first floor powder room, before she hooked a left at the back corner and nearly stumbled over the attacking fire crew, which was wrestling with hoses and donning their gloves and face pieces for their air packs.

Keeping far enough away not to interfere, she continued with her circle of the house. The conclusion of her tour proved to her that the kitchen, garage, mud room, and first floor guest room were all uninvolved in the blaze. The dining room, on the other hand, on the opposite side of the front door from the immolating living room, was fully involved in fire.

When she emerged at the front of the house, she found herself squarely in the middle of the firefighting activities— the very place that the teenager in the red hat was afraid that she would venture into. On the other side of the bedlam, Doug Kramer was pacing the sidewalk, obviously looking for her.

She waved, got a wave in return, and walked his way. He looked angry, but she didn't give him a chance to say anything. "This fire is arson," she declared.

Kramer took the news without emotion. "A little soon to draw a conclusion," he said.

"No, it's not," she said. "I just walked all the way around the house."

"I noticed."

"There is literally nothing in those front rooms that could have started the fire. The kitchen isn't burning— not yet, anyway—and neither is the garage. I don't have a fireplace up front. I don't have candles up front. That had to be started by an incendiary device of some sort."

Kramer blinked his response.

"You look like you don't believe me," Gail said.

"I don't believe one way or the other," he said. "Once the fire is out, there'll be an investigation, and then we'll know." He stuffed his thumbs into the top of his Sam Browne belt. "This is a terrible thing, Gail. A terrible day."

Gail heard his words and appreciated the sentiment, but she wasn't interested in his sympathy or even his empathy. She wanted to catch and hurt the sonofabitch who did this to her. Who was *doing these things* to her and to her friends.

"We've got bad people in this town, Doug. Not the ones who live here, but the ones who have invaded."

"I know y'all have been trying to connect the dots as to who these asshats might be," Kramer said. "What have you come up with?"

"Nothing worth sharing," Gail said. This was the dilemma they always faced with the work they did. Even as they drew conclusions, their hands were tied when it came to sharing those conclusions with the police. To share conclusions meant sharing means and methods, and that opened too many doors that needed to remain closed.

"What does that mean?" Kramer asked.

Gail turned it around. "What have your officers been able to find out?"

She listened as the chief talked about the identity of the known shooter, but he told her that didn't yet have information on his background. "Uncle Sam isn't always as fast as we'd like him to be," Kramer finished.

That's because you have to follow the rules, Gail thought. "What about the guys who ran Mama off the road?" she asked.

"We've been looking around, asking a lot of questions. You know, canvassing the area, but we haven't found anyone who can give us anything useful."

"No tire tracks or anything?"

Kramer hiked his shoulders to his ears. "It's a public road," he said. "We've got hundreds of potential tracks."

So, they had nothing.

Gail knew in her heart that the people who tried to kill Mama were the same ones who set fire to her house. She knew from Roman and his friend that the plan was to hurt the Security Solutions team and to hurt them badly.

As she watched her life being reduced to ash and smoke, she felt that the bad guys were winning the battle. At least for now.

Somewhere out there in the night, bad guys were lying in wait for their next opportunity.

Gail couldn't imagine that this fire would satisfy their bloodlust. If it started with a desire to kill, it wouldn't be sated by a fire. Not unless they thought that she was inside the building when they started it, and that wasn't reasonably the case because it was too early for most normal adults to be in bed.

She considered that perhaps they'd thought she'd been in the front room watching television, but she dismissed the thought. All of her lights had been out.

No, this was just the beginning of something else.

This really was the trap that everyone was concerned

it might be. Whoever the bad guys were, she was willing to bet now that the fire was the bait for a larger trap.

But with all the people around, it still seemed an unlikely opportunity to take a shot at her.

Maybe they wanted to get her out of the safety of the firehouse and into the open to catch her in transit. They wouldn't have anticipated that she'd commute with the chief, would they?

As the firefighters set up floodlights to illuminate the scene, Gail felt suddenly more exposed that she'd been before. Not only was she brightly lit, the night beyond the lights became invisible, rendered opaque in the glare.

"I'm going to step back a little," she told Kramer.

"Do you need a ride back to the office?"

"I'm not going anywhere yet," she said. "I just feel too much in the way here." She didn't know why she didn't say anything about the lights.

As she fell back into the shadows, on the far side of the closest fire truck, she pressed her elbow against the grip of her Glock for reassurance and turned her back to the fireground to scan the gathering crowd.

In a town so small, it would be nice to think that everyone knew each other on sight, but that wasn't the case here in Fisherman's Cove. Digger knew everyone, she supposed, but he had grown up here. It was the nature of this town like so many others of its size that to be a new arrival was to be an outsider. It didn't help that the work she did offered few opportunities to interact with the locals beyond buying sundries in their shops. She didn't have kids for other people's kids to play with, and her work at Security Solutions consumed pretty much all of her available free time.

Of the fifteen or twenty locals who had gathered to witness the spectacle, a crowd that was growing with each passing moment, she did recognize a few faces, but even their features were marred and twisted in the bizarre show of the emergency lights. For the most part, she saw only strangers. They watched the firefighters at work, pointing and talking among themselves. No one looked back at Gail, their eyes focused exclusively on the action. When she did make eye contact with a neighbor she recognized, the neighbor looked away and said something to the man standing next to her. Then he looked at Gail and looked away.

Gail wasn't sure what she was searching for as she scanned the faces, but she was confident that the monster responsible for her share of this very bad day was out there. He'd have to be. To set a fire and walk away would be like causing an itch and refusing to scratch it.

So, which one was he?

And she knew it was a he. Two men, actually, because that's what Mama saw as she was trapped inside her wrecked vehicle.

But they wouldn't stand together, would they? That would be foolish. Two strangers watching a catastrophe in progress would draw too many questions.

So, what was their plan? They wanted to hurt her. To kill her probably, now that she'd off'd their cohort. Whatever it was, she was confident she could beat them. She'd already done it once. How difficult could it be to do it again?

She took two steps farther away from the pumper and stopped. If someone were watching her, they'd react to this, right? They'd think that she was in motion, and they would do something unusual. Something suspicious.

That's what she figured, anyway.

But they wouldn't stand in the wash of the lights, would they? They'd want to hang back in the shadows, right? They'd want to watch yet still be invisible.

Gail changed her focus. There were, indeed, silhouettes back there beyond the ring of lights. Beyond them, the masts of the commercial fishing boats bobbed and waved in their berths, jostled by the rolling waves as they came ashore.

Keeping her right hand free, just in case, she cupped her left palm across her eyebrows in an effort to limit the glare even more.

The first silhouettes that attracted her turned out to be kids, teenagers no doubt drawn to the excitement. To them, she was invisible. Another watcher took a pull on a cigar, marking his place in the world with the glowing red cherry of his ash.

"So where are you?" she whispered. "If we're going to do this thing, let's do it here and now."

Movement beyond Cigar Man caught her attention for no other reason than the fact of the movement. She could make out the silhouette of a man but no real detail. He appeared to be wearing a down vest, and he was backing away from the rest of the crowd. He wasn't in a hurry, but he'd chosen to walk backward through the grass toward the walkway that led down to the marina.

Gail cast a glance back at the fireground, hoping to get Kramer's attention, but he was engaged in a discussion with a firefighter in a white coat and a white helmet, what she assumed was the mantle of command. She didn't want to yell because she had nothing to yell about.

In the five seconds that her head was turned, her person of interest had turned around and was walking normally down the slope that led to the water.

She checked that the Glock had not somehow magically disappeared, and she followed.

The man wasn't running by any means, but he was walking with focus. Determination.

"Excuse me!" she called. It wasn't loud. She intentionally kept her tone light, nondemanding.

The man kept walking. Same pace. Gail quickened hers.

"Excuse me!" she called again. "If you don't mind, I have a question I'd like to ask you."

The man started to run.

"Shit." Gail looked back once more for reinforcements, but she was on her own. She took off after him.

The guy was fast. By the time Gail got her ass in gear, he'd picked up an easy fifty-yard lead, and it was opening. Gail had never been much of a runner—PT had been the most miserable part of her training at the FBI Academy—and severe injuries a while back had left her dependent on a cane for a long time. She'd since ditched the cane, but the doctors assured her that her hip and her back would never be quite the same.

But that didn't mean she couldn't run. Even as the man gained distance on her, she never lost sight of him as he reached the gate of the closed marina and scaled the chain-link fence. She watched as he dropped to the other side and then disappeared down the second pier to her left.

As she ran, Gail pulled her Bluetooth transceiver from the pocket of her jeans, stuck it in her ear, then punched a speed-dial number on her phone. The other side rang twice as she arrived at the fence and started to climb.

"Hey, Gail," Venice said. "How bad is it?"

"I think I found the shooters," she said as she started to climb. "Call nine-one-one and get the police down here. Before you do that, though, pull up the security camera feed for the commercial side of the Cove marina."

"What are you doing now?" Venice asked. Clearly, she could hear something in Gail's voice. The effort of the climb, perhaps?

"I'm going after them," she said. "I can't let them get away."

"Suppose it's a trap?"

"I'm almost certain that's exactly what it is," Gail said. "That's why I want your spying eyes watching what's going on."

"Come on, Gail, wait for backup."

"I'll stay on the line," she said. "You can hear everything, and even make a recording, if you'd like."

The old cliché was one hundred percent true in Gail's experience: When seconds counted, the police were only minutes away. Trap or no trap, these guys—well, one of them, anyway, had put his back against the water, leaving himself an easy target until he thought of a way out.

If this was a getaway plan, then they wouldn't have gone through the effort to lure her in. On the other hand, if this *was* a getaway plan and she didn't follow, they'd, well, get away.

It had been a long time since Gail had climbed anything as challenging as a fence, and it proved to be more awkward than she'd anticipated. The toes of her shoes fit into the diamond shapes formed by the links, but the rusty surface of the metal tore at her fingers. Halfway up, essentially dangling in the middle of the fence, she realized what an appetizing target she would make if that were someone's plan.

She quickened her pace on the climb. When she got to the top, she thought, *Screw it,* and she rolled over the top rail, tightening her gut muscles against the points of the wire links. From there, she changed her grip to that of a chin-up and lowered herself to the other side.

Dropping to a low crouch, she drew her Glock and kept it close to her chest at low-ready. She remained motionless for a conscious five-count to steady her heartbeat and take in the surroundings.

This part of the marina was reserved for commercial fishing vessels, mostly shrimp trawlers to Gail's eye, but she was the first to admit that she didn't know one type of ship from another. The vessels were lined up nose to tail on each side of their respective piers. In between, the wide docks that would be teeming with activity in a few hours were abandoned. Each was dimly illuminated by a single pole light that rose from the center of the dock, halfway down its length. The ships themselves were quasi-lit with what she thought of as utility lighting, but it offered no visible detail beyond a few feet.

The air stank of dead fish. The ships themselves sounded like they were moaning as they rolled in the water and their fenders rubbed against the piers and pilings. The overall effect was anything but soothing.

"Do you have the security feed up yet?" Gail whispered.

"Not yet," Venice replied. "I'm good, but not that good.

I'm calling the police at the same time. Please wait for them."

Gail thought through the challenge she was facing. The piers ran parallel to each other, each with only one way in and out. She'd seen her mystery man disappear down the one on her left—she could see now that it was marked Pier Four—so that meant he was still down there somewhere.

"Gail, did you hear me?"

"All communication from here on out will be one-way," Gail whispered. "I'm about the enter the beast's mouth."

"Please wait."

Gail wanted to ask again for the video feed, but that would mean speaking. Mother Hen was very good at what she did. If there was a feed to be found, she would find it.

It was time to move.

She brought her pistol up in a modified CAR stance— Center Axis Relock, a two-handed stance that kept the firearm close to her body—and advanced to the bow stem of the vessel closest to her on the right-hand edge of Pier Four. That was a lot of steel to use as cover.

Shifting the pistol and stance to her left hand, she kept her elbows close to her body as she peered with one eye and the muzzle around the point of the bow and down the length of the ship's starboard side. She was looking for any signs of a person. Any signs of danger.

If this was a trap, this space was a great place to spring it. Sooner or later, she would have to step into the open and present herself as a target. She wasn't a regular on the waterfront, so it was difficult to know what was out of order when she didn't know what things usually looked like. She wanted to see movements or shadows, but none presented themselves.

She shifted her aim to the port side of the ship on the opposite side of the dock and watched as it moved with the waves.

Could he have boarded a ship? she wondered.

She supposed it was possible. And if he'd done that, she faced a much greater challenge than she'd originally suspected. The vessels were large, and there were four of them where he, or they, could possibly be hiding.

If her suspicions were correct, he was lying in wait. To take a shot means to have a clear lane of fire.

And a stationary target.

It was time to move again.

Pilings lined both sides of the dock, rising five feet above the decking every ten yards or so. They weren't much for cover, but they could provide some level of concealment.

She shifted to a right-handed grip and dashed across the open space of the dock to the port side of the bow stem of the trawler on the other side of the pier. Part of her hoped that she would draw fire that would reveal the location of the bad guy, but most of her was damned relieved that nobody fired a shot.

She waited and watched for another ten-count.

"Police are on the way," Mother Hen said in her ear, making her jump nearly out of her skin.

"I also have the security feed up," Venice said. "I see

you hiding at the front of one of the ships. I'm looking for others, too."

Good to know, Gail thought.

"I'm going to move to the next piling," she whispered. Staying silent made less sense now that he'd seen her dashing out into the open. "Don't watch me. Watch everything else. Look for anything unusual."

"Just stay put," Venice said. "Please. The police—"

"—still aren't here," Gail said. "I'm moving."

She couldn't decide if the dimness of the light from the poles was a boon or a curse. They cast just enough light to create shadows, but not enough to reveal what lay behind them. She considered shooting out the bulbs, but it would be a tough shot to make, and without night vision, she wasn't sure that darkness for everyone was any kind of advantage for her.

Pressing away from the piling, she dashed for the next, staying low and doing her best to observe her surroundings as she moved. When she stopped, she crouched and scanned again.

"Are you sure that someone is there?" Venice asked in her ear. "I don't see anything at all, and the cameras have pretty much all angles covered."

In the distance, Gail could hear sirens approaching.

Maybe this was a stupid idea, after all. Maybe it was time to regroup and reinforce. Let the police—

She never heard or sensed the presence of the man who grabbed her. He appeared out of nowhere, and her first awareness of him was when a wet arm closed around her shins and pulled her legs out from under her. The sweeping motion was faster than she could react to, and she hit the edge of the dock hard, her right thigh slamming into the wood, and then she was falling.

The world turned wet and black as she tumbled into the river between the pier and the hull of the ship. She hadn't had time to take a breath before she was submerged, and instantly, she needed air. Craved it.

She tried to kick toward the surface, but something remained tightly wrapped around her legs at her knees. She struggled against it but had no leverage. The water tasted like petroleum.

When the grip shifted from her knees to her waist, she realized that she was in the grip of her attacker. He must have been hiding over the edge of the dock and then dragged her in.

A searing pain erupted in her thigh and then again in her gut.

She sensed a gout of warmth flood the cold water, and she knew she'd been hurt. Stabbed, maybe?

God, she needed to breathe.

Could she be dying tonight? Right here in her hometown?

Could the bad guys really come out on top?

No, they wouldn't.

Her gut hurt again. She swung her left fist in the darkness and connected with hair and a skull. The guy's head.

At that instant, she realized that she hadn't lost her grip on the Glock in her right hand.

But she soon would. She felt her strength ebbing.

She knew now that he'd cut her and that he'd done a job of it.

In the inky blackness, Gail tightly grasped some of

her attacker's hair with her left hand, and with her right, she pressed the muzzle of the pistol against the bone of his skull and pulled the trigger.

The impact of the bullet reverberated through her arm and up to her shoulder.

The grip around her body relaxed, but she pulled the trigger again. And again. On the fourth shot, that man's body broke away from his skull, leaving her with a fistful of hair and bone.

She tried to kick to the surface but realized that she wasn't sure where the surface was. She was entirely disoriented. Up and down, left and right meant nothing.

Her lungs were going to burst. She tasted blood in her sinuses and at the back of her throat.

This was the end. It didn't hurt as much as she always imagined it would.

CHAPTER 25

The houses in this part of Hailey, Idaho, were built more to withstand the weather swings than they were for aesthetics. A mishmash of one- and two-story construction, each featured the same center hall design.

Jonathan and Boxers were about to pay a visit to Marlene Trainor, the proprietor and owner of Bitterroot Equipment and Vehicle Rental. You had to admire an unambiguous company name.

Boxers slowed the Sequoia to a crawl as he passed by the address they were looking for. "The numbers are right," Jonathan said.

"I'll park around the corner," Boxers said. One of their standing security rules was never to leave a piece of evidence as large as an SUV in a spot where people might remember it if a conversation went sideways and memorable things happened. Besides, they weren't going to be driving away in this vehicle anyway.

Jonathan wished that they looked less like soldiers in their camouflaged hunting gear as they closed up the car and started back toward the corner. "Cover the back, okay?" Jonathan said. He had no reason to suspect that Marlene Trainor would want to bolt out her back door, but a little caution was always in order.

"On it," Big Guy said. "Are we doing badges tonight?"

"Yes," Jonathan said. "Wolverine won't like it, but I think it's the shortest route to where we want to get."

They turned on their radios and did a quick check. Everything was working just fine.

Two minutes later, Jonathan was walking up the short front walk to the door when his radio speaker popped. "I'm in position," Boxers said. "I can see them watching television. Two adults, male and female and two kids. A boy and a girl, I think, but it's hard to tell from this angle."

Jonathan keyed his mic. "I copy. I'm going to knock now."

Before making contact with the door, he looked around the neighborhood to see if they had drawn attention. A community this small tended to notice everything that might be out of order, and he didn't want to make trouble for the Trainor family if someone overheard that the FBI was dropping by for a chat.

If looky-loos were watching, they weren't making a show of it.

Jonathan knocked softly. Sometimes, if a confrontation was expected, it was best to hammer the door hard to knock people off their stride and make them feel uneasy. He wanted exactly the opposite to occur here.

He had his credentials case out of his pocket and already opened for presentation when the door opened to reveal a bear of a man, every bit of six-four, wearing a Paul Bunyan beard and a flannel shirt.

Jonathan held up his creds. "Is this the Trainor residence?"

The man glanced at the creds and then glared at Jonathan.

"I'm Special Agent Neil Bonner with the FBI," Jonathan lied. "I need to speak with Marlene Trainor on an urgent matter."

"You got a warrant?" the man asked.

"No, sir, it's—"

"Come back when you've got one." He closed the door.

From inside, Jonathan could hear raised voices. He keyed his mic. "What are you seeing, Big Guy?"

"Looks like Mama is pissed, and Daddy might be a little drunk. Do you need reinforcements up there?"

"He wants to see a warrant," Jonathan said. "I'm going to try the easy way one more time before I go the hard route."

Jonathan rapped on the door again, this time a little more forcefully, but still more friendly than angry. The knock ignited more arguing from inside, and now the kids' voices were involved.

This time, when the door opened, Paul Bunyan looked ready for a fight. "I told you—"

"Trust me when I tell you that you don't want me to get a warrant," Jonathan said. "I am here only to ask a few questions of Marlene Trainor. Are you Mr. Trainor?"

Paul Bunyan took a deep breath to speak, but Jonathan wouldn't let him.

"If you close the door on me again, I guarantee that I will open it and that every set of ears in this neighborhood will hear what I have to say. You, of course, will be in handcuffs to be charged with obstruction of justice, at the minimum, and I'm pretty sure just from your demeanor now that resisting arrest would be part of the package, too."

The man of the house looked dumbstruck.

"Or, you could let us in and we could have a brief chat and then we would leave. It's your call."

A stout woman of about thirty-five stepped into view behind the large man blocking the way. "Just let them in, Dan," she said. "You don't have to be such an asshole with people all the time."

Jonathan keyed his mic. "Come around front now," he said. Replying to the curious looks, he said, "Talking to my partner." He forced a smile that probably looked more like a grimace. "Are you her husband, Dan?"

The man glared.

"No, he's not my husband," Marlene said. She looked just like her driver's license photo. "He's my baby brother, and he thinks he's scary."

"I think he's kinda scary, too," Jonathan said. "Are you going to get him to step aside? Maybe put him on a leash?"

Dan puffed up at those words, causing Jonathan to wish that he'd worked harder at de-escalation. Attitudes all righted themselves, though, when Boxers lumbered up behind Jonathan and stood at the stoop with him.

"This is Special Agent Contata," Jonathan explained. "My partner. Now, waddaya say, Dan? Can we come in?"

Dan pivoted out of the entryway and stepped back to allow Jonathan and Boxers to enter.

"What's going on?" Marlene asked. Her hands were clasped under her chin. She looked nervous as she led them into the family room, with Dan trailing behind.

The children were young—ten and twelve, maybe—and were totally absorbed in a cartoon that seemed to be about penguins.

Jonathan said, "Um, is there someplace we can chat away from the children?"

Marlene seemed confused by the question, but then her head cleared. "Oh, of course," she said. "Bobby, Bernadette, go play in your rooms for a while."

The request prompted the chorus of objections, counterarguments, and a final decree, as happens in millions of living rooms every night at bedtime.

When the kids were gone, leaving just the four adults, Jonathan said, "Before we start, I need to know if you're going to behave yourself, Dan."

The big man glared, said nothing.

"Keep an eye on him, will you?" Jonathan said to Boxers.

"Happy to."

Jonathan turned his attention to Marlene. "Can we sit down, please? I promise you're not in trouble. No one here is in trouble. I just need some information from you."

Marlene gestured to a matching pair of pale blue recliners. Jonathan waited till she was seated before seating himself. Boxers and Dan were enjoying a staring contest just inside the doorway to the room.

"What do you need?" Marlene asked.

Jonathan pulled his phone from his pocket. "I hope these images don't upset you," he said, "but I need information about these men." He pulled up the photos he'd taken of the dead men's faces from the mountain and showed them to her. He kept the phone in his hand as he swept from one to the other.

Marlene gasped at the more graphic shots but kept it together.

"Do they look familiar to you?" Jonathan asked.

"Why are they wearing uniforms?" she asked.

"Hunter's camouflage. Stay with me." Jonathan switched to the security photos that Venice had sent him from the ATMs. "Here's a less upsetting picture of one of them."

Instant recognition. "He bought a horse trailer from me yesterday," she said. "Maybe the day before. Is he one of the dead bodies?"

"Yes, he is. What can you tell me about them?"

"What dead bodies?" Dan asked. He started to walk over for a look, but Boxers blocked his way.

"Let's let them chat in private," Big Guy said.

Marlene made a face and shrugged. "I can't tell you much, I don't think. I mean, they handed me money, and I sold them the trailer."

Jonathan recoiled. "They bought the trailer? Outright?"

"It was so old, and they paid me a ridiculous amount for it."

"How much?"

"Why do you need to know this?"

"You've seen the *after* pictures of these men," Jonathan said. "And I showed you a *before* picture. I think you can imagine why I would like some details."

"They paid me over eight thousand dollars."

Jonathan didn't know if that was a good price or a bad price for a horse trailer, irrespective of age, but he did know that eight thousand bucks was way more than what they'd withdrawn from the ATMs.

"Did they pay cash?"

"They did, but that's not unusual around here. Lots of people in this part of the world don't like to use credit. Or, they don't have credit to use."

"Had you seen them before?"

"No," she said. "And frankly, we don't get a lot of strangers in these parts—certainly not ones with that much money to throw around. What did they do to get in trouble?"

"I'm afraid I can't talk about that," Jonathan said. "Do you have any idea where they were from?"

"I only really spoke with one of them," Marlene said. "The one in the picture. He had an accent. Mexican, I think. From somewhere south of the border, anyway."

"Did they say what they were doing here? Just passing through? Staying locally? What they needed the trailer for?"

"I presumed they needed the trailer to haul horses," Marlene said with a sly smirk.

Duh.

"But for the rest, they weren't a talkative group, not at all. And the one I dealt with was kind of a one-syllable guy. He asked how much for the trailer, and then he handed me the money."

In the silence that followed, as Jonathan thought things through, Marlene grew uncomfortable. "Is there anything else?" she asked.

"Actually, yes," Jonathan said. "What can you tell me about Victor McCloud?"

"Nothing you can't find from everybody else in town,"

she said. "He's richer than God Himself, and he mostly keeps to himself."

"Do you like him?" Jonathan asked.

That drew a big laugh. "This is a small town, Agent Bonner, but it ain't that small. We Trainors don't hobnob with the likes of the McClouds. Call it different social circles."

"He's an asshole," Dan said. "He's tryin' to buy up this whole valley, and anybody gets in his way, he crushes 'em like a bug. Total shithead."

Marlene blushed. "Well, I try not to talk bad about people, but Dan's got that pretty much right. Nobody likes Victor McCloud. As I understand it, even his wife didn't like him. She ran off with a ranch hand, and Victor had them both killed."

Jonathan reared back in his seat. "Holy shit. Really? And you don't want to talk bad about him?"

"Everybody here knows it. Nobody who knows him is the least bit surprised, either."

"Why isn't he in jail?"

Marlene rolled her eyes and looked over to her brother. "You gotta love outsiders, don't ya?" she scoffed. "I already told you he's got all the money in the world. He's got plenty enough to buy off every politician and cop in the whole damn world. Sheriff Usage would hold his own mother still while McCloud shot her if that got him a few bucks into his reelection fund."

"Tell 'em about Joe Belkoski," Dan prompted.

Jonathan waited for it.

Marlene explained, "Sheriff Sinclair Usage thinks he's got a birthright to his badge, know what I mean? He's had it for near long as I can remember, and he don't tolerate people tryin' to take it away from him. Well, young Joe Belkoski decided that the time had come for a change, and last election, he threw his hat into the ring. He ran against the corruption and the favoritism and shit, promising to bring truth and honesty back into the county government."

"I'm guessing his plans didn't go all that well?" Jonathan said.

"You know what they say," Marlene said. "If you come at the king, you better by God kill him. Belkoski was young and naïve and enthusiastic, never done nothin' wrong in his whole life, 'cept maybe drinking a tall boy too many from time to time, but even that he hadn't done for a long time—since he announced his run for sheriff. Well, wouldn't you know it? Turns out that that boy was sellin' drugs out of his car."

"And this was a surprise to you, I assume?" Jonathan said. He wasn't entirely sure what the relevance of any of this was, but she was into it, and he thought it best to let her run with her story.

"Damn straight it was a surprise, because it was a goddamn lie. Joe Belkoski wouldn't do somethin' like that. His record was clean, and then, just when he's challenging the way things are run around here, he suddenly becomes a cartel man? There's no way he would do that, but during a traffic stop out on the highway, deputies found almost three kilos of cocaine in his truck. In the tool chest."

"Three kilos is a lot," Jonathan said.

"No shit. Well, care to guess which cops found it?"

"Sheriff Usage's boys?"

Marlene pointed a finger at Jonathan's nose. "Bingo. Spot on. And wouldn't you know it? They had a TV news crew with them when they made the stop. They recorded his arrest, handcuffs and everything. Joe Belkoski ain't seen sunshine in over a year as I understand it. They sent him to jail and put him in some special category where it's solitary confinement for twenty-three hours a day while he waits for his trial. If he gets convicted, he could get life without parole."

"That's a federal crime, not a local one," Jonathan observed. "The sheriff can't—"

"Sheriff Usage don't want nothin' to do with the prosecution of this case," Marlene said. "That'd be actual work, and he don't like to do any of that. He's more than happy to hand it over to the feds for them to take care of it. He was able to get the evidence that will put Joey away for the rest of his life, and that's all he really wants. He wants to send a message to the rest of us that we'd best not cross him."

Jonathan was confused. "Are you saying that federal authorities are part of a conspiracy to make sure that a local sheriff stays in power?"

Another laugh, and then she withdrew a bit. "I'm sorry if that insults you," she said.

"Cuts too close to the bone is more like it," Dan said.

Marlene continued, "Agent Bonner, I imagine you don't like thinkin' bad thoughts about your fellow feds, but y'all are as corrupt as any two-bit street hustler. What is it they say? Just follow the money."

The last thing that would insult Jonathan was stating the fact of government corruption, but he had a role to play here. Moreover, he didn't yet see what she was trying to explain to him. "That's the part I still don't get," he said. "If I follow the money trail, where does it begin and end?"

"With Victor McCloud," Marlene said, drawing a laugh from her brother. "He's the beginning and the end."

Jonathan decided to regroup and try again. "Okay, then, where's the middle? What's the path of corruption?"

Marlene looked annoyed that it wasn't as obvious to him as it clearly was to her.

"Are you gonna let me sit down?" Dan asked. Then before he got an answer, he said, "Oh, the hell with you. I'm sitting down."

Boxers shot Jonathan a look, and Jonathan showed that he didn't care. As Dan sat on the edge of the threadbare sofa, Boxers remained standing, blocking ingress and egress.

"Think about it," Marlene said. "As I understand it, drugs are expensive. Three kilos of drugs are *insanely* expensive. Am I right?"

Jonathan gave a subtle nod.

"Well, where does Sinclair Usage get that kind of money? To plant drugs in Joey Belkoski's car?"

"You're assuming it was planted," Jonathan said.

"Yes, I am, because, yes, it was. I know it and everybody knows it. That's the simple truth that no one can prove. I told you that Joey is naïve. Good hearted and hardworking. Those drugs were planted in his car. So, I ask you again, where would Usage get that kind of money to buy the drugs and plant them?"

"I know you're going to say Victor McCloud," Jonathan said. "But why would he do that? Why would he risk that much—financially and legally—to help the sheriff stay in office?"

"So the cops look the other way when McCloud kills his wife and her lover," Dan said. "They were both shot in

bed by some *unknown burglar*"—he used finger quotes—
"who still ain't been caught. Like this is Chicago goddamn
Illinois, with a killer on every corner."

"That's kind of a long burn, isn't it?" Jonathan said.
"Pretty wandering route to cover up killing his wife."

"That's just one example," Marlene said. "Sheriff Usage
runs interference for McCloud on pretty much anything
you can think of. Zoning regulations, criminal trespass
when McCloud grazes his cattle on other people's lands
without consequence, and then arresting the people who've
been trespassed when they raise a voice or a hand in protest.
It's sickening."

"That doesn't even get to the trucks," Dan said.

"What trucks are we talking about?" Jonathan asked.

"The ones that run up and down the road at all times
of the night—but only at night. Wakin' everybody up."

"Are the trucks significant?" Jonathan asked. "Do you
know what's in them?"

Dan said, "Nope, and nobody does. Word has it that he
don't use any common carriers. That means that he owns
every truck and pays every driver, and nobody around
here knows who any of them are. They always come in
on the same road, and then when they leave, they go all
kinds of different places."

"Is this part of Chaps N Spurs Overland Freight?"
Jonathan asked. "His shipping company?"

"That's what the trucks say," Dan said.

"So what do you think is going on?" Jonathan asked.

"I got no idea."

"Well, you seem pretty spun up," Jonathan said. "That
means you must have a theory."

"I think it has something to do with drugs," Marlene said. "I think he's doin' some kind of sellin' or distribution or whatever. I don't understand how that business works. But I think that's what it is."

"Why that?" Jonathan asked. "I mean, there are lots of crimes in the world. Even if we assume that Victor McCloud is a criminal, how do you come to drugs specifically?"

Marlene said, "For one, it answers the question about Joey Belkoski. It explains how Sheriff Usage got his hands on the drugs. He just called up his buddy on the big ranch and asked for a favor."

"That's a big favor," Jonathan said. "Three keys is a shit-ton of cocaine."

"Better than the alternative, ain't it?" Marlene asked. "Better than havin' an honest sheriff that you gotta kill."

Jonathan sensed that she was being deliberately overdramatic, and he let it go. There were many ways to deal with new crises other than murder. But her passion was convincing.

"He's got a warehouse on his property, too," Dan said.

This just kept getting deeper and deeper. "Filled with what?"

"Marlene and me both think it's filled with drugs."

"But you can't prove that?"

"Hell, no. Nobody's allowed on that property. I only know about the warehouse because that's what I've heard other people say."

"There are lots and lots of items that could potentially be stored in a warehouse," Jonathan said. "It doesn't have to be drugs."

"You asked," Dan said.

"And I go back to Joey Belkoski," Marlene said. "It's the only thing that makes sense."

"And the federal connection?" Boxers asked from the doorway.

"Follow the money again," Marlene said. "Victor McCloud is a big contributor to every politician he wants to own. Big as in huge."

Then Jonathan saw it. And he knew they were right.

The decades-long so-called war on drugs—much like the war on poverty and the war for equal rights and so many others—were not wars at all. They'd never been intended to be won. If it weren't for the local drug dealers in downtown Big City and Small Town America, convenience stores and bodegas would have to shutter their doors because the drug trade was the only profitable industry left in the neighborhood.

Yes, drugs drove the gang violence that left hundreds of young people dead on the streets, but the violence itself was likewise useful to the political class. Health, peace, and harmony didn't sell. No one wrote thank-you checks to aldermen or congressmen. They wrote checks so the elected officials would pretend to fix the very crises that they had created in the first place.

They got away with it because the Fourth Estate had chosen sides and abandoned actual reportage in favor of pressing the narratives that their readers and viewers chose to believe as truth. News readers and news typists understood that clicks and advertisers were the only audience that counted, and all they cared about was selling stuff.

Follow the money, indeed.

What had Venice told him about Roman's conversation with his friend? The reward for providing information that would help someone kill Jonathan and his team was a reduced sentence for the friend's mother.

That was precisely the kind of influence a big money contributor could squeeze out of a politician he'd bought.

But Jonathan was not going to traipse through these weeds with the Trainors. They didn't need to know that the conspiracy theories that were so loudly denied by the elite political classes were, in fact, mostly true. He'd learned over the years that people needed that plausible deniability in order to sleep soundly.

Jonathan hadn't slept soundly in years.

He stood abruptly, startling the room. "I think we're done here," he said. "I can't thank you enough for your cooperation. Agent Contata, I think it's time we let these people have their evening back."

Boxers looked confused. "Okay," he said.

Marlene stood, too, but Dan stayed planted on the couch. "Can't you tell us anything about what is going on here?" she asked.

"Nothing that affects you," Jonathan said. "How's that?"

"Are you going to arrest Victor McCloud?"

Jonathan smiled. "It actually doesn't work that way. But we'll certainly give him a hard look."

"What about the men with the trailer?"

"We just need to figure out who they were," Jonathan said. "The fact that they're dead reduces the threat they pose to zero." He meant that as a joke, but it didn't float well. Even he heard the harshness in the sentiment.

But real FBI agents never apologize, never backtrack.

"We'll let ourselves out."

Marlene walked them to the door anyway. "I do have one question," she said.

Jonathan waited for it.

"I get to keep the money for the trailer, right?" she asked. "I don't have to give it back?"

Follow the money, Jonathan thought. "Have a good night, ma'am."

Boxers followed Jonathan out of the room, then they both passed into the night air and closed the front door behind them.

"Let's go jack a car," Big Guy said.

CHAPTER 26

Renaldo Vega cruised Lara and Aiden's Explorer to a stop alongside the Toyota Sequoia that had been stolen from him. It had been parked neatly and appeared to have been well taken care of. When the rental company got around to retrieving it, they would be happy.

He left the Explorer idling as he climbed out and peered through the Sequoia's windows. The thieves had left the equipment bags behind, but they'd been rifled. He harbored little doubt that the two men had taken whatever they would find valuable.

So, where were they now?

The fact that the car was parked meant one of two things. They had either holed up somewhere nearby, or they had found alternate transportation to wherever they were going to go from here.

Something about this place looked familiar to him. Very familiar, in fact. As if he'd been here before.

Then he remembered.

Renaldo hadn't paid attention to the wanderings early on as his team picked up cash at money machines and filled out their lists of necessary gear. None of that concerned him, really. He was the sniper, pure and simple.

His job had been to locate his target and kill it. He had every bit of gear that he would need to do the wet part of the job, and their benefactor provided the horse flesh for transportation.

The trailer. That's why this block looked so familiar to him. They'd been given the name of Trainor as the source of a horse trailer they could buy, and that moron driver ended up driving by the residence instead of the rental company itself. Renaldo had been trying very hard to nap at the time, but he'd opened his eyes long enough to see this strip of houses.

What an interesting coincidence, he thought.

This vehicle hadn't been abandoned here. Jonathan Grave and his friend must have connections with the Trainor family and decided for some reason to stay with them.

What else could it be?

A quick look at his phone revealed to no surprise that only one Trainor family lived on this street. He parked at a curb two blocks away and walked back to their front door. It wasn't that late, but all of the lights were off. Either no one was home, or they were all in bed.

Knocking would make too much noise, so Renaldo walked around to the back of the house. It was apparently built on a slab because he saw no basement windows or doors. A screened porch dominated the center of the back wall, flanked by what he assumed were the kitchen and dining room. See enough suburban American houses, and they all look alike on the inside. The porch led to a sliding glass door. Hopeful for a lucky break, he entered the porch and tried the door. They'd locked it. Entering through a slider wasn't any kind of a challenge, but it usually required making a lot of noise, and this was a quiet neighborhood.

He exited and walked farther out into the backyard, up to the fence that separated the Trainors' lot from that of their neighbor, and he scanned the second floor, where the bedrooms would be. In the far-right corner, flickering dim blue light spoke of someone watching television. The windows were all double-hung, and all were closed except for one—just left of center, near the edge of the porch roof. That one was open a few inches, leading him to believe that it was probably the bathroom. With the temperatures dropping, he couldn't imagine a reason other than odor release to have windows open.

That would be his way in.

He pulled his folding blade knife from the spot where it was always clipped to his pocket and cut away a four-by-four-foot section of porch screen, then climbed onto the railing, which gave him access to the leading edge of the porch's roofline. Checking to make sure his pistol was firmly seated in its holster, he grabbed the rain gutter with both hands and did a pull-up. His fears that the gutter assembly would pull away proved unfounded. The metal bent, but it remained attached.

He pressed himself up onto the roof deck and paused to see if he'd been heard. No lights came on, no dogs barked. He was good to go.

Staying low to present as small a silhouette as possible, he crawled up the shallow slope of the asphalt shingles to the open window. He tried to peer through into the darkness beyond, but the curtains blocked any meaningful view. Closing his eyes, he cocked his head and held his ear to the opening. He was less convinced now that the opening led to a bathroom. In fact, he now was convinced that this was a bedroom. In a perfect scenario, it would be the guest room occupied by Grave and Gigantor, but that was too much to wish for.

He heard nothing.

Deploying his blade yet again, he slipped it between the frame of the window screen and the window frame itself. A quick twist freed the screen, which he carefully paced on the roof deck.

Someone stirred on the far side of the opening. He hadn't made a lot of noise, but he'd made some, and apparently it was enough to make the room's occupant stir. After a quick snort of a snore, the room fell silent again.

Renaldo counted to thirty before moving again. Then he placed his palms under the edge of the window and lifted. The windows must have been newer than the house because it moved easily and quietly. He lifted his ever-present Mini Maglite from its pouch on his belt, covered the lens with his left hand, and turned it on. He played the beam through a slit between his fingers and scanned the interior.

It was a young boy's room. Clothes and toys littered the floor, and posters of anime characters that Renaldo didn't recognize stared back at him. The occupant of the room had kicked off his covers and lay in a fetal ball immediately below the windowsill.

Renaldo took care not to step on the child as he planted his feet on the mattress to make entry. The kid stirred again but didn't wake. He mumbled something unintelligible, and then his breathing became rhythmic again.

Once inside with his feet on the carpeted floor, Renaldo placed a hand on the boy's head and plunged the blade of his knife into his brain stem.

The boy didn't move.

"I'm sorry," Renaldo whispered in Spanish. "It's so much easier this way."

Children always complicated operations like this. Innocent of the crimes that brought vengeance onto their parents or siblings, they nonetheless were witnesses. The fact of their survival kept stories of killings alive in the media for much longer than if they merely died with the intended targets.

Renaldo told himself that upon his arrival in the next life, Saint Peter would pass no lesser judgment on his soul if he had killed only adults. They were merely children who had grown.

With his knife clutched in his left hand, leaving his right free in case he needed to deploy his pistol, he carefully opened the boy's bedroom door and stepped into the hallway, which was dimly lit by a deodorizing nightlight that looked like the façade of a cathedral.

On the far end of the hall to the right, the door was closed to the room where he'd seen the flickering light of the television. He had that pegged as mom and dad's room. Across the hall, on the front side of the house and a little to the left, Renaldo noted another closed door. He started there.

That door led to a girl's room. Impossibly pink and decorated with pictures of androgynous movie stars, the room looked too young for the size of the girl who slept under six inches of blankets and comforter.

She was sleeping with her face toward the door, requiring him to kill her from the front, which was necessarily bloodier, but she departed life nearly as quickly as her brother and, he was confident, with no more suffering than he.

Back in the hallway, he turned toward the master bedroom and crossed in front of the center hall stairway. He turned left and carefully looked around the opened doorway. In that bedroom, the covers here had been pulled aside, and it looked like someone had only recently risen from the mattress.

To his left, on the front side of the house, a toilet flushed, startling him and making him whirl. He saw no light inside the bathroom.

The door opened to reveal a large man wearing only a pair of black boxer briefs. The man jumped at the sight of Renaldo standing in front of him, and then he reacted with startling speed, rushing straight at his intruder. The man had his forearms up in the form of American football linebackers, and he drove them under Renaldo's chin, making him backpedal through the open bedroom door to land heavily on the thinly carpeted floor. The whole house shook from the impact.

The man was making guttural, animal sounds as he reared back to deliver a punch with a hand the size of a baseball glove.

Renaldo slashed his blade across the man's belly, spilling a loop of bowel onto Renaldo's shirt. In the same motion, Renaldo slashed again, this time in an upward motion that caught the big man under his armpit and then across and through his trachea. As the man reacted, Renaldo rolled him off onto the floor and then ended the fight by plunging the blade into his ear.

That's when he heard the scream.

He turned to see the woman he now recognized from the rental shop standing in the open doorway to her bedroom, backlit by the glow of the television. She wore baggy gray sweatpants with elastic around her ankles and a faded Darmond for President T-shirt.

"Don't yell," Renaldo said in English as he rose back to his feet. "I don't want to have to hurt your children."

His words froze her scream in her throat. Her eyes were huge, clearly beyond comprehension. She looked down at the mauled body on the floor . . .

"I had to do that," Renaldo said. "Strictly a case of bad timing. If he hadn't gotten up to go to the toilet, everything would be fine. I am here to ask you a few questions, and then I will leave."

"You talked about my children," she said.

"I have no interest in them," he said. "If you just answer my questions, everything will be fine."

He understood her confusion. How could she not be totally befuddled? "Please," he said. "Step back into your bedroom."

"Please don't hurt me."

"I'll have no cause to hurt you if you merely answer my questions."

"Why did you break into my house? *How* did you break into my house?"

Renaldo gestured toward her room and waited. As she started to move, he said, "Asking more questions is the opposite of answering them. It just prolongs my time here and increases the danger to you and your family."

"What kind of danger?"

He waited again as she got the fact that she was asking again.

"I'm sorry," she said.

"I understand how this is unnerving for you," Renaldo said. "Please have a seat on the bed."

She didn't want to. The prospect clearly terrified her. Renaldo considered telling her that he was not a rapist, but that would merely invite the question of what he *was* if not that. She sat on the edge of the bed, but barely. She kept her left foot on the carpeted floor.

"First things first," Renaldo said. "What is your name?"

"Marlene," she said. "Marlene Trainor."

"Is that gentleman in the other room your husband?"

"No, he's my brother." She looked away. "Was."

"I am so sorry it had to happen like that," Renaldo said. "Is there, in fact, a husband I have to worry about? I would hate for him to suffer the same outcome as your brother."

Marlene shook her head.

"No one else who might surprise us?"

"Only my children if they wake up." She started, as if she'd only just heard the words she'd said. "But you promised—"

Renaldo held up his hand. "I have no interest in them. Children sleep soundly, after all, and I should be here only a few minutes more. Do you recognize me?"

"You were with the men who were killed," she said. "The men who bought the horse trailer."

Renaldo's ears perked at her statement. "The men who were killed?"

"Yes. I mean, that's what the FBI agents told me."

Something fluttered in Renaldo's stomach. He wasn't

prepared for a battle with the federal government of the United States. In fact, his benefactor was supposed to protect him from that very thing.

"When was the FBI here?" he asked.

"Earlier today. This evening, really. Not that long ago."

"Why? What did they want to know?"

"They wanted to know about you and your friends," she said. "I assume that they were your friends. Please, if this upsets you, I'm just trying to answer your questions."

"You're doing a fine job," he reassured. "What did you tell them?"

"The truth," she said. "That you were here and bought the trailer with cash."

"Did that seem to make them happy?"

"Happy is the wrong word. But yes, they seemed satisfied. That's a better word."

"Of course," Renaldo said. "You can probably tell from my accent that English is not my first language."

She stared back at him. The fear was still pulsating from her, but she seemed to have settled down some.

"Did you talk about anything else?" he asked.

She scowled as she thought. "They seemed very interested in Victor McCloud. I think all of this might be an investigation into him."

"I see," Renaldo said. "What were you able to tell them?"

"Again, the truth. Not many people like him around here."

"That is very interesting. Do you remember what these FBI agents' names were?"

Her scowl deepened. "I don't," she said after a few

seconds. "I'm sorry. You see that badge and everything else goes out the window."

"Of course. Do you remember what they looked like?"

"The main agent—the one in charge—was muscular in a military kind of way. Very blue eyes. But his partner, oh my God. That man is huge. He, like, filled the doorway, you know?"

"I know these men," Renaldo said. "Very well, then. I think I have everything I need. Thank you very much. Now, please stand."

Her confusion morphed back to fear.

He gave a reassuring smile. "Don't be afraid," he said. "My work here is done. Please stand for me."

She stood. "Please don't hurt me. Let me go to my children."

He gestured through the open door to the children's bedrooms. "Of course," he said.

As she turned toward the hall, she unwittingly presented the base of her skull to him. With a single thrust of his blade, he fulfilled his promise. He sent her to join her children.

CHAPTER 27

"No!" A voice in Gail's head shouted it loudly enough that she swore she could actually hear it.

She wasn't going to die. Not today. Not like this.

She kicked harder, tried to relax her shoulders. She slid her Glock into its holster to free her right hand and let go of the severed scalp in her left.

She kicked again.

God, it hurt. Whatever he'd done to her, he'd done a good job of it.

She needed to make it to the surface. With a fresh lungful of air, she'd have options. Without it . . .

She kicked again. Her hand found a rope, at least that's what it felt like. She wrapped one fist around it, and then another. After two good pulls, she felt the night air on her face, and she gulped in a huge breath. That triggered a cough and a jab of pain that cut her in half. She tasted blood, mixed with oil and awfulness.

Another killer was still out there. She had to assume that to be the case.

Sirens peaked in noise, and then she heard scratchy

radio transmissions. Distant, but present. Had the cavalry arrived?

Could she stay alive long enough for them to reach her?

"Calm down," she told herself. Whatever was happening, it was bad, but she didn't yet know *how* bad. She had to keep fighting. She had to get out of this water. Even if she had no more than a hangnail, the infection risk had to be off the charts in this muck.

The rope she clung to—literally, her lifeline—dangled along the left-hand edge of a piling. From it, support beams ran horizontally to adjacent pilings, affording a better handhold. Since the first step toward not dying was to improve her chances of not slipping under the surface again, she wrapped the support member under her arm and shifted to her right.

Had she not done that, she would not have seen the ladder to the dock. It was a makeshift thing, little more than planks that had been nailed into the piling, but it gave her the handhold she needed.

Her gut really hurt. Climbing the ladder was going to be a bitch, but she felt her strength ebbing and knew that each passing second reduced her odds for survival. She got her hands and feet stable on the rungs, steeled herself, and raised her right leg to find the next rung.

An explosion of agony rippled through her insides, making her gasp. She grunted down and pushed up. The rough, wet wood dug into her palms, but she did her best to ignore it.

"This is a five-foot climb, you wimp," she told herself aloud. "Six at the most. Just two more times and you can mark drowning off the list."

Of course, there was still bleeding to death or getting jumped yet again by the bad guy's partner.

Where the hell were the police?

She moved her hands up to the next set of rungs, with the effect of stretching muscle facia that had been sliced open.

Don't look, she told herself of her injury. It was what it was, and if she saw something awful, it might freak her out.

She pressed up. It hurt even more.

She heard more sirens and more radio traffic, but none of it was coming any closer.

"Two more," she said. "One at a time."

Hands first, then feet, then press.

Her head emerged atop the pier's deck. *Oh, shit. Now I'm a target.*

"Speed it up, old girl," she said.

This next step was going to be a big one. She'd have to raise her knee to her chest to get a foothold, and then she'd have to grip the top of the piling with her hands to heave herself up those last few feet.

"This is the price for being impatient," she said. "For being stupid."

But she was not going to die tonight. She and God had already decided that, right?

"You can do it," she said. She closed her eyes and rested her forehead on the piling. "I don't know how, but you can do it."

For an instant, she thought she was falling back into the black water, but when she jerked in response, she realized that she'd lost consciousness for a half a second.

She was in trouble. Out of time.

Do it or die. Do it and die. There was only one way to find out which one it would be.

Letting go with one hand, she used it to lift her leg high enough for the final step. The effect was to overbalance her backward, and she had to snap her hand back to reestablish her grip on the piling.

"This is it," she told herself. "One of one. Make or break."

As she pushed with her leg and pulled with her arms, she heard a sound come from her throat that was inhuman, otherworldly. Part scream, part growl, and one hundred percent anger. She focused every brain cell and every neuron to pulling her ass up and over the edge of the pier. Something tore inside her, and the agony spiked to new levels, but it felt like the effort launched her airborne. She rolled as she rose and somehow landed on her back, soaked but alive.

From somewhere in the distance, she heard, "Police! Don't move!" A ripple of gunfire followed, but she realized it didn't matter to her. If she'd been hit, then getting shot hurt less than getting stabbed.

The darkness came quickly and out of nowhere.

Renaldo Vega stepped out of Marlene Trainor's shower and dried himself off. It was more of a quick rinse than a real shower, but he wanted to get the blood off his hands and face. He'd run his clothes through the washer, too. He didn't mind making a mess while doing what needed to be done, but he hated *wearing* the mess. You never knew when an overbearing cop or super-observant passerby might notice the bloodstains, and there would be no happy ending to a discussion that began on that note.

Before starting the cleaning regimen, he'd placed a phone call to the number he'd been given in case of an emergency. He knew it would take some time for the message to filter through the various feints and cutouts that his boss had built into his cybersecurity precautions. To make things even more frustrating for future investigators— if they ever got that far—he'd used the landline on the nightstand next to Marlene's bed.

It bothered him that she looked so uncomfortable in death. Normally, there was something very peaceful about being in the company of a corpse. The children, for example, barely moved when they died. They looked like they were merely in a deep sleep. Marlene, though, had fallen face-first onto the carpet, and her hair had flopped around her head like a stringy halo. He didn't like to look at her like that. But now that he was clean, he didn't want to touch her, either.

He was sitting naked on Marlene's bed, resting his eyes, when the phone rang. Per the existing plan, he answered in English and used the pass phrase, "What a fine good day it's been in this part of the world."

The male speaker's response from the other side was correct, though in a heavy Spanish accent: "Glorious sunlight and a brilliant moon."

Renaldo said, "Seven six five."

"Zero two two." The voice reverted to Spanish. "I will put you through."

Ten seconds later, after enduring a series of clicks, Renaldo heard Antonio Filho's voice. In Spanish, he said, "What is so important?"

"Things have not gone well," Renaldo said. "Thus far, I seem to be the only survivor among our team."

"Your duties remain the same," Filho said.

"I understand, but you need to be aware that my targets know about your friend, our benefactor here."

A pause. "And the reason that is concerning?"

"I am merely reporting the facts," Renaldo said. "In my experience, as secrets grow, they become unstable. The people you asked me to find turn out to be quite skilled, and I'm sure they can be very persuasive."

"What are you suggesting?"

"I suggest nothing," Renaldo said. He'd met Antonio Filho only once, and he'd found him to be an unstable man. Thus the reason for this call in the first place. Renaldo knew what he, Renaldo, would do in this circumstance, but he dared not act without permission from the boss. "But I do have it on the best information that my targets will be visiting our benefactor tonight. In fact, they may already be there."

"And what is it you are asking permission to do?"

"Again, sir, I am asking nothing. However, if you would like me to share with the benefactor the same gift that I bring for the others, I would be willing to do so."

Antonio Filho inhaled deeply on the other end, and let the breath go as a sigh. "Very well," he said. "I think that would be wise."

Renaldo sensed that the man was about to hang up on him, so he said this next part quickly: "Should I share with his family, as well?"

The resulting silence lasted a long time. "Tell me more."

"A grown daughter and her husband likewise live at the house with their two children, both young."

"Don't include the little ones," Filho said. "But the others, yes."

"There's the matter of cleanliness," Renaldo said. "After such a gluttony of gifts, small children will feel left out. They are likely to cause much attention that will live on and on. I worry about what others might be forced to do as word leaks out and outrage grows."

Renaldo knew that Victor McCloud was politically connected and that those connections were important to Antonio Filho. But while dead children were a homicide case, live orphans were a cause for the future. It was no different from that which befell the Trainor children.

When an answer didn't come for fifteen seconds, Renaldo said, "This will not be the first time that I have delivered gifts to children."

"Call me only if there are problems," Filho said. "If you are successful, I will know from many different sources."

After the line went dead, Renaldo padded naked down the stairs and through the kitchen to the laundry room, where his clothes were tumbling in the dryer. They were still moist, but they would have to do.

CHAPTER 28

Jonathan and Boxers had traded the Sequoia in for a ten-year-old dually pickup with huge hips and a ridiculously loud engine. The owners had been kind enough to leave the driver's door unlocked with the keys tucked into the visor. They'd pinched it from in front of a house three blocks away from the Trainors' that seemed to be celebrating something. Music blared, the house was overlit, and no one noticed a thing. They stopped first back at the Sequoia, where they transferred the hardware they thought they might need and left the rest for the police to find when they inevitably examined it for evidence tied to the mountain shoot-out.

"Do you really want to just go up and knock on the door?" Boxers asked. "That's not much of a plan."

"What's your suggestion?" Jonathan asked. "As if I don't know." Big Guy was a blow-shit-up kind of guy.

"Just because I ask a question doesn't mean I have an idea," Boxers said. "Generally, we have something beyond *knock-knock, who's there?*"

"I think we need to use our badges again," Jonathan

said. "Wolverine is already in the know, and I think that jolt people get when they hear *FBI* works to our benefit."

Venice had texted him floor plans for the ranch house and its outbuildings, along with the site plan that the ranch's original owner had submitted for his building permits. Most of it was public record, but the fact that she could tap into whatever she needed whenever she needed it was nothing short of stunning.

Going through the plans on his phone was a challenge, but there was enough detail for Jonathan to see that the ranch was almost a little town in its scope. The main house was classic ranch—single story construction with meandering rooms, all built in the log cabin style that he found ugly. With eight bedrooms and ten baths, that main house was huge. It would be hard to manage the angles if they ended up going to guns.

He noted the obligatory stables and barns, plus two workshops whose purposes were unidentified on the plans. He imagined, though, that on a spread this size, they'd need everything from a welding shop and woodshop down to their own farrier. The building that concerned him most was the one that the plans labeled as "BUNK HOUSE." The thought of a team of cowboys involved in whatever was coming troubled him.

"You have to call a building something when you're planning it," Boxers pointed out. "Doesn't necessarily mean that's what it's really used for. Could be a big storage building for all we know."

Either way, they would find out soon enough. On the positive side, that bunkhouse looked to be easily a half mile away from the main house.

The night out here was the kind of dark that Jonathan missed from his childhood. Perfectly clear and moonless, at least for now, the star field began at the visual horizon and spread like a cloud over all compass points. The roads and the topography reminded Jonathan more of a high desert than a mountain community, with long stretches of roadway that barely meandered. They hadn't seen another vehicle for the last ten minutes.

"I think I want to turn off the headlights and drive with NVGs," Boxers said. "They make me feel less exposed."

"Exposed to what?" Jonathan said.

"Did you forget about today's gun battles? I could have sworn you were there."

Jonathan's phone rang. Venice. "Driving with the lights off is a great way to attract attention from local cops," he said before putting Venice's call on speaker. "Hi, Mother Hen. What have you got for us?"

"I told you about Gunslinger's house burning. Well, they attacked her at the scene."

Jonathan felt a chill. "Who attacked her?"

"We don't know. She killed one, the police killed a second." Venice's voice broke. "They stabbed her, Scorpion. It's bad."

"How bad?"

"They flew her out to shock-trauma in Fredericksburg. I don't know anything beyond that."

"But she's alive." Baby steps mattered in these things.

"All I know is what I've heard from Doug Kramer. He said she was cut really bad, but that she was still alive. Had lost a lot of blood."

"What do we know about the dead attackers?" Boxers asked.

"Nothing yet. The police got there first and have control of all the evidence."

"Tell Doug to share it with you," Jonathan said.

"That might be a conversation you can have, but he and I don't have that kind of relationship."

"Ask him, then, don't tell him. All we need is a photo of the face, right?" Jonathan asked. "Then you can run it through your super-secret facial recognition software?"

"Well, yes, but if we do that, we'll reveal that we have the software," Venice said.

"This is Gunslinger we're talking about," Jonathan said. "Doug will understand the criticality of letting us in. He doesn't have to know why or how we're going to use it."

"But what—"

"Do it, Mother Hen. Big Guy and I are about to pay a call on our special target, and I need to know if Slingers' attackers are related to the ones who came at you earlier."

"You said there were two of them on Slinger," Boxers said. "It'd be helpful to have both."

"One is still somewhere under the boats in the marina," Venice said.

Jonathan and Boxers exchanged smiles.

"I've asked Charlie Keeling to go to the hospital and stand watch over her tonight," Venice said. "The rest of the security staff is working out a schedule to be with her for as long as it takes."

Jonathan felt his throat thicken. It was hard sometimes

to remember that kindness still resided in the world. It was particularly hard to remember on days like this.

"I have some information on your current target, too," Venice said. "With everything that's been going on, about all I can say is that he has very strong ties to President Darmond and his party. He's been a huge supporter for many years. There've been a few abortive efforts to associate him with transport-related crimes, but no charges have ever been filed against him."

"Do I need to know details?" Jonathan asked.

"I don't really have any," Venice confessed. "I've been drinking out of a firehose out here."

"I understand," Jonathan said. "And you know I appreciate it. Work on that photo as your first priority. Doug should be able to text it to you in a few seconds. Run it through your magical paces and let me know if I've got more ammo to use."

Twenty-seven minutes later, Venice called back. "That was easier than I thought it would be," she said. "You're right about Doug. He was happy to help."

"What do we hear about Gunslinger?" Jonathan asked.

"Nothing yet. She's on the way to surgery. The last word I heard was critical but stable."

"Tell me McCloud is part of it," Boxers said. "I want to bring some justice down on somebody's ass."

"I've got two more IDs for you," Venice said. "The rest is up to you. The man killed by the police at the marina is Cole Holman, thirty-eight, originally from Overland Park, Kansas. Five years in the Army, discharged as an E4, whatever that means. For the last six years, he has been on the payroll of OTX Security."

"That's the link," Boxers said.

Jonathan agreed. "I think you're right. And the other one?"

"This is a hit I finally got from one of the other guys you interacted with in the mountains. His name is Guillermo Torres." She spelled it out. "The whole world wanted him for various murders. Appears to be a free-lancer for the cartels—and for everybody else. Interpol is going to giggle themselves to sleep when they hear."

"What about the other guy who attacked Gunslinger?" Jonathan asked.

"Not enough left of his face to be recognized," Venice said. "Now, there's a picture I wish I could unsee."

"Thanks, Mother Hen," Jonathan said. "I think we have all we need."

"I have a question, but I don't want you to hate me," Venice said.

Jonathan groaned. "I hate setups like that."

"You're on domestic ground, Scorpion," she said. "If things get out of hand . . ."

Jonathan knew she let her words trail off because there was no need to complete her statement. There'd already been a lot of blood shed today—too much to keep the media out of it entirely and too much to keep local law enforcement authorities away from investigating these cases as homicides.

"You're suggesting we step back and hand it over to the locals?" Boxers asked.

"Or the FBI," Venice said.

"On what premise?" Jonathan asked. "We've walked this walk before. You can't share the facial recognition software, so how are you going to tell them who the bad guys are? How are you going to make the nexus between them and our target?"

"Maybe Wolverine could help."

"Maybe. Meanwhile, this is a very active, very fluid attempt to kill us all. We don't even know the scope of the plan. Hell, we don't know for sure that our assumptions are correct."

"Even more reasons to put the brakes on."

"I disagree. We're here. The problem is here. It's time to take care of it."

"Scorpion, I don't need any more angst in the day."

"Duly noted," Jonathan said. "We will do our best not to bring you any. Go hug your son. Keep tabs on Gunslinger. We're going to go black now. I'll call you when it's done."

Venice sighed on the other end. "I won't say it," she said.

"I appreciate that," Jonathan said. He refused to let people tell him to be careful. He thought it was a bad omen. Times like this were not about being careful. They were about being swift and being correct. Being vigilant. Careful people hid in their basements and pretended that things would become better. "I'll call you when I can."

He clicked off.

"How far out are we?" he asked Boxers.

"Even GPS is a little guishy out here," Big Guy said. "But I think we're getting close." After another mile or so, Big Guy pointed ahead and to the left. "I think those lights belong to the Sandstorm Ranch."

As they got closer, an elevated archway came into plain view. Lit from below, the sign, which sat atop twenty-foot metal poles, read "SANDSTORM RANCH" in the cliched block letters that mark so many ranches.

Boxers asked, "We just going to drive down the driveway?"

"That's where the front door is," Jonathan said.

The gravel driveway was longer than most city streets, tracing a straight line a quarter mile into the property, toward the house itself, which was lit like a stadium. To Jonathan's eye, every light was on, providing a clear view into the interiors.

"Not especially concerned with security, are they?" Boxers asked.

"Who are they going to hide from way the hell out here?"

Boxers slowed his approach. "I don't mean to be a pain, but all I know so far is that you plan to go knock on the door of a murderer and have a chat. Is that about right?"

"We'll be armed," Jonathan said.

"Oh, I knew that," Boxers said. "I'm curious about just *how* armed you expect us to be?"

"Just side arms."

Boxers' silence was his testament that he didn't like the answer.

"Our cover is that we're the FBI," Jonathan said. "We're not going to storm the place with guns a-blazing."

"Why not? See previous comment. He's a goddamn murderer, and he's cutting way too close to home for us."

"We don't know that it's him," Jonathan said. "We suspect that it's him, but we don't *know* that it is."

"How much closer to knowing do you want to get?"

"It's circumstantial," Jonathan said. "We're not about executing the bad guy."

"Speak for yourself, Tonto."

"We've *never* been about that," Jonathan said. "*Because* this one is so close to the bone, we need to make double-damn sure that we're right. We're not rescuing hostages here. We're not here to help other people. We're here because we think he picked a fight with us. That's what we need to verify."

"And then what?"

"And then it depends."

"Are you expecting him to come out and say, *Yeah, I'm the guy who ordered you to be killed*?"

"I don't expect it, but it'd be nice," Jonathan said. "And your whole premise is wrong from the get-go. I don't think for a second that this guy *ordered* us to be killed. I think Antonio Filho ordered that, and he is merely the executioner."

"A distinction without a difference," Boxers said.

"Here's our mission," Jonathan said. He was tired of talking options and decided it was time to be specific. "We're going to feel him out. We're going to let him know that we know. We're going to make him sweat."

"And then we kill him?"

"Jesus, Big Guy."

"Well, we're not going to arrest him. What the hell are we going to do?"

Jonathan had no idea.

CHAPTER 29

The driveway ended at a circular turnaround that was dominated by a large stone circular planter out of which grew a giant cactus. Jonathan had never bothered much with the names of flora beyond knowing which were edible and which were not. Given the number and length of the thorns on this one, he couldn't imagine ever being that hungry. A covered walkway led from the edge of the turnaround to the French-style double doors, through which he could see all the way through to the back of the house.

"Want me to go around to the back?" Boxers asked.

"Negative. If they decide to run away, they're going to run away. This is their sandbox, and we have neither the manpower nor firepower. Got your badge?"

"Yes, Mom. And my galoshes."

Boxers steered the pickup around the planter and parked to the side of the long walkway that led to the front doors. Jonathan climbed out and settled the leather holster for his prized Colt 1911 .45 just so on his hip. Boxers carried a HK 45. A hand cannon of the same caliber, but with twice the number of rounds in the chamber.

"I'll let you do the talking," Big Guy said as they started up the walk.

Jonathan smiled. Boxers hated talking to people. More to the point, he pretty much hated anything about people.

"Why is this place so lit up?" Jonathan wondered aloud. He didn't expect an answer and didn't get one.

"You see the cameras?" Boxers asked, nodding to the security installations in the corners where the ceiling met the front wall.

"I'm sure Mother Hen has worked her magic. The good news is, we're not being met by a bunch of security guys. That means they must not monitor their security feed real time." Most security cameras were about piecing together events after they had happened. In the end, it didn't matter much to Jonathan and his team because one of the gifts left by Derek Halstrom had been a program that could make designated faces unrecognizable to facial recognition software. It was a trick used by Uncle Sam to keep his spies from being recognized while plying their trade.

Jonathan pressed the button next to the door on the right-hand side and was greeted by the opening strains of "Greensleeves" on the other side of the door.

"I was expecting 'I'm an Old Cowhand,'" Boxers said under his breath.

"Behave yourself."

He could see movement in distant reaches of the house, just shadows, really, and he heard some shouting. Not the urgent kind, but the "Somebody's at the door" kind.

Jonathan was about to ring again when a boy around

Roman's age walked into view on the far end of the main hall. He was barefoot, and he wore mismatched black and gray sweats that Jonathan imagined to be his version of pajamas.

"A kid shouldn't be answering the door at this time of night," Boxers said.

Jonathan held his gold FBI badge up to the door where the boy could see it.

The kid stopped a few feet inside the door and squinted to see what he was supposed to look at, and then he seemed startled. He turned away from the door and shouted, "Dad! The police are here."

More shouting from the other side that Jonathan couldn't make out.

"I don't know!" the boy shouted. "There's two of them, and they've got badges!"

A few seconds passed as the kid listened, then he turned back to the door and opened it. "Hi." His smile turned to fear as he came to grip with Boxers' proportions.

"Don't worry about him," Jonathan said. "He's harmless. What's your name?"

"Jeremy McCloud." He wore glasses, weighed nothing, and adolescent skin issues would soon need to be addressed on his forehead and the bridge of his nose. Jonathan imagined him as an accountant ten years from now.

"I'm Special Agent Neil Bonner with the FBI," Jonathan lied. "This is my partner, Agent Cantata. We're here to see Victor McCloud."

"That's my father," said a voice from down the hall. A tall, skinny man of about forty stepped into view. It was rare in Jonathan's experience that father and son looked *that* much alike. He also wore sweats, but his were a co-ordinated set bearing the logo for the Chicago Bears.

"Is he here?" Jonathan asked.

"What's this about?"

"Would you get him for me, please?"

"Not until you tell me what's going on." He closed the distance to just a few feet—right to the borderline of Jonathan's discomfort zone—and gently pulled Jeremy back by his shoulder. Jonathan noted that both of the man's hands were empty.

"What is your name, sir?" Jonathan asked.

The man's eyes narrowed. "Alan McCloud," he said. "Listen, I don't mean to be rude, but it's late and anybody can pick up a gold badge from a store and pretend to be an FBI agent."

Jonathan reached to his back pocket and produced his mostly real creds case. He flipped it open and displayed his ID. "This better? Now, I need to speak to your father."

"This is unreasonable," Alan said. "I mean, the hour alone—"

"It's all right," said another voice, also male, also from the back of the house. That must be where the family room was, Jonathan figured.

"You're Victor McCloud," Jonathan said. He phrased it as a statement, not a question.

"I am," he said. "And if I may parrot my son, what is this about?" McCloud the elder wore gray trousers and a black cashmere sportscoat with an open-collared blue-and-white striped shirt under it.

"Is there someplace private where we can chat?"

"My son is also my lawyer," McCloud said. "Whatever you have to say to me, you can say in front of him."

Jonathan shifted his eyes to the boy and Alan got the hint.

"Jeremy," Alan said, "Go to the theater and finish watching the movie with your sister."

"How many other people are in the house?" Jonathan asked.

"Just Becky and Gramma," Jeremy answered. The words seemed to annoy his father.

"Becky?" Jonathan asked.

"Dad's new girlfriend."

"That's enough out of you," McCloud said.

"And are they in the theater watching a movie, too?" Jonathan asked. Before Alan could object to the question, Jonathan added, "I don't want someone sneaking up behind me."

As Jeremy left them, Alan said, "Do you have a warrant?"

"Do I need one?"

"You may very well," Alan said. "That's why I'm asking the question."

"Mr. McCloud," Jonathan said. "I have just a few questions. If you would prefer that I bring down a SWAT team to serve a warrant, I suppose I could do that, but do you really want your family locked into a police vehicle while we ransack your house?"

"Let it go," McCloud said to his son.

"Thank you," Jonathan said. "Is there someplace we can sit and speak for a while?"

"Come to the game room," McCloud said.

He led the way to an enormous glass-walled room at the back of the house that was dominated by a massive pool table covered in blue felt. Near the window, a beige leather group of love seats and chairs formed a conversation group. "Can I get you anything?" McCloud asked. "I'm very proud of my collection of single malts."

"Perhaps another time," Jonathan said. He helped himself to the man-eating chair that McCloud proffered, while McCloud and Alan sat next to each other on a love seat. Boxers stayed on his feet, hovering.

"How about you get right to it," Alan suggested. "It's late."

"Yes, of course," Jonathan said. From here one out, he'd be playing a big bluff, and he looked forward to it. "Would you prefer to start with Luciana Lopez or Eric Lonergan and Cole Holman?"

Color drained from McCloud's cheeks.

Jonathan allowed himself a smile. It's always gratifying when a shot hits center of mass.

Alan looked to his father, and then to Jonathan. "What is this about? Who are those people?"

McCloud said, "Alan, I think you should leave us alone."

Alan looked horrified. "What? No! What's going on here?"

"Please, Alan," McCloud said. He put his hand on his son's knee. "These men are here to discuss a very sensitive matter."

"They're with the FBI," Alan protested. "Everything they say is a sensitive matter. And everything *you* say—"

"Can and will be used against me in a court of law," McCloud said. "Yes, I watch television, too."

"Don't make light of this, Pops. Whatever is happening, you need me here to limit your damages."

"Please," McCloud said again.

Boxers took a step forward to speed the decision-making along, but retreated from Jonathan's look. *Let this stay between them.*

Alan turned his anger to Jonathan. "What is this about? You have no right—"

"I'm asking you," McCloud said. "You are not a party to everything I do in my life. Some things need to be discussed in private."

"Does this have anything to do with that toady from the White House that was here a couple of weeks ago?"

Jonathan hoped his poker face held through that surprise reveal.

McCloud stood. So did Jonathan, if only to not lose physical advantage. Boxers stepped closer. Alan remained seated.

Fifteen seconds or more passed without anyone saying anything. Alan grew progressively more uncomfortable, and he finally stood.

"This is a mistake, Pops," he said.

"If it gets into difficult territory, I will send for you, I promise," McCloud said. He reached out for Alan's hand and held it as he arose from the love seat. Then he folded his son into the kind of embrace that clearly made Alan nervous. It went on for too long.

"What's wrong, Pops?" Jonathan could feel the fear coursing through Alan.

"Everything will be fine," McCloud said.

Alan moved away, sent a blistering glare through Jonathan, then left the room, closing the door behind him.

With the McCloud mansion so brightly lit, Renaldo could see every detail of the interior down the center hall and every room in the front of the house. This job would be simple if he could shoot them all from here.

He'd pulled the Explorer off to the side of the long driveway and into the wide expanse of the yard. He'd been driving the final half mile without his lights on, thanks to the shopping mall-like illumination of the giant archway, and now that he was on the property, he angled the vehicle so it was parallel with the front of the main house.

He used one of the kid's suitcases as a barrel rest—a little black soft case with a picture of Batman on it. Keeping both feet on the ground, he stretched out over the hood, supported the forestock of his Remington 700 on the bag, then dialed his scope up to five-power, one up from his preferred setting of four. Any higher than that and he found the parallax difficult to deal with. He obtained a good cheek weld, pulled the butt plate into the soft spot of his right shoulder, and supported the stock with his left hand. The magazine was loaded with four rounds, and he had another in the chamber, for a total of five. He carried three more magazines in his pockets. With the safety on and his finger outside the trigger guard, he settled in to observe.

Two minutes ago, as he was approaching and still on the move, he saw people moving about in the foyer of the main hall, but now that he'd had a chance to set up, the space was empty. Just as well, he supposed. If he could set himself up properly, there'd be less chance of messing up a shot.

The first thing he noted was the pickup truck in the circle, which no doubt was the vehicle with which his targets had replaced the abandoned rental. Because Renaldo had parked off to the side in the grass, he had a good angle on the door and the space beyond. The heavy timber construction printed as yellow to him in the artificial light.

He watched for a solid five or six minutes as nothing happened. He noted the heavy glass in the front doors, which always posed a risk of knocking a bullet off course as it passed through, but he hoped that it would be less of a factor with his heavy seven-millimeter magnum rounds.

His plan at this point was a simple one. His boss had given him a kill order for every person inside that house. They were all family to each other, except for Jonathan Grave and his friend. Of the lot, those two were the only targets that concerned him. They'd proven their ability and willingness to fight. He expected none of that from the others.

Still, he couldn't write them off completely. The instinct to survive was an irresistible one. When cornered and threatened with imminent death, you never knew what people might do. It was always best to be quick and clean. When he saw a target, he would take it out. In a perfect world, his first two targets would be the professionals on his list, but there were advantages to members of the family going down first. They didn't have the discipline not to run into harm's way to help their downed loved one.

The cascading effect could pile a lot of bodies very quickly.

This bolt-action sniper rifle wasn't the best choice for this kind of mission, where multiple shots might be necessary in rapid succession, but there'd be no denying the effectiveness of the weapon on anyone he touched with it.

Because he could see into the front rooms, he figured that his targets must have retreated into a back room. Now he had to decide whether to move around to the other side of the house to get that shot or if he could just lie in wait here. Sooner or later, they'd have to show themselves.

In this line of work, patience was always rewarded in the end.

From off to the left, a thin man in a black sweat suit stepped out of what must have been a hallway that Renaldo couldn't see. In five-power magnification, he appeared distraught. Angry, maybe. He didn't look like he wanted to be there. He seemed torn about whether or not he should return to wherever he'd come from.

The man stood still, his hand over his mouth.

Renaldo settled the reticle of his scope on a spot in the middle of the man's chest, thumbed off the safety, and placed his finger on the trigger.

When they were alone, McCloud sat back down. So did Jonathan, and this time, Boxers planted himself in the other overstuffed club chair.

"Who are you really?" McCloud asked.

"Who might you imagine me to be?" Jonathan asked. He pulled his phone from his pants pocket, opened it, and pulled up pictures of the men they'd killed in the mountaintop shoot-out. "I believe this man's name is Alroy Montoya," he said. He swiped past the screen and brought up another corpse. "And this is Guillermo Torres."

Eric Lonergan and Cole Holman were next, and with each photo, McCloud's shoulders sagged more.

"These faces look familiar to you?" Jonathan asked. "What's left of them, anyway?" That last part felt gratuitous as soon as he said it.

"Are you them?" McCloud asked. His eyes stayed focused on a spot on the floor.

Jonathan waited.

"Are you Graves? And the man with the Dutch name?"

"Look at me," Jonathan said.

McCloud rocked his face up. It was a mask of fear. Tears balanced on his lids.

"When you dispatch killers, you should have the plain, common decency to know your victims' names."

McCloud's jaw worked, but no sound came out.

Jonathan didn't offer to correct him.

"Please don't hurt my family," McCloud said.

"We're not here to hurt anyone," Jonathan said.

Boxers stirred but said nothing.

"We're here for information," Jonathan continued. "You didn't have the courage to try to kill us yourself, and I don't believe that the kill orders started with you in the first place. Am I close so far?"

McCloud had gone back to staring at the floor.

Jonathan clapped his hands once, causing McCloud and Boxers both to jump.

"Pay attention, McCloud."

"Yes, that is correct."

"And your orders came from Antonio Filho?"

"How did you know that?"

"Tell me about this meeting with a guy from the White House."

McCloud looked like he'd been slapped.

"Don't deny anything," Jonathan warned. "Alan just confirmed that he was here. I want a name."

McCloud looked terrified.

"I know who it is," Jonathan bluffed. "I need it from your mouth."

Silence.

Boxers spoke for the first time. "We're not here to hurt you. but that doesn't mean we won't. Do yourself a favor and don't try our patience. Ask my partner. If it were up to me, you'd be a sticky smear of goo already."

Generally, Jonathan hated being interrupted, but Big Guy's words seemed to hit the target.

"Charlie Aisling," McCloud said.

Jonathan's brain shouted, *Holy shit!* But he covered it. Aisling had been Darmond's right hand since forever.

This could only be about one thing, he figured. "Did the pardon come through for Luciana Lopez?"

Fear, confusion, and anger passed across McCloud's features. "How can you know these things?"

"Your friends betrayed you," Jonathan lied. Why not fan the flames of his paranoia?

"I don't know," McCloud said. He jolted back in his chair, as if expecting violence. "I'm telling the truth, really," he said. "I told him what we wanted, but he left without making a commitment. He said he'd talk to his boss."

"The president of the United States," Jonathan said.

"He only said *the boss*. I presumed that to be—"

The sound of a gunshot startled them all.

From beyond the closed door of the game room, Alan McCloud shouted, "Oh, my God. I've been shot. I'm . . . I'm bleeding."

Victor McCloud leapt to his feet, but Jonathan pushed him back down. "Stay there," Jonathan commanded as he drew his Colt.

Boxers was already on his feet, his pistol in his hand.

"No, Becky!" Alan yelled from beyond the door. "Don't. Stay back."

Another gunshot, and a lady yelled.

Renaldo cursed under his breath as he jacked a third round into the chamber of his Remington. The man was down but clearly not dead. The lady, on the other hand, had taken a solid hit to her neck. From the spray of blood alone, he knew that if she wasn't dead on impact, it would be only a matter of seconds before she was.

CHAPTER 30

"Get those goddamn lights out!" Jonathan yelled as he dashed to the closed double doors to the hallway. He sensed movement behind him and heard glass breaking as lights went out one at a time.

"Stay in that seat!" Boxers yelled, presumably to McCloud.

Out in the hall, Alan McCloud lay sprawled on his back, surrounded by a halo of blood, and the lady Jonathan presumed to be his girlfriend was clearly dead on the floor next to him. Across the hallway, down a short alcove that matched this alcove to the game room, an older woman and the two children dashed out of a darkened room that he presumed to be their home theater.

"Alan!" the woman yelled. "Becky! Oh, dear Lord."

"Stay back!" Jonathan yelled. This hallway made for a perfect shooting lane.

The old woman either didn't hear or didn't care. She started moving.

"Goddammit, no!" Jonathan yelled. He sprinted across the open hall as he heard glass break. The woman made a barking noise and spun on her own axis as her knees buckled. She was still falling when Jonathan hit her at a dead run and snagged her middle before she could fall. He accidentally hit the two kids, and they went down like bowling pins.

"Gramma!" Jeremy yelled. Then he looked into the hallway and got the bigger picture. "Daddy!"

The kid tried to go out and join their father and Becky, but Jonathan snagged him by the collar of his sweatshirt and shoved him back into the theater. "This house is under attack," Jonathan said as he laid their grandmother's body on the carpet in the theater entryway. "Your father and his friend and your grandmother are all dead. I'm sorry to be so blunt, but it is what it is. If you go out there, you'll be dead, too, do you understand?"

Jeremy gaped. How could anyone understand such news, especially at that age?

"Is this your little sister?" Jonathan asked.

She nodded.

"What's your name, sweetheart?" Jonathan asked.

"Carrie." Her pajama sweats featured a cartoon cat that looked vaguely familiar to Jonathan, but he couldn't say who it was.

"Carrie and Jeremy, listen very, very carefully to me. I know this is really scary—"

"Scorpion!" Boxers boomed from across the hall.

"I'm over here with the kids!"

He looked back to see Big Guy in the game room doorway. "Jesus."

Jonathan turned back to the kids. "This is scary, but for right now, you have to promise me that you'll stay here in this room."

"Is Daddy going to be okay?" she asked.

Jonathan turned his attention to the boy. "Listen to me, Jeremy. Your sister needs you now. Probably more than you'll ever need each other again. You need to take care of her. But I'm going to make this all stop. At least I'm going to try to."

"Who is doing this?"

"Jeremy, not now. That's not important."

"Scorpion!"

"What?"

"We need the long guns."

"We need to kill the power first," Jonathan said. "Find out from McCloud where the main breaker is."

Back to Jeremy: "Does your daddy or grandfather have any rifles in the house?"

He nodded and pointed toward the front. "They're locked in a safe in the library."

Shit. That would be like stepping onto a stage to get shot.

"Where is the back door?" he asked.

"Which one?"

"Hopefully one that won't make me walk out into the front hallway."

Jeremy pointed vaguely to a place around the corner of a cross hall that still required him to dash out into the kill zone.

"So, if I go out there and do a quick buttonhook around to the right, I'll be where I need to go for the back door?"

"It's down the hall. There's the kitchen and then the back door."

"Okay," Jonathan said. "Do you promise to stay here with your sister?"

"Are you going to kill the person out there?"

"I'm going to stop him," Jonathan said.

"Scorpion!"

"What!"

"I've got to get to the basement. It's on your side of the house."

"Of course it is," Jonathan said. "Okay, here's the plan." They could see each other now across the expanse of the main hallway. "He's only firing single shots. No double taps, so I'm guessing his rifle is bolt action. I've got to go down that same hallway, but I'll only be exposed for half a second. I'll draw his fire. You make your run while he's reloading."

Boxers stared back. "That plan sucks."

"You got a better one?"

"No, but I want it on the record that your plan sucks."

"Duly noted," Jonathan said. "On my count?"

"Wait. What about McCloud?"

"Do you really care?"

A beat. "Okay, on your count."

Jonathan settled himself. He looked to Jeremy. "Remember, your sister needs you."

The boy wiped away tears. He was trying to be strong. He got a nod out.

"Okay, Big Guy!" Jonathan said. "Three . . . two . . ."

Renaldo Vega had not anticipated his primary target dashing across the width of the hall as he sent his bullet downrange for the old woman. He'd been so focused on his target picture that he didn't even know that Jonathan Grave was on the move until he was there and gone.

Patience paid off every time.

He dialed his magnification back down to four-power to give him a wider view of the kill box he'd created. Grave remained inside the alcove where he ran. Renaldo wished that he'd seen where Grave had come from, but he guessed that it had to be from across the hall, where the guy in the sweat suit had emerged from.

He considered sending a round through that wall just to keep them on their toes, but decided against wasting a bullet. He didn't have that many to start with.

Minutes passed. Sooner or later someone was going to have to do something.

Renaldo jumped and almost jerked the trigger when Jonathan Grave stepped out into the open, paused a second or two to extend two middle fingers toward Renaldo, and then disappeared around a corner.

"I fell for that once," Renaldo said aloud. "I will not do it again."

He shifted his aim to his left, to the other alcove. "Come on out, Mister Brian. This is enough bullet even to take down an elephant like you."

"I told you your plan sucked," Boxers said. "He didn't fall for it."

"Yeah, I got that," Jonathan said. "Okay, I'm going to try it again."

"No, you're not," Boxers said. "It's my turn to play with him."

"He's going to be waiting for you."

"Probably. But we've got shit we gotta do." Boxers took a deep breath. "Hey, Boss," he said in a softer tone.

"Yeah?"

"If I don't make it, I want you to remember that I really thought your idea sucked."

Jonathan hated this. Hated the vulnerability. He couldn't remember the last time he was shot at when he didn't have the power to shoot back. He had his .45, of course, but it would be useless in this circumstance. What he needed was a way to lay down covering fire so that when Big Guy moved—

Boxers darted out of his alcove and ran toward Jonathan. Halfway, he hook-slid to the floor, then reversed direction as more glass in the door broke and a wood panel splintered in the spot immediately behind where Big Guy had been.

Half a second later, Boxers had found his feet again. Jonathan had to jump out of the way to keep from getting slammed.

"Shit!" Renaldo shouted it. He didn't fall for the first fake out, but he bit right into the second one.

The rest of the family would have to wait. The professionals were displacing. That meant that they had a plan, and Renaldo needed to be somewhere other than where they expected him to be.

He left the Explorer where it was and moved toward the house, keeping low to limit his target profile.

* * *

"You'd have made a helluva dancer, Big Guy," Jonathan said.

"You know, Boss, I've always dreamed of mounting your head over my fireplace."

"Now that he's missed us both, he'd be a fool to stay in position," Jonathan said. "If I were him, I'd go for our truck, where the gear is."

"He doesn't know there's gear there. I think he'd go for a better angle on the house."

"Either way, we need to not be on the X. Where is the electrical panel?"

"Down in the basement."

"Okay," Jonathan said. "You go down and make this place disappear into the night, and I'm going to go out and grab the rucks and rifles."

"You'll be an easy target," Boxers warned.

"If he couldn't hit your fat ass, I figure I'm okay. I'll meet you with the gear at the red-black corner of this building."

They took off together down the hall that led across the back of the house to the kitchen. Jonathan had never seen a place with so many windows. Or so many goddamn lights on.

Once they crossed the threshold into the kitchen, Boxers broke right for the door to the basement and Jonathan broke left for the back door. He hit it hard, found it was locked, fumbled with the dead bolt, and then stumbled out onto the brick patio, where fiesta lights had been strung around the brick pavers and outdoor kitchen, highlighting the fancy outdoor furniture.

Jonathan noted all of it as stumbling hazards and

barricades to make him slow and become an even better target.

He dipped as low as he could and still be able to run his zigzag pattern to make himself as difficult to hit as possible. He had no reason to suspect for even a second that he hadn't been spotted, if only as a backlit silhouette. Now, all he had left was to be a difficult target to hit.

That and for the damn lights to go out. What the hell was Big Guy doing?

When Jonathan reached the black-red corner, he dared a stop as he pressed himself against the heavy timber wall. If the thick logs wouldn't stop a bullet, they sure as hell would take away a lot of its energy.

He scanned the horizon. He didn't think that the shooter had had enough time to come all the way around the back of the house, but he sure as hell had had plenty of time to ease into the side yard.

And who said there was only one shooter?

He thought that one shooter was the most likely scenario, if only because of the slow pacing of the shots, but there was no guarantee against others.

He also had to worry about whoever lived in the bunkhouse, if anyone. Even though it was a long way away, anyone there had undoubtedly heard the shooting. If they came down to investigate, they wouldn't know a good guy from a bad guy. In their minds, that would put everybody on the same bad-guy footing.

He saw nothing that concerned him. And that very fact concerned him. Too many years in this line of work gives you a sense of paranoia that was more helpful than harmful.

He'd stayed still for too long. He had to get to the

truck. Had to get to the rifles. Most important of all, he had to get to the night vision goggles. The ability to see in the dark would be the edge he and Boxers needed to bring an end to this.

He started down the side of the house, moving toward the truck. "Come on, Big Guy," he mumbled. "Don't let me down."

Renaldo Vega moved out to his right about twenty yards away from the Explorer and lay on the cold, frosty grass. He kept the suitcase as support for his barrel and assumed a prone shooter's position. Grave and his friend had proven themselves to be worthy opponents. They would be on the move, and the one place they would have to go sooner or later was to their truck.

Patience.

He wondered at what point he would need to turn his attention to responding police officers, but he would handle that in time, if it became necessary. He imagined that response times out here were slow at best.

Movement on the right front corner of the ranch house caught his attention. He pivoted his rifle to assess the situation. At first, he didn't see anything out of the ordinary. Perhaps it had been a bush stirred by the breeze or a small animal.

Or perhaps it was a human being. A target.

If it were a human, it was one with great self-control. It remained very still.

Renaldo waited.

He concentrated on what looked out of place, looked wrong for the situation. That was how—

It moved again.

It showed itself to be Jonathan Grave, squatting small and trying to make himself invisible.

Renaldo thumbed the safety off.

His finger moved to the trigger.

The world went black.

CHAPTER 31

The children screamed when the lights went out. "Papa!" Jeremy called. "Papa, what happened?"

"Stay where you are!" Vic commanded. "Don't come out! You know what the FBI agents said. They'll take care of this."

Only they're not FBI agents. They were the men that Vic had agreed to have killed. That made him an accessory. Before the lights went out, while he was cowering under the pool table—the most substantial piece of furniture in the room, perhaps in the entire house—he had his phone in his hand.

He'd even dialed in the digits to call 9-1-1, but he couldn't bring himself to press SEND. How would he ever be able to explain this in a way that would keep him out of prison for the rest of his life? There were limits even to what Tony Darmond could do. When news of this broke, everything would be over.

Who would raise his grandchildren?

"My God," he whispered through a sob. "I've killed them all."

* * *

Jonathan sprinted out from his corner at the same instant the world went dark. Boxers had found the breaker box.

Half a step away from his hiding place, he heard the *whiz* and whip crack of a passing bullet at the same instant he heard the boom of a rifle. It was close. The shot and the shooter.

Jonathan dropped to his hands and knees and scrabbled across the lawn toward the bed of the pickup truck.

As he moved, he drew his Colt again. At this range, while it was anything but the perfect weapon, it was at least relevant to the fight.

In the darkness, there was no follow-up shot. To Jonathan, that meant the attacker had no night vision. That made sense, of course, because he and Big Guy had stolen their rigs.

The darkness seemed absolute at first, thanks to the vision-ruining illumination of the house. He was as blind as the shooter, but the shooter had the advantage of knowing exactly where Jonathan was.

Jonathan didn't see the pickup until he was there. He damn near collided with it.

The time for caution was gone. He needed to move as fast as he could on the assumption that the shooter was going to charge the truck.

With a single-shot, bolt-action rifle, the gunman didn't have the luxury of a spray-and-pray strategy. He needed to see his target to have any chance of hitting it. That was where Jonathan would soon have his second edge.

He never slowed as he reholstered his pistol, grasped the edge of the truck bed, and heaved himself over.

He hit with a loud metallic thud that had to alert his attacker to where he was.

In the darkness, Jonathan's hands found a rifle in the bed, under the tarp they'd laid over it for concealment. From there, his hands worked on their own. Grabbing the rifle's pistol grip in his right fist, he worked the charging handle with his left hand, slid the switch from SAFE to FIRE, and shot randomly out into the night. One shot per trigger pull, he sent ten 7.62-millimeter rounds downrange in under three seconds.

He hoped that would keep the shooter's head down for the five seconds it would take for him to sling the other rifle and two rucksacks over the bed and onto the ground. He followed them and landed hard.

Seconds counted now. Hell, milliseconds counted now.

Placing his rifle on the ground, his hands tore at the Velcro closures of his rucksack. From the big pocket on the outside, he pulled out tonight's Holy Grail: the two-tube night vision array. For now, he didn't bother with the headband. He flipped the ON switch and brought them to his eyes like a pair of binoculars. The quality of the goggles' image was nowhere near as clear or advanced as what he was used to with the four-tube arrays they usually used, but they brought light to the dark.

Nobody posed an imminent threat, and as he dared a peek over the truck's bed, he saw a Ford Explorer parked in the middle of the yard, but he didn't see any people.

He battle-slung his rifle against his chest and slipped the suspension headband into place to hold the NVGs in front of his eyes.

The rucksacks themselves would have to stay behind. They were too cumbersome to carry and still be able to engage targets. He grabbed Boxers' rifle and the second set of NVGs and headed back the way he had come.

He moved more slowly now. A hunter was still out there, and he was still the hunter's prey. And the hunter was no doubt pissed at himself and at Jonathan for the whiffed shots.

He worked his way down the red side of the ranch house—the right-hand side—keeping his rifle at his shoulder and his back to the wall as he approached the back corner where Boxers would be waiting for him. He swept his field of view one hundred eighty degrees, first one way and then the other, continually scanning for the threat.

He was easily still twenty feet from the red-black corner when he started whispering, "Big Guy, don't shoot. Big Guy, don't shoot."

After six iterations, Boxers said, "If I haven't shot you already, I'm not going to now."

Renaldo knew now that he was outgunned. The fact that the night vision goggles were missing from the Toyota Sequoia told him that Grave and his pal had them now. That was why they cut the lights. That long ripple of gunfire was their way of trying to intimidate him, to scare him with the knowledge that they could send far more bullets downrange than he could.

They wanted him to think that he no longer had a chance of winning.

And he knew now that they were right. That he would die tonight was a near certainty.

He felt a certain freedom in the realization.

He'd retreated back to the Explorer after his shot into the night. He didn't know if he'd hit his target or missed it, but he had to assume the latter. At least until he could be reasonably certain he'd made a kill.

Now that he knew his fate, sitting here with his knees drawn up behind the engine block for cover felt unmanly. It felt cowardly.

Renaldo Vega was no one's coward.

Now that he was certain to die, he was free to take chances. He was free to take them all with him on his journey to the next life.

Speed was his only friend now, his only advantage.

As he got up and ran straight at the front door, he pulled his Mini Maglite from its pouch. Let them have their night vision. He'd do just fine with bright white light.

With the glass shot out of the front door, all he had to do was reach through the opening and turn the knob.

Jonathan handed Big Guy his gear, and within a minute, they were both ready to go.

"Where's our guy?" Boxers whispered. "I thought maybe you had an unfortunate event when I heard the shot."

"It was close."

"Do your shorts stink now?" Boxers asked. "We can't let this guy get away."

"I think I knew that," Jonathan said.

Big guy pointed down the back of the house toward the green side. "If you didn't see him out front and you crossed all the way back here down the red side, he's got to be over that way."

"Or he's really well hidden." Jonathan thought it through for a few seconds. "You know what? I'm tired of playing by his rules. Instead of chasing him all over creation, let's wait for him inside. We can take up positions—"

"You can come out now," a voice called from inside. "We killed the gunman. You're safe now."

"No!" Jonathan and Boxers yelled it together. "He's lying! Stay where you are!"

They ran to the back door they'd come out of just a few minutes before.

When Renaldo kicked the double doors at the end of the alcove on the left, they exploded open as if they'd never been locked.

He shined the light into the darkness and first saw the massive pool table, but he didn't see any people.

"Seriously, Mr. McCloud, the threat is over. You can—"

He saw what appeared to be the light from a smartphone screen reflecting off the floor under the pool table.

Renaldo lowered himself to one knee, his rifle gripped in his right hand. He nailed McCloud's face with the impossibly bright beam from the Maglite. That face came apart an instant later, blown off his shoulders by a seven-millimeter magnum round.

Renaldo left the rifle on the floor and drew his Glock 23 from its holster.

The men who would kill him would be here in seconds. He needed to move quickly to find the children who were screaming from behind the doors at the end of the alcove across the hall.

He didn't bother to avoid the blood as he stepped over the bodies he'd dropped there.

Jonathan had just crossed the threshold into the kitchen when the house shook with the report of a gunshot.

"God *damn* it!"

At the far end of the cross hall, he saw the sweep of white light. A flashlight.

If he did the calculations right in his head, the shooter was moving from the game room across the hall to the theater. He was going to kill the children.

He heard the crash of splintering wood and a crescendo of screams.

Jonathan turned the corner in time to see the shooter holding his flashlight aloft with his left hand while he leveled a pistol with his right.

Jonathan didn't have time to bring his rifle up. He hit the shooter hard from behind, sending the Maglite flying and the man flailing into the cushioned seats that were far better than any you'd find in a public movie theater.

The pistol fired, but Jonathan didn't know where the round went. He grabbed the firearm by its barrel and twisted it in the attacker's hand. It fired again, but Jonathan's grip kept the slide from cycling all the way, jamming the weapon and turning it into a paperweight. Or a hammer.

Jonathan threw an elbow into the man's face. The blow connected, but the retaliatory punch knocked the NVGs off of Jonathan's face. They were both blind now.

Behind him, the kids continued to shriek.

Jonathan's slung rifle was in the way, a thing to get

tangled in as they tumbled from the seats onto the floor between the seats.

Jonathan's right hand found soft tissue on the man's face that he assumed to be his eyes. He jammed his fingers in deep, and the man howled.

The damn rifle kept Jonathan from getting all the way to the floor, so the guy was able to scramble out. There were sounds of stumbling and gasping as the gunman pulled away.

"Scorpion freeze!" Boxers yelled. Two muzzle flashes strobed, and then all the sound went away, except for the continued wailing of the children.

CHAPTER 32

Twelve Days Later

Catholic or not, to live at RezHouse meant attending the 9:00 A.M. Mass every Sunday at St. Kate's, where Father Dom was pastor. At 8:40 A.M., Roman had finished drying himself after his shower when somebody knocked on his door.

"Two seconds," he said, and he stepped into his boxer briefs. He was still reaching for his prescribed gray trousers when the door opened and Mateo stepped inside.

"You're not ready yet."

"No shit."

Mateo wasn't just showered and dressed. His shoes were polished to a high gloss, his shirt was pressed, and the seams on his trousers were sharp enough to cut flesh. The knot in his tie was perfect.

"Don't make us late." Each class filed into Mass as a group.

Roman pulled last Sunday's still-buttoned shirt out of his closet and pulled it over his head. He stuffed the tail into the waistband of his pants, then slipped the noose that was his perpetually knotted tie over his head. He stuffed the striped fabric under the wings of his collar and cinched the knot up under his chin.

"There," Roman said. "Done."

"It's cold out," Mateo said. "Shoes and socks are a good idea."

Roman rolled his eyes. He shoved his bare feet into his leather church shoes. "Socks are for wusses. Let's go." He started for the door.

Mateo hesitated. Something was on his mind.

"What's wrong?" Roman asked.

Mateo leaned his back against the door panel and looked at the floor. "I wanted you to know that I confessed to Father Dom. You know, what I did to . . . well, you know."

Roman didn't know what to say. If ever there was anything in the world that was none of his business, it was the content of Mateo's confessions.

"How is Miss Gail doing?"

"She'll be okay. She's back home. Well, she's living with Mr. Jonathan now." Roman sat on the edge of his bed. "I get it, you know? I get why you did what you did."

Mateo still avoided eye contact. "It was all a lie, too. They were never going to let my mom go." When he rolled his head back up, his eyes were red. "Everybody lies."

Roman stayed silent. That seemed like the right thing.

"Can I tell you something? And you won't think I'm a shit?"

Roman waited for it.

"Well, any more of a shit than you already think I am." A tired smile broke through.

"Oh, okay, well, that'd be easy," Roman said.

"I'm glad it didn't work out. With my mother, I mean. I don't want to go back to that life. It's better here."

"You like living in a fortress?" Roman didn't know why he said it that way. He kind of liked it, too.

"It's better than living in a war zone," Mateo said. "Back then, I saw things you couldn't imagine. Violence. Death. It feels safe here."

Roman had no argument with that.

"Am I a shit because I don't love my parents enough to miss them?" His voice caught on his words. He swiped at his eyes. "Ah, shit, look at me." He turned and pulled the door open. "God, now *I'm* gonna be the one to make us late."

Roman stood. He knew he should say something. He wished he had the words. He wished he knew even what the words should convey. Something about friendship, about sharing the shitty times. Something about also being happy that Mateo didn't leave.

But the moment passed. Roman hurried out the door and headed off to Mass.

When Jonathan remodeled the firehouse to be his home and office, he designed the kitchen to reflect what it looked like when he used to hang out here as a kid, playing mascot to the firefighters. He knew now that the massive picnic table didn't work well as a dining space, and maybe he'd change that one day.

But he loved the eight-burner gas stove and the old-school cast iron pots and pans. He didn't get to cook for others as often as he'd like, and now that Gail had moved back in to recuperate from her bowel resection surgery, he found himself with not only the duty to play chef but also the challenge to add flavor to bland foods.

Her wounds turned out to be serious, but less so than they could have been. Her attacker had cut deep into her gut but had missed all the major blood vessels. As Jonathan knew from experience, God blesses us with more intestine than we really need to survive. She'd be on antibiotics for a while to combat infection, but other than that, her gut problems now were mostly about weaning her back onto real food.

Breakfasts were easy. You didn't get much easier on the system than eggs and white toast. The bacon and sausage would have to wait for another week or two.

Jonathan welcomed the downtime.

He just wished that he could spend more of it sleeping. He'd seen a lot of shitty images in his life, but the looks of terror in the faces of Jeremy and Carrie McCloud haunted him. After Boxers killed the shooter—who turned out to be a bad bit of business named Renaldo Vega—the gun smoke still hung in the air as they hustled the kids out to the pickup truck and on up to the bunkhouse, which was occupied by a groundskeeper couple who slept with ear plugs to cancel out each other's snoring.

Jonathan was able to roust them from their sleep long enough to have them take custody of the children and to issue instructions for them to call the police. That done, he and Boxers had raced off to the airport.

Jonathan didn't know what befell the kids after that. He told himself that they landed with a special aunt, or maybe their maternal grandparents, but he knew better than to ask such questions.

He loaded the toaster and cracked four eggs, which he eased onto the surface of the frying pan.

"I think I'd like to try something a little stouter than eggs this morning," Gail said from the kitchen doorway.

Jonathan jumped at the sound of her voice. He put his hand on his heart. "Jesus, Gail, if there's anyone who should know better to do that . . ."

She grinned as she hobbled in on her cane. "I thought I was done with this thing," she said.

"It won't be long," Jonathan encouraged. "Just a muscle tear."

She gave him a look.

"Okay, a muscle laceration. Is that better?"

Gail sat at the near end of the picnic table. "So, are you going to tell me about this morning's news?"

"You mean that bit of justice south of the border?" Jonathan said with a grin.

"Is that your euphemism for vaporizing Antonio Filho in a drone attack?"

"I had very little to do with that," Jonathan said.

"*Very little* as in *everything*?"

"Somebody might have had a persuasive conversation with Charlie Aisling," Jonathan said. "He might have been led to believe that the world would soon know of a link between Victor McCloud and the president that led directly back to a Colombian murderer."

"Might he have been encouraged to launch a drone strike on a friendly nation?"

Jonathan flipped the eggs. "There's a very good chance that he ended the conversation convinced that the only way for him and his boss to stay out of jail was to make the problem named Filho go away."

The toast popped up, and Jonathan set the slices on the plates. No butter because healing guts didn't like butter all that much.

"Are you proud of yourself?" Gail asked.

Jonathan killed the flame on the burner and scooped the eggs onto the plates. "Are you disappointed that cool stuff was going on while you were lollygagging in a hospital bed?"

She grinned. "Maybe a little."

THE END

Acknowledgments

Over the years, I've learned that many people believe that writing is a lonely pursuit. I think the romantic image involves a novelist holed up in a dimly lit garret as he struggles to tame the voices in his head and herd imaginary friends into a readable storyline. Some of that is true for me, I suppose, to the extent that the plotting buck stops with me, but it's anything but a lonely, solitary effort. I believe that success in any artistic endeavor (whatever that means) is dependent in large measure on the team on which the artist (in this case the novelist) is able to lean for expertise and support.

My team begins with my lovely bride, Joy, who's been sharing my life for nearly forty years. She is my rock. My love. The best thing that ever happened to me.

Without the patience of experts who are willing to listen to me and answer my phone calls, Jonathan and his team would look nowhere near as capable as they do. Thanks to Jeff Gonzales, Rick McMahan, Chris Shaw and Steve Tarani for their expertise and training in tactics and weaponry. Special thanks to Robbie Reidsma at Heckler and Koch for sharing his knowledge about that wonderful weapons platform.

Thanks, also, to Chris Thomas, for his help in things

aircraft related. It's hard to believe how much time has passed since we road firetrucks together.

I've mentioned before that I am part of a critique group that calls itself the Rumpus Writers (aka Rumpi). I don't remember how we found each other, but I have had the honor of sharing the company of Ellen Crosby, Donna Andrews, Art Taylor and Alan Orloff once per month for the past eleven years. We've never missed a session. To commemorate the formation of the group, Ellen did a bit of research and found some stunning statistics. Among the five of us, we have published (or have under contract) 92 books, 53 of which came out during the period when we have been meeting. Collectively, the Rumpi have edited 12 anthologies and written 109 short stories. The group's works have won 36 mystery/thriller awards and have been nominated for 55. (Full disclosure: my work contributed precious little to a few of the categories.) That's pretty heady company, and I am indebted for their help in making my books better than they otherwise would be.

On the subject of making me look better at this stuff than I really am, I bow to my longtime editor Michaela Hamilton. A dedicated slayer of adverbs, Michaela has a sense of story and pacing that never ceases to amaze me. That, in turn, is made possible by Steve Zacharius and Lynn Cully. Special thanks to Ann Pryor, Vida Engstrand, Lauren Jernigan and Alexandra Nicolajsen for all they do.

And, of course, none of this would be happening without the efforts and skills of my longtime agent and friend, Anne Hawkins of John Hawkins & Associates in New York.

Don't miss John Gilstrap's newest series, starring Victoria Emerson, a former congressional representative who leads survivors to freedom after an unthinkable disaster.

Keep reading to enjoy an excerpt from

BLUE FIRE

A Victoria Emerson Thriller

Available from Kensington Publishing Corp.

CHAPTER 1

Hell Day + 34

Victoria Emerson heard the urgency in the tone before she understood the words. She pivoted toward the back door as she rose from the table that she'd transformed into a makeshift desk in what used to be a diner called Maggie's Place. Since the days immediately following the war, Maggie's had served as an ersatz city hall. Victoria's knees scooted her chair across the wooden floor as she stood.

"What on earth is that?" asked Ellie Stewart. They'd been meeting about the status of the clothing bank, now that the air had begun to smell like winter.

"Whatever it is, it sounds important." Victoria opened the door.

A horse approached at a full gallop. Its rider—her fourteen-year-old son, Luke—hung tight to the saddle horn with his left hand, while he slapped the reins with his right. Never having sat a horse until a few weeks ago, he'd taken to it well, but he was pushing the beast way too hard on the asphalt roadway.

"Blue fire!" he yelled. "Coming down the river! Blue fire! Coming down the river!"

Victoria's heart doubled its rate.

"Is he shouting blue fire?" Ellie asked, standing. Everyone understood *blue fire* to be the code phrase for the highest level of alert. It meant imminent danger from deadly forces, whether man-made or from natural causes.

Victoria didn't answer. Instead, she reached back inside the door and grabbed the M4 rifle that was never more than a few feet away from her. It was a sad fact about feral, terrified humans that violence came more instinctively than kindness. That was a lesson hard learned in the first days after Hell Day—after the war.

Slinging the rifle over her shoulder, she adjusted the pistol that always rested on her hip to make room for the stock, and stepped the rest of the way outside. She waved, trying to get Luke's attention, but he was focused on spreading the word of imminent peril. She shivered against the chill of the autumn air and jogged around the side of the building toward the intersection of Mountain Road and Kanawha Road, the spot that had evolved, by silent consensus, to be the social and governmental center here in Ortho, West Virginia.

This unincorporated little burgh had never had its own town government, instead taking leadership from a county whose real leaders had evaporated, either killed in the attacks and their aftermath, or just choosing to flee. Those who remained had survived the unspeakable destruction of Hell Day—the eight-hour conflict that left the world in ruins—but all the technology and conveniences of the twenty-first century were gone. Even the previous century was beyond reach. Electricity was a memory, and without it little else worked. Most of the homes that existed on Hell Day had propane in the tanks buried in their backyards, and as long as pressure remained, the gas could flow. But the clock was clicking down on that, too.

Equipment that utilized microcircuitry, or was even moderately computerized, had been transformed by electromagnetic pulse into paperweights and doorstops. A few ancient cars still worked, but without electricity to power pumps, it was a daunting challenge to raise gasoline from underground tanks, where it languished unused.

As she hurried toward the square, Victoria looked across the street and caught the eye of Army Major Joe McCrea, who returned a look of dread. He had not made the progress he'd been hoping for on the construction of barricades to provide some level of protection from miscreants and marauders. The town still reeled from the attack from the Grubbs gang, just a few weeks before.

Rifle in hand, McCrea jogged to intersect Victoria's path to the square. She slowed, but only slightly.

"This better not be a mistake," McCrea said, making a broad gesture to the dozens of people flooding the square. "That would be a bad way to start."

The emergency response protocol was new to everyone. Most agreed that swift action was key to mitigating any emergency, and they'd voted overwhelmingly to arm themselves while outside their homes. Those with access to long guns—in this part of the world, that meant just about everyone—agreed to keep them close at all times.

McCrea's biggest fear about the new protocol, which

he'd voiced only to Victoria, was overreaction and alarm fatigue. People had different opinions of what emergencies looked like, and if miscalculations resulted in a series of false alarms, especially in the early days, the system would quickly fall apart.

The fact that Luke Emerson was the first Paul Revere to trigger the alert protocol made it even more important that the emergency be real. Victoria had risen to leadership in Ortho by default rather than by election, and while her support remained strong among the original residents of the town, the daily flood of newcomers placing demands on the community's already-limited resources were forcing her to make decisions that were increasingly unpopular.

"He's a smart boy," Victoria said, even though the past weeks had all but obliterated his prewar boyishness.

Luke continued his gallop in a wide loop down Kanawha Road, then left on Charleston Street, where he disappeared and reemerged from Fourth Street. As seconds passed, the shrill squeal of whistles billowed like a cloud of noise as residents reacted to Luke's warnings. Another critical element of the emergency plan included the distribution of a recently discovered cache of coaches' whistles from the basement of Ortho Hardware, so that selected residents could spread the news of danger even farther. Whoever heard the whistle—the sound of which traveled many times farther than the sound of shouting—was instructed to blow their own whistle as they hurried toward either their designated rally stations or the town square.

Victoria felt embarrassed that her whistle remained dangling from its chain behind her flannel shirt. As she ran the last few yards to the square, she fished it out and gave it a sustained blow, adding her own noise to everyone else's.

By the time Luke pulled his horse to a halt at the square, nearly thirty people had assembled, and more were rushing in.

Victoria stepped forward and raised her hands. In the distance from behind, she heard a familiar voice shouting, "Wait! We're almost there!"

She turned to see her sixteen-year-old son, Caleb, sprinting toward them as best he could, his M4 carbine slapping against his unbuttoned coat. He'd taken a bullet through his butt cheek during the dustup with Jeffrey Grubbs and his gang and still moved with an awkward gait. Rory Stevenson, the town's only doctor and Caleb's nominal boss, kept up, step for step.

Victoria knew they'd be next to her by the time Luke got to the point. "What's going on?"

Luke struggled to catch his breath as he leaned over his saddle horn. "People in boats," he said. "Lots of them. All with guns. They're coming this way."

"What does *a lot* mean?" McCrea asked.

"I didn't count," Luke replied with an adolescent flash of *duh*. "Maybe fifty?"

"How many boats?" Victoria asked.

"I didn't count those, either. Ten, maybe?"

George Simmons, once the owner of Simmons Gas and Goodies, stepped forward. "Were the boats under power?"

"I don't think so. I didn't hear any motor noise. I think they were riding the current."

"Why is this an emergency?" Victoria asked. She

thought she probably knew, but she wanted to hear it from her son.

"All the guns," he said. "And the way they looked at me."

"They *looked* at you?" Caleb asked. He was incapable of speaking to his little brother without a silent *you idiot* attached to the end. "How close were you?"

"I was on the shore," Luke replied. Victoria knew from his tone that he'd been doing something he shouldn't have, but she didn't want to press him on it now.

"I thought you were hunting," Caleb said.

"Do you want to hear or not?"

"Boys!" This from Joey Abbott, whose pawnshop had once been a major form of credit for locals, back when paper money had value. "For God's sake. Are we being invaded, or aren't we?"

"One of them pointed a rifle at me," Luke said.

McCrea seemed to inflate with anger. "Did he fire on you?"

"No, sir. But I think he wanted to scare me."

"Looks like it worked," Caleb said.

"Up yours."

"Stop!" Victoria was forever amazed by her sons' cluelessness about how interactions like that made them look small in the eyes of others. So much for the departure of boyishness.

"How far out are they?" McCrea asked.

Luke shook his head. "I don't know. A ten-minute gallop."

"One mile," Simmons said. "Maybe two."

"That's not much time," McCrea said. "We need to take this seriously. It could mean nothing, or it could mean everything." He raised his voice to address the crowd. "Most of you know where to go. If you don't, find some cover and get behind it. Snipers, don't be trigger-happy, but be sure and accurate." At those words, five of the assembled residents—the Emerson boys included—peeled off and trotted off to their sniper's nests. The others headed off to their assigned defensive stations.

As head of town security—by default rather than by choice—McCrea had trained every resident older than fourteen (older than twelve in the cases of some of the kids who wandered in from the country and were skilled shooters) always to fight from defended positions.

"Where is Paul?" Victoria asked, referring to First Sergeant Copley, the other half of Victoria's security team on the night the world ended.

"He was helping in Church Town, last I heard," McCrea said. It turned out that Paul Copley was damn near a master carpenter. With the constant influx of new people, and the approach of winter, the need for housing had become critical. Church Town was an eight-acre plot of land surrounding the Church of the Redeemer, about a mile down the road, on which Copley was overseeing the construction of at least twenty cabins.

As if on cue, the fast-approaching clatter of hooves drew their attention that direction in time to see First Sergeant Copley at a dead gallop ahead of a line of others on bicycles racing in to respond to the whistles.

Copley pulled his horse to a stop and dismounted a few yards away.

"Everybody to your assigned stations!" McCrea yelled. "Move quickly. We don't have much time!"

"What's going on?" Copley asked.

Victoria took ten seconds to fill him in on what they knew.

Copley turned to McCrea. "So, what's the plan?"

"That's up to them. If they sail by, they sail by. If they stop, here at the boat launch is pretty much their only option. In that case, we have a chat." Victoria imagined that in the before times, everything from bass boats to rowboats to houseboats lined up for their turn to launch from the concrete ramp that sloped from the street to the water's edge.

"Suppose they unload before getting to the launch?" Simmons asked. The way things shook out in this un-elected management structure, George Simmons and Joey Abbott were both part of the unofficial government.

"There's really nowhere else for them to go," Joey said. "I guess they could pile out into the trees along the river-bank, but why would they?"

"Because they mean to do us harm," Simmons said.

"If that's what they do, then we'll know," McCrea said. He'd only recently abandoned his Army uniform in favor of a hybrid of camouflage uniform pants with a warm plaid flannel shirt.

"I don't like not having a plan," Copley said.

"We do have a plan," Victoria said. "People know where to go and to keep an eye on what's happening."

"That's more a standing procedure than a plan, Vick," McCrea said.

"Call it what you like," Victoria said. "We've got good people in this town. Smart people. And they will do what's necessary to defend it. If I didn't feel that way, I wouldn't be here. I certainly wouldn't put Luke and Caleb in harm's way."

"I worry about overreacting," McCrea said. "With everybody spun up since the last attack, I worry about somebody on our team picking a fight unnecessarily."

"We trained 'em," Copley said. "I thought they did pretty good." Victoria guessed him to be in his midthirties, and he looked like he'd been born to wear a uniform. Built like a weight lifter, he was a zero-bullshit straight shooter, and perhaps her boys' best friend in town.

"I see them!" someone yelled from one of the surrounding buildings.

Victoria admired the simplicity of McCrea's action plan. Not knowing what might come, he'd settled on a one-size-fits-all strategy. Whether the threat was coming from the road or from the water, Victoria and McCrea would serve as a greeting party. If all worked out peacefully, newcomers would never know that crosshairs had been settled on their brainpans. If things went other than peacefully, the attackers would be caught off guard by the number of hidden fighters facing them.

A flotilla of pleasure boats appeared one at a time from concealment behind the trees, first visible from about one hundred yards. Victoria didn't know one boat from another, but these were a mishmash of watercraft of the sort you'd pay for by the hour at a midlevel resort. At first glance, Victoria saw that Luke's estimates had been spot on. Fifty people, more or less, occupied exactly ten boats. While the watercraft were clearly civilian, the people on board appeared otherwise. The majority, if not all of them, wore green camouflage uniforms. Victoria had never seen so many firearms outside of a gun show.

"I don't have a great feeling about this," she mumbled. "I see a grenade launcher."

"This could get interesting in all the wrong ways," McCrea agreed. "Spread out a bit and be ready."

Per the plan, Simmons and Abbott spread out to the flanks, taking positions at the far edges of the boat launch ramp. Victoria and McCrea stayed in the middle, but separated by twenty feet. At times like this, you never wanted to bunch up. It was much harder to harm individuals than it was to harm a group.

The occupants of the boats used oars—some real, some makeshift—to turn toward shore. When they closed within fifty yards or so and showed no sign of stopping, Victoria shouted, "Stay away from the shore!"

"Stop or be fired upon!" McCrea yelled.

A man in the lead boat with captain's bars on the front tab of his uniform shirt called back, "I am Captain Roy Magill, of the Maryland National Guard. Put down your weapons or you will be arrested." Midthirties, with leathery skin that clearly had seen no sunscreen, his high-and-tight haircut had grown out over his ears. He projected menace in a way that Victoria had seen in many cops and military officers.

McCrea shouldered his M4. "Last chance!"

Captain Magill brought his weapon to bear and McCrea dropped to a knee. "We represent the United States Army!" the captain called. "Put down your weapons!"

"What is happening?" Victoria asked no one as she darted to her right toward a tree that might provide cover.

"Do not advance!" McCrea yelled. "Don't turn this into—"

Victoria stepped forward and raised both hands into

the air. She intended it as a gesture of mitigation, not surrender. "Stop this!" she yelled.

McCrea hissed, "Vicky, what are you doing?"

She didn't answer. She stepped closer to the water's edge. "Put your weapon down, Captain Magill. We've already had one war. We don't need another."

She sensed McCrea moving to her left, keeping his field of fire open. "You too, Major McCrea."

Magill clearly didn't know what to do. He broke his aim, but not by much.

"The next choice is yours, Captain," Victoria said. "Trust me when I tell you there are many more guns leveled at you than you think."

McCrea snapped his rifle back to his shoulder. "You in the second boat!" he yelled. "Put your weapon down!" At a whisper he added for Victoria's benefit, "You're giving them advantage."

"You can see how fragile this moment is, Captain," Victoria called. "If people die in the next few minutes, it will be because of you, not because of us." She wondered how far away people needed to be to hear the hammering of her heart.

"This is a mistake, Vicky," McCrea said.

"Hush, Major." Victoria watched as Magill worked through his options.

Magill never shifted his eyes from McCrea as he shouted to his troops, "Everyone stand down! Drop your muzzles. Let's not have a fight. Not now."

"Thank you," Victoria said, taking a step closer, until her boots were in the water. "I am Victoria Emerson. We need to start over again. First of all, you will arrest no one. And you will not help yourself to our stores. If that is your sole intent, then you need to move on."

Magill's eyes narrowed as he listened. "Victoria Emerson," he said, tasting the words. "Have we met?"

"Not that I remember," Victoria said, "but we may have."

"You look familiar."

"I get that a lot. Would you like to come ashore so we can talk?"

"What about my troops?

That depends on how our talk goes. You pointed rifles at my son. That's a crappy first step in a new relationship."

"How many people do you have in this town?"

Victoria said nothing.

"Are you the leader?" Magill asked. "The mayor or something?"

"Or something," Victoria said. "Captain Magill, we've arrived at the shit-or-get-off-the-pot moment. Either you come ashore and we talk, or you and yours press on. If you choose to fight, I guarantee you will lose."

"You've got a lot of swagger, I'll give you that."

"Call the ball, Captain."

"All right, Lieutenant MacIntosh, row us ashore." His eyes never moved from McCrea, his hand never left the grip of his M4.

An unhealthy-looking man behind Magill engaged his paddle and pulled them closer to shore. As the bow of their pleasure craft scraped onto the launching slip, Magill threw a line to Victoria.

She made no effort to catch it as it splashed into the water. She was the leader of Ortho, not his crewman.

"It's like that, is it?" Magill said as he hefted himself

over the gunwale to land in shin-deep water. "Mack, come with me. Elliott?"

"Sir?" That came from a third man in Magill's boat.

"Keep everyone close. If this is a trap, we'll know it soon enough. Safeties on, but weapons at the ready."

That didn't sound good. "Major McCrea, come with me, please. George and Joey, you too."

McCrea called out, "First Sergeant Copley!"

From somewhere behind them: "Sir?"

"You know what to do."

"Yessir."

"Are you ganging up on me, Vicky?" Magill asked.

"It's Mrs. Emerson to you, Captain." She turned her back on Magill and headed back toward her office in Maggie's Place. Entering through the front door, she stopped at the second table she came to, turned and waited for them to join her.

When MacIntosh and Magill were in place, she pointed at the two seats that would put them with their backs to the door.

"Who's your second?" Victoria asked, indicating the wan lieutenant.

"Hunter MacIntosh," the man said. "People call me Mack."

"What are you in real life?" McCrea asked. "Outside the Reserves?"

Victoria bristled at the question. This was her meeting, not the major's. She was surrounded by military hotheads driven by testosterone, and she needed to exert civilian control.

"I worked in a warehouse. Shift supervisor."

"Forgive me for saying this," Victoria said, "but you

don't look well." His eyes seemed to have sunken into his head, his color wasn't right, and he looked like he'd lost weight faster than his skin could accommodate.

"You don't have to say anything to her," Magill said.

"I think I might have been a little too close to the radiation," Mack said.

"How big is that problem with the rest of your people?" Victoria asked.

"Why is our health any concern to you?" Magill asked. "Radiation sickness, if that's what this is, is not contagious."

"No, it's not," Victoria agreed. "I don't believe I said it was. I was concerned about your friend's health, so I thought I'd ask him about it." That was not entirely true, of course. Sick people sucked up rare and valuable resources. Terminally sick patients could be a particularly difficult drain, and these folks were not from around here.

She decided to shift gears. "What are your intentions, Captain?"

He cocked his head to the side, but said nothing.

Victoria clarified her question. "We've had people wandering into town ever since Hell Day. You're the first group that came in threatening the other residents. Why would you come in hard and fast like that, threatening to arrest people?"

"I saw your weapons, and drew the wrong conclusion, I suppose."

McCrea shifted his stance as if preparing to speak, but backed off from Victoria's glare. "That's not true, Captain," she said. "You announced yourself as representing the United States government, and you ordered our townsfolk to put down their weapons or face arrest. You came in with a plan, and I want to know what that plan is."

"You're imagining things," Magill said with a dismissive flick of his hand. His eyes grew large as a thought occurred to him and he snapped his fingers. "Aren't you a congresswoman? I've seen you on television."

"I used to be," Victoria said. "We're not changing subjects. You say you think I'm imagining things. If that's the case, let me share those imaginings with you. I think you and your band of soldiers are on a foraging mission."

Magill made a puffing sound. "Don't be—"

"I'm speaking," Victoria said. "I'll tell you when it's your turn."

Magill's ears turned red.

"In my world, foraging is another word for stealing. You're not doing that. Not here in Ortho."

They glared at each other for a few seconds, and then Victoria said, "You may speak if you wish."

"I don't know who made you Queen Bitch—"

"Careful." George Simmons took a half step closer.

Magill stood. "If you really want to have a fight—"

Victoria slammed the table with her hand. "Stop it! Captain Magill, you can sit back down or you can leave. We can continue this chat or you can take your troops elsewhere, downriver."

Magill planted his fists on his hips and cocked his head again. The head thing clearly was a tell, but Victoria hadn't yet figured out for what.

"Look, *Mrs*. Emerson. Are you really so delusional

that you can defy a lawful order from the United States Army and think that there will be no consequence?"

Victoria stood, taking her time doing it. "That sounded remarkably like a threat, Captain."

"My troops need stores," he said.

"So do the citizens of this town," Victoria said. "If you want your own meat, hunt it. If you want fresh vegetables, you're screwed till spring. If you want fresh water, pull it out of the river and purify it. What am I missing?"

Magill's shoulders sagged as some of the bravado bled away. Victoria didn't believe it. "You're talking about skills that we don't have."

"If you've got guns, you can shoot game," Victoria said. "Boiling water is not an advanced skill."

"But preparing meat that you've hunted is," Magill said.

"Then learn."

"Excuse me for interrupting, ma'am," McCrea said. "Do you have orders, Captain? Or are you just wandering?"

Magill seemed startled. "We're trying to help people."

"Bullshit," McCrea said. "First of all, you've just admitted that you have no help to bring. You're not the Army. There is no Army anymore, at least not in the way we used to think about it. Just as there's no longer a police force or a Department of Health and Human Services."

Magill's jaw set. He was losing his temper again.

"Pretty much everything that was, just isn't anymore, Captain. You may *think* you're on a noble mission—though I don't believe you do—but what you really are is a roving gang. You're a team of former military people who are looking to survive, just like everybody else, but you're not willing to work for it."

"I did not come ashore for a lecture from you."

"And your words reinforce what Major McCrea is saying," Victoria observed. "That's an insubordinate tone."

"Fine," Magill said. "Think what you want. Say what you want. You say we need to learn, so teach us."

Victoria cast a glance to both George Simmons and Joey Abbott. They both shook their heads. They were subtle movements—twitches, really—but their meaning was clear.

"I'm sorry, Captain," she said. "I wish you well, but not here. There are other towns downstream, and maybe they'll help you—if people are still alive there. But once you pointed guns at my friends, you surrendered trust." She pointed her forehead at McCrea. "See to it that they leave, please."

"You don't have the right—"

"We're done here," Victoria said. She turned to McCrea. "See the gentlemen back to their boat, please."

George and Joey joined McCrea to form a loose circle around Magill and Mack. "Time to go, gentlemen," McCrea said.

Mack rose with considerable effort. "Any sympathy for the sick guy?" he asked.

"I wish you a full recovery, Lieutenant," Victoria said. "Just not here."

Magill's demeanor changed as he left Maggie's Place. His back straightened and his swagger returned.

Victoria followed at a distance, her rifle still slung in front of her.

Visit us online at
KensingtonBooks.com
to read more from your favorite authors,
see books by series, view reading group guides, and more.

Visit us online for sneak peeks, exclusive giveaways,
special discounts, author content, and engaging
discussions with your fellow readers.

Betweenthechapters.net

Sign up for our newsletters and be the first to get exciting news
and announcements about your favorite authors!
Kensingtonbooks.com/newsletter